Praise for Lindsey Da

'Enter the feisty, savvy and continues her wonderful p itants, and the delightful element – the complicated women

The Times

'Lindsey Davis's many fans will have been made anxious by the news that she is embarking on a new series with a new sleuth. They need not worry. Marcus Didius Falco's adopted daughter, Flavia Albia, is a wonderful creation, rendered with a surprising tenderness . . . Just as closely researched and yet light-hearted as the Falco novels, *The Ides of April* is more touching'

Book Oxygen

'As Flavia Albia takes over from Falco, the twisting plot mixes high politics and low life with all her classical aplomb'

Independent

'Davis conjures up this teeming, vigorous era with such verve that the trip in time she offers is irresistible'

Express

'Davis was *primus* and still has no *pares* . . . The auguries promise a long, successful series'

Telegraph

Also by Lindsey Davis

The Course of Honour
Rebels and Traitors
Master and God
A Cruel Fate

THE FALCO SERIES
The Silver Pigs
Shadows in Bronze
Venus in Copper
The Iron Hand of Mars
Poseidon's Gold
Last Act in Palmyra
Time to Depart
A Dying Light in Corduba
Three Hands in the Fountain
Two for the Lions
One Virgin too Many
Ode to a Banker
A Body in the Bath House
The Jupiter Myth
The Accusers
Scandal Takes a Holiday
See Delphi and Die
Saturnalia
Alexandria
Nemesis

THE FLAVIA ALBIA NOVELS
The Ides of April
Enemies at Home
Deadly Election

Falco: The Official Companion

DEADLY ELECTION

Lindsey Davis

HODDER

First published in Great Britain in 2015
by Hodder & Stoughton
An Hachette UK company

First published in paperback in 2015

1

Maps by Rodney Paull

A CIP catalogue record for this title is
available from the British Library

ISBN 978 1 444 79418 2

Printed and bound by CPI Group (UK) Ltd, Croydon, CR0 4YY

Hodder & Stoughton policy is to use papers that are natural, renewable and recyclable products and made from wood grown in sustainable forests. The logging and manufacturing processes are expected to conform to the environmental regulations of the country of origin.

Hodder & Stoughton Ltd
Carmelite House
50 Victoria Embankment
London EC4Y 0DZ

www.hodder.co.uk

DEADLY ELECTION

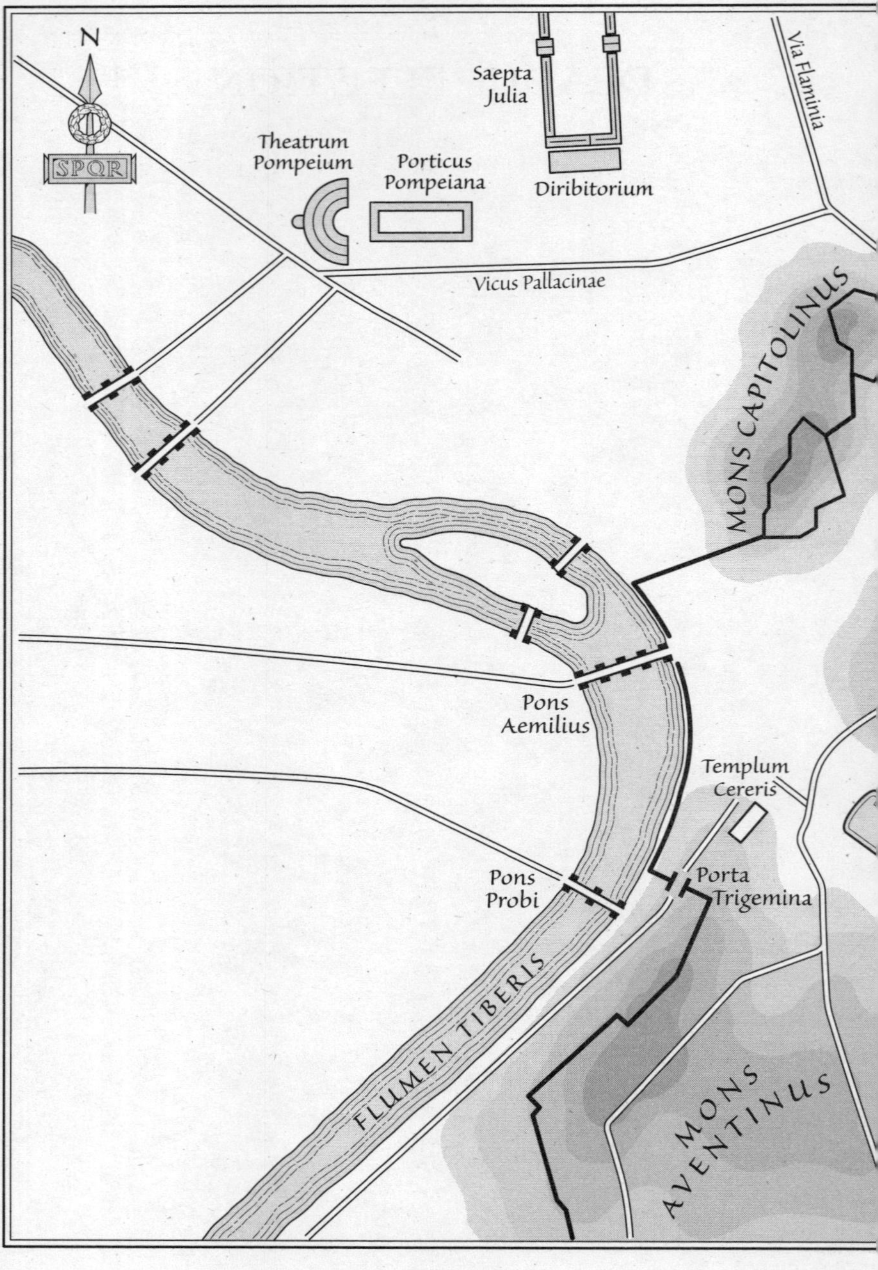
N
SPQR
Saepta Julia
Via Flaminia
Theatrum Pompeium
Porticus Pompeiana
Diribitorium
Vicus Pallacinae
MONS CAPITOLINUS
Pons Aemilius
Templum Cereris
Pons Probi
Porta Trigemina
FLUMEN TIBERIS
MONS AVENTINUS

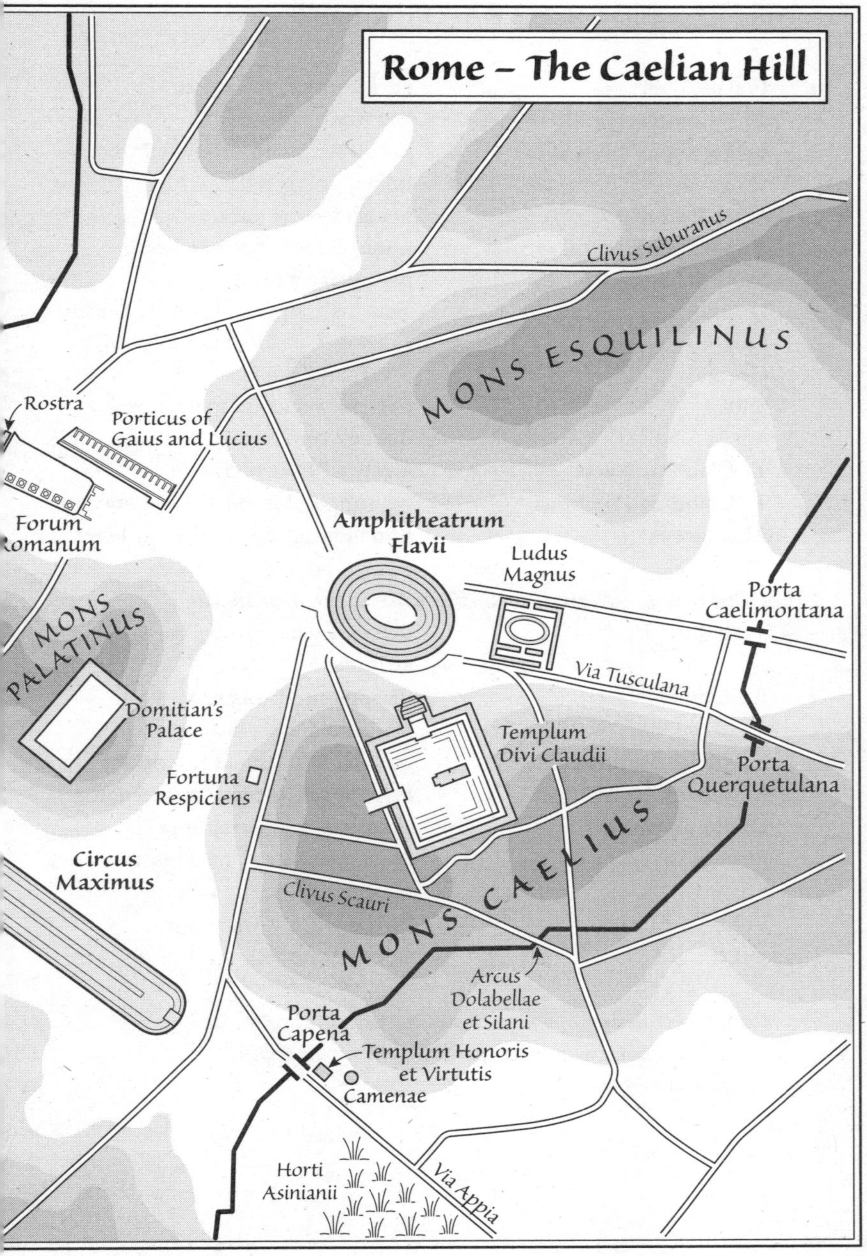

Rome – The Caelian Hill
Clivus Suburanus
MONS ESQUILINUS
Rostra
Porticus of Gaius and Lucius
Forum Romanum
Amphitheatrum Flavii
Ludus Magnus
Porta Caelimontana
MONS PALATINUS
Via Tusculana
Domitian's Palace
Templum Divi Claudii
Fortuna Respiciens
Porta Querquetulana
MONS CAELIUS
Circus Maximus
Clivus Scauri
MONS CAELIUS
Arcus Dolabellae et Silani
Porta Capena
Templum Honoris et Virtutis
Camenae
Horti Asinianii
Via Appia

CHARACTER LIST

Flavia Albia	an informer, feeling seedy
The Camillus brothers	her useful uncles
L. Petronius Longus	her father's old crony, another uncle
Maia Favonia	her laid-back aunt
T. Manlius Faustus	a magistrate, not her lover
Tullius Icilius	his uncle, with big plans
Dromo	Faustus's slave, with little sense
Laia Gratiana	Faustus's unforgiving ex-wife
Gornia	a very old auction porter
Staff	porters, security, messenger, donkey boy
T. Claudius Laeta	a retired bureaucrat
T. Claudius Philippus	his son, a chip off the old stylus
Abascantus	a mandarin, on gardening leave

Candidates for Plebeian Aedile and their manifestos:

Trebonius Fulvo	devoted wife, strong core, harsh attitude
Arulenus Crescens	disappointed mistress, weak principles
S. Vibius Marinus	missing wife, good intentions
L. Salvius Gratus	loyal sister, cynical manipulator
Dillius Surus	rich wife, convivial appeal
Ennius Verecundus	quiet wife, stern mother, no hope
Volusius Firmus	loving wife, thwarted hope, standing down

Callistus Valens who has gone to the country

And his family – sons, nephew, wives, ex-wives, granddaughter, slaves

Julia Verecunda	the mother-in-law from Hades
And her family – daughters, son, in-laws, grandchildren	
Marcella Vibia and her husband	proud parents
Strongbox Man	a mystery
Titus Niger	an efficient agent
Claudia Galeria	his wife, a good manager
'Puce Tunic'	a loafer with a terrible dress sense
Fundanus	an undertaker with a horrible job
Priestess of Isis	a wounded plaintiff

The financial fraternity

Nothokleptes and Son	Egyptian bankers
Balonius	a Gallic banker
Other bankers	Greek, Syrian, unavailable
Claudia Arsinoë	a different kind of banker

Miscellaneous

Consul/'Incitatus'	a spirited hound
Venus with the Big Behind	popular art (in quadruplicate)
Boy with a Thorn in His Foot	unpopular art
Ursa	a mouldy bear, unsaleable
Patchy	a deplorable donkey

ROME, the Caelian Hill: July AD 89

I

Never hold an auction in July. In Rome, who's around then? People who can escape will have fled to rural retreats in cooler parts of Italy. The rest are on their deathbeds or have stayed here to avoid relatives.

Hopeless. Everybody's tunic is sticking to them; sweat pours down their greasy necks. Porters drop things, then storm off in a huff. Sellers vacillate and buyers renege. Dockets go missing. Payments ditto. Wild dogs invade and scatter the punters. Afterwards, somebody points out that no advertising notice was ever put up in the Forum. Rival auctioneers are not bothering to gloat at your poor takings: it's too damned hot.

My father owns an auction house and in high summer he hides away at his seaside villa. His staff keeps the family business chugging along. It's always a quiet period.

Nothing was different in the year of the consuls Titus Aurelius Fulvus and Marcus Asinius Atrantinus, except that before one sale in July our workers found a corpse.

I was in Rome. I had been at the coast, carried off there by my mother – 'rescued', she said – during an illness that had nearly killed me. She plucked me from my apartment and took me off to the family spread, south of Ostia. After three weeks of people fussing, I was longing to come back.

A friend had originally found me lying half dead and gallantly saved my life, so I wanted to thank him properly and believed I was now strong enough for city life.

You may be thinking this friend and I were lovers. How wrong you would be.

It was an all-day journey by rackety cart down the Ostia Road to Rome. That really drained me. As soon as I stepped into my stuffy and silent apartment on the Aventine, I knew I was too weak. I stayed in bed for two days, fortunately sustained by a hamper of dainties from my mother. Lonely and tearful, I propped myself on pillows and munched my way through everything. I thought I had no appetite, but I had been a starving street child once. I hate waste.

All too soon, I licked out the last little dish of aspic salad. I would now have to fend for myself – or crawl back to the parents ignominiously. No chance of that.

Still, I love them. They adopted me when I was lice-ridden and desperate, a difficult teenager to whom they were loyal and affectionate when others would quail. They had turned a lost soul from far-away Britain into a fairly normal Roman daughter. I was now twenty-nine and an independent widow, but I had whined and argued to come back from the coast, worming away at it like my two younger sisters when they wanted new sandals.

'Go, then. We'll keep your bed made up!' the parents scoffed. So now I had to live up to my claim of being fit.

I forced myself to drag on a tunic. Slowly, I descended a flight of outside stairs towards a balcony walkway. This half-rotten structure, a so-called fire escape, was inaccessible to most tenants. It ran around the bare interior courtyard, once a laundry but nowadays deserted. I lived in the Eagle Building, Fountain Court: one of many dark, creaking, stinking tenements in which miserable, poverty-stricken Romans – most of us – endure what passes for life. The edifice was full of inadequate apartments and prone to extremely odd smells. Father owned it, I regret to say. This did not add lustre to his reputation, though since he was a private informer, it was low to start with. People were amazed he had the money to possess a building – though much less amazed once they heard he was also an auctioneer, a profession that is famous for wealth.

I was an informer myself. Public opinion was even harder on me, because a respectable woman ought to remain at home all day. I should be weaving at my loom in a gracious atrium, between beating my inoffensive slave-girl or screwing a litter-bearer rather than my husband. Stuff that for a game of knucklebones. 'Loom' was a dirty word among my mother, sisters and me. I didn't own a slave-girl and my husband died ten years ago. I worked. Not that I felt like it at the moment.

I crept down the steep stairs a few at a time. It was always worth taking care in this building in case part of it fell down on you. Who wants a broken back and dry rot in their hair?

I was testing myself. If I felt faint, I had a one-room bolt-hole off the first-floor walkway, where I could fall onto an old couch and recover my strength. Otherwise, I could shout myself hoarse, which just might summon the building's porter, Rodan. Given clear instructions and some loose change, he would go for help.

Not needed. I made it down to the walkway. I felt better than expected. Aspic salad is full of goodness. Helena Justina might be annoyed with me for running off, but she knew how to impress on me that I still needed a mother. I was the craziest of her four stubborn children, but she would not let me fade away.

I leaned on what passed for a handrail, though I applied my weight with caution. Particularly unpleasant lichen gave clues to the rotten bits. Touch it, and your hand came up covered with grey-green slime. Something about its texture was even worse than the pigeon guano, although there was plenty of that too.

For once Rodan was in sight. An elderly ex-gladiator, scarred by rent-collecting among the violent poor rather than by fights in an arena, he was a heavy lump of lard who stood in the porch, arguing (his reaction to any request). He was with a runner I recognised from Father's auction house. I watched them.

Messengers in Rome are used to hassle. This man, Cyrus, stood in silence letting Rodan's pointless pushiness wash over him. If Cyrus had come from the Saepta Julia, where the office was, he would have had a good walk here, with a steep climb up the Aventine at the end of it. He was taking a breather in case he had to turn around and go straight back, mission unaccomplished. In contrast to Rodan's ugly shaved head and the huge sweat stains on his ragged tunic, Cyrus was neat. In his forties, he had trimmed hair, laced footwear, a white tunic that was limp in the heat though not grimy. He was slim, though not from going hungry. My father still remembered what poverty was like, so he was a decent employer. Nor were his employees crushed by constant beatings, unlike many in our supposedly civilised city.

Father employed Rodan too, but Rodan was beyond help.

I called out. Rodan immediately slunk back into his smelly cubicle. Cyrus came across the courtyard and gazed up at me, one level above. Still light-headed, I was trying not to sway.

'Flavia Albia! We heard you were home.' He looked relieved to have found me. 'I don't suppose your father will be city-bound himself any time soon?'

'Sorry, Cyrus, it's July. Falco is out in a small boat every day, with one hand glued to a fishing rod and the other clasping a wine gourd.'

'Any fish biting?'

'No, he just likes wearing a silly hat and dreaming. But once in a while he lands a very beautiful statue that he claims he found floating on a current . . . He's turning into his old man.' My grandfather had often rowed home from a day on the water, towing a small skiff full of gorgeous Greek art that had 'fallen off the deck of a ship'. Such a good way for an auctioneer to avoid import tax. Wide-eyed and shameless, Geminus could make the story sound almost true.

The auction staff knew Father gave me authority to act for him, so I apologised briefly, 'Cyrus, you're stuck with me. How can I help?'

The messenger shrugged. 'Oh, it's nothing we can't handle, but the head porter thought we should tell someone. They are getting ready for the Callistus sale. One of the lads heaved up the lid of a big box – and next thing, he's gazing into the eyes of a dead body curled up inside.'

That revived me. I said if Cyrus whistled for a hired carrying chair, I would come at once.

2

The best way to endure a journey by chair is to close your eyes, take a tight grip on any part that is not too splintered and ponder the meaning of life. I normally shun philosophy, but I needed to take my mind off the bearers flinging me around. As we jogged downhill on the craggy Aventine, which has bad roads and a slope like a hypotenuse, I was afraid of being tipped out.

What is this? – a woman who mentions hypotenuses? Well, when Falco and Helena adopted me, they gave me education as freely as if it were one more new kind of food and drink. I gobbled it up until I knew more than most women and many men too. I happily consult encyclopaedias and I can write my own notes; if I want to show off, I can jot them in Greek. Sometimes even with the accents.

Another thing is that Apollonius, the head waiter at the Stargazer, our local poisonous eatery, once taught geometry. Since he was forced out of teaching years ago, he had served a large amount of fake Falernian in my aunt's bar, waiting for conditions to improve so he could open a new in-the-street primary school. Under our current emperor, Domitian, that was never going to happen. People do not waste education fees on their children when a tyrant might have them executed as soon as they grow up. Try discussing Euclid with the gaoler in a death cell:

the bonehead will thrash you until you can hardly totter to the lions.

So, thanks to parents and waiter, musing on triangles saw me down to the level and onto the Field of Mars. In between, I prayed that no feral dogs ran out and caused the bearers to drop me. Or to start running. That's worse than being dropped.

In fact I was safely carried right into the Saepta, an elegant galleried exchange on two levels, where my father, like his father before him, rented a fortified lock-up for their best antiques. Upstairs they also leased an office that filled up with trash they couldn't sell – a batch of terrible stuff they grew foolishly fond of.

I had been deposited in one of those grand monuments at which Rome excels. Still new, it combined flagrant expense with beauty and functionality – in so far as anyone could remember what this building's function was supposed to be. It had been a counting house for election votes but emperors can't risk democracy, so nowadays real elections were never held. In place of voting, men-about-town came here to be seen, and to buy jewellery for their mistresses to be seen in. Though no longer needed for political purposes, the Saepta Julia had been rebuilt lavishly by Domitian after a huge fire swept across this area in the reign of his brother Titus.

Titus had lasted barely two years. Some thought Domitian saw to that. In my family we kept quiet because insulting Domitian was suicide. He called himself a god, therefore we became deeply religious. With luck, either the real gods or some angry human agent would deal with our monstrous ruler. Quack fortune-tellers prophesying when Domitian would die were as common as garlic salesmen. Occasionally a prognosticator was good enough to see him coming, so hopped it. But mostly Domitian did put them to death – along with a lot of other people, one or two of whom were genuinely plotting to assassinate him.

Somebody would do the deed. You could smell plots in the air.

Cyrus led me up to the office, where I flopped on a stone throne that the auction house had owned for so many years nobody could bear to sell it, not even if some idiot with a monarchy complex offered cash and his own transport. The throne was one of many items saved from the city fire by my cousin Gaius who, when the inferno started, had carried out stock methodically then returned to the Saepta to help save lives, losing his own when the vast cedarwood roof collapsed. I had been fond of Gaius. After he perished so heroically, I never really liked coming here.

Today my unease was short-lived. As soon as I sat down, the head porter, Gornia, informed me that the corpse was in fact at Pompey's Porticus. That was where the Callistus auction would be held. I had passed it on my way here.

Another thing at which Romans excel is making you waste your time. It is not my style. I am crisp. I am organised. I save energy – dear gods, especially when I am still recovering from virulent dysentery. However, I know never to show impatience, because that only makes these maddening people worse.

My chair had left, so I said they would have to find me another. The porticus was only a short walk round the corner, which was why the Didii favoured it for auctions, but I was feeling whacked. The staff knew I had been very ill; it had caused family turmoil. So Gornia, who these days himself had the papery aspect of an underworld ghost, said he would summon our driver, Felix, with his mule, Kicker; they would take me to Pompey's monument in the delivery cart. I agreed. Felix had never warmed to me, but he was a good driver. Kicker was sweet.

Most wheeled transport is banned in Rome during the day. Felix kept a plank and a pile of dirty buckets in the cart, to look like a builder; they have permits.

Felix knew I wanted to hurry, so he meandered about like a tourist guide. Instead of a quick run round the corner, he went in a big loop round the Pantheon and Agrippa's Baths. The usual crowds kept getting in his way, slowing us to a crawl. At last we arrived at the Theatre of Pompey, which was entirely the wrong end of that large and busy complex, then trundled slowly down one side of it until I was finally dropped by an entrance, pretty well where I had started from in the Saepta. Thank you, Felix!

Pompey's monument had also been rebuilt by Domitian after the fire. Every new ruler should reconstruct the city in his own taste, putting up his name on big inscriptions. If he wants to look extra benevolent, he can spend his private money on projects, or claim he does so. I imagine there are Treasury officials who know the true version.

The Porticus had its gorgeous stone theatre at one end, beneath a high-rise Temple of Venus Victrix; behind the theatre lay an enormous arcaded garden where crowds strolled in the shade of plane trees and, famously, a very large public lavatory on the tainted spot where Julius Caesar was murdered while going to a Senate meeting. To the Roman mind (well, the pinched mind of the Emperor Augustus), the crime scene was too horrific ever to be used again as a curia. Brutus and Cassius were commemorated, so far as it was legal to remember them, in a really fine latrine.

My father, a republican to his marrow, sometimes muttered that people ought to remember it was not just Brutus and Cassius but sixty other forgotten anti-dictators who had bravely stabbed Caesar. We had to hush him. Any spy might report him to Domitian for discussing daggers.

Users of the lavatory could gaze out at the large garden square, which was surrounded by cool colonnades. On one side was a gallery of Greek statues, curtained off with famous gold brocade drapes. This was one of the few places where females could be out and about in public on their own. Men could therefore have a relaxing pee, then eye up women who were eyeing up nude Greek statues and getting ideas. No wonder Pompey's Porticus was popular.

Romans loved to come and walk in the arcades. As well as the art gallery, there were shops to browse. Open areas were used for public gatherings, including auctions. My grandfather had favoured the Porticus for sales; according to him, it had nothing to do with the fact that he was a legendary womaniser. Father, a happily married man, continued the practice because the Porticus was so convenient for the Saepta Julia. As far as I knew, we had never before had a corpse turn up while a catalogue was in preparation.

I was glad to see the container was standing well out in the open air. It was a huge rectangular armoured chest, the kind rich people keep at home for their valuables. A show-off householder plonks his strongbox in the atrium, so as soon as they enter visitors will be wildly impressed.

Members of our staff were loafing in the shade among some topiary, several of them eating filled bread rolls. It takes a lot to put them off, but I noticed they were all well back from the chest. They had draped it with heavy cloth, which looked suspiciously like the famous gold curtains from the art gallery. This was to mitigate the heat of the sun on the decaying contents, but the minute I arrived they whipped off the cover to display the box.

It was a seriously banded and studded affair, on four stocky legs. The locks looked fierce. I wondered why anyone would sell this, unless they were bankrupt, which was not what I had heard about the Callisti: they were well-known businessmen. Then I noticed the wooden parts had signs of old fire-damage.

The staff politely offered to show me the corpse. Even though I had made no complaints about them eating on Father's time, I noticed they put their lunch away. I guessed what was going on here. Whatever waited inside the box was revolting; they had taken bets that I would throw up.

Well, that warned me. I motioned to have the lid raised, bracing myself. I looked inside, saw all I needed, smelt the gruesome stench, then gestured frantically. The porter slammed the lid down. He sprang back, gagging. I had stifled a squeal but just about managed to maintain my dignity. A stiff bout of dysentery gives you good practice in self-control.

The staff looked disappointed.

'You must have jumped when you found that.' Still wanting to vomit, I brazened it out. In my job either you are tough or you are lost.

'Yes, he's a bit ripe!' The cheeky blighters were still hoping I would be sick or pass out.

'About a week old,' I speculated. 'In Rome in July even an embalmed body would stink . . . How long have you had this dodgy sarcophagus?'

'Came today.'

'Didn't you notice the niff? You should have sent it back.'

'We're used to pongs. And nothing oozed out at the bottom. It's too solid.'

'Some of the weight must be him inside. He's not skinny.'

I forced myself to think about him.

The man folded up in the chest looked at least fifty. He had all his hair and was clean-shaven. The hair was almost grey, thick and curly; it looked matted, though that was probably a nasty result of putrescence. My rapid glance had taken in that he was of solid build, normal height, wearing boots and a blue tunic. I could see ropes tightly tied round his chest, pinning his arms to his sides. Even though his facial features had started to decay, enough expression remained to make me suspect he might have been alive and struggling for air when someone closed down the lid on him. If so, he would eventually have suffocated.

A foul thought.

'What are the Callisti dreaming of? And don't you ask people to check items they are putting in for sale?'

'Never. Then anything we find is ours!'

'Does my father approve?'

'Falco's instructions.'

'Oh, really?

I bet they had been up to this trick since my grandfather was the auctioneer. Geminus might have started the practice – though it could just as easily date back aeons to the estate sale after Romulus the Rome-founder killed his twin brother Remus. A few forgotten coins must have dropped out of moth-eaten old wolfskins on that occasion, only to be palmed by innocent-faced auction porters. Centuries of scavenging 'lost' valuables followed. It was a recognised perk. But in the trade we were not so keen on acquiring dead bodies. As I remarked to the staff, that lowered the pre-sale estimate.

'Maybe not,' a porter disagreed cheerfully. 'We can bump up the value by trading on notoriety.'

'Oh, well done! . . . Now, look. I know this will be a nuisance, so don't whine, but we have to find out who he is and who locked him in there.'

Falco would have said the same. They knew he would. The staff glumly agreed that, even though he adopted me from the ends of the earth, I was my father's daughter.

Since foul play was so obvious, I had to investigate, rather than simply let our porters tip the corpse into the Tiber after dark, which they were longing to do. If he knew about this, Father would be in there, identifying the man and discovering who had dumped him. I wouldn't tell him yet. I always enjoyed beating Falco at his own game.

I authorised calling for an undertaker to collect the remains. We would pay for that, then add the fees when we billed the Callisti for our commission. Our fees were so high, they might not even notice anything extra. 'Once he's tipped out, wash the chest and keep it closed during the sale. Say you don't have the key to hand, but any buyer will be given it on completion.'

'We can keep it at the office as a precaution. "Just in case it goes astray during the viewing".'

'Convenient! Have we had a lot of keys disappear on us?'

'Used to be regular. Now we never put them out.'

'Good. Tell the undertaker I need to know anything he discovers on the body. Any clue to who this is. Arm-purse, amulet, wedding ring, signet. Take a note of funny warts or birthmarks . . . He'll know the routine. People are always being found knocked down by carts or drowned in the Tiber.'

'Do you want any items to be kept for you?'

'I suppose I'd better.'

'Brave girl!'

Luckily I was no longer a girl, but a tough raisin who had seen life.

3

The delivery driver had taken his cart and bunked off. That was typical of Felix.

Fortunately the head porter, Gornia, was now so old my father had supplied him with a donkey to travel to and from his home. Though frail, Gornia still insisted on starting work at dawn and not leaving until dark. I knew his rented room was so dismal he preferred being at work. During the day, the others often used the donkey; keeping it busy was their idea of animal welfare. So it was here at the Porticus and I could borrow it. A wizened boy led the creature about; he could come with me, wait outside and make sure nobody stole the beast or spoiled it by offering carrots while I was indoors at the Callistus house.

Prosperous people, they lived on the Caelian Hill. Dominated by the massive Temple of Claudius on its northern side, this was an old aristocratic enclave near the Forum and Circus Maximus, where plebeians were now muscling in. Livening it up, according to the incomers, or, if you were old-style nobility, lowering the tone.

The Callisti had taken over a whole block on the western slope, though they leased shops, laundries and bars on all four sides, leaving only their own entrance actually on a street. Outside the house I vaguely noticed a large advertisement space hired by some election candidate's supporters, though I had not bothered to take in whose name was painted in. I thought the Senate voted in January, so was it old news? The Callisti might simply have hired out the wall, or they could have supported someone themselves. *The Tiber oar-makers like Idiotus* . . . One of them might even have been standing. Our auction might be necessary to pay for an expensive campaign. Only the rich can stand for office.

This had once been a beautiful area, near the Vestal Virgins' shrine at the spring of Egeria, the Camenae as it is called, and the Temple of Honour and Virtue, although these days the concepts of honour and virtue were much debased. A relay station for watering horses had been built at Egeria's sacred spring, then the entire shrine and grove had been rented to Jewish entrepreneurs, ex-prisoners, to exploit for grass and wood. On the Caelian, property prices had slumped from exorbitant to almost reasonable.

Even so, most people here had more than a few sesterces. The Callisti were prosperous because they were gritty men of commerce, the kind who would sell you your own cloak if you'd let a footman take it when you visited. As it was July I didn't have a cloak, and I kept my stole loosely over my head to look modest.

I don't normally hide behind my father's name when I am working, but in this case I said firmly that I was Didius Falco's daughter, here on auction business. When the porter still looked reluctant, I added, 'I prefer to see one of the family, but if that is inconvenient my complaint is very serious. I can go to the authorities instead.'

It stopped being inconvenient.

They had a row of stone benches outside their front door, where clients hoping for patronage could wait every morning for a handout, letting the world see how important the Callisti were. However, I did not have to sit out in the sun. Once I hinted I might report a misdemeanour, I was hustled indoors.

I knew the occupants were a father, two sons and a nephew. They were the kind of family where you never heard about their womenfolk, though presumably they existed. The Callisti were a masculine, business-oriented bunch. Still, I guessed they had a venerated old mother who made nice soup with her own arthritic hands, and daughters who were married off at twelve to dim sons of colleagues.

I was kept waiting, inevitably. One of the younger Callisti was at home, but he was 'in a meeting'– having his beard shaved, screwing a kitchen boy, prostrate with a hangover, or even studying a scroll of deep Greek thought, though I doubted the last. All sorts of unlikely people are self-educated, but probably not these. Their family money came from running a fleet of heavy barges on the Tiber; one branch built river-navigable craft. A hobby of racing chariots absorbed much of their cash, but there was plenty to spare; it was easy come, easy go, with them. I had been told all this by Gornia; our auction house did not accept a sale without financial checks. As an informer, my papa specialised in that kind of investigation for clients – and in checking up on his clients themselves, before he accepted them, unless they were attractive widows, in which case he was notoriously trusting. I learned informing from him, though I was more sceptical of widows, being one myself.

I had been popped into a small waiting room with the doors closed, but once the porter left I sneaked back into the corridor and looked around. I listened, too. The house had a well-occupied ambience. Thick walls were absorbing noises from the busy streets outside. Any staff indoors were behaving discreetly. The entry mosaic had a clichéd beware-of-the-dog message but it was a standard floor package, just for show. Tesserae don't bark.

I went back and waited. Nobody brought me refreshments. I was trade. I wanted something from them; they had no need of me. I would have to ask for even a cup of water. They would let me have one, but asking would mark me as a chancer.

When he was ready, Callistus Primus, one of the sons, appeared. He was in his late thirties, wide-built, confident. A well-swathed tunic and heavy gold rings. Nothing too bad. If he had married my best friend, I wouldn't have stopped going to see her. But I might have visited when I thought he would be out.

Polite enough, he summed me up in turn; I guessed he thought sending a woman along meant our auction house was cheapskate. I was dressed to look businesslike, but with a gold necklace to show I represented management.

Once I'd told him about the corpse, Callistus sharpened up. He denied all knowledge; no surprise there. Although he raised eyebrows at my news, his immediate reaction was to remove himself and his family from being linked to the death in any way.

Nevertheless he told me about the armoured chest. After the Mount Vesuvius eruption it had been dug up from their buried villa on the slopes. They safely rescued its contents – money and treasures – after which they put the damaged container in a warehouse in Rome. It had stood there untouched for the past ten years. Now they were disposing of unwanted items. An agent had visited the storeroom recently to make a sale inventory, although the man would have had no need to open the box because it was known to be empty. I was not invited to interview this agent and I judged it premature to make a fuss.

Callistus reiterated that he had no idea who the dead man could be, or who might have put him in the chest. We agreed it was someone who had known the chest existed, but that told us little because it could be a number of people. Callistus stressed the likely involvement of warehouse staff, rather than anyone connected with his family; I made no comment.

Either way, the perpetrator must have thought the chest would continue to be stored there while the body rotted until identification became impossible. Callistus insisted the killer could not be close to his family; otherwise whoever it was would have heard the auction being discussed. In the way of families, they had had argy-bargy about the sale over breakfast every day.

I asked if Callistus Primus would take a look at the corpse while we had it, but he refused.

I didn't blame him. I smiled and said so.

Looking curious, he asked why I was bothering with this. I explained how my father and I took responsibility for the mysterious dead. Somebody had to. 'You may like to think that if your wife poisons your mushrooms, someone will expose her crime before she grabs the inheritance.' Callistus Primus's expression changed. So he had a wife. I did not necessarily assume she wanted to kill him off. 'The work suits us,' I went on drily, still thinking about his faint facial twitch. 'We meet a lively cross section of society and we solve puzzles. We hope to console people. Perhaps the strongbox man had a worried old mother or little children who are now crying for their missing breadwinner.'

'You must be crazy,' Callistus disagreed. 'Why don't you just shove the remains on a rubbish heap like anybody sensible?'

I smiled again. 'We may yet do so.'

His question was a good one, of course: why hadn't whoever hid away this corpse simply secreted him under a pile of dung on the streets or weighed him down with rocks in the river?

An answer might be that the dead man was somebody who would be searched for, his disappearance perhaps reported to the authorities, notices asking for help put up in public places. If such a corpse happened to be found, it might be recognised. Perhaps that would make his killer or killers obvious. Maybe there had been bad blood with someone. A clear motive. So leaving him to rot in a box might have seemed safer.

This was good news. If the corpse was identifiable, the incident was worth looking into. I stood some chance of solving the mystery – and if I did, a grateful associate of the dead man might even pay for news of his fate.

Don't start going all self-righteous. I have to think about fees. Being an informer is not an act of public benevolence. Nobody does it to win approval from their gods. It's a job. It's supposed to pay your rent. It puts bread on the table. If you are good enough, it even buys all the wine you have to drink to make you forget what a horrible job informing is.

The sight of that body in the chest was a disturbing memory.

4

The Callisti hired storage space in an old granary a couple of streets off the Via Tusculana; it runs on the east side of the northern peak of the Caelian, not quite as far along as the Querculana Gate with its lovely little grove of oak trees. People choose such storage places because granaries are specially built to be secure, dry and comparatively fireproof. They have thick walls and strong floors raised on brick columns for aeration, with a certain amount of fortification against vermin – although any smart rat knows granaries are food containers. It was lucky the box containing the corpse had been so strong, despite the fire damage, or he would have been nibbled.

The biggest granaries and stores are situated along the river, but Rome is packed with warehouses. This was freedman-owned and not enormous, just one courtyard, with only a single entrance beneath a modest brick pediment. Rooms led off the courtyard on three levels, with ramps instead of stairs to the upper floors to assist loading. There was a small lodge near the entrance, then rows of other rooms that I could see were all barred with wooden beams, secured with heavy padlocks after they were slotted in. You could not squeeze a cart through the entrance (a security measure) so there were loaders to hand-manoeuvre goods. They looked foreign. Slaves, I presumed.

Callistus had given me a letter of introduction. This caused more suspicion among the granary guards than if I had simply turned up and asked questions. For one thing, they were unable to read. I had to untie the tablet strings and recite the contents. If the letter had really been a recipe for turnip soup they would have been none the wiser.

They were a pair of Syrians who had only broken Latin, perhaps because few people ever spoke to them. I mimed an attempt at translation, before we all gave up and they waved me in. Being on guard was so boring they fetched keys and were soon happily taking me round and showing me what valuables everybody had in store. That was interesting. Bullion boxes. Jewellery caskets. Lifetime records. Mildly hideous paintings.

Why would anybody want four identical statues of Venus with the Big Behind? Try not to be lewd when answering. Send suggestions to the procurator for art tax fraud at the Imperial Treasury. Don't hold your breath for a reward.

While the guards were being so helpful, a clerk bustled up, returning from a late breakfast or early lunch. I could smell wine on his breath from four strides away. Someone must have let him know I was there, so he came tumbling back from his all-day bar vigil. He looked nervous. Was that because he knew there had been foul play?

The clerk was a tufty, paunchy, bleary-eyed disaster. He shooed away the guards and himself showed me to the ground-floor room where the Callisti kept their unwanted stuff. It was almost empty after their recent clear-out, though various dud bits still remained, no doubt rejected by Gornia as unworthy of sale. Short oars, mostly. Nothing that appealed to us: we specialise in reproduction marble wares with not too many pieces missing, or furniture we can describe as high-end, even if that's pushing it. We don't handle stupendously barnacled planks.

Gornia must have accepted the fire-damaged chest because it had once been really good quality. People who attend auctions will buy anything if it is correctly talked up. There had been a period when we needed to conceal from buyers the fact that something had emerged from the volcano eruption, but its sad associations had not been a deterrent for long. 'Vesuvian' was now attractive, because people thought it meant 'owner lost; item going cheap'.

A large rectangular patch in the dust on the floor, with various scuff marks, showed where the great chest had stood and how it had been dragged out. There were footprints in the dust, none meaningful now. Our auction staff would have trampled about, unaware they were compromising evidence. If the dead man had been seized and tied up here, there was no way now to tell. Nor could I deduce how many assailants had been with him.

The door to the room was protected with a hefty padlock, for which the clerk had produced a key when he let me in.

'Where do you keep the padlock keys?'

In his little office by the gate, all hung on hooks, all labelled. I asked what happened if anybody called unexpectedly, wanting access to their store, while he was off the premises, as he clearly often was. The lying lump swore the guards turned people away, but I already knew better from their guided tour for me. All you needed was an air of authority. I bet those guards would even let anyone charming take a key for themselves. The lodge with all the keys was not locked.

We walked back to the gate, where the guards were pretending to look busy. I quizzed them about any visitors a week ago, but as far as I could tell through the language barrier they remembered no one. It seemed pointless to ask the tipsy clerk, but I dutifully raised one eyebrow and inevitably he shook his head. I asked if records were kept of when storerooms were opened and by whom. Of course not.

Irritated, I told the clerk he had to go to the undertaker's and see the body, in case he recognised the man. He tried to wriggle out of it, but I said if he refused to cooperate I would report him for negligence. Even a habitual drunk could see that having a corpse dropped there without his knowledge counted against him.

'Go today,' I said, adding cruelly, 'He's in a horrible condition, so we can't delay the funeral. Have a good look at him, before he gets any more putrid.'

It struck me that, since this granary was so cool and airy, I might have underestimated how long Strongbox Man had been dead. The Callistus storeroom was not so chilly as a cave or cellar, but inside three-foot walls its temperature felt even and low. I had arrived at the building flapping the top edge of my tunic to fan myself, but cooled off comfortably while there. This atmosphere might have kept the body fresh. Not long enough for me to be very far out, though; not in Rome in July. Call the corpse ten days old, rather than a week.

I was about to leave, feeling despondent and tired.

In the shadow of the entrance gate other visitors were loading scroll boxes onto a handcart wielded by a grumbling slave. I recognised the cart first, next the slave, then his master. The master wore formal dress, a rich white tunic with wide purple stripes on the hems. It makes magistrates stand out anywhere, which presumably is the intention.

His name was Manlius Faustus. He was the noble friend who had saved my life when I was ill. I was surprised to find him here; he looked perplexed to see me.

'Oh, no!' grumbled the slave, whose name was Dromo. 'Now I'll have two of them bossing me!'

'Shut up, Dromo.'

I said that. Faustus, always a silent type, was too preoccupied. He was inspecting me tetchily – a man who had put himself out for a woman whose foolish behaviour was now jeopardising his good work. I began to feel hot and queasy, enduring the scrutiny.

5

'You look ready to pass out!' Faustus dropped the merciless Medusa stare. He ran his fingers through a head of dark hair in an exasperated gesture. He had seen me at my lowest ebb, and I now felt shy with him. 'What happened to convalescing? Please don't tell me you are working, Albia.'

Even though we were in the dank shade of a large gatehouse, sunlight came whacking in off the street outside with its full midday glare. He must have seen I was finding it too much.

'Just an errand for our family business,' I hedged. 'My father is still at the coast—'

'What can be so important? Look at the state of you. You need to sit down and rest.' He was visibly agitated. 'I can't stop now. I dare not leave Dromo on his own – he'll be mugged in minutes . . . I'll have to take you with us.' Seeing I meant to object, he interrupted. 'We're only going three streets – is that your donkey?'

'How can you tell?' I murmured.

'By how hopeless it is.'

Gornia's donkey stood with its head down, apparently too careworn to bray. He was of mixed colouring, with uneven brown patterns, and known to our staff as Patchy. 'Kind-hearted Tiberius, the mangeball is acting. I know how much he costs in hay.' I stroked the beast's long ears; it leaned on me confidingly. I staggered, as it nearly pushed me over.

Faustus shouldered Patchy off me. He was a naturally sturdy plebeian; he probably exercised, though never seemed unbearably athletic. I would call him strong but sensitive – except 'sensitive' fails to fit the whiplash rebukes he often launched at me.

He smacked the donkey on the rump, probably because he was too buttoned-up to do it to me. He was anxious. He cared, really. Too much for his own good, other people might say.

While Faustus and I had our tussle of wills, the boy with Gornia's sad animal put out his tongue at Dromo, who gurned back so hideously I was afraid his eyes would pop out. After these formalities the lads seemed to tolerate one another. Faustus also settled down. He turned back to the granary clerk. 'I hope we can count on you to support Vibius Marinus for aedile. He is holding a little reception for loyal supporters, so do come. Bring your friends – well, bring a few.' Faustus grinned affably so the dipsomaniac grinned back, won over by the offer of a free drink.

I was glimpsing how Manlius Faustus and his uncle had behaved with the public when he stood for office himself this time last year. It was a new side of him. I was not sure I liked it.

'Remember – give your voice to Vibius!'

Before I could dodge, Faustus put his warm hands on my waist and lifted me onto the donkey. Allowing people to save your life makes them very free with you.

He had put me up side-saddle. Of course there was no

saddle, only a threadbare cloth. Faustus had a glint in his eye as he realised I was considering whether to ride astride. Normally I do, but getting into position reveals bare legs. Manlius Faustus would really enjoy disapproving of that.

Since it made talking easier, I stayed put. Patchy moved off and we ambled along, trailed by the donkey boy and Dromo.

'Is that granary one of your uncle's buildings?' I asked. Faustus's Uncle Tullius owned commercial warehouses.

'No, but he keeps his old accounts there, rather than waste our own space. My uncle likes high-grade retail tenants who will pay heftily for decent security. That place is cheaper – but just a dump. I'm picking up documents for Sextus Vibius.'

'What are they?'

'Mortgages and leases his father wants to call in for cash to lavish on potential voters. A lot of influential senators are about to be spoiled – let us hope they are grateful.'

'And who is Vibius?'

'My old school friend,' he explained. 'I persuaded him to stand as an aedile. I am his campaign adviser.'

'Hard work?'

'Harder for me than him, it seems. I feel like a biffed fly, madly zizzing on the floor . . .' Actually, Faustus seemed cheerful enough. We had worked together on a couple of inquiries. He had energy and tenacity; I enjoyed sharing a case with him.

I had only known this man for three months, but when he seized my donkey's rein from the boy and led it himself, I knew he was after something; he probably wanted to work with me again.

* * *

He took me to an apartment on the Clivus Scauri, close to that gate in the Servian Walls where the Arch of the consuls Dolabella and Silanus stands. His friend lived in modest, though elegant, rooms on an upper floor with a wife I did not meet. His elderly parents had the ground floor, the original family home, from which the campaign for Vibius was being run. Apart from the extra space available, working downstairs was more convenient. There was constant coming and going. The house was very well placed for business in the Forum; depending on which way you turned, you could walk down easily through either of the valleys around the Caelian. It was obvious why aristocrats, and now other people with money, should want to live thereabouts.

The Vibii had money, judging by their furniture – for instance, a large round table with exquisite figured veneering, a table whose cost would have paid lifetime bills for poorer families. Trained by my father, I reckoned that on the right day it would make a good price at auction.

Faustus introduced his friend: Sextus Vibius Marinus. He was around the same age, thinner, with floppy hair. He had a jumpy manner, where Faustus was watchful and still.

It is odd how you can balk at your friends' friends. Faustus assumed I would love Vibius as he did, and be equally thrilled by their campaign. To me, Vibius seemed much less mature. I felt lukewarm about him and, had I been entitled to vote, I would have picked another candidate.

Vibius wandered off to take the mortgage scrolls to his father's study. Faustus, well at home there, ministered to me. He indicated a daybed (bronze frame and head pad, lavish cushions) and arranged refreshments. Resting with a long cold drink of water helped me recover quickly.

Reassured, Faustus apologised for being churlish with me earlier.

In theory there was social distance between us: I was a private investigator and he was a magistrate, whose remit included monitoring dangerous people like me. Some aediles were a problem in my line of work. If he wanted to be awkward, Manlius Faustus could have hampered my activities. But once someone willingly holds a sick bowl for you and sponges up your mess, perhaps he is unlikely to fine you or limit your activities.

'I overdid things today,' I admitted meekly.

'Promise to take care.'

I found it hard to choose the right words. 'I wanted to tell you how grateful I am—'

Faustus brushed aside my stilted thanks. 'Own up, you scamp. What *were* you doing at the granary?'

Reluctant to keep secrets from him, I explained about the body in the box and confessed my plan to investigate. Faustus pulled a face. 'Trust you!'

His friend reappeared and listened, intrigued, as Faustus tried to dissuade me. 'Just call in the vigiles, Albia.'

I claimed that my father would expect me to carry out enquiries. Faustus saw through that. 'Nonsense. You nearly died. This is too soon!'

'I promise I shall only make gentle enquiries. I haven't explored enough yet. All I have had time to do is question a certain Callistus Primus, who owns the box but denies knowledge of the stiff inside.'

To my surprise, Faustus and Vibius exchanged a glance. Faustus only said to me, 'We know Primus.'

I asked, 'So?' They both shrugged.

'Through Julia, my wife,' added Vibius cagily.

I left it. Faustus, for one, would have seen that I noticed the atmosphere.

'You must be busy,' Vibius suggested, trying to send me home.

Faustus overruled him. 'I asked Flavia Albia here on purpose.' He told me, 'You could help us.'

I knew his commissions. 'I need to solve the box-man problem.'

'That's heading nowhere . . . Listen, before you refuse.'

I owed him that. 'What, then?'

'You remember that tract I was reading – the advice to Cicero, supposedly written by his younger brother?'

I had a vision of lying ill in bed at my apartment, while Faustus sprawled in a wicker chair close by, choosing to entertain an invalid by reading aloud a published letter full of frank advice for political success. He made an unusual nurse. Very unusual. I blushed to remember.

Cicero's brother had been sufficiently cynical to keep me from drowsing as I howled at his proposals for getting a 'new man' elected as consul in traditional Rome.

'Oh, I remember, Faustus: keep your friends happy with promises in case you win, even though you may never be able to fulfil the promises, and probably don't intend to. Ruthlessly call in old favours. Talk sweetly, even to people you despise. Make yourself visible in the Forum on a daily basis. And – my favourite – brutally blacken the names of any other candidates. Is that devious tract your campaign manual, Tiberius Manlius? And you such a person of principle!'

His friend Vibius guffawed quietly.

'It worked for Cicero,' Faustus reminded us. 'I have lined

up all Sextus's family and friends, we visit the Forum at the same time each day so people now recognise us, we have lists of all the guilds and trade organisations to canvass, we are smooching special-interest groups, we give dinners and banquets, we attend public entertainments—'

'Tut! I hope you are not neglecting your own valuable work as aedile!' I was mimicking the tone in which he often criticised me. 'Who is chasing down dangerous animals and rounding up gamblers?' Faustus compressed his lips, his way to hide a smile if I ever wriggled under his defences. 'Oh, I get it.' Light dawned. 'You want me to dig out sleaze?'

'The Cicero brothers discovered that one of their opponents had murdered someone.'

'Lucky them!'

'I don't expect to unearth any serious crimes,' Faustus assured me, 'but I need you to advise where to look for scandal.'

Vibius, who was to benefit from this, muttered anxiously, 'All respect to your clever associate, Tiberius, but could my reputation be damaged if I use an informer?'

I was used to rudeness. 'Set your mind at rest, Sextus Vibius. The informers you have heard about are seedy men who collect information to prosecute victims. As a woman, court work is barred to me. I help private clients on personal business; many are women. I am, hopefully, invisible to the rest of the public.'

Faustus looked embarrassed. 'Show Flavia Albia more respect, Sextus. Her father is an equestrian. He outranks us – and therefore so does she.'

I countered that gently: 'Falco remains a plebeian at heart – and therefore so do I . . . Your opponents will be checking on you too,' I pointed out to Vibius, wanting to demonstrate my skills. 'Try to spot who their informers are. Ask me, in case I know anything against them. Then use my father's trick – march straight up and greet them by name, cheerily suggesting they question you directly. Since openness is your policy, you will gladly supply the full facts.'

'And shall I?'

'Olympus, of course not! If you are to be a politician, your natural medium is lying. Surely your agent has explained that?'

Again, Faustus had to control a smile. 'So, what should we be looking for, Albia? And what will the opposition try to uncover against Sextus?'

I had plenty of ideas. 'A good informer will closely shadow a rival candidate, monitoring his life. The informer will be very persistent. Where does this man have lunch – does he go home, or slip down a quiet side-street to a pretty apartment that is occupied by a vivacious young woman, not his wife? When he attends a harp recital, does he take his honoured spouse – or does he spend time in close conversation with the wife of his best friend?'

Both men nodded gravely. Faustus had not always been pure and I wondered about Vibius. There would be no point in criticising his opponents if they discovered worse things done by him.

Personally, I would not think Vibius Marinus was worth a rash affair. Still, other women constantly surprise me with their crazy choice of lovers.

Faustus, on the other hand . . . But I had tried to get him into bed. No luck.

'For really juicy titbits,' I went on, 'winkle out who the candidates bank with. Have a quiet word. Are they in debt?'

More nods. 'When they parade their so-supportive family in the Forum, who is quietly missing? Have they behaved badly to a sibling, wife or child? Do they have a complicated history of divorce?' I tried not to look at Faustus, who himself had that. 'We must cosy up to their slaves and ask how popular they really are. And don't be fooled by the business associates who are supporting them. Look for associates who have *stopped* doing business with them. Then we'll find out why.'

Faustus exclaimed admiringly to Vibius, 'I told you! Flavia Albia is superb. She has even more gristle than Quintus Cicero. You see why I want her with us.'

'Oh, you just want to supervise my convalescence,' I murmured.

He quickly gleamed at me, not denying it. 'Sextus, listen to her and don't let me see you slipping down any side-streets for libidinous lunches! You must have an immaculate reputation. Which, of course, you do,' he assured his friend, sounding as if he fully believed it. A true politician.

I was privately glad of this chance to work with Faustus. I asked who the other candidates were, the men I had to lumber with grubby reputations. Faustus supplied names. I wrote them in my note tablet. Vibius mentioned someone else, Volusius Firmus. 'No, he dropped out,' Faustus said. 'Don't know why. Run out of money? Salvius Gratus is pooling resources and working with us,' he told me.

'A joint ticket?'

'A coalition.'

'Is that legal?'

'No, but everyone does it.'

'What is Gratus like?' I asked.

'Surprisingly amenable, given he is your ex-brother-in-law,' chuckled Vibius to Faustus. That was unwelcome news.

I knew how Faustus had come to be divorced. I had had recent dealings with his ex-wife, Laia Gratiana. She was bound to be supporting her brother but her grudging presence as a campaign collaborator held little appeal for me.

I wondered how much Vibius knew. Faustus had confided in me the story of his split from Laia: his fault, due to a fling with the wife of a patron. Ten years ago, he must have told his best friend something, though the scandal was hushed up. Had he been as frank with Sextus Vibius then as he had been more recently, after his wounds had healed, with me?

Faustus looked uneasy so I changed the subject. 'I am puzzled, Tiberius. I thought elections were no longer held. Our emperor pores over the lists and controls new appointments himself. If Domitian has the final veto, what is the point of campaigning?'

Faustus groaned bitterly. I saw him check around with a glance, making sure there were no pottering slaves to overhear. 'Good question. Domitian certainly chooses the consuls. But years ago electing other magistrates was passed to the Senate.'

'Domitian loathes the Senate!'

'But, remember, a tyrant hates to admit he is one,' Faustus said quietly. 'The worse he is, the more he claims – and even believes – that traditional religion and democracy matter to him deeply and determine all his actions.'

That was true. Some of Domitian's worst cruelties had been carried out in the name of upholding some ancient practice or in supposed devotion to the gods. His favourite excuse for executing people was to claim they were 'atheists'. (This could have been macabre humour on his part: the god that people didn't believe in was Domitian.)

'Candidates announce they are standing,' Faustus continued, 'then lobby important people, including senators.'

'It is taken seriously? But canvassing who? Emperor or Senate?'

'Hopefuls ascertain that the Emperor has no objection to them – and, if possible, even get him to call them "Caesar's candidates". That makes success certain because, obviously, Domitian's choices are voted on first.'

'Why are you campaigning now?' I asked. 'Don't the Senate vote in January?'

Faustus scowled. 'In the old days, elections for aedile took place in July. The job starts on the first of January, so a successful man had six months to prepare himself. Now people still campaign in July even though aediles designate are appointed for the following twelve months.'

'Hades! You could have fallen under a cart by then!'

'Or simply lost interest.' He seemed depressed. 'If we are especially unlucky, by January the Emperor will have returned from Pannonia and he will turn up to preside.'

'Don't worry. He hardly ever goes to the Senate. But I assume you can't canvass Domitian directly. You work on his officials?'

Faustus groaned. 'Endless imperial freedmen.'

'So you ran your friend's name past some stylus-pusher?'

'We tried. They are all jumpy. Their chief, Abascantus, has been sent away under a cloud. Currently no one knows who is in charge.'

I nodded. 'Domitian could have any of them removed tomorrow. The old "mismanagement of funds" charge, no chance to defend themselves, then swift execution . . . My father knows one who may help,' I volunteered. 'Claudius Laeta – he is elderly now, but bureaucrats never entirely retire.'

'Would your father mediate for us?'

'No need. We can take along some invalid porridge and I'll introduce you to the tottery scroll-master myself.'

Faustus raised his eyebrows. Turning to Vibius, he said, 'Flavia Albia always amazes me. The other thing I have not mentioned is that she has two uncles in the Senate.'

Vibius was certainly not grateful. 'Just another five hundred and ninety-eight to win over,' he grumbled self-defeatingly.

Faustus had met my uncles, Camillus Aelianus and Camillus Justinus, when they advised us on a case. I would make no attempt to coerce them. Let other women work behind the scenes for political favours; I had never seen that as my role. Faustus would have to persuade them himself. But I did suggest I would let him know next time I intended to visit so he could tag along.

Faustus eagerly suggested he bring Vibius, too. I agreed, though somewhat coolly.

The conversation ended. I took my leave, since I wanted to conduct research on all the candidates before anything else.

I had another motive. Manlius Faustus seemed to think he had diverted me, but I was still interested in the dead man found by the auction staff. I pretended I was going home to rest, though in fact I intended to visit the undertaker.

Faustus had sent away Gornia's donkey earlier; he now produced a carrying chair, I think borrowed from his friend's mother. 'Take Flavia Albia wherever she wants to go,' he ordered the bearers. Then to me he pleaded, 'One diversion, Albiola! Promise me not to tire yourself – just one sly errand, then please go straight home.'

He knew me too well.

6

I had had the body sent to Fundanus. He was a barbarian. I don't mean he came from a country outside the Empire where they cannot speak Greek and eat their children. His forebears had had premises by the Circus Maximus for generations, believing that narrow-minded opinions were their ancient right as Roman males. From conversations Fundanus had inflicted on me about his filthy views on life, I knew he thought slaves were less than human, foreigners not much better, that all men should beat their wives and all women were sluts. He called this traditional. I called it rats' piss. I deduced he had a forceful wife he was scared of.

He organised slave-torture for the state and for private individuals, so he was bound to be crude. It did make him an ideal undertaker after foul play, an unflinching brute who could cope with any unpleasantness.

Fundanus was cheery. Coming from Britannia, I happen to know that true barbarians tend to be morose. They stand around flicking fleas out of their curly beards and moaning that if the rain doesn't let up the crops will fail. Sometimes it snows in Britain, which they find very exciting since iced-up beards don't itch so much, and it gives them a chance to drown, falling into frozen lakes.

A true barbarian engages in human sacrifice, but for the

best of reasons. Fundanus was horrible because he liked it. I was not looking forward to talking to him about the man in the chest while I was still feeling seedy. There was a good chance I would snap at his diatribe, grab an embalming tool and shove it down his throat. Never helpful. I tried to be more mature, these days.

Perhaps it was lucky Fundanus was out.

One of his staff, a pyre-builder, talked to me. He had probably absorbed his master's hate-based bigotry but he had a fluffy little beard and came across as a sweetie. He may not have noticed I was female and a foreigner. If he had, he knew I was paying the bill and respected that.

He told me they had learned little more than I had seen for myself. Fundanus had put the dead man at fifty-five or sixty, older than I had thought; he was generously built and well fed, enjoyed his drink and could afford it. In so far as his gooey remains could be inspected, the funeral people had found no distinguishing scars, misshapen bones, tattoos, birthmarks or amputated limbs. His teeth were ground down and half missing, just like everyone's. He had no obvious signs of disease, having died from being trapped in a confined space. Fundanus thought the man had been thumped, probably to stop him struggling while his arms were being bound, so he was unconscious when he went into the box. He probably never woke again and the expression I had thought I saw on his face meant nothing.

I was relieved. 'That makes it a kinder death. I bet Fundanus was disappointed; he loves to imagine pain . . . But when his assailants put him there, the man was alive?'

'Possibly – they could not tell.'

'You are very fair-minded! And this was a respectable citizen?'

'Barbered and manicured. Nice tunic and undershift – regrettably we had to burn them. White mark from a signet ring that someone had removed. There was a plain wedding ring they didn't bother to take. We had to cut his finger off, but the ring is here for you.'

'Please tell me the finger is not still in it.' I knew funeral directors' ways.

The pyre slave grinned. 'I can pull it out.'

I nodded weakly. 'My hero!' The slave considerately turned his back. There was a slight thump as he chucked the finger into a rubbish pail, then he handed me a metal object. He had the courtesy to place it on a scrap of material in which I could wrap the unsavoury takeaway; best not to wonder whose tunic they had cut up for rags or what that person had died of.

I scrutinised the ring, which was narrow and undecorated. 'Real gold, or mainly so. Half of Rome has one like this, except when they are chatting someone up so take it off to hide the fact they're married . . . Was there anything else?'

'Do you want to see his belt?' The slave unbuckled a decent leather effort that he was himself wearing. It looked standard and difficult to trace so I gave it back to him.

He had on a pair of good boots too. He saw me looking, but we did not mention those.

They did not fit. As he saw me out, he walked in an awkward, bandy-legged way.

While I was being taken home, I thought hard but could see no way to go forward with this odd mystery.

Even so, I was not ready to admit failure. The auction staff, and Manlius Faustus, were all waiting for me to drop the case. I would delay as long as possible before I caved in.

7

When I returned to Fountain Court I felt tired, yet more stable climbing the two flights back to my apartment than I had been that afternoon coming downstairs. Work had given me a boost. Informers are tragic people.

I slept soundly, rose early, then went out for breakfast. On my way, I told Rodan to send a message down to the auction house, asking for use of Patchy every day until my stamina improved. The others would curse me, but old Gornia would be thrilled because he could sleep at the Saepta Julia. He would be happier there, cramped among the dusty stored furniture, than in his terrible doss. I made a note to tell Father to give him a mattress and not make him go home all the time. That way, if Gornia was taken ill in the night, someone would be there to help him in the morning. If he died, we would soon find him.

I ate at the Stargazer, my tiresome aunt's terrible bar. Sometimes Manlius Faustus happened along and joined me in a bread roll, though not today. He would be busy with his friend. Until the election was over, we would have to shelve our habit of meeting 'by chance' as I took breakfast. Today I chatted with Apollonius while he served at the counter, but it wasn't the same.

I told myself working with Faustus was fine, but I must not grow too used to it. Better the pleasure I used to take in waking up slowly over my dish of olives in my own quiet company.

Then I kicked the table leg and thought, dammit, I liked breakfasting with Faustus.

To work.

I wanted to size up the rival candidates. The best place to start would be in the Forum where I could take a look at them parading with their retinues. If they had read that tract by Quintus Cicero, they would appear good and early. None would have read it personally, but all their advisers would have pored over the thing. Like Faustus, the men behind the other candidates would be crazily searching for ways to success, looking for the magic charm. I remembered when my family was plotting to get my uncles, the Camillus brothers, into the Senate. They were hopeless. We had to do everything.

People with asthma should avoid men who are running for office. They are called candidates because on formal occasions they wear robes whitened with chalk. The Latin for 'white' is *candida*. I found this year's contenders by following the clouds of white dust and bystanders coughing . . . I am not entirely joking. But the commotion made by the chalkies' supporters, together with the hoary jeers they were throwing at each other, helped identify them.

What a glorious crop. (Now I *am* joking.)

Vibius Marinus had already set my teeth on edge, even though the respectable Manlius Faustus could be heard assuring onlookers that his friend was a man of grit, integrity and flawless ancestors, who would be a hard-working, honourable magistrate. Vibius smiled graciously. Any swine can do that.

Trebonius Fulvo and Arulenus Crescens were working a ticket in partnership, and doing so effortlessly. They looked a pair of bullies. Surrounded by bull-necked cronies, one had fistfuls of finger-rings and a lazy eye; the other carried three times his proper weight, rolling through the crowds with a side-to-side sway, like a sailor. I decided on sight that neither had an interest in public service for its own sake; both would use any office for their own advancement. They would pick on people for petty misdemeanours, then take handouts in return for not punishing them. But their campaigning style was so smooth it made me groan. They could talk like fishmongers pushing last Thursday's rancid octopus. I quickly identified the slick duo as having the morals of the brothel and the habits of the gutter. The electorate love that. These two were the serious opposition for Vibius and Gratus.

Dillius Surus appeared to have only just crawled out of bed, so I made a note to look into the tousled layabout's drinking habits. With luck, his late-night antics would involve flute-girls of the good-time kind. Well, any flute-girl would do. Even if she's virginal, nobody believes it. Needless to say, the crowd were being kind to Dillius. They adore anyone debauched.

Ennius Verecundus smiled constantly and was supported by his mother. She wore one of those old-fashioned outer tunics with thin straps over the shoulder, and had her hair screwed back so hard it hurt to see. Traditional: she could have whopped the warlike Volscians single-handed. I would have voted for her. I would have been frightened not to.

And, finally, here came Lucius Salvius Gratus, significantly wealthy brother to Laia Gratiana. Neat and trim; well organised and bumptious. The type my father hates on sight, my mother, too. He had fair hair with pale skin and looked as if he were constantly blushing, though I guessed he was as shameless as the rest. His pale, thin, elegant sister stood loyally beside him, though was too snooty to shout his praise in public. She would work on people in private, not wanting to be mistaken for a loud-mouthed manicurist – as if anyone ever would. Manicurists are lovely girls.

Famous herself for show-off religious duties at the Temple of Ceres, Laia was expensively dressed, heavily jewelled and naturally blonde. These traits amount to star voter-appeal. If Faustus's ex-wife helped get his best friend elected – which she would, if people were as daft as I thought – it was not for me to quibble.

I wanted Faustus to be happy. Which was exactly what Laia Gratiana had probably never cared about, and almost certainly the reason that, as her husband, he had been lured elsewhere.

Titan's turds, if I had seen him married to Laia, I would have lured him myself, as an act of religious duty.

Each candidate was called a *petitor*, because he was petitioning voters, so his opponents were his *com*petitors. Latin is a pleasingly constructed language. (I speak with British irony: imagine how it felt to come from stealing crusts on the unmade streets of Londinium to having the passive periphrastic, otherwise called the gerundive of obligation, explained to you, even by a patient woman. Helena was lucky I was bright.)

I was lucky. I know the exact moment when a stolen crust becomes too mouldy to eat. If you are starving, that is much more useful than the four conjugations of verbs.

Latin is the argot of despots, intended to confuse people. *Domitianus adoranda est.* The tyrant must be worshipped. Our master and god. Well, yours maybe. Some of us have taste.

I digress. Is this a tiresome Roman habit, or delightful British naïveté? Either way, I have it.

In the manner of my mother, I will now patiently explain elections, otherwise called an obligation of democracy. (Helena Justina explains things satirically.)

In Rome, when such things as elections were allowed, competitors paraded before their fellow-citizens for several weeks beforehand. Wearing their whitened togas, they were attended by tribes of supporters, whom they were not allowed to hire in. Back then, candidates had to persuade the entire public to vote for them, which included going to towns and villages outside Rome. Now candidates only had to make themselves look popular enough to impress senators.

Supporters would be of their own status, or higher if possible, although candidates were also followed around by poor citizens; this was supposedly because the poor had no other way to show their feelings. Those of the poor who bothered to turn up had two ways to make their support known: force of numbers and rioting. Everyone was having a rest from rioting today. It was too hot.

I was listening intently for any insults thrown by members of the crowd, hoping to discover usable sleaze. People were too exhausted for that too.

There would be scandals, and I would find them. I was a good informer. I stayed confident.

The candidates' campaign process was called 'going about'. They had to be continually on show, endlessly pleading for support. This was tiring for them and a bore for everybody else.

I watched the men taking their walks through the Forum. Each was accompanied by a helper, who told him the names of those they met. This was done openly, yet to be addressed familiarly was always taken as a compliment. The Roman public was pitifully easy to please. The candidate's false intimacy was sealed with a handshake. I never managed to spot money being passed over. It was illegal. That never stopped it.

Of course money was paid for support. To keep it secret and avoid legal penalties, agents were employed. They made their bargains in street-corner bars, then stakeholders kept the money until payment fell due. Laws against bribery were numerous – a testament to how prevalent it was.

Candidates had to deposit a sum of money before they started, which they would forfeit if they were convicted of corruption. That was a joke, though even the mildest competitor would not shrink from taking his opponents to court. Sextus Vibius had been right to complain that some informers made an income from litigation. Going to court over something or other was a regular sideshow, almost a duty; Vibius would expect to prosecute rivals soon, if Faustus had proper control of their campaign. I might find evidence for them. It was usually a farce and came to nothing. All the judges had been candidates for office themselves, so tried not to let anyone be disgraced.

If a candidate used violence, he could be exiled. That never happened. Black eyes and split lips were everywhere this morning, but those could be merely the after-effects of banquets.

I did wonder whether the man found in the auction chest

had been uncooperative over promising his support. Murdering him seemed extreme . . . Even so, feelings can run high. I wondered facetiously which candidate might stoop to murder.

Trebonius and Arulenus, the smooth-talking bruisers, looked the most likely. Dillius Surus, white-faced with his hangover, seemed too washed-out, though he might possess friends who were fixers. The mother's boy, Ennius Verecundus, I dismissed. He had the mark of a man who would fail to get elected through simple worthiness – despite which, I thought he would make the best aedile. Throughout his year in office his mother would make it her business to patrol the streets, reporting problems to her son. If he didn't know what to do about antisocial behaviour, she would soon tell him.

Salvius Gratus, Laia's brother, seemed unlikely to load a man into someone else's strongbox, or even to use an agent to do it by proxy. And Vibius Marinus had been turned out by Faustus looking utterly decent and trustworthy. Mind you, Vibius and Faustus had said they knew Callistus Primus, the owner of the chest . . . Still wondering how that was, and why they were reticent about it, I began the gentle process of making candidate-enquiries.

I moved around, standing quietly on the edges of crowds, listening at first. When I had the feel of things, I murmured questions to fellow bystanders.

'That one sounds all right. Nice speaking voice. I'll tell my husband to vote for him. Is he rich?'

'Must be.'

'Promising! I wonder who he banks with?'

Given how dearly people like to keep their business confidential, it was surprisingly easy to winkle out background.

Helpful members of the public passed on dirty details. Soon I knew Trebonius Fulvo was involved in a lengthy wrangle about mortgages (a law case brought by his own elderly grandfather, who had a terminal disease, poor man, and feared he would not live to see justice), while his colleague Dillius Surus had been accused by a heartbroken mistress of fathering a daughter on the promise of marriage and (this was the real eye-waterer) stealing her jewellery, including a valuable necklace that another lover had given her . . . As I found out later, much of this was unreliable.

Rumours would do. When you blacken someone's name in politics, hearsay can be freely deployed. Scandal needs to be colourful, not true. Vibius was never going to win if he had a conscience.

'Surus looks like a lush to me,' I suggested.

'Oh, he's a wonderful character. Laugh a minute, really enjoys life. We need a breath of fresh air in Rome.'

Nobody knew who financed the candidates but I think that detail is always telling. I had to find out for myself. I would ask a banker.

8

On the left side of the Forum, as you face away from the Capitol and just after the Curia, lies the two-storey Basilica Aemilia, adorned with a colonnade called the Porticus of Gaius and Lucius. This was the Emperor Augustus honouring his grandson heirs through fancy shops. Gaius and Lucius died, but their fine arcade was still here, still smart enough to be frequented by bankers pretending to be upmarket. Our family used Nothokleptes, which Father claimed means *thieving bastard*, a pseudonym bestowed by my uncle, Lucius Petronius. There were now two generations in the firm, and we used the son even though wicked Uncle Petro said that for him we should add *useless*.

Young Notho still kept chained deposit chests in the main aisle, on the lower level where desperate debtors could rush straight in from the Forum, into the arms of the kind-hearted financiers who were waiting to save them from creditors. For a huge fee.

The banking stations graced a lofty interior that had massive floor-slabs of marble in beautiful, expensive international varieties. There I found the folding bronze stool Nothokleptes used, standing empty beside a change table, guarded by an ugly Pisidian bouncer, under a frieze with scenes from Roman myth and an enormous statue of a barbarian. I assume this was commissioned in gratitude, for it symbolised the origins of Rome's wealth: crushing peoples from provinces like mine.

I am generally Roman, but portrayals of sad, defeated nudes in torcs soon turn me back into a Briton.

I went straight upstairs, ignoring the Pisidian, apart from a mild jibe of 'Who are you staring at, pig-face?' (This was not prejudice, but factually accurate: his snout was squashed, he always stared and I always said it.) Nothokleptes Junior was at his barber's in the upper colonnade. He was shady, even by the Egyptian standards from which he took both his monetary heritage and his crazy hairstyle. His rings were so chunky they kept his fingers splayed. Born and bred in Rome, he still managed to find tunics that were too long and too tight over his big belly, so he looked Oriental. Which in any lexicon is another word for dubious.

His father was sitting with him, now reduced by age to watery smiles and silence. Always a heavy man, Nothokleptes Senior had spread slowly into a vast blob of smooth flesh. They had pegged a barber's napkin under his chin, even though he was not being shaved, in case he dribbled. He didn't know the time of day, but if you put a bag of mixed coins in front of him, he would rapidly sort it into denominations while palming a percentage by some sleight you could never spot. Most of his brain was far away, but his essence persisted. He still loved the feel of copper and silver under his clever fingers.

His son was having his beard painfully scraped off with pumice, a daily routine that nevertheless left him permanently blue-jawed. 'Nothokleptes! Yes, you, the useless one!'

Junior gave me the family glare, a mix of blatant ingratiation and mild rebuke for *useless thieving bastard*. He would never get us to stop and, thanks to Uncle Petro, half Rome believed it was his real name.

'Flavia Albia.' His father had taught him to be reverently formal. This was supposed to set people at ease while loans they could not afford were seductively pressed upon them. It must work. They had pots of lucre to use for making more. Nothokleptes Junior had collected at least three priesthoods to show how highly the public valued being fleeced by him. 'And how are you this fine day, Flavia Albia?'

'Too hot. You can drop the fake politeness. I don't need you. I'm solvent.'

He pretended to laugh. 'So like your dear father.' He turned to his own and shouted, 'Look, oldster, it's Falco's daughter!'

Nothokleptes Senior dribbled with what might have been delight.

'Didius Falco sends his regards,' I told him gently. That was nothing like what Falco would have said, but the old man was past insulting.

'So, daughter of the esteemed Marcus Didius, our favourite client,' smarmed Junior, jumping up from the barber's chair in the hope that he was tall enough to look down my tunic (he wasn't but he never learned), 'if you don't want financial advice . . .'

'Your advice is always "Borrow a lot of money from us at wincing rates of interest"! I can do without that kind of sorrow. No, I am working, Notho.'

I told him about both my lines of enquiry. The man found in the chest fascinated him more than the election rivals.

'It's always possible the deceased in the strongbox had reneged on a loan with one of your more vicious colleagues and was punished as an example,' I suggested. 'He looked respectable before he started rotting, so if you hear of any punter who's gone missing unexpectedly I'd like to know.'

'You don't need the ones we *expect* to disappear?'

'No point. Your flight-risk bankrupts will have planned their exile – besides, they will come sneaking back, once they get tired of hiding on Greek islands. This man has met a surprise fate, I believe. I have no clue to his identity. He could be anybody. Even, in fact, a banker.'

'Flavia Albia, if a banker goes missing, everyone will know.'

'Yes, you're right. Cheers would resound from here to Tusculum.'

Junior was insulted too often to react. 'I have been eagerly waiting for your proceeds from the Callistus sale, Flavia Albia, but who will bid, when the goods are contaminated?'

'Fear not. Our staff say close contact with a corpse brings added value.'

He cheered up. 'So, any plans to have a body in every sale?'

'No. Restraint, Notho, is the motto of our house. Anyway, the market is too volatile – you can never get hold of a good gloopy cadaver at the right moment.'

He blenched. Changing the subject as a courtesy, I asked what he knew about the men standing for aedile. Even though Uncle Petro called him useless, he knew quite a lot. I obtained the names of all their bankers, plus confirmation that Dillius Surus had inherited the best wine cellar in Rome but it was now known to be empty, due to his diligent testing of vintages. 'It doesn't matter. He married a rich woman. Terentia wants to be the wife of a magistrate so, until he is one, she will humour him.'

'Into his grave, by the sound of it.'

'Could be her plan. They reckon he is about two days away from seeing eight-foot rats climbing walls. She'll find a new husband easily. Horrible woman, but she has exceedingly pretty investments. I'd love to acquire a client with such placement in Baetican olive oil and shipping squid-in-brine. Her broker is a magician, even though his armpits are hairy and his feet stink . . . Which of the fine upstanding bastards are you working for, Flavia Albia?'

'Vibius Marinus.'

'Handsome lad? Are you trying to get him into bed?'

'Notho, my father would kill me if I went to bed with a magistrate.' Well, only if he found out. 'No, his agent has employed me to dig dirt on the others.'

'Oh, you're going for easy labour, these days?' We laughed. 'What have you turned up so far?'

'After one morning's work and picking your brains, I think they are all unspeakable.'

Notho made an Egyptian gesture of amazement. 'Even your client? Mind you, Falco's customers were never up to much and I haven't noticed you choosing better. You want to start earning real money and build up some decent savings, Albia, or you'll never attract a new husband.'

'I want one who thinks I have a wonderful mind.'

'That's why you have been single for the past ten years.' Notho was wrong. I could have been married. I simply preferred to keep looking for a man whose habits and personality did not fill me with rage. 'Marinus, you say . . . I still fail to place him, Albia. Is he the wife-beater?'

'I hope not!'

'Well, somebody mentioned that one of them is. I forget exactly. Maybe it's Marinus whose dog bit a priestess of

Isis. And on her birthday, poor slut! The word is, she ended up with gangrene and has only days to live.'

'Ooh – lovely details. Thanks for that, Nothokleptes. I'll trace the dog and ask for his side of the story . . .'

Notho went on to say I had been misled about Dillius Surus suing his grandfather (the sick man who would not live to see justice); Notho claimed that was Trebonius Fulvo, one of the bullies. 'Are you sure?'

'Hard-arse who does weight-training? My cousin has the grandfather's account. It was all he could talk of last Saturnalia.'

'Thanks again, then . . . May I ask whom the banking fraternity have decided to support? I presume you have put your heads together and chosen your favourite?'

'Trebonius and Arulenus.'

'Surely not! They look like dangerous men.'

'Exactly.' Notho Junior was unrepentant. 'Looks are not everything – though Arulenus would do well to get that eye fixed. Weird appearance puts people off more than he thinks. But we cannot be complacent, Flavia Albia. These men are tough. They know how to govern. Firm hands on the tiller, that is what Rome needs. Not whimpering simpletons who will fail to collect any fines.'

Ah! Bankers would be involved in investing fines income – or even, when some aedile believed public office existed to help him amass bribes, they would launder the money. Either entailed fees for them.

Trebonius and Arulenus were perfect for bankers. Apparently they gave legendary dinners for their supporters and had promised they would change the law to allow higher interest rates.

They looked unbeatable. But were usury laws even in

the aediles' remit? I would consult Faustus. If not, Vibius Marinus could gain ground by announcing that his rivals not only sued their granddads and cheated on their fancy women but made impossible promises. Shocking!

All right. I am not that naïve. But if he accused them of lying, everyone would believe it. The rivals would never sue him; defamation had to diminish the plaintiff's reputation. Nobody would think any the less of Trebonius and Arulenus for the customary sin of fibbing.

There were probably no votes in this. But Vibius Marinus would look like a man who was enticingly outspoken. Rash claims about opponents can only help.

Slander was promising, but sleaze would be better. I must try to find some.

9

Talking to your own banker is hard, but it's nothing like trying to squeeze information from somebody else's. Juno, you might almost imagine that bankers are bound by confidentiality rules. This cannot be true. My father has many tales of ravenous creditors learning exactly when he had a few denarii – information only his banker could provide.

Yet they are picky who they speak to. Do you, an ordinary person, desire to check whether someone is creditworthy? Ask their tailor or their fishmonger. Their banker will never help, not even if the person in question owns vast unmortgaged estates and squillions in a strongbox in the Forum – no, not even if he wants you to believe he is sound so has himself given you his banker's name as a guarantee.

To tell the truth, if someone offers his banker as a reference, all the investigators in my family assume he has prepaid the banker to lie.

Nothokleptes and Nothokleptes certainly counted fake credit ratings as a service they provided. Rates were in their business prospectus. It came in cheaper than them sending bail money to get you out of prison. If you pleaded for that, the bastards charged a sky-high fee. Best of all for the Nothos was producing a witness statement in a claim for divorce – which they did *pro bono* because if they saved your dowry from a grasping spouse it enhanced your value to them.

How do I know these things? Because I am the one person in Rome who always scans notices and price lists. If words are written, I read them. Helena Justina brought me up that way.

Perhaps I should have clarified earlier that Notho and Son were not *my* bankers. They believed they were. Even my darling papa presumed it, although my mother was more astute. So the Nothos continued to suppose that if I ever had money to save I would tuck the coins into my father's strongbox, as an unmarried or widowed daughter ought to do – while (surprise!) no funds of that sort ever materialised.

My work rarely produced large sums. Such as it was, I needed my income right away for essentials, like laundry bills and food. Not to mention new earrings to cheer myself up. I had a secret place in Fountain Court where I stashed any spare cash – which was what most ordinary people in Rome did. It was the easiest way to please your neighbours in the burglary profession.

But years ago, when Lentullus and I first took up together, we had been given money by both Father and Quintus Camillus, for whom Lentullus worked. Once the family stopped viewing us as a ludicrously incongruous couple, they surprised us with a dowry. It was more cash than either of us had ever conceived of owning, and we regarded it as magic gold. We felt it wasn't really ours. We lived rent-free at Fountain Court and our outgoings were so modest that when my husband died only two years later, with us both still young, we had never touched the dowry money. Nobody wanted it back. I asked Uncle Quintus, who said that it remained mine. He was a lawyer, so he should know. I left it where I had put it.

That was, in a bank owned by a quiet Greek widow who had inherited this business from her own husband, a man who had died of apparently natural causes on a trip he made to Sardinia for reasons that were never explained. His will had left everything to Arsinoë, with instructions that she should marry one of their freedmen. That was traditional. Greek bankers did not want their widows to be left undefended. And I am assured there are Greek widows who do see being alone with large sums of money as a curse.

Amazingly, tragedy struck twice. As if poor Claudia Arsinoë had not enough to contend with, only four days after she heard her husband was dead the freedman she was promised to went out to buy a mullet for a nice Greek dinner and mysteriously disappeared. Ever since, Arsinoë had borne her sadness bravely; she ran everything herself and, like Penelope, fended off other suitors with pleas that she could not commit herself to them, sweet as they were, in case her missing fiancé one day reappeared.

She was cheerful despite being left in the lurch and I found her an excellent businesswoman. My dowry had trebled in the past ten years, thanks to her investment skills. I left it with her, accumulating. On the rare occasions when I had a love-life, I always forgot to mention that I possessed this money.

My love-life since Lentullus had died on me had been pitiful. I could not boast about it. Men who were attracted to the idea of a rich auctioneer's daughter soon fled once they met Falco. Even I could see this saved a lot of heartache. Father always kindly explained the situation to me. He was a thoughtful man and good with words. Words like 'A complete wastrel arse. Just dump the bugger, Albia.' In most cases dumping was either pre-empted by the wastrel having fled of his own accord after a chat with Falco, or I had seen through him anyway and already told him to get lost.

I intended to visit Claudia Arsinoë to pick her brains, which I knew were of fine quality. But first I went through the normal process. I tried the men with whom the candidates banked. It had to be done, though the results felt like waking in the middle of the night with unbearable heartburn.

Trebonius Fulvo and Arulenus Crescens both used the same firm. It was one of those money tables in the Clivus Argentarius where the proprietor never puts in an appearance; the slippery owner is always off somewhere, having mint tea and sticky Greek sweetmeats with equally sticky cronies, leaving peculiar underlings to run his bank. For him, that is the point of prosperity: he no longer has to engage in the dirty trade that established him.

The business was traditionally Athenian. The workers were completely unhelpful to a Roman woman. The banker had them trained to deflect questions. I dare say plenty of gossip was exchanged elsewhere over the pastries, because bankers need to do that, but not here. And even if I tracked him down, the best I could hope for was a ferocious Athenian grope, getting honey and crumbs on my dress. I skipped that.

What the flash banking table did tell me of its own accord was that the hard men, Trebonius and Arulenus, must be rich. Only people with serious assets can interest that kind of bank, or afford its rates.

They imported wine and oil. Nothokleptes had told me. Say no more.

* * *

Dillius Surus, the candidate with the drinking habit, banked with a fellow from Antioch, who also wasn't there. Maybe they drank together. Maybe the Syrian was sleeping it off.

The rich wife of this Dillius, his real financial backer, invested her large fortune with a scruffy-looking Gaul called Balonius, who favoured tunics with huge sleeveless armholes. These gaping spaces demonstrated that Notho had not lied. The broker had extremely hairy armpits, where his hirsute arms met hideous knobbly shoulders. He smelt as foul as he looked. He had extremely ugly feet too, clothed in the shabbiest sandals I had ever seen on a professional man. One had a broken strap so it hung off his instep.

He lolled in the shade of a statue of Scipio Africanus, that heavily togate hero with his firm mouth and a big nose. Men with expensive belts and women in tightly sealed carrying chairs visited Balonius to massage their healthy portfolios. A child would be sent to fetch them refreshments. I received a dish of olives and a fruit cordial, even though I admitted I was there on spec.

It slipped by me at the time, as it was meant to, but I realised afterwards that Balonius never said a word about his client, the wealthy wife of Dillius. He might look disgraceful, but he was efficient. On Dillius Surus himself, Balonius was more forthcoming. First he told me Forum gossip was wrong: it wasn't Dillius who was suing a dying grandfather. Balonius first thought that was Arulenus Crescens, the one who had recently abandoned a mistress and who had previously left his first wife when she was pregnant, but on reflection he decided the family litigant was Salvius Gratus, Laia's brother.

Balonius then happily gossiped that Dillius was impotent, had tapeworms, had been sued by a man to whom he owed thirty thousand sesterces (for an apple orchard where the trees had been felled by a jealous neighbour) and apparently it was also Dillius who owned the uncontrollable dog that had bitten the Temple of Isis priestess.

'Oh, this fine specimen will get elected!' I murmured.

'He will. Done deal. His wife gave Domitian a troupe of performing dwarfs whose act is deemed the most indecent ever seen outside an Alexandrian brothel.'

'That will be very useful information for my clients.'

Or not. There was no way the pious Manlius Faustus would encourage his friend Vibius to compete in gift-giving lewd performers. Faustus had the tenacity to find out where you could buy rude little men, and the guile to get them for a good price, but he would disapprove too much to do it.

'Now, what can you tell me about Trebonius or Arulenus?'

'Nix. More than my life's worth.'

'Do they frighten you?'

'Don't they frighten you?'

'I hope I am beneath their notice.'

'Don't be too sure. If you are asking questions, they will soon know.'

I gulped. To some extent it was for show. Not entirely. 'Well, never mind them. What about Vibius Marinus and Salvius Gratus?'

'I thought you were working for them?'

'Indeed I am – which is why I need to know exactly what libellous gossip is attaching to their glorious names.'

'You are a sly one!' Balonius scrutinised me with new respect. 'Marinus seems to keep his head down. Seems to be relying on the "good family man" posture. Fathering babies is a talent, so who needs moral stamina? Gratus is so invisible I've never even heard of him.'

'He won't like that! He bounces around like someone who wants to be famous.' And his sister thought herself wonderful too.

'So what does your man Vibius want to be known for?' asked the smelly broker, looking at me sideways.

I gave him a mysterious smile and said that remained to be seen.

Which was the truth. He was the friend of my most admirable friend, yet I had no idea.

10

I was tired, though not as tired as I had feared I might be. I spent a little longer in the Forum watching the candidates as they went about, giving fine performances of men who could be trusted with public funds, religious duties or other people's desperate hopes for the future: smiling, shaking hands, asking after the families of complete strangers, endlessly promising favours they would make no attempt to remember.

As they criss-crossed between the temples, arches and statues, the men nodded to one another if their paths met, while their womenfolk looked daggers. Prostitutes catcalled. Slaves cursed. Busy freedmen on urgent errands weaved in and out among them adroitly, dodging the more obvious pickpockets and the snack-sellers who carried enormous trays, often above their heads and at a dangerous angle. It was midday, with the sun relentless. Everywhere that didn't smell of frying oil stank of bloody meat or fish. There was so much uproar coming from stallholders in the colonnades, even the harsh bray of a distressed donkey was lost.

This was Rome, a huge, casual madhouse that made Londinium look staid. I had never quite grown used to it.

Everyone paused, trying not to show annoyance, as a short procession of Vestal Virgins moved sedately from the sacred spring outside the Capena Gate to their own Forum temple, snooty dames bearing half-full water jugs on their shoulders and expecting the pungent populace to move aside for them. They made no eye contact with anyone, but I had two teenaged sisters so I knew for sure when women were secretly scanning the streets, hoping to view muscular workmen with extremely short tunics and visible buttocks.

I was thinking this and smiling to myself when someone put a hand on my shoulder. Before I had time to sink angry teeth into the hand, Manlius Faustus pulled me round so I could see that it was him. That hand, which he hastily removed, was scarred on both sides where I had once speared him to a table with a metal kebab skewer. His fault: he insulted me unpardonably. I come from Britain where the wild tribes are proud of their hot tempers.

Faustus looked at me as if he knew what I was thinking about those buttock-loving Virgins.

'Tiberius! I have been about your business.'

'Any luck?'

'Lots.'

'Brilliant. Lunch?'

'Lovely.'

We started to walk. Then my good spirits died on me. Faustus had been with Vibius and other people when he had seen me and come over. Now he was heading back to them. Vibius was talking to his colleague, Salvius Gratus, whose horrible sister accompanied him as stubbornly as a bailiff. I was starting to feel sorry for her brother.

Laia Gratiana glared. She did not want me besmirching his campaign. I restrained my aggravation. While I would have liked to apply strong kitchen implements to delicate parts of her, the gadget had not yet been invented that would grate up that woman finely enough for me.

For a grim moment I thought Manlius Faustus intended

we would all go to lunch as one large party. I was bound to get stuck next to Laia, who would blank me, and I knew the men would drink all the wine they ordered, ignoring us women.

Vibius appeared to think a big sociable lunch was on: he invited everyone home to his parents' house; those parents were quiet elderly people who had come to support him and were now waiting nearby in a litter. Happily Faustus excused us. 'You go ahead. Albia and I need a strategy meeting. I'll come along to the house later.'

The Grati were promised elsewhere. As they left, I heard Laia ask, 'When shall we be seeing your wife, Sextus Vibius?'

'Ah, please excuse her. The poor girl really cannot abide crowds.'

I wondered if, like me, she could not abide Laia Gratiana.

'*Darling Julia!*' Laia cooed, so I wanted to vomit – and I did not even know Vibius' wife.

Faustus wheeled me away in his brisk manner. The others were all walking one way around the Flavian Amphitheatre, past the Sweating Fountain, but he headed around the ellipse in the other direction. Once we shed them, he let out an oddly triumphant whistle between his teeth. (He had teeth a dentist would curse, none in need of extraction.) 'Smart getaway!'

He grinned. I hid my surprise. Still, if Manlius Faustus thought I had news, he would want to assess it with me in private. Vibius was impetuous; Faustus liked to prepare a plan thoroughly before talking to him about it.

We were at the south end of the Forum. On the far side of the amphitheatre, Faustus muttered with mild annoyance. He had spotted a senator he needed to beard while he had an opportunity: the man was, for once, unencumbered by mistresses or hustlers trying to sell him things. With a quick apology Faustus left me for a moment while he darted over to canvass the senator's vote.

I watched him go, a relaxed figure in the formal dress he was obliged to wear for business. Many men found it hard to endure a toga, but Faustus shouldered the heavy folds easily. He refused to let it interfere with whatever he wanted to do. He looked the perfect campaign manager, efficient and intent.

I waited in the shade. For personal reasons I rarely came here, or rarely stopped to look around. The great, glorious drum of Vespasian's triumphal arena rolled away on both sides, clad with Travertine marble from its specially opened quarry and decorated with statues that my father and grandfather had helped source. From street level nobody noticed that some were substandard: legs, spears, even heads had been missing, but the damage was expertly repaired for my naughty grandpa.

I felt slightly daunted. Three monumental levels of the great arena towered above me, each ringed with one of the classical orders of columns, then above them soared the topmost level with its huge flashing bronze shields; even that was crowned with yet another feature, the awning that shaded spectators. It was the highest building in Rome. With the sun at full strength, I felt heat throbbing off the gleaming marble.

Standing there below the grand entrance, I let myself gaze up at the big bronze four-horse chariot that dominates the imperial archway. This is what you are supposed to notice. I should never have looked: I was overwhelmed by a great gust of melancholy.

Faustus returned. I brightened my expression. He paused. 'Was I too long?'

'No, no.'

'You look subdued.' He, too, glanced up, a little surprised. 'Do you have an aversion to the Victory quadriga?'

I don't know why. He cannot have expected it, but I blurted out why I was sad. 'This is the spot where my husband was killed.'

'Here?'

'Right here.'

He was shocked. 'Oh, my dear, I am so sorry. I would never have left you anywhere so painful . . . Quickly, let's go somewhere else.' When I stayed put, Faustus grew still. 'I never liked to ask you what happened, but do you want to talk about it?'

'That's brave! Don't worry, I won't cry.'

'Cry all you want. Share your trouble.'

He had done quite enough for me, but maybe I was still so weak I needed his offer. That was unusual for me. My husband and I had kept our joys private; after he died I clutched my bereavement to myself in the same way. People had worried over me, but I never let any of them come close. All my life I had managed grief by myself.

'Tell me,' urged Faustus. 'You and I can tell each other anything, you know that.'

That was news to me. Still, for once breaking my silence seemed right.

'Well Lentullus, my husband, had a badly damaged leg. He had been wounded, defending Uncle Quintus in a fight. He could walk and do most things, but he often struggled and his movement was hampered. If he attempted sudden turns, he would even fall down.'

Faustus listened.

'There was a freak accident. You are allowed to see this as a funny story,' I assured him, smiling wanly. 'Lentullus would have found it hilarious. It was grim for me, being left behind so unexpectedly. But the accident could only have happened to him and I am easy with it nowadays . . .'

I pointed. Faustus and I stared up again at the vivid sculpture placed above the main gate. The four enormous reproductions of galloping horses, heads up, straining, manes flying, as Victory urged them on. The fabulously decorated chariot with its rapt driver. Each horse with one proud hoof raised, to give an impression of furious galloping movement forward.

'What happened, Albia?'

'Farm Boy, as I called him, was watching the sculptor's men erect the four horses. He would have been fascinated. Lentullus had a childlike personality. We used to say, if ever there was a hole in the road with a notice saying, "Danger, keep out", he would go straight over to see what the danger was, and fall in . . .'

His personality would never have altered, but I had changed in the intervening years. Although we were close to begin with, I would have grown out of him. It would have been a tragedy. He would never have understood why, and would have been heartbroken.

'Go on,' Faustus persuaded me gently, as I faltered.

'Everybody laughed about him, but he loved me and I needed that.' Faustus nodded. 'To him, everything in the world seemed wondrous. He was always thrilled to watch things happening. He would have been completely absorbed here . . .' I hesitated, then carried on unprompted. 'The bronze horses' legs had been cast as separate pieces, I presume because of their weight. They were being fixed to the bodies, which had already been winched up there. Something went wrong.'

I saw Faustus breathe, anticipating.

'A leg fell. Witnesses said my poor daft boy made no attempt to move – he just stood with his mouth open, watching, while the enormous piece came down. If I had been there, he would have squealed, *"Coo, look at this, chick! They've dropped a bit."* Marvelling. Unaware of his danger. Unable to move, anyway. So the bronze smashed down right on him. He was killed outright.'

Faustus looked at me.

'By a horse's leg,' I said, permitting him to laugh, to laugh with me about it.

We did so gently. Farm Boy would have chortled with us. Then, although I had long ago learned to cope with my grief, I dropped my head forward onto the aedile's shoulder, hiding an unbidden tear. Faustus let me bury my face in the folds of his toga. I wiped my eyes dry on its white woolly nap and stepped back quickly. He murmured that formal dress has some uses and I found his lack of fuss comforting.

We went and had lunch.

11

We walked down the ancient Via Tusculana via the Ludus Magnus, Domitian's new gladiators' training school. He had built it for the fighters in the Flavian Amphitheatre, to which it was linked by an underground passage. You could always hear exaggerated huffing, whacks, thumps and raucous shouts of encouragement, as big stupid men inside showed off.

Once we had passed the milling gawpers, who were trying to gain entrance to the restricted viewing facilities at the Ludus, and the huddle of off-colour bars that the fighters and their crude associates favoured, the street climbed a little at the beginning of the Caelian Hill, then soon became quieter. We found a civilised thermopolium. It had an interior garden courtyard. A few other people were there but we had arrived ahead of the crowd.

We decided against the stuffed vine leaves on offer. Quality depends on what they have been stuffed with. While Faustus unwound himself from his toga, I selected flatbread and chickpea paste. He ordered mulsum, the invigorating drink that is given to soldiers – and to invalids, though I accepted his choice. It was too hot to drink wine at midday, unless you were at home and could fall into bed afterwards for sticky lovemaking.

I did mutter a muted apology for my upset earlier,

admitting I was not myself. That led Faustus to quiz me about my health. I described my stay at the coast, talking nonsense about life at our seaside villa. We were a still-young family. My brother, whom Faustus had met, was only eleven and although my two sisters were in their middle teens they often behaved like silly schoolgirls.

'I hope everyone spoiled you.'

'Depend on it.'

'It was hard to let you go,' Faustus said, chewing and playing nonchalant.

It had been hard to leave.

Time for work. I described all I had learned in the course of that morning about the rival candidates. My companion winced at some of the details, yet seemed prepared to use the information. He was the speech-writer. From what I had seen of Sextus Vibius, that did not surprise me.

'You write it out and he reads the scroll?'

'No, I make him learn it.'

'Are you going to share these stories with Salvius Gratus?'

'Not the obscene dwarfs.' He showed amusement, teasing me. He must know I was jealous of Laia. 'Don't you think his upright sister would be shocked?'

'Well, you know her better than I do!' I sniped, gently by my standards. 'It isn't for lofty Laia to poke her nose in. We have to discredit the opposition where we can.'

'That's what I say,' agreed Faustus, placidly, giving me grapes. 'The dwarfs are in.'

This was him. He would not give way to Laia, though at the same time he never criticised her. He showed pain whenever he referred to their divorce, but I had to look closely to see it. He took the blame, so he always spoke of

Laia with scrupulous good manners and there was no point in trying to make him exhibit rancour. Anyway, the marriage had been over for ten years.

Besides, I bet he had never taken Laia Gratiana to a friendly lunch like this. I had seen how she loathed watching us go off together today.

He went to the counter to fetch more mulsum, coming back with a new nibbles saucer. 'They have cheese!'

We both loved cheese. Manlius Faustus measured by eye then divided the piece into two, being carefully fair. We shared a smile at the way he did it, before enjoying the treat in silence.

After lunch Faustus went to the Vibius house to work on the campaign. He had drawn up a list of senators, marking any who might be favourable to our candidate, which were cemented to rivals, which remained unknowns. He was making little headway with them. He wasted effort scurrying around and was depressed because even if he managed to approach them nothing they said could be trusted. They might assure him they would vote for Vibius – but many simply lied to escape being canvassed.

'The really devious ones keep me talking for ages, even though they have no intention of supporting us, just to prevent me going off and seeing someone else.'

'Well, the task is not impossible. You got in last year.' I had better taste than to say Faustus was not well known generally and I could not see why the Senate had chosen him.

Manlius Faustus had somehow managed to obtain votes – even though he was a single man with no children, which put him at a disadvantage because husbands and fathers took precedence. He must have organised sufficient support in the Senate, not to mention avoiding Domitian's veto.

He did a sound job now. He had been a perfect choice. Maybe senators had good judgement after all. No, all right. His Uncle Tullius had simply bought them.

Faustus threw back his head, as if enjoying the sunshine that filtered through the canopy of vines on a trellis above us. 'Yes, I got in, thanks to my uncle. Fortunately he is helping again. He is very close to Salvius Gratus, always has been.'

'What's behind that?' From all I had heard, Tullius verged on crude; he seemed a poor fit with the staunchly respectable Grati.

Faustus grimaced, then explained, 'Uncle Tullius, as you know, owns a great many warehouses. A number of his best are in a certain street, where one building plonk in the middle has always been owned not by us but by the Gratus family.'

I saw where this was heading.

'The warehouse in question,' Faustus rasped, with a new edge in his voice, 'formed part of the dowry when Tullius married me to Laia Gratiana.'

'Neat,' I said. I kept it neutral.

'Neat, though not for long. I had to hand it back when she divorced me.'

So: neat until everything had turned nasty . . . and that was his fault. 'Tullius can never have forgiven you?'

'For him, poor man, that was the worst aspect. He could live with the shame of me cheating on my wife, the inconvenience I caused him – even the expense. But he could not bear to lose that warehouse, not once he had triumphantly acquired it. I suspect he had hopes the whole road would be renamed after him, the Vicus Tullii . . . He still yearns to retrieve the situation. His cosying up to the Grati never stopped, first the parents and then Laia's brother, even though it's impossible to take me when he visits them and he cannot lure them to our house.'

'What have they to fear? – You would go out!' I sniggered.

Faustus growled, 'I'd stay out all night if I had to – I'd sleep under a bridge . . . I don't get involved, but Uncle Tullius still swarms around the Grati socially. Biding his time. Looking for an opening. Elections, for manipulators like my uncle – who, believe me, is impressive when he goes into action – are always a chance to reposition.'

'With favours and promises.'

'Exactly.'

'You say you keep out of it, but you are working with Salvius Gratus now.'

'Not to do so would be unfair to Sextus.'

'What about being fair to you?'

'Ah, you are very sweet to say that.'

No, I was very annoyed with his uncle, his friend and the damned Grati for putting Faustus in this position. 'Nobody calls me sweet and gets away with it.'

'We'll see!' chuckled Manlius Faustus, as if he thought he could get away with anything. From anyone else it would have been flirting.

I said I was sorry not to help with his campaign work that afternoon. I needed to rest. And the next day I would be caught up in my own family's business: tomorrow was the Callistus auction. I wanted to be there. I assured Faustus I would be required to do nothing that would tax me; I would only be an observer. 'Oh, really!'

I strolled with him as far as the Vibius house, after which I would make my own way home. We parted with a light kiss on the cheek – good manners between acquaintances.

I found the energy to walk all the way to my apartment. It was not a long distance: along the Clivus Scauri and around the far end of the Circus Maximus, on the flat at first, though followed by a slow climb up the Aventine. That was steep, especially with food inside you, but I knew how to pace myself. I was in a good mood. The streets of the thirteenth district were quiet while everyone was lunching, at home or out in company. Businesses were shuttered now until early evening. Even the most excitable dogs were resting in the shade. Children had been called in. Beggars were taking a snooze and hustlers could not be bothered.

So I went home, and was happy to be there, even though I was alone and there was no chance at all of an afternoon's sticky lovemaking.

12

Auctions begin at dawn, indeed often earlier. It was barely light when movement started. By hoary tradition professional dealers come along for first pickings, pawing your stock, tossing items around as they scavenge like particularly arrogant crows. These men, and occasional women, regard it as their right to make pre-auction bids, which are always preposterous. If rebuffed, they are annoyed, even though everyone knows they are trying it on. Many are shifty-looking; some bring unpleasant half-starved dogs. Father calls them the warts.

Today's warts were on good form. They sauntered up, glum-faced, with no greetings for our staff, let alone me, although some exchanged curt nods with one another. As soon as they arrived, in dribs and drabs because they were solitary beings, they started inspecting the lots as if we were invisible – yet they scoffed, loud, derogatory comments for us to overhear.

'Settle down!' Gornia soothed them. He had seen it all before. He kicked one of the whippety dogs away from sniffing the big half-burned strongbox. 'If your hound pees on anything, we'll want compensation . . . You know it's always hard going in July. We are lucky to have put together a sale. Falco wasn't at all keen . . .'

Falco didn't care that much. Falco regarded the auction

house as a colourful, temporary hobby. He hankered to be back informing, but had to lie low and look as if he had retired because Domitian was known to be rancorous towards him. There was a reason. Father never said what.

With Domitian, nobody asked questions, in case merely mentioning his name should put the thought of you into his head. He brooded on slights long past as darkly as on offences now. Everyone scurried about with their heads down. The people of Rome were terrified of him, and the monster enjoyed that.

A snotty woman dressed in odd raggedy skirts and scarves pointed out that Falco had not even put in an appearance. 'Exactly,' smirked Gornia. 'Gone fishing. Like I said, it's July!'

The warts moved off, still without proper conversation. They dispersed to harry some other auctioneer if they could find one, despising his goods as much as they apparently despised ours. Once our bidding started, some would slide back. They had decided what pieces they wanted; indeed, if the items were small, the warts had surreptitiously hidden them under larger things, away from other eyes. At the auction, warts usually made fierce bids. That was why we let them poke through the lots. They looked like paupers, but they were out to buy and had plenty of cash hidden about their skinny persons.

So far it was chilly in the dark colonnades inside Pompey's Porticus. The dawn atmosphere felt ominous, as if anyone who was lurking out in the central grove of plane trees must be up to no good. We went about our business, hoping they would stick to theirs. We usually employed big fellows to act as security, but they would arrive later, just before the auction started.

I huddled in a cloak while I kept an eye on proceedings. I was being the auctioneer's daughter today. I would sit on the sidelines, on a stool or a chair. Regulars knew who I was. The decent professional dealers would give me a nod, possibly even come over to send their regards to Father. I would be called upon to adjudicate any problems, though Gornia could have done it, if none of the family were present.

In a plebeian family business, women have a valued place. They share the work. My Aunt Maia had kept the auction accounts for years. I wondered if I would see her today, though mostly now she worked at home where she could combine the figure-work with looking after her husband in his retirement. Somebody would take a big basket of receipts to her when it was all over, then Maia would squeeze in alongside Petro and his wine flagon on the sun terrace, where she would deal with record-keeping, send out bills and pay off the sales tax.

All over the Empire this was how it worked, even though in theory women were cyphers. I myself was fairly well informed about the art and antiques we sold. Fakes too. I had been tutored to recognise counterfeiting, 'marriages' and overdone distressing. I also knew how to let someone down gently when they brought along a ghastly heirloom, hoping their cracked item would be worth a fortune. I would even be careful what I said because, perversely, if a worthless dud went into a sale, some idiot might pop up and pay a lot of money for it.

I liked being allowed to take part. I would have enjoyed having my own family business, but that presupposed a husband to run it with me. I had stopped expecting either. Being an informer, a loner's profession, would suffice. I did not fret about my life. I saw enough unhappy frustration among my clients.

In the dull patch before things started, I inspected today's lots.

The Callisti must have had that granary storeroom crammed to its ceiling. Much of their list was furniture, one or two pieces with Vesuvian damage but otherwise simply goods they had grown tired of. Their taste was heavy – too much gilding and too many animal paws for me. They were parting with a whole chest of lewd lamps; someone had made a collection of flying-phallus chandeliers that a wife must be making him throw out. A matched pair of decent alabaster side-tables had been ruined by a neglected water spill on one (Gornia put up a notice that optimistically called it 'restorable'). A generation ago some hapless ancestor had blessed them with misjudged art. I had seen reproductions of Greek sculpture that were almost better than the originals, fine work from Campania, but still the world contains far too many inferior gods and athletes in marble that is less than pure and Parian, or sometimes only painted plaster.

We called this the Callistus sale, but there were smaller lots from other people, right down to a single platter from a hard-up old lady. We accepted those because Father was so soft: whenever a sad-eyed grandma came bearing a pathetic treasure, he lied about the price it achieved, making up the difference from his own pocket. The grandma, hard as nails, would scuttle off to tell her cronies that the daft son of Didius Favonius was an easy mark.

As usual we had one or two pieces from our own family inheritance; it was years since my grandfather had died, but a lifetime of fervent collecting had been stashed in houses and warehouses. From time to time, Father discovered more, then faced the sorry decision whether to own up to his belated windfall and pay inheritance tax on it. Many a long hour in the evening was spent with furrowed brow as Didius Falco wrestled with his conscience – or so he said, as he called for another beaker of Falernian (from Grandpa's cellar) to help him deliberate. He seeded an auction with choice pieces whenever he needed cash to fund a project. He grumbled and called it 'dowry money', though in fact these sales more often paid for funerals, education or travel. That was how he had helped to back my uncles, the Camilli, when they were entering the Senate.

Today Father was selling a fine large silver urn and its even finer little brother, plus a number of eastern carpets. Otherwise, not much attracted me, though I admired a weathered stone bench with dolphin ends that I chose as my perch for the day. Gornia said he could pull it out of the sale for me but I had nowhere to keep it.

Oh, look. Some wild hopeful was trying to offload a statue of *A Boy Pulling a Thorn out of His Foot*. Good luck with that, deluded person!

Our security arrived, silent musclemen from a local gymnasium, bearing breakfast rolls for all. The day brightened. The Porticus warmed up. Members of the public began strolling by, at first idlers who looked alarmed and moved on rapidly if we spoke to them, then people with a genuine interest, who were prepared to stay and make bids.

As soon as we had attracted a small crowd, Gornia began selling. The hour was still too early, but no use waiting around like shrimp-girls outside a gladiators' barracks: we needed our event to sound lively, as if something unmissable was happening.

I installed myself on my bench with a pile of waxed tablets, the catalogue, which I marked up whenever an item sold. I was part of the scenery. Ideally, to look like the auctioneer's daughter, I would have fixed up complicated hair and cosmetic work. Having had to leave my apartment in the dark, I had simply thrown on a fine tunic with rich hems, big earrings and lashings of necklaces – the kind of outfit that makes your mother shriek you look like a travelling trapeze artist. Otherwise, I had my usual work uniform: a plain plait and a clean face. Laced shoes, a stout satchel, a brightly woven belt. Helena would have groaned if she saw me going out of the house like that, but I felt the look was a good mix of the exotic and the businesslike . . . In my heart, I had remained fifteen.

Once we started, no one took any notice of me.

Quite a few punters slunk around as if they had sinister motives, but that's the way of crowds. There were a few genuine sneak thieves, sly idlers with big patch pockets, all closely watched by members of our staff. The rest looked genuinely respectable, which could hardly have been true. This was Rome.

I was convinced that whoever was responsible for Strongbox Man would have heard his container was in this sale. Whether they knew we had opened it and found him was an interesting point. We had kept quiet. Would the Callisti have let any news out? Did the killer think the corpse was still curled up inside?

I had my eyes peeled for anyone suspicious. Unluckily for me, many people turn up to auctions out of curiosity. They convince themselves they won't bid – before, inevitably, they lavish more than they can afford on a wild offer for something they don't want. When their wife back at home says she hates it, they are stuck . . .

This vigil was useless. I failed to spot any likely suspects. I had to pass the time somehow. Musing, I developed a witty theory that auctions are like politics. In an auction, you let yourself be fooled by appearances, get carried away and commit yourself rashly; then, as soon as it's over and you take your so-called sound investment home, a leg drops off. Just like electing some sham who turns out to have neither talent nor morals . . .

Not Sextus Vibius Marinus, friend of my own honest friend Faustus, clearly. I must try not to be satirical about the lovely Vibius. Otherwise I would let an incorrect opinion slip, causing his chief supporter to take offence. Naughty girl, Albia.

I was bored.

Towards the middle of the morning, everything warmed up. I had shed my cloak and the porters were starting to glisten as they hauled stuff about. The Porticus of Pompey was at its most elegant. Fountains splashed attractively. The golden curtains on the art gallery shone with determined refulgence. Bright, unremittent sunlight was now flooding into the gardens, where every arcade had a full complement of flâneurs and women who fancied a fling – or who wanted to fool themselves they were risking their reputations, although they would dart away in horror if any sinful adventurer sidled up to them. Even the slave-gardeners seemed happy to be trimming up the box hedges.

Gornia had moved on to selling decent lots. The donkey boy fanned him. I could have used him fanning me.

There was serious interest. Warts had returned and were intently bidding against one another. Even unlikely objects found new owners. A nice young couple had snapped up a good table that they dearly wanted, at a price that seemed to surprise them (auctioneers have hearts: we are more pleased than you think to see customers go away delighted). The table had no hidden defects either. Joyous.

I scrutinised a man in a poorly dyed puce tunic, hanging about near *The Boy with the Thorn*. He pretended to look at the statue, then kept sidling off elsewhere.

From where I was he seemed good-looking and sturdy, but too indecisive to be a murderer. Still, he could be a sidekick sent to observe. He didn't look as if he cost much to employ. He would have cost *me* nothing at all because I would have sent him packing. As soon as he saw me watching him, he beetled away guiltily.

Callistus Primus arrived. He was accompanied by two other men whom he brought across and introduced, his brother and cousin. Secundus, the brother, looked just like him but several years younger. They moved to one side where they stood in silence, watching their items come up. A good price left them expressionless. The few things that failed to sell, or failed to sell for what they had hoped, left them visibly disgusted. I dislike such men, but among auction clients they are common. People expect too much. If they don't achieve the price they want, they blame the auctioneer.

Gornia was actually on good form. He had learned his trade from my grandfather, though no one will ever surpass Geminus at coaxing bids from the shy public. Didius Geminus could sell shit to a dung farmer – and get him to come and collect it in his own cart.

* * *

Gornia put up *The Boy with a Thorn in His Foot.* Puce Tunic did not bid. He just lurked unhappily behind some topiary. The statue failed to reach its reserve and was not sold. Surprise!

At this point, Gornia winked at me and did a little jiggle, signalling that I should go over to where he was standing on a box, his tribunal, and temporarily take over. When he needed to use the Porticus lavatory, we all knew it had to be regarded as urgent. He was an old man.

I surrendered the catalogue to the boy who normally marked it up. As Gornia nipped off, looking anxious, he passed me the hammer; according to family tradition, this implement came from an arena in Africa where it had been used to test if gladiators were dead or shamming.

Some of the audience were surprised when I jumped on the box and composed myself, but it was not the first time I had been left in charge of a gavel. My father had started to bring me with him after Lentullus was killed, wanting to lure me out from brooding alone. Falco said I was bossy enough to control an auction. He trained me.

I quite enjoyed taking charge. I always felt nervous initially but if there was a murmur among those watching, by the time I took the first lot it was over. All you need is a quiet, efficient manner. Punters don't care, not if they are fired up to buy.

'Gornia's gone for a comfort break. You just can't get the staff, these days. Be calm, my friends, this isn't a Greek auction, no fear of accidentally acquiring a new wife – I am Falco's daughter. Good afternoon.'

Some actually answered obediently, 'Good afternoon.'

‘First item is this robust garden-god statue, fully equipped in every sense.’ The evil porters had set me up with a stone Priapus. Luckily I do not embarrass easily. I talked it up. ‘A fine feature to impress friends at your peristyle supper parties. I had a close look and his dibber shows very little trace of wear!’ I had them. ‘A slight chip in the foreskin, best not to think how that happened. Let’s face it, there must be women here who have been saddened by worse sights . . . I’ll take a thousand.’

They bid. Not a thousand, but enough. A woman bought it. We had a laugh. She was fifty and took the banter in good part. Perhaps a widow. Free to have what she liked in her garden now, without her husband picking at her.

The audience were mine and the porters had had their moment, so I could continue in my own style, being serious and direct. The job is easy, in my opinion. You only have to make it clear whose bid you take. ‘I am with the red tunic. Any advance? Sir at the back, thank you. Are we all done?’

Drop your hammer decisively. Move on.

‘Next, please, porter. Now this is lovely. Who will start me at five hundred?’

I sold several routine lots, to let everyone feel comfortable with my presence and pace. The Callisti stopped looking nervous. The regulars had never been bothered anyway. It must be close to lunchtime. We had a large crowd and I even spotted a haze of ultra-white on the outskirts, as if we had been joined by election candidates. People were fanning themselves, some drinking water, a couple of lads trying to cool off in the fountains.

The Boy with a Thorn limped round again. He failed to

sell a second time. 'Oh dear. If nobody takes him home soon, this poor wounded lad will end up with gangrene!' Enjoying myself, I was soaring like a seagull on a thermal. I called the no-sale. Almost without intending to, I heard myself say, 'I'll take the handsome strongbox next.'

Perhaps I should have waited. But, Hades, it had to go some time. It was just a half-burned chest.

13

Some people knew its history. There was a rustle of anticipation. The three men of the Callistus family gave away little, though I saw them grow tense. This was the best vantage-point for me: right at the front, raised on my stand and, by virtue of my task, looking directly at everyone.

Puce Tunic was back, lurking. A couple of fellows pushed in closer to the strongbox. People do that. People who have no intention of bidding like to approach the lot you are taking, stand alongside and gawp. Lunatics. I hoped the smell choked them.

'This is a fine antique chest of exceptional size and armouring, with a good provenance of south Campanian workmanship, only ever in the possession of a single family. It shows some singeing; buyer takes it as found. There are working locks; a handsome key goes home with it.'

As one, the burly Callisti had folded their arms, subconsciously defensive. People were shooting sly glances in their direction. People knew all right.

On the edge of the crowd, I definitely identified Manlius Faustus, with Vibius and Salvius Gratus. The brutes, Trebonius Fulvo and Arulenus Crescens, were in their group too, surprisingly. They were all pretending to be on good terms with each other. Anywhere out on the Field of Mars was a suitable haunt for candidates. Strolling into a porticus to watch an auction was an acceptable activity. They kept turning to people nearby, shaking hands and causing a disturbance. I enjoyed myself calling out, 'Less noise over there, please. Give the bidders a chance to make up their minds!'

I saw Faustus and Vibius walk over and shake hands with the Callisti, but the next time I noticed, they were back with the other chalk-whites.

I concentrated on the chest. I named a price, well above its value, and found no takers. Anyone who had viewed the item properly must have seen it had substantial damage. I brought my price down in stages, gently, without excitement, as you do. The trick is never to sound desperate. Like love, really, as my sisters would say.

The two loons by the box were jostling like village idiots. A serious buyer would remain quiet. If this ridiculous pair had been sent by the killer to observe, they were drawing too much attention to themselves. I had seen tribesmen in round huts show more sophistication.

'Somebody start me.'

Near the front a hand lifted, barely a movement of the fingers. Probably only I noticed the gesture. Even though he was professional – I recognised this dealer – he had weighed in too soon and would probably end up not buying. I called the bid, which encouraged someone else. We were far too low, but there was time. A third and fourth joined in, but half-heartedly. Number three dropped out at once. Four could be a possible. I made sure I kept eye contact.

Numbers two and four went at it against each other. They slowed. A new bidder entered. Four perked up, hiking his price with a big jump. Excellent. Another new bidder gave me a nod, over by Puce Tunic, though not visibly associating with him.

A pause. I rested and went with it.

'Come now, we are surely not all done yet? Do I have any more? If not, I am selling. Last call, fair warning . . .'

The lull seemed about to continue. When I raised my hammer, teasing them, bidding resumed as I expected.

I love the rise and fall. I love the sense of steering the event. Dull days are depressing, but here in the sunlight we were having fun today. I understood why my grandfather had loved his work.

I sold the box. I got a good price. The hammer came down on a high figure, considering how damaged the item was. I saw what the staff had meant about notoriety. This old chest had caused a frisson that had been missing at the sale all morning.

A thin man with a heavily acned face was the buyer. He wore an unobtrusive beige tunic and joined the bidding late on: a type I recognised – almost certainly not working on his own account, but acting on instruction either for a dealer or a private individual. He had bided his time, then come in once the rest were tiring. It was skilfully done.

'Thank you!' I said to the audience, polite but firm.

Gornia reappeared. He must have deliberately let me take the strongbox. As he passed me, he muttered something.

I looked over. The Callisti – Primus, Secundus and nephew – were leaving, as if they had seen all they came for. That was understandable. The buyer, who still had to complete the purchase formalities with us, did not even look in their direction. Yet I believed what Gornia had said to me: the skinny man was their negotiator.

The Callisti had secretly bought back the strongbox themselves.

14

It was not a unique event, though buying back was rare. Anyone sensible who changed their mind simply withdrew their item from sale.

Relieved of gavel duties, I went up to the negotiator as he made payment. He wanted to give us a banker's draft, which needed family authorisation. 'That's acceptable,' I instructed our finance clerk. 'Sir, we need your note by tomorrow. We keep the goods until the payment arrives.' I congratulated the man on his purchase, making my remarks sound routine. Then I slipped in, 'I am told that you act for the owners?'

He scowled but did not deny it. As he finished the formalities, I leaned in, letting him see me read his signature. He was a lanky strip of wind who went by the name of Titus Niger. I drew him to a quiet corner. 'If you work for the Callisti, Niger, was it you who went to that storeroom they use and prepared the inventory for sale?'

'Yes, I did that.'

'I've been hoping to talk to you. At the store, did you look inside the strongbox?'

'No.' The tall skinny man was very sure of that.

'Did you notice anything odd in the room where it was kept?'

'No.' Despite his brief replies the negotiator was keeping

a polite manner. He had a weaker voice than his trusted position and confident air suggested. I put the squeak down to nerves. The Callisti had warned him I was trouble and that he must watch what he said.

'Footsteps in the dust on the floor, for instance? Or a nasty smell?' I prodded.

'Nothing that caught my attention. The light was poor. I had a lamp to write my list by, but it was dim. Everything smelt musty, but that was to be expected. Stuff had been in store for years.'

I said I presumed he knew I had discussed the chest with Callistus Primus. 'He will have told you what our people found inside?' Beige Tunic nodded. He was probably fifty, long in experience. 'So may I ask what your principals were thinking when they made you bid for the old chest?'

'They changed their minds. It is allowed.'

'Of course! But if they want to keep it, why not ask us to cancel the sale? People have second thoughts. My father is always obliging. I assure you there would have been no comeback.'

Looking uncomfortable over his strange buy, the negotiator gave in. 'Primus decided not to let the strongbox go to some inquisitive ghoul who wanted the thrill of finding bloodstains.'

'There was nothing left to find inside,' I said. 'There never had been blood. The poor victim suffocated.'

'Primus thought people wouldn't know that. And he feels whoever killed that person and dumped him in their storeroom gave them responsibility.' That was certainly not how Primus had reacted when I talked to him. His brother and perhaps his cousin may have persuaded him have a rethink, but they looked similar types, all unsentimental. 'I was told to buy it incognito. When it comes home, someone will burn it and make a proper end of the thing, rather than let it become some ghastly souvenir.'

'Well, that will be respectful to the dead.' I kept my face neutral. 'So why did the Callisti come here today, when it might have been better not to draw attention?'

Niger gave me a look. 'They wanted to watch and see who else was interested in their box.'

I, too, was pinch-mouthed. 'You should tell them that even if the killer hoped nobody had found the body he would never buy the chest himself – too dangerous.'

'So you don't think he was here?'

'Oh, certainly! He was here – or someone acting for him was.'

'And wanted to buy the body back?'

'They probably realise we found the corpse. No, I think any culprits will have wanted to discover today what is known about the dead man. After all, if somebody identifies him, the finger of suspicion may point at them.'

The Callistus agent gazed around the audience. Most were intent on Gornia selling Father's carpets. 'So who is it, Flavia Albia?'

'My guess is he or they have already left.'

The negotiator went off, too, without another word.

I felt Niger had no connection with the killing. Mind you, being plausible was his job.

My next task was to move casually about the audience, making a closer inspection of everyone who had bid on the chest unsuccessfully. I took one of the porters to introduce me to them. I still thought the killer would have been crazy to attempt to purchase the box, but you never know. Killers can be stupid.

I found that those who had shown interest were all regular dealers and bidding for themselves, apart from one shipper we had not dealt with before, but he had only arrived in Rome two days ago, giving him an alibi.

Out of politeness I went and said hello to Faustus and company. They were still fingering goods and making themselves agreeable to all and sundry.

None bothered with warm greetings for me. Laia Gratiana applied an expression of austere distaste. 'Do you often do that, Flavia Albia?'

'Take an auction? Not often – but, as you saw, I know how.'

'Quite a skill!' blared Trebonius Fulvo, not bothering to introduce himself – a man who assumed everyone knew him. He was the one with the odd eye and knucklefuls of self-promoting jewellery. He came and stood too close.

'It just requires a little theatre work,' I murmured, with an unobtrusive sidestep.

'I like a girl who does Priapus jokes!' Trebonius trowelled on lewd insinuation.

'As she said, acting for the punters,' said Faustus, moving in to support me. 'Flavia Albia is perfectly modest by nature.' Somehow he sounded as if he meant that.

Laia snorted.

I shot Faustus a grateful look. 'We have some superb items still to come. I hope you will all stay and enjoy more of the auction – maybe you would like to buy something!' I spun on one heel, my sensible shoe staying on firmly, as I moved off to continue my circuit.

I strolled around representing my father: shaking hands, smiling, enquiring about business, asking after families. 'We were all very sorry to hear about your wife, such a lovely woman and far too young to go . . . Your youngest must be walking now . . . How is your brother getting on with his new business?' Occasionally with newcomers I introduced myself, 'Hello, I am Didius Falco's daughter. I hope you are enjoying the sale. Do talk to any of our staff if we can help at all . . .'

I was 'going about' like the candidates. The only difference was, I paid for no favours and made no fake promises.

I returned to the dolphin-ended bench. The catalogue boy had been there but he moved off when Manlius Faustus approached, clearly about to speak to me.

'So this is a big-earrings day!' Manlius Faustus could be a man of surprises; he seemed to like my jewellery.

He sat down with me but the bench had reached its turn for bids. As we rose from it, Faustus must have seen my rueful glance and how I stroked the worn head of one of the dolphins. 'You like it?'

'Nowhere to keep it.'

'You may have, one day. Put it in the courtyard of your building until then.'

Gornia called a starting bid; Faustus raised his hand. It was a firm gesture; no auctioneer would miss it or wonder if he was just waving to a friend. Gornia saw that Faustus was with me and did not seek more offers. Nobody was keen; even Gornia had said the piece had been 'well used', which can be auction shorthand for falling to bits. Faustus secured it.

'Lucky I can afford the money!' I mumbled.

'Not you. Albiola, this is a welcome-home present. You just have to promise to let me come and sit on it.'

'You should not give me presents,' I half complained, but I really liked that bench.

'Yes, I should.' With no explanation of that cryptic remark, he breezed off to formalise his purchase, then returned to report, 'It's coming to you this evening. I shall try to be there to oversee delivery.'

Faustus waved goodbye, before leaving with Vibius and others.

Coming in the other direction, an unmistakable figure rolled up, signalling to me: Fundanus the funeral director.

'What, Fundanus – you here? Hoping to see the famous wooden tomb? Thank you for cleaning it for us.'

Fundanus was an awkward character to deal with, big-bellied and full of his own ghastly opinions. His face was disfigured with pustules that suggested he had much too close contact with bodies that had been infected with plague. I had never seen any evidence that he practised necrophilia, but it would not have surprised me.

His opinion of the living was low. 'Which of the disgusting types you have lured here today is the killer? I suppose he came. Couldn't stay away. Might be anyone, by the look of their ugly faces. I wouldn't want to plug any of their nasty arses. Your father needs to bring in a better crowd, then he'd make more money.'

I wished he would speak more softly, but Fundanus always boomed as if he were the only man on the planet.

I ran through with him what his pyre-builder had told me yesterday about the corpse. Fundanus sniffed at his lad's effrontery in helping me behind his back – a member of the public, one who paid him money – though I noticed he made no corrections.

He was the worst kind of witness. He had no further facts,

yet plenty of stupid ideas. 'This boxed-up stiff has got to be a cheating husband who shagged one bloody-meat-stained floozy too many in the Cattle Market.' Fundanus was inventing this so vividly he convinced himself it was all true. People in his line of business always think they have a special understanding of human nature, despite the fact most humans they encounter are incapable of self-expression due to death. Even the living, the bereaved, are in crisis so not themselves. 'He was found out. The wife got her lover to suffocate him, and now those lovebirds are enjoying his money together. That lover wants to watch out. As soon as he runs through her cash, he'll be in for exactly the same treatment.'

'Well, that will give us a lead,' I managed to interject. 'Two deaths the same is always helpful. We could leave a chest with its lid up helpfully, somewhere in that granary storage place.'

Fundanus beamed with patronising approval. 'Well, that's better, girl. You're learning!'

I was glad to see the back of him.

I lie: his padded rear, swaggering across the porticus as his fat legs bore him off to lunch, was a foul spectacle.

The thought of a man who had such intimate dealings with the dead eating lunch always made me queasy. He prodded human offal, then looked as if he never washed his hands.

The Boy Taking a Thorn out of His Foot came up on offer again. Most of the punters were wandering away by now and took no interest. The man in the puce tunic plucked up his courage and bought the statue. That was all he had wanted, all along.

Apparently.

15

The sun was high overhead. In the post-noon bake, I began to flag. The marble-clad porticus buildings sweated heat from every stone, until my heart was pattering uneasily.

Gornia noticed me looking flushed. His ninety-year-old frame was exhausted too. We conferred, carrying out an inventory by eye: there was enough stock to continue the sale tomorrow when staff and buyers would be fresh, rather than struggling on when everyone was past caring. So we finished for today.

I made Gornia ride Patchy back to the Saepta. Our people stayed in the porticus to guard the lots overnight. I left and walked wearily towards the Aventine. After passing the civilised Porticus of Octavia, the closed Theatre of Marcellus, the teeming vegetable and meat markets, I came level with the Circus Maximus and faced a choice. Maturity struck me. Instead of forcing myself to make a suicidal climb up the steep hill, I went gently along the Embankment to my parents' house and rested there.

A slave let me in, then left me to myself; they all knew me as the peculiar one, often reclusive. With my family still away, the empty house felt melancholy but I made good use of the coolness and peace. Reflecting on the auction, I wondered again about the interested parties, those I had spotted and others who might have escaped my attention.

I mulled over the two idlers who had parked their stupid bodies by the armoured chest while I was selling it: were they not so stupid as they looked? I considered other faces. I even paid attention mentally to the man in the puce tunic, the strange loafer who had bought the thorn-in-foot statue.

Getting nowhere with that, I chewed over Manlius Faustus bidding for the bench. I failed to solve that puzzle either – or not in a way where it felt safe to venture.

Early in the pleasant summer evening, I went home. No one I knew was at Fountain Court. I tidied my apartment and carried out chores. I collected old food scraps to feed to a fox who visited a local enclosure, gathered laundry, went down the alley to leave it, carried on to Prisca's Baths and asked Prisca's trainer to give me a few exercises, steamed myself, bought fresh provisions, then swore at Rodan on my way back in, just so he knew life with me at home was back to normal.

'Something came for you,' he grouched. My new bench. Anyone would think there had been no delivery man or any competent person to supervise. Of course there was: he was still here, out on the bench, working on a scroll. I could tell Rodan had never lifted a finger when the stoneware was lugged into the courtyard. He was moaning because he hated change. 'We never had to have a seat before! We'll get people sitting on it.'

'Juno, that would be terrible! It's only for me. I don't want anybody else parking their dirty bums on it.'

'Tell him, then!'

'We'll allow him. It's his bench.'

The slave, Dromo, had been taking his ease alongside Faustus, but he was turfed off when I walked out into the courtyard. They had positioned the bench where the old teasel-carding racks had once stood when this was Lenia's laundry, famous for its owner's drinking habits and for losing people's best belongings; the two were directly connected. Now nothing occupied the deserted yard except my cheeky-looking dolphins, the generous man who had bought them and his awful slave. 'Where am I supposed to go now?'

'Quit moaning, Dromo. Sit over there quietly, in the porch.'

'Oh, no! Master, don't do that to me, not with smelly Rodan!' Dromo knew he had to go, but made his way as slowly as possible, dragging his feet in their scruffy sandals and glaring back balefully. He shouted out, 'At least from here I don't have to look at you two mooning over each other.'

'Get lost or I'll beat you.' Dromo knew there was little chance of that. His master made the mistake of adding, 'Albia and I do not moon!'

'You would, if I wasn't looking out all the time to catch you at it.'

Manlius Faustus gripped his belt with both hands, gave up on his slave and spoke through gritted teeth to me: 'Sorry!'

'No need.'

'I could sell him.'

'You never will.'

'Perhaps not. He is mine. He is rude, he is defiant, yet he is my *familia*.'

'Counts as a relative. Bound to be maddening . . . Be calm, Tiberius.'

He made a gesture of acquiescence. He had high standards, yet tolerance of those who had a reason to be truculent. He believed that finding yourself a slave was an unfair accident of Fate.

He was tolerant of me too. I could get away with anything. I knew that.

'Now they're saying, "What shall we do about Dromo?" I bet,' scoffed the boy, so we were bound to overhear. Faustus ignored it. However, I heard pent-up growling from him.

The aedile rolled up the scroll of senators' names he had brought, too jaded to continue making notes. Instead, we discussed the auction and my failure to gather any useful clues.

'Now, Tiberius, I saw you speaking to the Callistus brothers and their cousin.'

'Good manners. We just said hello.'

I mentioned how Callistus Primus had inexplicably ordered the repurchase of the armoured chest. 'The family is presenting this as an act of respect, in order to stop anyone else taking an impious interest in the victim. I don't believe their explanation.'

Faustus looked sympathetic but proffered no ideas.

'I think they know who the dead man was, but I'll never get them to say.' I changed the subject. 'The strongbox is my problem . . . Laia Gratiana was jibing at your friend today and actually has a point. Sextus is married. Why do we never see his wife?'

Faustus shrugged. 'I suppose for the reason he said. She dislikes large groups of people. You cannot make a shy person enjoy public campaigning.'

'Do you know her? *"Darling Julia"*?' I quoted Laia Gratiana, though was less sarcastic in tone. Anyone Laia was catty about was a friend of mine.

'I have met her. Quiet girl. Never has much to say for

herself, but she has always been devoted to Sextus – she is famous for it.'

'In that case,' I mused, 'you might expect her to be brave and turn out to support him sometimes.' Faustus made no comment. 'Is it not part of your duties as his manager to try to persuade Julia to appear among his supporters?'

'I can have a word. I don't know her very well.'

'Did you go their wedding? How long ago was it?'

'Yes. About eight years.'

'Do they have children?'

'A boy and a girl, I think.'

'Don't you know? Old friend of their father, are you not their jovial Uncle Tiberius, always spoiling the darlings?'

'No!' Faustus moved suddenly, adjusting position on the bench as if I had made him uncomfortable with my questions.

'Sorry.'

'It is your work. You can't help it . . . But, Albia, when you start prodding, I automatically fear you have a problem in mind.'

'No.'

'Well, good . . . Two rumbustious little tots, last time I saw them – which was not all that long ago,' Faustus insisted defensively. 'I do visit them. Sextus and Julia simply like being private.' He paused, then suggested awkwardly, 'Well, you know, sometimes a married couple don't issue many invitations to a friend who is single.'

'I see.'

'Inevitably we have less in common.'

'Right.'

'Their social life tends to concentrate around similar young families.'

'So true. And a bachelor will not seek out occasions where all the talk is of running a family home and educating children?' I spoke gently, touched by his hint of loneliness.

'I can endure family chatter.'

'Yes, if you have to, but I said you don't *seek* it.'

'I don't avoid it,' he persisted. After a moment he suddenly added, 'There must have been a third child. I once heard Julia in discussion about an older daughter. I never asked, in case it's a tragedy. Anyway,' Faustus concluded, 'I am seeing enough of Sextus now. He turned to me for help with his campaign, after all. We work together on a daily basis.'

He unrolled the scroll again, an act of punctuation: a full stop firmly positioned in my nagging interrogation.

New paragraph. I can take a hint.

For some while we talked, as he ran a finger down the endless list of names. This was discussion as he and I practised the art: with serious purpose, balanced, highly productive of ideas. We contributed equally, both intent.

I fetched out the waxed tablet that I always carried, making notes for him. Since I had run out of leads on Strongbox Man, I offered to be available tomorrow to take Faustus first to see the Camilli, then to consult the retired Secretary of Petitions, Claudius Laeta, with whom Father used to work. 'Or work against, I should say – the man was an intrepid manipulator. Always so subtle we could never deduce his real objectives.'

'So it will be all straight answers!'

The aedile's humour was interrupted by his slave, as Dromo shouted, 'Master! I'm supposed to yell out when you have to go off to dinner!'

'No, Dromo, you are supposed to approach discreetly and whisper in my ear . . . Sorry, Albia.' Faustus smiled a rueful apology, although in truth I had no claim on his time. 'He is right. I have to go. More necessary socialising. Dinner, probably lousy, with one of the possible senators . . .'

'Time I let you leave.' I made it sound as if I was happy to be rid of him. My true feelings were probably visible. 'Is your Sextus going too?'

'Yes, he will be on display. That is the purpose of it.'

'Will his wife accompany him?'

'I am not sure.'

'Salvius Gratus, your coalition colleague?'

Amusement crinkled around the aedile's grey eyes. 'Yes – and before you ask, Laia Gratiana will drag herself along as well, to demonstrate her support for her brother.' I applied an uncaring expression. Faustus gazed at me. 'Would you like to come as my guest, Albia?'

Gulp.

I said taking along their informer might not assist Sextus Vibius. Ours is a despised profession. I heard myself add that it would look as if Faustus had brought along his mistress, which was only useful if the mistress had a great deal of political influence and was publicly known to have slept with very famous men.

Faustus reckoned it depended on the senator: some, he claimed, would find me very interesting. I laughed drily. Then he sensibly accepted my refusal.

I walked with him to the gatehouse. He touched my hand lightly. I watched him march off down Fountain Court, Dromo lolloping in his wake, like a disabled rabbit. The way Dromo fell over his feet reminded me of the slave who worked for Fundanus, the pyre-builder, struggling in a dead man's stolen boots.

I recrossed the empty courtyard and resumed my bench. Pleasant early-evening sunlight warmed the spot where the aedile had positioned it, bringing me a sense of well-being.

My new seat aroused lively interest among the other apartment-dwellers. They were fewer than they once had been: my father was intending to sell the decrepit Eagle Building for redevelopment. It was one of those drawn-out sales that take several years, with a sluggish buyer who keeps you guessing; everybody knew it was planned, but his tenants would scream with indignation when the buyer suddenly came good and Father had to evict them.

Most lacked balconies but managed to lean out of windows, calling, 'Ooh, get you, Flavia Albia!' By tradition, any people who lived here were appalling.

I already felt this bench was a crucial acquisition. One of those items that become central in your daily life, the one crazy possession you make sure to save if a fire breaks out . . . Silly: it was in a courtyard and made of stone. All I had to do was keep burglars away from it, especially strong ones.

I was an informer. I lived alone in squalor here. I had done so for years, never expecting change. Yet Manlius Faustus had planted the idea that I might begin to strive for a better life.

Still, he was a political campaigner. That is what they always say. All lies. It never happens.

16

We rendezvoused next day at my uncle's house. Since Faustus had met the Camilli before, I let him make his own way there. I could have suggested breakfast first at the Stargazer, but as he had spent the previous evening in his ex-wife's company, I felt cool towards him.

We had to wait. My uncle, the most noble Quintus Camillus Justinus, was in the midst of dealing with a child, one of six he had fathered. The infant must have behaved so dreadfully that for once even Quintus and his wife Claudia felt that playing the heavy paterfamilias was required. Quintus had probably had to look up how to do it. An efficient mother, his wife was bound to possess a child-education manual.

Claudia was somewhere else in the house, trying to stop their five other little fiends giggling. Nearby, we overheard a small boy shrieking defiance, then heartbroken sobs and muffled contrition. Silence fell.

Faustus winced, though I could not tell whether he was sympathetic to the boy or to my uncle. To cover the hiatus, I did ask about the dinner, to which he replied that the swinish senator had promised his favours but was obviously wriggling and that, yes, Laia Gratiana had been present but, no, he had not spoken to her. 'Thoughtful hostess. Did not put me next to her.' A hostess who knew their story, then.

'I didn't ask.'

'But you were dying to know.' He sounded scratchy, so I wondered if he had a hangover.

Quintus joined us, looking ruffled. At the same time my other uncle, the equally noble Aulus Camillus Aelianus, appeared from his own house next door, making smug comments about children who misbehaved, goading Quintus. These squabbling brothers were supposed to be acting as Romans of influence, greeting clients at their morning levée. For us they were not in their togas but casual white tunics. Neither appeared to have combed his hair that morning, though in other respects they were turned out neatly.

To me, who had known them from my teens, they were still the boyish relatives I had first met when I was about fourteen and they were in their twenties. Both had been despondent and unsettled then, due to career setbacks even when Vespasian was emperor; I had thought them glamorous, though now I saw they had both caused their parents great anxiety before they settled down.

We got them into the Senate at the same time, about ten years ago. They were just shy of forty now, and typical of second-generation senators who tried to act well yet felt increasingly hampered by the current regime. Domitian distrusted the Senate, working against it where he could; he had killed or exiled many of its members, some of them prominent. My uncles had sought to join this body out of ambition, a sense of duty and, in both cases, a genuine love of law and law-making. They found the Curia frustrating and unsafe. They could not leave. Nobody resigned. Domitian weeded out people, but his way of doing so was deadly.

According to traditional early-morning practice, we ought to flatter our hosts, so they would be gracious, possibly donating small gifts. But Faustus and I were not standard clients and that was not expected.

Quintus seemed fraught after disciplining little Constans; Aulus was characteristically glum. I left Faustus to canvass for Vibius. He had not brought his friend, preferring to speak for him. He made a good case. He was easy and direct. He admitted that he was unable to offer favours, though he could promise that Vibius Marinus would work hard and keep his assigned districts in good order. There was an unsaid hint that Faustus would supervise him.

The Camillus brothers politely assured him they would give thought to his candidate. Everyone knew what that meant. Faustus could not conceal a despondent sigh.

'Is it always so hard to get answers?' I asked sympathetically. 'It must be especially difficult to excite senators over mere neighbourhood magistrates – I mean, they don't put their noble noses out into the street much, in case the proletariat abuse them, so why should they care whether pavements are muddy and metal jugs displayed on pillars biff you in the face? – And then, of course, the position of aedile is optional in the senatorial course of honour.'

'Not "one of us", Albia,' agreed Aulus. He spoke in his usual dour way, though his intention was satirical. These were my mother's younger brothers; they had been brought up with the same wry attitude.

To emphasise how worthy Vibius was supposed to be, I ran through the scandalous stories I had unearthed about his rivals until I felt the Camilli might support our candidate at least by default. 'Remember, my mother won't like you if you vote for a man who hands out lewd dwarfs to Domitian.' Mention of Helena Justina made them both wince in a way I thought silly. Typical brothers.

'The outcome depends on the order for voting,' said Aulus. Of the two, he was the legal tactician and he was prim about scandal.

'I agree.' Faustus leaned forwards, equally ready to expound on technical issues.

Aulus interrupted: 'The word is, we must first elect some puppet called Volusius, "Caesar's candidate".' The brothers had taken *some* interest then.

'Volusius Firmus dropped out. Nobody seems to know why. I don't know him personally, so I can't ask.'

The uncles sat up. 'Lost it with Domitian?' suggested Quintus, quickly. The uncles glanced at each other. If I knew them, they would ask questions of colleagues, poking at this mystery. That would save me having to do so.

Aulus mused further about the listing until Faustus said he believed that now Firmus was gone the order for senators to vote would be: Trebonius Fulvo, Arulenus Crescens (the two bruisers), Dillius Surus (the drunk), Salvius Gratus (Laia's brother), Vibius Marinus and finally Ennius Verecundus (the mother's boy). Apparently his uncle had been digging: this list emanated from Tullius. There were four posts. The men were voted on one at a time. Once four obtained a majority, the rest lost out. None of us commented but that that meant, however worthy he was, in fifth position Vibius might lose.

He could stand again, but it was expensive and he would lose his chance of serving 'in his year' (at thirty-six, his first opportunity); also, all Faustus' campaign work would have to be repeated. Personally I thought that would be a bad idea for him. He needed to do this now, then be rid of it.

'And do you always vote as you are told by Domitian?' I demanded of my uncles.

'I am not ready to die.' Aulus was taciturn.

'Who instructed you to favour Volusius Firmus?'

'Hints and whispers.'

'The Emperor doesn't gather you in a bar, offer drinks all round, then name his choice, I take it! But the Senate does what he wants – even when he is abroad?' (No wonder he despised them, I thought.)

'Out of sight, yet never out of mind,' said Aulus. 'He'll be back for the vote. He won't put up with a Pannonian winter.'

Quintus soothed me: 'If we were told that wild Dacian tribesmen had rushed over the Danube and murdered Our Leader, we might have second thoughts. Though he likes to tease so awfully, he might well start such a rumour himself in order to see our reaction. To be safe, I would want to see the bier carried home. I might even need a peek at his cadaver before I felt free to vote independently.'

We tended to forget that Domitian was absent from Rome. That was because his influence never left. Last January, around the time Manlius Faustus first took up his role as a magistrate, the Emperor was challenged in a revolt by the Governor of Germany. It had been ill conceived and was brutally suppressed, the trouble all over before Domitian himself could arrive there. My family had paid special attention because the brutal suppression was carried out by Ulpius Trajanus, the crew-cut Spanish general to whom Falco was trying to sell Fountain Court – for heaven's sake, we did not want this man Trajan distracted while we were urging him to sign our property contract . . .

Domitian only made it as far as Pannonia, where restless tribes from over the frontier had taken advantage of the upset on the Rhine. The Emperor was now embroiled in fighting those tribes at the western end of the Danube frontier, while also making a highly unpopular settlement with the King of Dacia, a more formidable enemy further east. He had harried Rome for some years past. As Quintus alluded, there had been massacres of whole legions, defeat in battle of the Praetorian Guard, and slaughter of Roman high officials by Dacians marauding across the river. They liked to behead significant officials, though had failed with Our Leader. He was rumoured to be out of their reach, safe in a fort, screwing sinful boys and eating specially imported oysters.

As you can tell from that, Domitian liked to see himself as a great military leader in the mould of his father and brother Titus, though he approached it rather differently. These barbarian opponents were tenacious. He could be kept busy in foreign parts for a long time. Despite that distraction, his morbid shadow fell on Rome. The tyrant controlled everything – including the election of minor officials at home.

My uncles moved on. They encouraged Faustus to talk about progress so far. He spoke fluently; one thing he mentioned was that he had canvassed a few senators from overseas because, as an owner of warehouses, his uncle Tullius had contacts among provincial traders. Senators were not allowed to trade directly – that did not stop them, just accounted for the numerous negotiators and agents in Roman society. The father of Vibius Marinus owned land in Gaul, where he had once served in the army, so they had started with Gallic senators.

Quintus and Aulus volunteered that they might be able to interest the small number of Spanish senators (though clearly not Trajan, our building purchaser, who was away governing Spain when not crushing rebels). Aulus, when young, had assisted a previous governor, and Quintus had married a Baetican. Claudia really came to Rome to marry Aulus, but nobody blamed her for transferring to his sunnier, better-looking brother. Aulus's own first wife was Athenian and he still associated with her so, unexpectedly, he offered Faustus an introduction to Greek members of the Senate.

I was seeing how a good campaign was put together. This approach was all the better, Faustus said, because nowadays most candidates rarely bothered to court anybody outside Rome and never provincials. As a result, the foreign senators were grateful when he did so.

Romans are great snobs. Was this what Quintus Cicero had meant when he instructed his brother to talk even to people they despised? In deference to my uncles, with their foreign wives, I kept quiet. Quintus apparently loved Claudia. Aulus was on better terms with Meline since they divorced than when they were married. (Well, ever since he divorced two later wives, when Meline for some weird reason came back and helped him through it.)

I was probably foreign myself, though could not offer to cajole any senators from Britain. Hades, I dread even to think what they would be like.

17

The Camillus brothers lived immediately beyond the Capena Gate, which was also convenient for our next call. Like many imperial freedmen, my father's old contact Claudius Laeta had acquired a large, elegant villa outside Rome, though not far outside. It was as if, even after they were allowed to retire, palace servants felt they must remain near the court. This often came in handy when there was an imperial assassination, because the loyal freedmen or women would make their beautiful gardens available for otherwise-awkward funerals. Phaon had let Nero commit suicide in his villa garden. Dispossessed emperors or their disgraced relatives never had to lie unburied. The freedmen stepped in when a state funeral was out of the question, thus avoiding any disrespect for the once-important.

Laeta's villa happened to be down the Via Appia, which exits the old Servian Wall through the Capena Gate. After we left my uncles, Faustus and I went straight there. I had Patchy the donkey, though I walked alongside. We strolled out past the Gardens of Asinius Pollio in warm sunlight without conversing until we reached the old man's handsome spread.

As far as I knew, this property had never yet hosted a cremation, though someone might one day have to salvage the bloody corpse of Domitian . . . Once, Claudius Laeta had been the kind of administrator people might turn to for removing a despotic ruler (my father always thought that in his younger years Laeta must have worked behind the scenes when Nero was ousted). He was past all that now. Retirement meant Domitian should leave him alone – although the Emperor did bear grudges against ancient freedmen, and notoriously executed them, even decades after their perceived sins. A despot may well brood over anyone who has a history of removing despots.

We arrived, wormed our way in past the defensive team who cared for Laeta and were led to him in his long chair. We may have looked like a pair of would-be conspirators. Our host would have been used to that in younger days. Plotting was in his blood.

Tiberius Claudius Laeta had had a long career as chief secretary, a post where he reckoned he ruled the Empire using old Vespasian as his mouthpiece, while the easy-going Vespasian valued him enough to let him think it. Laeta could be any age between sixty and seventy, older than average. At the palace he had led a pampered life. He still had all his hair (dry-looking grey stuff, cut short and straight); his face was an unhealthy red; his eyes were dim and watery. He wore a white tunic that fitted awkwardly on his slack frame. On one liver-spotted hand he kept the wide gold ring of the middle class, but he twisted it uneasily as if his fingers had grown too fragile for the weight of the metal.

My father had told me Laeta's aims were always long-term and his motives devious. He was intelligent and could be vicious, a man who consistently disposed of his rivals, generally before they saw him coming. For instance, with my father's assistance, he had won one long-standing feud, with a dangerous Chief Spy whom nobody else would have managed to oust. Don't ask how, or how I knew. It was still unsafe to mention.

Many of Laeta's schemes had been like that. His relationship with Falco had lasted many years, on both sides a mixture of reluctant admiration and steely distrust. If there was one man on earth who had wheedled out the truth of my father's own troubles with Domitian, this was he – but, if so, it was not Falco who had told him.

We had met before, though in view of his frailty I introduced myself anew. 'I am Flavia Albia, eldest daughter of Didius Falco and the noble Helena Justina. I know that you and Father worked together.'

For a time it seemed he would not respond. Could he even remember Falco? He seemed to need to recall the memory, but he suddenly piped up, 'Plenty in common. Much we disputed . . . I sent him to Baetica.'

'He often speaks of it.' The words 'olive oil' still made Falco groan. 'And to Britain.'

'Hah! I never count Falco's escapades in Britannia as real!'

I did. That was how I came to be adopted and made Roman. Just in case this devious man would query my citizenship documents, I kept quiet. He liked to know something against everyone. My position was legal, my adoption duly certified, but once you have been outside acceptable society, you never relax.

'And who is this?' Laeta was staring, his face alert and inquisitive.

'This is my good friend Tiberius Manlius Faustus, one

of this year's plebeian aediles. He wants to talk to you about the next election.'

'Take him away! No one talks to me, these days. I have absolutely no influence.'

'Flavia Albia thought you might nevertheless have advice for us. Better advice than we can obtain from your successor.' Faustus knew how to get along with stubborn pensioners, apparently. 'I am acting for one of the candidates.'

'You want me to subvert senators.'

'I couldn't possibly—'

'Then I am glad you are not *my* agent!' This was proving harder than I had hoped. 'Get the buggers on your side. It's no use hoping they will just like the look of your candidate's scrubbed face. Bribe them!'

Faustus had become rather stiff. 'I am aware of your past work, sir – and your legacy to today's state servants.'

'Bloody Abascantus! Scented fool.'

'Domitian has sent him away, sir.'

'In irons?'

'I believe not.'

'Suggested he top himself?'

'Perhaps a temporary seaside sojourn?'

'Domitian's gone soft! Abascantus will creep back. Long-haired lightweight. No sense of tradition. They say his wife pushes him. The man is unbelievable . . .' The old stylus-pusher added waspishly, 'You know the type: *poets* think him wonderful!'

Faustus must have been aware that Abascantus, until recently the most powerful freedman at the palace, was generally regarded as a talented young man. While Laeta was still sniggering to himself over poets, my friend pressed on valiantly: 'Sir, even if his exile proves to be temporary, Abascantus is no use to us if he's on gardening leave. I can find nobody of his calibre, let alone of *your* calibre. You are sadly missed.'

Laeta took some thick invalid drink from a redware beaker. He swallowed it with studious care, very slowly, then grimaced to himself. 'What do you want from me?' Before Faustus could say anything, the old man answered himself: 'Who does Domitian support? Why that one? What is wrong with the others? Will he damn your own man? Which way will the Senate jump? Does anybody dare cross Our Master-Who-Believes-Himself-A-God?'

Faustus gave a wan smile. 'All those questions, please. We originally understood that Our Master supported Volusius, though Volusius has inexplicably pulled out.'

'Volusius Firmus?' Laeta was on it immediately. 'Family in oar-making, or some watery industry? Married to Verecunda's daughter? Has, therefore, the mother-in-law from Hades? That woman is loathsome, and all her girls are Furies – she brought them up deliberately to be full of hate.'

'You are still well informed!' I commented.

'I keep up. Somebody has to. Abascantus never has any idea what is going on. Does what his wife tells him – not my way! No contacts. No initiative.'

'No subtlety,' I said, smiling. Laeta gave me a sharp look as if he suspected satire. Manlius Faustus did the same. Our eyes met. Faustus understood: I believe that 'subtlety' equates with fraud.

'Dear me, I shall have to investigate Volusius Firmus,' Laeta decided, fussing, fretting, agitated not to have the gossip. 'This simply will not do. The Emperor's favourite stands down? Somebody failed to foresee that. He should never have been on the list in the first place. Standards are slipping . . .'

'So why was he Caesar's candidate?' I asked. 'How would Domitian know him?'

'Domitian has never met him, depend on it.' Laeta was crisp. 'Abascantus must have pushed Firmus, for some reason.' Money changed hands, I presumed. 'Now that Abascantus has been nudged aside, Firmus is wise to step down. Just in case Abascantus is out of the picture permanently,' Laeta said, clearly hoping for it.

'Do you then approve of the Senate being given a steer from the Emperor?' asked Faustus, shifting ground.

'Provided the Emperor has been steered by wise counsel first.'

I laughed. 'Claudius Laeta means, Faustus, the Emperor's choice should be steered by his freedmen. Government by secretariat. Democracy through bureaucracy.'

'Long-term planning,' Laeta decreed. 'A suitably strong briefing note.' He must have written hundreds of those. 'They need it!' he scoffed.

'And how do you see the current mood in the Senate, sir?' asked Faustus.

'Abject terror.' This was despite the fact Laeta cannot have visited the Senate for some years. 'Their anxiety is heightened by the Saturninus shambles.' That was January's military revolt in Germany.

Faustus was settled on his stool now, enjoying the debate. 'I thought the received wisdom was that Saturninus failed because he omitted to organise Senate backing? He was in Germany, raiding legionary funds, but here in Rome he had worked up no support. So, everyone assumes the Emperor regards the Senate, for once, as innocent?'

'Just because the Emperor has not dispatched swords at dawn, do not suppose Domitian exonerates them,' Laeta answered. 'My sources say his suspicions have, if anything, increased. He believes the members *were* coerced – but it was cleverly covered up.'

'Does Domitian blame Abascantus for that?' I asked; it would explain the freedman's sudden exile.

Claudius Laeta gave me a long, purse-lipped gaze. However much he despised Abascantus, as two bureaucrats they were bonded. He would not snitch.

Faustus then supplied the names of the other candidates, seeking Laeta's views.

'Whoever devised such a dreadful list?' Laeta snapped crossly. 'Someone should receive a reprimand! It's the Caelian Hill mob, all clubbing together – when they are not feuding. There ought to be men from other districts and backgrounds. Variety. Choice. This selection has had no beneficial management. A list should be elegant, pleasingly simple so voters can navigate with confidence.'

I was intrigued that Laeta saw an election list as something to be supervised by officials. I had foolishly supposed that candidates personally decided to stand, then had to make their own way. 'No, Flavia Albia, there are rules, of course there are. This is a stupid pickle. We may live in a city where family counts, but you don't want all your magistrates sharing a bed. Especially if, every time one turns over on the pillow, the one behind stabs him in the back.'

Faustus sounded anxious: 'I suppose you mean that my candidate is paired up with my ex-wife's brother . . .'

The oomph went out of the freedman. 'Did I say so? No. Thank you for telling me. I did not know that. Manlius Faustus . . . who are you? I know nothing about you. Where have you arrived from?'

'Falco's daughter, has your father completed a background

check on this "good friend" of yours?' he demanded of me abruptly. He had remembered my words of introduction. He remembered Father's methods too.

'Ah, Falco is always suspicious of his daughters' friends.' I chuckled.

'Well, thank the gods someone still has standards! The election is murkier. I shall have to think about the implications. It is all too much for me today.'

'Sir?'

We had lost him. In a moment Laeta faded before our eyes; he seemed to become confused and drowsy, an old man in his dotage, losing all vestiges of his past powers. We felt like intruders, harrying the man in his declining years.

I lifted the beaker from his hand. As we tiptoed from the room, Tiberius Claudius Laeta, one time behind-the-scenes steersman of government, seemed sunk in his chair, dozing, a lumpen shadow.

I did not entirely believe it. From what I knew of his history, nodding off may have been an act. I thought there was life – and mischief – in Claudius Laeta yet.

I apologised to Faustus that the interview had gone rockily. He thought about that, as we walked back to the city between the roadside tombs that grace the Via Appia. He surprised me by saying that in his opinion we would hear from Laeta. The old freedman would not forget our visit. After we had gone, Laeta would deploy whatever contacts he undoubtedly still possessed. Then, sooner or later, he would send us information.

We walked some distance further. Suddenly Faustus demanded, not breaking his stride, 'Well, has he?'

'Has who done what?'

'Has Didius Falco carried out a check on me?'

I kept it light. 'Of course. He made up an excuse about the auction house and came back to Rome for three days on purpose.'

Faustus said nothing. That was Faustus.

'Tiberius, I strictly instructed him not to.'

For a while Faustus remained quiet. I dared not look at him. His voice was taut: 'He loves you. He wants to protect you.'

'Rubbish. I told him you are not interested in being more than a friend.'

I did turn and look at him then, only to find Manlius Faustus laughing. 'Oh, oh, I shall never be allowed to forget that!' He meant, as I had meant, the time I wanted to go to bed with him but he turned down the offer. 'I must have been crazy!'

I stared straight ahead and kept walking.

After a moment more, Faustus murmured, 'I like it.'

'What?'

'Having an embarrassing story that I shall be teased about for years to come.'

'Years?'

'Better get used to it.'

Again, I kept walking and made no answer.

Some time later, inevitably, the aedile wanted to know what my father had found out about him. I claimed that Falco had refused to tell me.

18

Back at the Capena Gate, Faustus turned left towards the Arch of Dolabella and Silanus, intending to visit Sextus Vibius.

Laeta had said, 'the Caelian Hill mob'. What did he mean? I asked Faustus but he either did not know or chose not to tell me.

I continued straight ahead on my own towards the Flavian Amphitheatre. I passed along the Sacred Way to a place where my father kept an advertising space on permanent hire. Since the Callistus sale was virtually over, I scrubbed its details from the wall, found the chalk we left behind a loose brick, and neatly wrote up a description, all we had, of the strongbox corpse. I appealed for information about the man's identity. I gave my contact details, and promises of gratitude, although I stopped short of offering a reward. I could not face all the chancers who would turn up at the merest sniff of money.

People would look. They might gossip initially. All too soon they would ignore the wall, taking no more notice of my appeal. Still, I might as well try.

Occasionally someone responds. I do it myself. I had met Manlius Faustus when I answered a notice he had put up, asking for witnesses to a street accident.

* * *

At a loose end, I decided to walk on to the Porticus of Pompey and check how the auction had finally ended.

Most lots had been sold. Everything had petered out. Yesterday's items had been taken away, either collected by buyers at the time or dragged off before dawn by Felix in our own delivery cart. The professional dealers had gone on their way; only a thin crowd of casuals remained, no one taking too much interest in the last selection of distressed goods. Further down the porticus, a fool who didn't care if he disturbed the peace stood on a barrel telling dirty jokes; most of the idlers had moved up there and were craning their necks. Anyone morally offended would complain to an aedile. By the time the aedile came to fine him for obscenity, the comedian would be long gone.

I thought about Vibius, also Gratus, Arulenus, Trebonius, Dillius and Verecundus, wondering how each of them would cope with a situation like this. Poorly, in my opinion. Mind you, that was traditional. Even the mighty Vespasian, a future emperor, had been hauled up for failure of duty when he was an aedile; the folds of his toga were loaded with mud from the streets he had failed to have properly cleaned.

It must be just before lunchtime. It was hotter even than yesterday.

Some of our workers were packing up; they were being discreet because the auction was still running, just about. I saw Gornia, looking more harassed than usual. He had only the last few items, which had been collected together around his tribunal.

I recognised a moth-eaten stuffed bear we had been trying to shift for months, which kept failing to attract any bids and we all knew why: interested parties had only to wander up for an inspection and her mouldy smell made them recoil. Until we found someone with a sinus infection, Ursa would remain ours. There were a bunch of ceramic comports with uneven stands, a huddle of barnacled fish-pickle amphorae, a dog kennel for a very small dog that didn't mind being rained on, and an old friend.

The mediocre statue of *The Boy Taking a Thorn out of His Left Foot* had come back.

19

'I do not believe this!'

Taking a breather, Gornia mopped his brow. 'I know. It did seem too good to be true.'

'What happened?'

'Defaulter.'

'The bulgy man in the puce tunic? I don't understand it. He'd been hanging about all day waiting for his chance to bid, hoping no one else would have a go.'

'I wish they had. I wish we'd had a good underbidder that I could drag this bloody thing along to . . . In fact I'm ready to give it away.' Gornia was bitter. 'Buyers have to see the docket boy. Everyone knows the routine. He never even tried to complete. Must have waved his hand and made his bid, then scarpered. Strolled off straight out of the porticus. No money, no delivery instruction, and a no-show this morning. It happens,' the unhappy old fellow told me, trying to defend the situation. 'We were all so tired, nobody saw it. Your pa will understand.'

'My pa will get on to him about it, surely – assuming we know who he is?'

'Falco won't bother. No point, not if he really made up his mind he didn't want it. Once they've gone off the scene, we don't usually chase them. He'll never pay. We still have the goods. We'll just sell the thing next time.'

'And do we know?' I insisted. 'Do we know who Puce Tunic is?'

'Absolutely no idea,' said Gornia flatly. 'Never seen the swine before.'

He gave *The Boy with a Thorn* a kick, then went back up on his stand to try to sell Ursa, the seven-times-attempted mouldy bear.

However, half our staff had been listening in. They love to watch an upset. 'Puce Tunic was talking to that other one,' the money-clerk told me, taking a break from his lunch. 'That skinny one. Him who bought the strongbox.' Titus Niger.

Gornia brought down his gavel on a no-sale for the stuffed bear. He leaned down from his box. 'And that's another thing, Flavia Albia. We had a bad day yesterday – the skinny man still has not sent his banker's draft. Looks like the old Callistus chest is staying with us, too. It's lunchtime. We're never going to see him bring a purse now.'

I sighed. 'I suppose you are going to tell me this is what comes of holding auctions in July.' I spoke mildly. I had no wish to offend Gornia.

'Bad payers don't care. It's bloody ridiculous,' he snarled back. He seemed a sweet old fellow, but he had a furious side. 'I'd like to know what's going on – what games are these jokers playing?'

I thought it felt more complex than games. I was suspicious of two defaulting buyers talking to each other. Were they really unconnected, or was this a concerted scam? Anything involving the chest seemed significant, while the puce-attired man had looked dodgy from the off – and not just in his taste for tunic dye. If he and the Callistus negotiator knew one another, that certainly caught my attention.

'I always thought *The Boy with the Thorn* was ours for keeps. The strongbox is really outrageous, though,' Gornia raved. 'I had good bids on that.'

Neither of the no-shows was our fault. You conduct your sale as best you can, then there has to be trust between auctioneer and bidder. Defaulters are a menace; if feasible, you ban them from attending again. Rome has a tradition of allowing goods to go home with people on credit, but shrewd auctioneers don't allow it. Too many strangers. Too many peculiar buyers.

I still felt I was the family representative. I said I would go to see the Callisti and, if I could not discover what was going on, at least I would give our clients some colourful language.

'Now you be careful!' Gornia had heard me before when I sounded off. He sent a porter with me, Lappius. The large one. The Callisti were used to taking the lead in their business affairs. They were not used to anyone arguing. Especially anyone like me.

First, though, I went to see their skinny agent. He, unlike Puce Tunic, had foolishly left us an address.

20

Niger lived off the Via Tusculana, a small side-street on the lower edge of Oppian Hill. He was not entirely daft: in case anybody angry called, he had gone out.

Luckily for me, he had one of those strange wives who like to be at home all day, mopping floors. I made sure not to step on the wet part.

Broad of beam and wide of features, this put-upon woman assured me she had no idea where her husband might be or when she could expect him home. Many marriages, I knew, are run on these pathetic lines. (Not mine!) It flagrantly flouts the definition that marriage is the agreement of two people to live together. 'Together' being the crucial word. If he goes out, either he takes you with him – if you definitely want to go – or he damn well tells you where he is off to so you can turn up there later and catch him with his arm round that dumpy barmaid nobody else would look at.

I commented politely that Niger's woman kept the place nice for him, so she said it was expected, wasn't it? In the Manlius Faustus style of discussion, I made no reply. If she had been brighter, she would have seen my silence as dissent.

I managed to extract from her that Niger had been highly upset last evening when the Callisti sent a curt order not to honour his bid. She said he was so angry, he raved around the house all night, shouting his objections to the way he had been treated – which at least meant his wife had discovered what was wrong. She explained the issue: Niger was worried that our auction house could count him as liable. If we came down on him for the money (and my presence now hinted that we might) it was too much for him to find. Even if he could pay up, he was landed with a rubbishy old chest.

If we let him off, defaulting on his bid was bad practice; Niger had an image to keep up. It was important because he was not salaried to the Callisti but worked as a freelance; he relied on having a good reputation and references to obtain other work. He needed to look like a man who knew what he was doing.

I expressed fellow feeling; it went over her head. Niger's wife had no concept of a woman working, let alone working for herself. She thought I was just a messenger today. 'Your husband had been hired by Callistus Primus on other occasions, I presume?'

'Well, actually, I think recently was his first time with them. Niger was hoping it would lead to bigger things.'

'He struck me as very experienced.'

'Oh, yes.'

'Then he can live without the Callisti in his portfolio. People who let you down are a nightmare . . . Who does he work for otherwise?'

'Oh, you would have to ask him that.'

'I will if I can find him.'

'He acts as an agent for some *very* nice people,' the wife assured me, though I did not take this as reliable. Nice people are pretty hard to find. 'Good payers, most of them, as well.' Probably true. His income would impact on her household budget, so she would keep an eye on it. 'They all think very highly of my husband as their agent. Julia Terentia gave us a beautiful set of glass beakers last Saturnalia.' Presumably not much use if Niger was never at home to drink anything out of them.

'That was thoughtful of the lady . . . I am not sure I know Julia Terentia?'

'Oh, you must do,' Niger's wife insisted. 'She is one of that lot on the Caelian. The rich, bossy one. Niger will tell you. Just ask him.'

I said I would come back later when Niger could give me the low-down on what Laeta had called 'the Caelian Hill mob'.

Niger's wife had told me little. In my work, I have many conversations that are utterly frustrating; I have learned never to lose my temper with the witness. No point. If they drive you nuts, you can ease your feelings later at home by throwing a bucket at a wall. Just make sure to use an empty one. You don't want to end up scrubbing floors all day.

I hoofed it out of there and found Lappius, the big minder Gornia had imposed on me. I had left him in the street when I went up to the negotiator's apartment. Now I had seen it, I knew it was decent, in both size and amenities, and only on the second floor. That fitted what I had just learned. Whoever he worked for other than the Callisti, Niger made a good living. So he had reputation, a nice home furnished with gifts from grateful clients, and an uncomplaining wife. This is the life all freelance professionals hope for. Not many of us achieve it.

Nobody in that position had much to gain by killing a

man and stuffing him into a chest, especially when Niger knew from preparing the inventory that the chest was about to be auctioned, with certain discovery of its contents.

Lappius and I set off to see the Callisti.

21

Callistus Primus was not at home. I wondered if he was out with Niger, although if the agent was annoyed with him, that seemed unlikely. It was tempting to suppose that, like Niger, Callistus wanted to hide from me, but we informers have to beware of assuming other people's lives revolve around us. Callistus was entitled to go out on business. He had probably forgotten I existed.

His brother and cousin were out too. Neither had been home the last time I had called, so this was routine for them. I had not met the father and saw no point in asking after him. He wasn't in. I worked that out for myself.

I told the door porter I would wait like a morning client on their stone bench until somebody or other came home. As I was now a returning visitor, he brought me a cup of water. Things were looking up.

I had no real intention of hanging around for long, but was keen to sit down. I had walked a lot today: down to the Capena Gate, out on the Via Appia, back into Rome, across the Forum, on to the Porticus of Pompey, and now back again, first to the Oppian and then around the Caelian to here. The 'bench' was a simple ledge, but had a fine view across the main road from the Forum towards the big shrine of Fortuna Respiciens that sits at the base of the Palatine. Gazing at the temple saved me having to look higher up at Domitian's flash new palace, with its élite stadium and private gardens occupying the crag.

I had a wary respect for the goddess of fortune, patron of good luck or bad, bringer of benefits by chance. 'Respiciens' meant looking over her shoulder, wise woman. In the past she had laid much misery upon me, yet from time to time she sent unexpected joys. Like all those heavy, big-hipped Roman deities, Fortuna had her quirks. That suited me. I possess a few myself, I am proud to say.

While I sat resting, I noticed again the large advertising space on a wall of the Callistus house. There had been slogans before, but it was blank now. I was sure the previous notice had been political, so it seemed premature to remove it. Was an election candidate slyly obliterating rivals' claims? (That gave me ideas.) Most likely, someone had crept up and painted in a notice without paying the hire fee. The wall's owner had scrubbed off the offending advert, while the culprit moved on to some other empty space.

Still pondering, I thought about how Claudius Laeta had said this year's candidates were too close-knit. I ought to look into that, because to me few links were obvious. Faustus had failed to see what Laeta meant, too, or so he maintained, though I sometimes had a vague feeling Faustus and his man Vibius were keeping things from me.

It would not be the first time a client had held back vital information. Then when you finally discover the truth and point out how vital it is, they go fluttery, or they even turn on you: they protest that they thought it was not relevant; they did not want to hurt their mother; they wanted to shield you from unpleasant information; the truth was embarrassing; they simply forgot . . .

The first thing to know about clients is that they never help themselves.

Sometimes it pays to wait for things to happen. As I mused, the Callistus door porter popped out from the house, exclaimed at me being there still (though he had clearly come on purpose), picked up my empty cup and offered that if I was really desperate Julia could see me.

He had an odd expression; I noticed and was forewarned. When he led me indoors, a couple of other slaves were standing about in the atrium, as if watching to see what would happen. They reminded me of the auction staff just before they opened the strongbox for me, with the body still reeking inside it.

Remembering that Niger's wife had spoken of a 'Julia Terentia', who had given her the Saturnalia glassware set and who lived on the Caelian, I wondered if by coincidence it would be her. Not so. This was Julia Laurentina, a Callistus wife, married to the cousin of Primus and Secundus. According to the porter, she was at home, sleeping off her lunch.

I swiftly said I would wait until she woke of her own accord. The last thing I wanted was an irritated interviewee. But the porter had already arranged for her to be woken.

As soon as I saw her, I knew it made no difference. Julia Laurentina was always annoyed, that was the reason her servants had been glancing at one another and, without doubt, were listening behind the door, to see just how rude their explosive mistress would be to me.

I jumped in quickly: 'I am *so* sorry. I was too late to stop your people disturbing you.' The sneaky bunch deserved to have the blame.

'I don't suppose you tried too hard!'

Oh dear.

I sat down, unasked, and composed myself with folded hands. If she raged, I would let it wash over me.

She was about thirty years old, sluggish as she rose from a rumpled couch. 'Sleeping off her lunch' could have meant she hit the wine flagon, though I detected no sign of that. She wore white, with gold embroidery. When she shook her head to clear her drowsiness, the earrings that tinkled against her long neck were highly fanciable droplets, each sporting a couple of large oyster pearls and what looked like a heavy garnet. I guessed she was given a lot of presents, in the hope of keeping her happy. It failed.

'Who are you and what do you want?'

I stuck with being Falco's daughter, on business from the auction house, and said there seemed to be a mix-up over paying for their bid.

'Oh, my husband sides with his ridiculous cousins. Apparently, we're now not having the thing back.' It seemed Julia Laurentina despised her menfolk, even more than she looked down on me. This at least made her all too willing to complain about the men.

She stretched out a hand, surveying her manicure, which looked professional. She said there had been a row last night. It was a common occurrence in their house, she admitted. 'Mind you, yesterday set a new standard.'

'Why was that?'

Julia surveyed me down a long sharp nose and this time decided she would rebuff me. Was it caution or bloody-mindedness? 'Mind your own business!' she snapped.

This was my business. 'The three men seemed to be of one accord at the auction. I assume they had prearranged for their agent to bid. At that point there must have been consensus; did something happen afterwards so they changed their minds?'

'First they wanted it, now they can't bear the sight of it. Who knows, with men?'

'Julia Laurentina, I would normally agree with you – but this sudden alteration seems odd, even allowing for male perverseness.'

The woman gave me a nasty look. 'I don't think you should come into our house, calling my husband perverse!'

No, she was the perverse one, suddenly defending him. I kept my temper, in case I could still squeeze any information out of her. 'Please believe I have no intention of causing offence. I am only trying to find out what happened and what your family members want us to do with the strongbox.'

'That bloody strongbox!'

'So?'

'Do what you like with it.'

I could see Julia knew enough about the quarrel to be thoroughly exasperated by whatever had occurred last night. But I acted all innocence and explained, 'You may not know, the strongbox has a history.'

'I know you auction people say you found a body in it.'

Say? 'We did, madam. I saw the poor man myself. That was a ghastly experience.'

She stared. She sat up straighter and blurted out, 'What did he look like?'

The interview swung. It was as if *she* was keenly interrogating me. 'In his fifties, well built, wearing a blue tunic.'

'His fifties?'

'I could hardly look at the body. I thought him a little younger; the funeral director said he had lived well and taken care of himself, so he put the man between fifty and sixty. I have used that firm before, so I trust the verdict.'

'No clues as to who the victim was?' Julia Laurentina sounded merely curious, yet I suspected there was more to it.

'Any clues had been carefully removed – he had on an ordinary wedding ring that is impossible to trace, but there were clear signs that he once wore a signet ring that someone had taken off, no doubt his killers to prevent it being identified.' I did not bother to ask why Julia was interested; she would never tell me. I was watching her instead. She was posing, acting casual, though I glimpsed some dark mood. Without undue emphasis, I asked, 'Do you recognise the description? I don't suppose anyone like that is missing from among the people you know?'

Julia stared again. 'No,' she said. Then she repeated, 'No. No one.'

'Are you sure?' I had detected unease. She nodded so quickly, it seemed unwise to press her.

While she looked introspective for a moment, I zapped in a few extra questions quietly: 'Do you know Niger, the agent?'

'I have never seen or spoken to him, but he came on the recommendation of one of my sisters.'

'*She* knows him?'

'He acted for her husband and now her.'

'Why did your menfolk want him to back down over the bid?'

'My husband says we have no need of a beaten-up, burned-out old chest; that was the whole point of trying to get rid of it at auction. Against him, Primus lost his temper and said he wants no more to do with it but he isn't going to let strangers get their hands on it. His brother Secundus thought Niger paid too much.'

'Bidding was brisk.' I thought it best not to say I had been the auctioneer. She would have recoiled, just like the wife of Niger. I didn't suppose the wives of Primus and Secundus concerned themselves with the river-transport business that brought in the cash for their finery. Julia Laurentina's husband owned a boat-building yard, but she had probably never been there. I was sure none of those women could recognise their boat captains, let alone understand a lading docket. That would not have done in *my* family. 'Niger had been instructed to buy the chest. If he had stopped bidding too soon, he would have lost it,' I said. 'He paid enough, though not over the odds, in my opinion.'

Julia said nothing.

'Since there was other interest,' I mentioned coolly, 'we intend to approach the underbidder and see if he still wants it.'

'Well.'

Well what? I raised my eyebrows. Mine were rather nicely shaped. The talented brow-girl at Prisca's Baths could even do it painlessly. Well, not quite, but she was better than the usual damage-wreakers.

Julia had had her brows plucked into thin arches; I always find that artificial. It must have hurt, but she seemed a woman who would not acknowledge pain.

'My husband is right for once. That strongbox has been used for something terrible, and we can do without it.' She shrugged it off, her gesture too exaggerated. She was unused to acting. I suppose she normally flared up and said whatever she wanted, then people backed away. I was a different commodity: she could not handle me.

'I just don't understand the change of heart here,' I persisted. 'I was told the strongbox would be privately bought back, then burned to prevent ghoulish interest. An act of respect, Niger the agent called it. Piety towards the dead man . . . whoever he was.'

'You seem to do far too much talking to other people's agents!'

'I belong to the auction house,' I told Julia gently. 'Talking to agents happens all the time. It is also good business practice for us to make enquiries when items seem odd, or people's behaviour feels wrong.'

Julia got a grip. 'Well, you must do your job,' she answered me, equally quietly.

The uncharacteristic restraint was fascinating. I would have expected sarcasm. This woman can rarely in her life have chosen to show so much control. Julia Laurentina was secretly fascinated by the corpse. I was sure she had heard her menfolk discussing it. Might they know who the dead man was?

Julia, I felt, had not been told his identity, hence her questions about his appearance. But she was harbouring suspicions. With the Callistus brothers and her husband, did she hide her curiosity? Was she trying to find out for herself what had happened, perhaps before confronting them?

Whatever the truth, Julia Laurentina was visibly anxious. She hardly gave the impression of a woman who was perturbed by family troubles. Yet it seemed to me the identity of that dead man and what had happened to him mattered more to Julia Laurentina than she would admit.

She dismissed me. I was surprised she had found the patience to let me stay for so long. It only confirmed her private interest in the strongbox corpse.

As I left the room, a young girl entered. About thirteen, she was not introduced. After the doors closed behind me I heard a low murmur of female voices. The talk sounded subdued, as if the speakers were discussing me. In my business, that is something you expect. It seemed friendly enough in tone.

I asked the porter if that was Julia Laurentina's daughter. He said no, she belonged to Callistus Primus, his only child with a first wife, long divorced; her name was Julia Valentina. She lived with her father. He wanted to bring her up himself.

That was unusual, but fathers had a legal claim to their children after marital separation so it happened. Some men were determined to exert their right of possession, even of a daughter, even if the child was very young. I sometimes had to help divorced mothers argue for custody.

I also asked the man about the advertising notice outside. He said the family owned the wall space; they had supported Volusius Firmus for aedile, the candidate who was forced to stand down. So removing the notice made sense.

When I stepped out from the house, I passed two other Callistus wives being delivered home in chairs. Dressed in the same highly embroidered style as Julia, they had clearly been shopping; it was obvious from the train of slaves carrying baskets and parcels. I gave them a formal nod, but did not interrupt their happy dash indoors, calling for cold drinks and their feather-fan girl to revive them.

'A goodly haul!' I nodded at the packages, smiling.

'It will all have to go back!' muttered the porter, darkly.

I dallied, pretending to adjust my sandal. 'Primus and Secundus are mean with money?'

'Not when they have it, but there's none to spare at the

moment. Everyone has been ordered to cut down.' The two young wives had obviously failed to hear the message.

'Has it happened before?' I remembered Gornia saying the men gambled heavily on chariot races.

'Time to time. They always get a windfall eventually, then it's joy all round again.'

I said drily, 'They ought to buy themselves a big strongbox where they can put away a nest egg for times of crisis.'

The porter missed the joke.

I wasted no pity on the Callisti. They must have picked the wrong team. They would have their auction proceeds coming in shortly to ease their money worries. If funds were tight, I imagined they would not admit openly that they were poor managers. They would want to keep quiet publicly and might even try to bluff a new agent. Embarrassment about their cashflow might explain why Niger's bid for the old chest had been overturned.

It would have been sensible to warn him not to go so high. But when do most people act sensibly?

22

I convinced myself I needed to see Faustus. It was a short walk round the Caelian to the Vibius house so I went there, on the excuse that we had not fully discussed what Claudius Laeta told us.

Excuses were unnecessary. Faustus was writing a speech. He welcomed me, knowing I would listen, help him line up his thoughts and make good suggestions. The candidate, who had to deliver the oratory, ought to have done this but Vibius was nowhere to be seen.

'Where is he?'

'Oh, he'll turn up. Let's get the speech done. It's time to make things personal.'

'Insults!'

'Yes, I thought you would like that.'

I would have liked to insult his friend Sextus for using Tiberius unfairly, but was too wise.

We had to blacken the rivals' characters. It would involve information I had gathered, buffed up with dramatic rhetoric that Faustus was now contributing. Written out, most of my gleanings seemed to be about Dillius Surus: he not only drank, he lived off a rich wife who had given Domitian a troupe of obscene dwarfs, had tapeworms, was impotent, sued a man over an orchard – and if that wasn't enough, he owned the dog that had bitten the priestess of Isis (on her birthday).

'No, that's wrong,' said Faustus. 'Latest information is—'

'It was the priestess who bit the dog?'

For a moment I had him, then he smacked a cushion as he realised the joke. 'Oh, and it was the *dog's* birthday . . . No, I traced this malign canine. One of my colleagues had to deal with a public-order complaint from the priestess. The dog-owner is really Trebonius Fulvo. It's some horrible hunting creature in a spiked collar that he keeps to make himself look menacing.'

'What does he want a hunter for in Rome? Rat-catching?'

Faustus wrote that into the speech. For added sneers, he changed it to 'Mouse-catching?'

Trebonius and Arulenus would be characterised jointly as antisocial citizens. Sextus would say not only did the pair show no respect for age, religion, decency or dog-control, they were physical degenerates. One did too many gymnastics, the other was both fat and effeminate, a double shame. Faustus had (he claimed) once seen Arulenus in a long striped tunic, with fringed sleeves, an outfit that no manly male would wear.

I smiled. 'I had not envisaged either of those boors as chasing boys.'

'No, but we can make the fact they are such close partners look suggestive in itself. "This pair practically roam the Forum holding hands – an insult to the stones where our ancestors walked!"'

'You are surprisingly inventive, Faustus . . . Can't they then say the same about Vibius and Gratus?'

'Anyone can see Gratus would be scared to do anything outrageous and Sextus looks clean-living.'

'I hope he is!' I murmured.

'Trust me. Then we point out Trebonius acquires his muscles by over-exercising in some sleazy gym.'

It was tricky for a Roman to strike a balance between looking after his body and not. A politician needed to be healthy and strong; he would be admired if he took care of himself, which implied he could be trusted to take care of his office. However, too much weight-training put him on a par with gladiators, bloody brutes who were social outcasts. Being muscle-bound could only be for sordid purposes in Roman eyes; there was a suggestion that what went on in gymnasiums (with their sinister Greek origins) might be sexually outrageous.

I eyed up Faustus, who shifted on his couch as I assessed his physique. 'Nice!'

He concealed any embarrassment. 'Arulenus wearing exotic clothes implies he's a beast who lives for bodily pleasure – such an easy target. Everyone knows people in fancy dinner outfits go to all-night supper-parties with singing and dancing, leading to lascivious sex games. They wear perfume and depilate their bodies, all to appeal to the wrong kind of sexual partner. From a long tunic it's a short step to a man who has wasted his fortune—'

'Loose belts mean loose morals; fringes equal fornication . . . But the fringes are hearsay,' I murmured. 'And has anybody ever seen him with a pretty boy?'

'I saw the fringes! Dangling right on his hairy wrists.'

'Tiberius, I don't doubt your eyesight. But please only have Sextus report he heard this from "a trusted friend". Those two will make bad enemies. Trebonius and Arulenus might well send shaved-head heavies to thrash you senseless.'

'Thank you for caring.'

I acknowledged his thanks. 'Trebonius Fulvo wears ordinary tunics – though he is bursting out of them. He is also laden with finger jewellery. The rings look stuck on his fat fingers so if Sextus points them out Trebonius can only twist them helplessly, while everyone stares right at him. Arulenus seems much worse, totally immoral – isn't he the one who cheated on a mistress, promising her marriage, then stealing her jewellery? And apparently he abandoned a wife when she was pregnant.'

'Yes, he's poison. We can imply the hypothetical pretty boys are the reason he reneges on decent marriage. He breaks the heart of an innocent woman – well, fairly innocent. It is said half the Senate have slept with her. He fails to become a respectable husband who sets about fathering children or if he gets one he leaves the mother in the lurch. Completely decadent. Is it too extreme to suggest his pretty boys are eunuchs?'

'Stage too far,' I warned him. 'Given that you invented them!'

'Me? Glyco and Hesperus, handsome young bucks who gild their nipples, everybody knows that degenerate duo . . . '

'You made them up.'

'That's oratory.'

'Be sensible. Go back to Trebonius. He's *too* masculine?'

'A brute!' Faustus was fired up. 'For comparison, I read up on Catiline – once the evil hard man of Republican politics. Cicero said Catiline made himself able to endure cold, hunger, thirst, lack of sleep – but then there was an argument against him that he was too dangerous to trust.'

'My father rails against him for trying to overthrow the Republic, using the plight of the poor for his selfish advantage. Many of the poor still admire him, but those fools won't be voting. Senators who actually remember who Catiline was will think of him as attacking the aristocracy. They will shudder and vote against that, hopefully voting *for* Sextus.'

'Cicero calls Catiline an enigmatic figure,' mused Faustus. 'A good leader, but lustful and self-serving.'

'Enigma is always viewed as dangerous. Mind you, some senators probably think lust is commendable in a strong politician.'

Faustus laughed. 'I cannot call Trebonius ambiguous. He's transparently ambitious for personal power.'

'Say that, then. And don't forget to mention how Trebonius and Arulenus dined out the bankers so they could make promises to increase interest rates. Many of the Senate are struggling in debt. That will rile them.' Faustus made more notes. 'Now, doesn't that heartless swine Dillius have a vicious lawsuit against his dying grandfather? He cannot wait for his inheritance because he is desperate for more money for his exotic Greek wines.'

'Greek?'

'Bound to be. Unpatriotically ignoring Italian vintages.'

'Well, it's not him,' I said. 'Latest information puts that charge against Gratus, so you won't want to use it.'

'Ah! . . . Pity.'

The only candidate against whom we had no ammunition was Ennius Verecundus, the loner who went around smiling too much, with his mother running his campaign. Faustus remarked, 'A candidate's mother, if she is alive, should back him, though a man needs visible male supporters. Since Rome reveres strong mothers, we cannot call that reprehensible. But we may insinuate that if they elect Ennius Verecundus we'll have a woman running a magistracy.'

'*So* unacceptable!' I scoffed fiercely.

'Depends on the woman, in my opinion,' Faustus answered. 'But this idea will terrify the greybeards. Many are scared of their own mothers, and they will have seen Ennius being led around virtually on a leash by his fierce mama. When Sextus speaks, the frightful woman only has to stand there glowering and she will make our point herself.'

Having seen the mama, I allowed that. 'I hate the way Ennius Verecundus smiles all the time. And I wonder, Tiberius, where are the rest of his family? Does he have other relatives? If not, be careful, or he and his mama will turn into the brave lone widow and the poor fatherless boy she lovingly does her best for . . . I'll try to find out. If he does have relatives, are they too nervous to be near his domineering mother? I doubt if I can prove he lives a wild life – he doesn't look as if she has ever let him out of doors to enjoy life at all.'

Faustus wrote that down.

We had reached the end of what we could achieve, and at that moment we were joined by the mother of Sextus Vibius. The grey-haired elderly woman had brought home-made mint cordial for us, with her own hands carrying in a tray and delicate little cups.

I had not properly met her before. She was well dressed but looked worn. She had a mentally ailing husband. He was regularly brought out to support Sextus, but never left the litter. I found myself wondering about those mortgages Sextus had had fetched from store; did his father really have legal capacity to sign financial documents? Was he truly aware of the resources being spent on his son's campaign (was he even aware of the campaign)?

Marcella Vibia spent all day looking after him, rarely out

of his company. An old-fashioned wife, she took his care upon herself, even though they had domestic staff. I had often heard him fretting and her soothing him. She looked like someone who spent her days fearing the worst.

Now she sat down with us as if glad of other company; she said the old man was asleep for once. She fanned herself gently with her hand, feeling the heat. I leaned over and served out the cordial. Then, as Marcella Vibia only smiled and sipped, I took up what had caught my attention earlier and asked, 'Have you enjoyed being aedile yourself, Tiberius?'

He nodded, but did not elaborate. Vibia spoke up. 'It has changed him visibly, Flavia Albia, in only a few months. The magistracy has helped this young man finally discover what he is made of.'

I could see that, having no mother of his own, Tiberius was sometimes taken under this kindly woman's wing. She talked freely about him and he let her do so. 'You mean,' he said, 'I was an idle scamp but I have learned to be useful.'

'We were all a little surprised!' she teased. 'That is why we wanted to see Sextus follow in your footsteps.'

I wondered whether that meant his parents saw Vibius as an idle scamp himself . . . Personally, if we managed to have him elected, I could not see it turning out so well.

Then, more seriously, Vibia spoke to me: 'I have known Tiberius Manlius from childhood; his family had the next estate to ours near Fidenae and the boys went to school together. We were so upset when his parents died – such lovely people – both carried off by the same summer plague. That meant his uncle took him, which of course was for the best, I would never say otherwise, but Tiberius went away to Rome at that early age and we almost lost sight of him.'

'Well, we are all together in the city now,' Faustus soothed her.

'But Tullius has you up there on the Aventine, so far away from everyone!'

Faustus chuckled. 'Not everyone. Flavia Albia lives there too.'

'Obviously a great attraction,' responded Marcella Vibia, only a little sarcastically. 'I hope you don't haunt the streets looking for girls to follow about, Tiberius.'

Faustus liked to tease stern women – I had seen him do it before, with my mother. Possibly he even did it to me. 'Perk of the job! I still remember when I spotted Flavia Albia, trotting to and fro on her business. It brightened my day.' That startled me. I liked him, but not the idea he had regularly tailed me. I could not believe it. Surely I would have noticed.

'So you told yourself, "This is the life"?' asked Vibia, coolly. 'Streets full of pretty women?'

'Well, I made sure I found out who this one was.' Faustus turned to me, aware I was glowering. 'Pull your claws in. Of course I did not follow you about.'

'Scary!' I agreed. 'And I believe it's a crime . . . So you love exercising your powers?' I nudged, lightening the subject. He made no reply. 'No, that's unfair. You want Sextus to take up the torch because you believe in the city being well run, its neighbourhoods tidy and safe, its people content because they live in a decent environment, its gods honoured through good management.'

'Tiberius is extremely capable and he needs to have something to do,' Vibia declared. 'His uncle has never employed him enough in their business. You know I am right,' she told Faustus firmly, as he prepared to argue. 'Now you have stepped away from him and learned to enjoy responsibility. You will not want to go back to having him control you. Either he must change or you must break away.'

'We shall reach some accommodation.' Faustus was squirming.

'You will. You're ready for it. And the point is,' Vibia told him, 'I have known you for a long time, and never seen you happier.'

Manlius Faustus bowed his head and looked embarrassed.

He was spared a further lecture because a maid came in, seeming anxious: she said the master was awake. Marcella Vibia jumped up and went to attend to her husband, as if frightened what would happen otherwise. On her way out, she ruffled the aedile's hair fondly.

Left alone, Faustus and I sat in tricky silence.

Smoothing down his hair again, he said, 'Vibia is a good woman. She worries about her husband constantly. He finds his condition frustrating and I slightly suspect his loss of mind and memory makes him lash out. She only rarely lets herself relax as she did just now.'

I realised that this was why Faustus had taken so much upon himself with the election. Yes, he and Sextus were old friends but neither of the parents could be much use at the moment: the father would never regain his capacity and the mother was run ragged. So Manlius Faustus had stepped in.

All the more reason why the candidate's wife ought to have been at his side.

Hmm!

23

I felt more sympathetic now about Faustus's support for Sextus, but it was time-consuming. I knew he was privately fretting about his duties and offered to polish the speech so he could go over to the Aventine and work.

'Go and rake some fines in. Inspect baths. Order pavement repairs. Register more prostitutes, so our rivals may have recourse to them and we can point that out . . . Don't worry,' I said grimly. 'I know Sextus won't like to think an informer has written his rhetoric. I can ask one of his parents' scribes to produce a fair copy to my dictation. He need never know.'

Although he screwed his mouth up, Faustus accepted I was right. 'You think of everything.' He also knew I did not blame him for his friend's prejudice.

He went off. I finished the speech. I borrowed a secretary, who wrote out the final version then promised to give it to the young master to learn that evening.

It was hard-hitting. We were a good team. Faustus had created a draft with structure and attack; I edited the skeleton into a strong piece of work. It read so fluently Sextus could not fail to remember his lines or to speak them naturally. No one who heard this would imagine he had had speech-writers. Even he might convince himself it was all his own work.

I wondered if that was what had happened when those two were schoolboys. Did Tiberius complete their teacher's projects while Sextus plagiarised him, moved a few sentences around, then pretended it was his own composition?

I bet their teacher knew.

I sat on by myself in the campaign salon, thinking.

I was glad Faustus had trusted me with the speech. He ought also to have realised what I might do, left alone at the Vibius household. I was determined to make the acquaintance of the candidate's wife, the elusive Julia.

Faustus would have been furious at me nosing. That did not stop me.

It was mid-afternoon on a baking hot day. Most people were resting. The ground-floor apartment, so handsomely furnished, lay almost silent as everybody tried to conserve energy while waiting for the sun to sink lower so the temperature would drop. The slaves were at rest. Wherever Marcella Vibia was sitting with her husband, he had probably nodded off again, calmed by her presence; she, too, might have allowed her eyes to close in relief as she patiently guarded him.

Sextus had not appeared since I arrived. He could be upstairs in his own apartment, yet I took a chance.

Now that I was learning about this family, I saw that the parents' ground-floor apartment, so busy during the campaign, must have been extremely quiet at other times. That gorgeously veneered table would stand with an empty urn on it, unused. Marcella Vibia and her husband occupied only a small proportion of the gracious spaces they presumably rented. A bedroom where he fitfully passed the night while she only let herself doze in case he woke up and wandered. A dayroom where they had comfortable chairs and a couple of side-tables. Little else in regular occupation, as far as I had seen.

The neat but barely used central courtyard had a stairwell in one corner, leading to upstairs accommodation. I had noticed Sextus Vibius taking those stairs sometimes, so I made my way up. The treads were clean natural stone, spaced evenly and well designed. Small windows lit them. A handrail, so rare in Rome's ramshackle tenements, made the climb easier. These steps would be safe for Vibius and Julia to allow their two small children to visit their grandparents (I was sure Marcella Vibia was the kind who kept small toys and a supply of daily pastries).

Those children, I was certain, must be up and down here all the time. They would bring treasures to show their grandparents, while Vibia would find their visits a welcome break in her lonely routine of caring for her husband. It was odd that I had not yet seen them.

Well, I might do now.

The pleasant Clivus Scauri building was about four storeys high. Only this first-floor apartment was accessed from the courtyard, as if designed for an extended family. Other, less elegant, rooms had more basic stairs from the street outside. Sextus's apartment was secure, protected by his parents' door porter downstairs. Perhaps for this reason he had not bothered to lock up. I know, because when nobody answered my tentative knock, I gently tried the handles on the decorated double doors.

I went in and stood just inside those doors, pulling them to behind me. I cleared my throat. When that produced no reaction I called out, with the same result.

Where were the slaves? In a home like this there would normally be people everywhere. There were certainly plenty in the ground-floor apartment. When, or if, he became an aedile, Sextus Vibius would also rely on his duties being covered by an extensive team.

So where were the people who cared for Sextus and Julia?

They must all be busy or taking a siesta. Then the deep stillness of the upstairs rooms told another story. Nobody was here.

I felt emboldened to look around. My father had taught me, never miss a chance.

There were five rooms and a couple of service lobbies. The rooms were finely painted, with creamy white moulded-plaster ceilings. Rugs lay on the wooden floors, all centred, no creases. Couches and side-tables were pushed back tidily against walls. None had been left askew after somebody had pulled them out for use. Cushions were plump. There was no mess.

There was no sign of life at all. I found no used dishes; nor was there fresh fruit in the endearingly battered basket that lived on a sideboard. Nobody had left an unfurled scroll or an open inkwell. Nobody was coming back to drain their unfinished goblet. Nobody had been practising the lyre in a few spare moments. Certainly there was no evidence of children.

I deduced that Sextus did sleep in the master bedroom. The bed was made, though the cover and pillow were slightly less neat on one side than the other. I could not believe Sextus had tidied his own bed, but whoever came and did it for him had only pulled the coverlet straight. On one side-table stood a beaker for water; it was empty, dry in the bottom, accompanied by no flagon or jug. A masculine tunic was hung up with a pole through the shoulders. Spare male sandals lay under a stool. When I lifted lids on two similar clothes chests, one had a man's belongings and paraphernalia (why do all men think they need four identical belts and a folding knife set with a camping spoon?). The other was empty. A faint trace of a woman's perfume could be detected. I found no jewellery in the room, no silly shoes nor wispy scarves, no chatelaine with household keys, no dainty ring hung with tweezers, nail cleaner and cosmetics grinder. Neither creams nor cosmetics. No hand mirror. No comb.

One of the other bedrooms contained two little beds but it was so neat it felt like a guestroom.

Back in the reception room, I stood listening to the silence. I tried to gain some feeling of the young family whose home this supposedly was. Only one thing struck me. I would not be meeting Julia today.

I saw now how things were working. Sextus either ate his meals with his parents or he dined out. While he was campaigning, Faustus was constantly taking him to canvass people so it was easy to disguise what happened at home. Sextus slept alone up here, or at least he did sometimes. It would not surprise me if otherwise his mother let him stay downstairs in whatever room he had had when he was younger.

Faustus, I was absolutely sure, had no inkling about this; Sextus was keeping it from him and, of course, from me. That meant this situation had probably arisen recently. I could not tell where the two children were, or who was looking after them. For Julia, I made an intelligent guess.

She must have gone back to her mother – or, according to Roman legal definitions, back to her father's house. The evidence seemed clear to me: the wife of Sextus Vibius Marinus had left him.

24

Closing the doors carefully behind me, I returned to the ground floor. Had this been anybody else, I would have tackled him about it without a second thought. Since Sextus was such friends with the aedile, I had to consider what Faustus would want to do. He would be circumspect. I knew that without asking.

Marcella Vibia came through the colonnade while I was still staring at the courtyard, perplexed. 'Albia! Still here?'

'I am leaving now. I had a rest, I hope you don't mind.'

'Of course not!'

She walked me towards the exit, as a politeness. I said casually, 'Marcella Vibia, I do believe I have never seen your grandchildren.'

Did I detect hesitation? But Vibia answered calmly, 'They go to a little school close to the Capena Gate. Our baby girl is only five; the boy is six, almost seven. Their father will be bringing them home any time soon. Of course they have a pedagogue who escorts them, carrying their tiny satchels and keeping them from harm along the route, but Sextus likes to pick them up himself and spend time with them.'

'That's wonderful.' Actually, it was quite unusual.

'He takes good care of them.'

There was no mention of their mother. I reflected sadly

on little old ladies. Even this warm, civilised woman would lie, by omission at least, if it suited her.

However, she had told the truth in some respects: while we were talking, Sextus Vibius did come home, preceded into the house by two tousled children, full of pent-up energy after their release from lessons. They hurled themselves on their grandmother with joyous hugs, then charged off to a room in her apartment from which they produced toys.

They lived down here. Their grandmother was looking after them. Nothing was said about that.

Marcella Vibia went to fetch drinks for the children and a damson in honey each – 'One! Lucius, just the one or you'll spoil your supper.' The pair sat quietly side by side on a low colonnade wall to drink from beakers under her supervision. They were well behaved. Lively. Cheery. Not visibly upset by their mother's absence; I compared this to how disturbed we all used to be if Helena Justina was away from home even for a day. Maybe when it came to bedtime they would whimper and miss Julia, but until then they managed well enough.

I wondered what they had been told. Of course, no ethical informer would ever try to get such small children on their own and question them . . .

They finished eating and rushed off to play. I delayed my departure, keen to see what happened in this family. While we stood and watched the boy and girl, I explained to Sextus why Faustus had left earlier, saying only that I had stayed to attend to 'notes'. Sextus was intent on his children, clearly a good father. He was popular and natural with them, constantly catching balls they lobbed at him or warning them to be careful when they clambered on balustrades.

Suddenly he turned to me, all smiles. 'This is the first chance I have had to pry – Tiberius certainly kept you quiet!'

I did not trouble to answer. I preferred it when he was sniffy about my profession.

'Own up!' urged Vibius. 'How long has this affair been going on?'

People were bound to misinterpret our odd friendship; I was none too clear how to interpret it myself. 'Nothing is going on. We work together sometimes.'

'Oh, so he has not made his move yet!' his friend exclaimed, now grinning broadly. I found his attitude annoying. He was so sure Tiberius was my lover; there was no way to persuade him otherwise.

I gathered myself together as I prepared to go home, smoothing my skirts and tidying my jewellery, tucking in a wayward wisp of hair. 'You have two delightful children, Sextus Vibius. Such a pleasure to see them. I would really like to meet your wife also.'

He was a good politician. He smiled as if this was the most natural thing to ask. 'Of course!' he replied, as smooth as almond custard. 'We shall have to arrange it very soon.'

'I look forward to that,' I replied lightly.

If he wondered what I had found out about his wife, Vibius gave no sign. His mother had listened in from nearby without appearing to do so; it was impossible to judge what she was thinking.

Vibius had the cheek to wink at me as I left. 'Remember, I want to be the first to know! *Tiberius*!' he spelled out, as I looked blank. Apparently this had become a joke between us. 'You make sure to tell me when he makes his move.'

25

Vibius disconcerted me, though I would not complain to his friend.

It felt urgent to see the fabled Tiberius, that refined man who never in fact made his move, in order to discuss his candidate's missing wife. Whatever had happened, any separation affected Vibius's electoral claims to be a happily married man, with the right to take precedence over the unmarried in the voting order. Judging by pointed remarks people had already made (including that missile Laia Gratiana had launched), he was close to being exposed. Any rival who caught wind of this could make a complaint to the Senate: Vibius Marinus was faking his marital status.

Even if it was not his fault his wife had left him, he could only lose. In the minds of the public he had tried to mislead them, while senators would love to denounce a man of such unsound background.

My brain throbbed as I rode Patchy at his leisurely pace back towards the Aventine. I should myself have challenged Vibius straight away, but I wanted Faustus to take up the matter. Let him ask the precious Sextus what he was playing at.

I was assuming Faustus was unaware of the situation. I hated the thought that maybe he knew, maybe he had known all along, but had not told me. Would his relationship with his close childhood friend matter more to him than being honest with me? The hard truth was, *I* wanted to be his confidante. I had fooled myself I was.

If he did not know, Faustus would want to be told immediately.

Since he was working, he could be anywhere. Faustus never stayed in the magistrates' office placidly signing documents. He interviewed wrongdoers personally and if there were none waiting to be dressed down when he arrived, he would go out and try to catch some. I went to the office, by the Temple of Ceres, but he had been and gone. Staff thought he was expected back, but they could not be certain and they would soon be closing up for the day. I left a message anyway that I needed to speak to him.

I could have walked around looking for him, but he moved surreptitiously when patrolling his patch. In the crowded Aventine alleys I could easily miss him. Anyway, by now he had probably gone to the baths, then on somewhere to dinner.

In the street outside, while I was pondering what to do, the tricksy goddess of fortune placed a chance in my way. Up in the Greek-style portico of the temple, the temple where she had made herself a prominent member of the élite matrons' cult of Ceres, I spotted Laia Gratiana. Normally I would have headed off fast in another direction. But I had heard Laia seeming to hint that she knew the missing wife had gone away. *When shall we be seeing your wife, Sextus Vibius? . . . Darling Julia!*

She knew. The nasty piece of work knew his wife was never going to appear.

I called out to her and marched up the temple steps. At

first, Laia had the advantage, able in the most literal way to look down on me. She had been standing between the heavy columns, enjoying a survey of her realm, the Aventine. Meanwhile the Hill went about its business untroubled by her scrutiny.

'Why! Here is Manlius Faustus's latest bit of rough!'

She must have spoken in this insulting way about the woman with whom Tiberius had had an affair. That had been a rich man's wife, very beautiful, and I guessed that whatever her morals, she had actually been cultured. Still, low-minded people were always snobbish about me.

Refusing to look wounded, I reached the same level and addressed Laia briskly. 'I don't like you, you don't like me, but I believe in your affection for your brother, so stop being vicious and hear me.'

'What an outburst! What has my brother to do with you, Flavia Albia?'

'Nothing. I wouldn't take his dog out for a shit. But he is partnering Vibius Marinus in a joint election bid, and I suspect they have a status problem, so listen.'

A row of silver bracelets tickled with indignation along Laia's arm. Chin up, I looked her straight in the face; she probably thought I should gaze down deferentially. She had good bones. Her face could have been pretty, given a lighter expression. She glared at me, a cold-blooded soul, who was a punishment to herself. She had never had to suffer as I had, yet she would never be as carefree as I was. Perhaps she saw that. Perhaps that was what annoyed her.

'Laia Gratiana, do you know the wife of Sextus Vibius?'

'I have met her.'

'My impression is that none of his friends have had much opportunity to get to know her.'

'Friends? My brother only knows Vibius through Manlius Faustus and his uncle. Tullius suggested him as our campaign partner.' Laia was forcing herself to answer, only doing it because she was consumed with curiosity. 'What is this about?'

'You see it as I do,' I suggested. 'The non-appearance of the Vibius wife has become significant.'

'It detracts from our campaign. She should be ashamed! He ought to be ashamed too, standing for election when his personal affairs are in disarray.'

'What disarray?'

'You are the informer. Find out.'

'I will! Before I start, do you agree you share my suspicion about Julia?'

Laia sniffed theatrically. 'It only takes intelligence, Flavia Albia. One does not have to be *paid* to see what is amiss.'

I wanted to poke her eyes out but I let it pass. 'You think she has left him?'

'Well, I do not suppose he has hit her over the head and buried her in the garden,' sneered Laia.

Neither did I. Even so, to be quite sure, I might walk around the courtyard next time I visited, and look for disturbed patches of soil . . . 'What do you know about their relationship?'

'Nothing.'

'Faustus says she is obsessively devoted.'

'Huh! What would Faustus know about devotion?' More than Laia realised, in my experience. 'Well, I have heard similar. But maybe Julia learned something that changed her.'

'Do you know for sure there is something to discover?'

'No, I do not mean that!' Laia became angry, suddenly

uneasy about what she was saying to me. Spreading scandalous suggestions was unworthy of a devotee of Ceres. People might think badly of her. (Vibius might sue for defamation.) 'There can be many reasons why a marriage ends.'

'So, you share my suspicion it has ended? I had a quiet look around their home and she is definitely not living there.'

'Remind me never to let you into my house, Flavia Albia!' I ignored it. 'This could be a disaster,' Laia grouched. 'My poor brother is fatally stuck with the man now. How can they campaign as respectable people if Vibius is covering up his marital split?'

'Is your brother married?' I asked, guessing not.

'No. His wife died. They had no children. But my brother will be making a happy new wedding announcement shortly. He will time it so his engagement appears in the *Daily Gazette* on the day names go forward to the Senate.'

'Perfect. How romantic!' How clinical. 'I would like to find out where Vibius's Julia has gone. Possibly I'll visit her.' If only I could pinpoint her whereabouts, I would certainly do so. 'Do you know her parents? I assume she has returned to them. Indeed, I hope so. If she has run off with a lover, it will cause an even worse scandal. It certainly will if Julia – Julia what? – if Julia has fled with a gladiator or an actor.'

'I met her. She was perfectly sweet and decent, not that type at all.' Laia was oozing more snobbery.

'Oh, no fun!' I shot back, feeling wicked.

Laia looked frosty, which she did with aplomb. 'Her name is Julia Optata.'

'That's a start. Do you know her parents?'

'No idea.'

'Not even their names?'

'No.' Laia had answered immediately, being truculent with me by instinct. 'Oh, of course I do! Her mother, anyway, is Julia Verecunda.'

'Verecunda?' Where had I heard that name recently? *Married to Verecunda's daughter? Has, therefore, the mother-in-law from Hades? That woman is loathsome, and all her girls are Furies . . .* Thank you, Claudius Laeta! While complaining about how the candidates were linked he had mentioned this woman: 'Volusius Firmus, the man who dropped out, is married to a daughter of Verecunda too. So Julia Optata is his sister-in-law?'

'I hadn't considered that,' said Laia, seeming to think it unimportant.

'It matters in one way. My sources call Julia Verecunda a loathsome woman. So it's more likely Julia Optata would take herself off to a consoling lover, rather than go home to her hideous mother.'

'Well, that would be extremely selfish!' snapped Laia. She judged people and events on a simple basis: their effect on Laia Gratiana.

'And do you have any idea where I can find Julia's mother?'

'None at all. That's your job, isn't it?'

She had no more to tell me, so I left her at the temple and decided to go home.

It was a warm, still evening, bright but no longer oppressive. Happy voices everywhere. Sociable smells and noises. I made my way to Fountain Court, deposited Patchy and his boy at a local place with stabling, then took the scenic route through our fabulous mud and rancid puddles to the grim hulk of the Eagle Building. We needed an aedile to take an interest in our alley. It had never happened yet, and I saw no chance of it.

I called hello to Rodan. He belched a reply.

I walked to my bench, its stone seat warm and comfortable after a day baking in the July sun. If I had a proper apartment, with a courtyard, I could go in and fetch cushions. Snacks. Whoever lived there with me would come out and talk before dinner . . .

Fantasy, Albia.

Here, if I wanted any dinner, I would have to go upstairs into my apartment and hunt for stale leftovers. Deferring that unappealing moment, I became lost in thought. I had had an intensely busy day and realised how exhausted I was.

Drifting, I had a new idea descend on me. As I leaned back, with the last pale sun on my tired face, I suddenly made an extra connection. Verecundus, Verecunda. These matching names were too much of a coincidence. Claudius Laeta had not mentioned to Faustus and me that, as well as several daughters, the woman called Julia Verecunda had a son.

Now I saw it. Her son must be the 'mother's boy' candidate. 'Ennius' must come from his father's name, then Julia had called him after herself. Her driven, protective support suggested to me that he had no brothers. Mother's special. Poor unlucky boy! He might easily have turned into a cruel, pathological serial killer. He could have gone from pulling the wings off birds in attic rooms to sexual torture and perverted murder . . . Instead he looked like a weakling who never stood up for himself.

So here was a curiosity: the forceful mother of the constantly smiling Ennius Verecundus was also the mother-in-law from Hades, one of whose daughters was the wife of Volusius Firmus, Domitian's temporary favourite, while another was the absent wife of Vibius Marinus, our candidate. I wondered whether she had any other daughters and, if so, who were they?

I had no clue whether this would be important or, if so, how.

The day had been long enough for me. I went indoors, found a few scraps to eat; then, while the Aventine bars were still thronged with merrymakers and the blackbirds still singing challenges to one another in the few old groves of trees, I took myself to bed.

Alone again. Too tired to care.

Wrong, Albia. I cared.

26

I had breakfast at the Stargazer and was not surprised when Manlius Faustus hove into view. He always followed up on messages from me. That was how he had come to notice I was missing, the time he found me ill.

'Tiberius! Don't you need to be with Sextus?'

'He can manage. I was told you needed to speak to me.'

The waiter, my deaf cousin Junillus, brought more bread and cold sausage to the rustic table where we sat. This wasn't so much that Junillus had learned our favourites: it was the only choice. Some fashionable eating houses have a limited menu because they only serve that day's freshest produce at market. The Stargazer gave you whatever had been available two days ago at the cut-price bakery and run-down stalls my aunt frequented, searching for giveaway items with not too much mildew.

Aunt Junia did not believe in spoiling her customers with variety. Her attitude was that if they never came back it meant fewer people to annoy her by expecting service. She rarely served at the Stargazer herself. She said people were rude to her. Even if we told her why, she failed to hear the message.

The aedile and I gnawed our rolls. Choosing words with care, I explained my discoveries about the missing Julia, and about her mother and relatives. Her family links to

Volusius Firmus and Ennius Verecundus caught Faustus by surprise. Watching him, I felt satisfied that he had known nothing either about Sextus being abandoned.

'Now I am cursing myself. Oh, Albia, I should have seen there was something wrong – I have been visiting the house for weeks. He said nothing. Nor did his mother.'

'But she obviously knows.'

It would not be the first time a mother-in-law actually connived at shedding her son's wife, though I refrained from saying so. Faustus was too fond of Marcella Vibia.

'I can't understand it.'

'The upstairs apartment is neat, the children seem happy,' I told him. 'It looks as if, whatever happened, they have all settled into a new routine. There is no sign of Sextus feeling agitated, or worrying about how to be reconciled.' I dropped my voice and asked, 'Will you take it up with him?'

'I have to. If this comes out, we need to have our reply prepared . . . Are you absolutely sure?'

'She has taken all her things. The children came home from school and never asked after her. They appear to be eating and sleeping downstairs with the grandparents, Sextus as well, to some extent.'

I confessed what had happened when I met Laia Gratiana. Faustus groaned.

'Now don't blame me too much. I know she'll tell her brother but, Tiberius, isn't it better to come clean, rather than have Laia and Gratus find out from other sources?'

Faustus decided he must go and speak to Sextus now, before Gratus and Laia turned up fuming. He wanted to waylay Sextus on the way to the Forum, before he made his speech.

'Should we cancel the speech?' I suggested.

‘Problematic. We have stirred up an audience. It’s too late.’

I said he could borrow the donkey. Patchy must like him: Faustus rode off like a prime jockey on a fine-bred Spanish mare. The donkey boy could hardly keep up, running along after him. Dromo did not bother to try.

I chewed my way through the aedile’s unfinished sausage. Junillus threw in a free gherkin, but it failed to cheer me.

Only then, too late to mention it, did I remember Nothokleptes saying of Vibius Marinus, ‘Isn’t he the wife-beater?’

27

That shocked me. Could it be true? Had Sextus been knocking Julia about? Had she gone because he hit her?

I felt doubtful. Vibius Marinus had been boorish about informers (who wasn't?) but on the whole he seemed too bland; he lacked the kind of intensity that I associate with violent men (I had encountered enough to know). I summed him up as impetuous, though only in the sense of misjudgement. He jumped in without thinking. He lacked measure and gravitas – but that is not the same as exploding with rage and using your fists.

I had seen him with his mother, with his children. All the same, how many violent men seem to outsiders to behave normally? In public, they conceal their brutality under a show of utter decency. How many friends and neighbours tell you, after a tragedy, that they had no idea? They are stunned. They would never have allowed it to continue – or so they maintain.

And how many times have I heard that while standing beside the pyre for some miserable, skeletal victim after the undertaker has told me privately that the poor woman had sustained many broken bones and scars over the years, before the attack that killed her?

If Vibius beat his wife, it explained why she might leave

him – though if she was any kind of mother, why had she left behind her still-young children with a man who hurt her?

Even if Vibius hit Julia, Rome might be slow to call it reprehensible. Historically, Roman men had the right to chastise their wives and children, and if they committed crimes that shamed the family, to kill them even. The paterfamilias had been king, trial judge and executioner in his own household.

In theory he still was. Wives found ways around that system, mainly by ignoring the supposed rules.

We no longer lived in traditional times. Cruelty was frowned on, at least if the bruises were visible; love – or a pretence of love – was applauded. Even in cases of adultery, a husband or father was not legally permitted to put his wife or daughter to the sword, although if he caught her with a lover in his own house, he could slay the lover. Adulterers had to be quick at shinning out of windows. Women were wise to conduct love affairs in friends' houses. The friends had to pretend not to know about it, else providing a love-nest was pimping.

Suppose a man went too far and did kill his wife or daughter. He was virtually let off if it happened in the heat of the moment. However, husbands who battered their wives for pleasure, or for no reason, or to hide their own guilt at screwing a prostitute, or when too drunk to know what they were doing, or too drunk to care, were denounced. Husbands had to protect the weaker members of their households. After all, if a man really needed to take out his temper on someone, he was supposed to knock the lights out of his slaves.

Wives could leave. Divorce was easy. Fathers had to take

back brides who found married life unbearable. We were civilised nowadays. Fathers might curse but, after all, they could always find the returning daughter a new husband and offload her again. Under the rigid Augustan marriage laws, a divorced woman was supposed to re-wed promptly. She lost her right to receive legacies otherwise, assuming that bothered her. Really unhappy wives might think money did not matter.

There was a moral code, too. If people thought Vibius had caused the break-up of his family, the kind of family the law directly encouraged, that would lose him votes. He had two children; he was supposed to persuade his Julia to let him father three. In the kind of senate we had, some would disapprove of violence yet others would actually envy a man who had dared to chastise his wife. But the governing fathers would never let him get away with his deception.

What about the other candidates?

In general, I had thought marriage was so much the norm for would-be politicians I had not even asked the question. To be an aedile, a candidate must be thirty-six; since men tended to marry first in their early twenties it was likely they had all done so at one time. The only one I had ascertained as married was Dillius Surus, who notoriously lived off his very rich wife. Presumably, since she paid his bills, he paid her respect, though perhaps he drank so hard simply to endure having to be grateful to a woman some called unpleasant. Arulenus Crescens stood accused of refusing to marry his mistress, so he must be single now but had been married before and left a wife pregnant; it was possible he had ditched the latest mistress (a woman with a blowsy reputation) because he had wanted a more suitable wife for show. Laia's brother, a widower, was making a new marriage, unusual only in cynically timing it for the election.

I decided to establish more facts, double-checking with the banking fraternity. No one else had so keen an interest in a man's domestic background. I could either make a return visit to Nothokleptes or call on my own financier, Claudia Arsinoë. I did that. Arsinoë could be relied on to give me mint tea.

She lived and worked not in the Basilica Aemilia or anywhere else in the Forum, but above one of the bookshops that quietly inhabit the Vicus Tuscus at the back of the lawcourts. Her bank had a change-table among the élite financiers in the Clivus Argentarius, but private clients saw her at home. This was like visiting an auntie. I took flowers and had the posy tied with ribbon.

You had to allow for eastern formality. First, we pretended this was a catch-up on friends and family. She called for the mint tea. Sipping, she spoke well of my mother, and I asked after her health. Then we ran lightly through my investments. The weather came up for notice; we fanned ourselves wearily. I gave my opinion of her newest patisserie provider. She pressed more tea upon me. And another cake.

Arsinoë was a forty-year-old native Athenian, putting on the pounds. As a widow, she wore dull clothes and covered up. However, her hair, still naturally dark to all intents, was rarely veiled and held in place by a pointed gold stephane that any goddess would have coveted for her temple statue. She was deeply religious but she enjoyed worldly pleasures. Waiting for her missing fiancé never interfered with her colourful Greek social life. I had been invited to these gatherings. There was laughter, throbbing lyres, lashings of traditional food, resinous wine and utterly sad singing. Arsinoë loved a good cry. (Yes, I know: it's hard to envisage a banker in tears.)

She was a good source. From her, I learned that Trebonius Fulvo had been married to the same woman for years, quite happily; she did not let him bully her and like many tough men he appreciated that. The louche Arulenus Crescens had had a couple of wives and several long-term mistresses, shamelessly overlapping these creatures and leaving behind children. Dillius Surus was the second husband of a woman who had married first extremely well – at least, well in Arsinoë's terms: he had enviable pots of money and he left it all to his widow.

'Being dead is good – why did she spoil everything by taking on an idiot?' Arsinoë wondered.

Ennius Verecundus had a sweet young wife of a few years and a baby.

'I bet they live with his mother?'

'I believe they do, Flavia Albia.'

'Disaster.'

'Surely there can be good mothers-in-law? Kindly women who will help a new bride while she is learning, and become fast friends with her?'

'Is that irony? This kindly woman is called Julia Verecunda.'

'Oh, that witch!' Arsinoë made a sign against the evil eye – well, that was what I assumed the gesture to be.

'You know of her?'

'Who doesn't?'

'Has she money?'

'None worth mentioning.'

'She is putting her son up for election.'

'*He* has cash. From his father, Ennianus. Verecunda is not allowed to touch it. I have heard she finds her husband's prudence galling.'

Salvius Gratus was about to announce his engagement to an Aventine hide-importer's daughter. (Arsinoë knew the details, even though Gratus had yet to announce it.) And Vibius Marinus, as I knew, was married with two children.

'Ah, yes. Arsinoë, have you heard any rumours?'

'Why, no! Tell me the gossip.'

'One candidate is said to be a wife-beater. Since his Julia has gone missing from home, can it be Vibius Marinus? At least, that is the slur from Nothokleptes.'

Arsinoë made a short noise of disgust. 'Nothokleptes is a useless bastard.'

'Really!' I chortled. 'Have you heard any hint that Julia Optata may have left Vibius?'

'No, I have not.'

'By some coincidence, *her* mother is Julia Verecunda also.'

'Pallas Athene!' cried Claudia Arsinoë. 'The mother-in-law has caused the rift. She is famous for quarrelling. She makes her daughters treat their husbands badly, leave them for better ones. She loves to see families disintegrate and to know she is responsible.'

'What makes her like that?' I wondered.

'A wicked nature. Hating is her character.'

'And she brought her children up to be the same? Are they all aggressive?'

'No need to teach it to them,' scoffed my banker. 'Venom came with her milk, like a sorceress. But the family character was there before their birth. Their very blood is poisoned.'

Even allowing for Greek drama, this boded ill for Vibius.

I felt sympathy for the other son-in-law, Volusius Firmus, and more still for Ennius, the natural son in this unhappy-sounding family.

'You know your road,' declared Arsinoë. She tended to declaim like a fortune-teller, though her fees were cheaper and you didn't have to watch her handle mummified gizzards. 'You better go and see this horrible cow. Tell her I send a howling Fury in hot wind if she harms one hair of you.'

'Thank you, darling.'

Arsinoë jumped on me and smothered me with hugs as if she thought she might never see me again. I took that as her Athenian love of the theatre. If she really had been a fortune-teller, I might have found it worrying.

28

What was I trying to prove here, and would anybody thank me? Deciding no to that, I opted to be cautious.

It was mid-morning. I walked down the Clivus Tuscus past the Temple of Augustus, heading into the Forum. This temple had been destroyed by fire and rebuilt by Domitian; the neat edifice was newly released from its scaffold, so I paused to admire its eight spanking columns and glimpse the interior statues of Augustus and Livia.

Considering my next move, I would look again at the various candidates, including the now-problematic Vibius.

It seemed very quiet. If the rivals were on their daily walkabout, either I kept missing them or they had floated off to a new venue. None was at the Rostra, the main point for formal oratory, where Sextus Vibius was to make his speech today. Had he done it? Had the jibes hurt the others so deeply they had crept home to lick their wounds like defeated athletes? I did not suppose so. I am a realist.

'Anybody been on the rostrum today?'

'One of the fools was up there spouting. I took no notice.'

Great.

So much for being a political speech-writer. Nobody thanks you. Even the dummy who is reading the words misses the point of your best jokes; your fine sentiments will be superseded by events and forgotten by tomorrow;

anyway, the crowd don't even listen. No one is impressed. Get a new career. Sell fish-pickle.

Perhaps because they were always somewhat isolated from the main group, I did run into Ennius Verecundus and his mother. If the other rivals had moved off in a body, these two had missed the picnic invitation. He was the boy nobody else wants to play with.

I watched Ennius lavishing those smiles on everyone he met. He had a rectangular face with a pointed chin and a slightly receding hairline that made his forehead extra square. His eyes looked more intelligent than fitted his humble stance. If you met him out of his election robes, you might identify him as a disillusioned secretary. One who had been pensioned off because he was no good.

Mama did not steer her son quite as blatantly as I had originally thought. He moved around of his own accord, even though she was constantly watchful. She must know he had no real aptitude. He launched himself towards people and dutifully shook their hands; that smile of his was not exactly false, though meaningless. If someone had called him a lying cheat, he would have kept smiling.

Surprisingly, people were oddly patient. He would join a group and pose as he shook the hand of the leading figure, smiling around at the others. He acted as if they were all like-minded. They let him.

At least no firebrand tackled him with aggressive questions about what was wrong in their neighbourhood. Nobody expected he would do much about anything. Nobody had the energy, on a hot day, to engage with him. No one threw goose eggs. They just waited for him to move on again.

It was true that his baleful mother looked a woman not to cross. That was partly because of her resolutely old-fashioned dress and deportment. Today she again wore the *stola*, that sleeveless over-tunic that had once been reserved for respectable matrons but which now no younger woman would be seen in. Her hair, turned back in a topknot, with three precisely pinched waves down each side of her head, also harked back to the cult statue of the Empress Livia I had seen earlier.

In imperial art, Livia wore the *stola*, and was frequently veiled. She had an oddly sweet face, yet, even if you disbelieved the lurid tales of her poisoning people, she had been another dame to treat with caution: a wife who, while pregnant, had left her first husband when she saw that Augustus was a better deal. Thereafter she had tirelessly devoted herself to polishing his reputation, grabbing the seal and conducting business if he was away. A matriarch to chill the blood. Another mother who had pursued the claims of her son, the weird Tiberius. Wife, mother, grandmother, great-grandmother of emperors (some wicked, others mad). Deified, yet still viewed nervously.

Julia Verecunda had assembled a matching outfit and the hair. She copied Livia's wide eyes and beyond-reproach expression. Her features were naturally plump and might have been sweet but for the firm unsmiling lips. *Respect me or I break your legs.*

Subservience to the male was, of course, her public persona. Their campaign was for Ennius, about him and (apparently) led by him, as it should have been. No one could doubt that she advised him, which probably meant nagged him.

Even if he did what he was told, he gave no real sign of feeling hen-pecked or bossed. He had learned. He knew to avoid trouble.

He had his own money, Arsinoë had told me. Presumably his mother knew that meant, if he was ever brave enough, he had an escape.

I now saw that a small, quiet party of faithfuls followed them about. These included a young, pale, decent-looking woman who must be the wife, mother of his baby. The babe had not been brought to woo the crowds, however cute it was. Today was far too hot; the child would have been wailing. Either the pale wife or someone else must have sense. The decision probably had not emanated from Julia Verecunda, the grandmother from Hades; such a one would surely expect infants to behave impeccably on all occasions – or would make the pale wife feel she was a useless mother if a fretful baby cried.

The wife had on an attractive sky blue gown, elegant on her slim figure. Though pale, she looked quietly composed. Mind you, the downtrodden learn to stand straight to avoid drawing more trouble on themselves. Perhaps she and Ennius were well matched in submissiveness.

I was heartened when Ennius, speaking to a man who had his own wife there, called forward the pale thing and introduced her; the two wives then talked. It was undoubtedly about babies. The wife of Ennius was not exactly animated, but assumed a polite, politician's helpmeet manner. Ennius kept a hand on her shoulder. It looked almost affectionate.

Playing the politician's partner was what Julia Optata, the supposedly devoted wife of Vibius, ought to be doing.

The rest of the party looked like family slaves and freedmen. Perhaps there were a few friends and relatives but, if so, they were very discreet.

I cornered one of the freedwomen. She had been trained

to answer questions from the public and she welcomed me as a potential influence with male voters in my family. (She did not know my family or me.) Introducing myself by name though not by profession, I spoke admiringly of Julia Verecunda. I said I believed she was a woman of importance in this election. 'I have heard she is not only mother to Ennius, but has two daughters married to other candidates. She must hardly know which train of well-wishers to join!'

'Oh, she supports her son, of course.'

'But it would be an accolade for any family to have more than one candidate elected the same year?'

'Maybe, but Julia Verecunda is not thinking of that.' No: she allegedly despised the sons-in-law.

'Your young master will be elected, I feel sure.'

'Yes, that's what his mother wants for him.'

The freedwoman was turning away. I laid a hand on her arm, just enough to detain her yet remain good-mannered. 'Excuse me, could you just tell me one thing? Someone said that one of her daughters, whom I need to speak to, is living with her mother nowadays. Julia Optata. Will I find her at your house?'

'Oh, no – whoever told you that? Julia Optata is married to Vibius Marinus. You must ask for her where he lives.'

'I wonder why I was told otherwise. Of course, as a good daughter she does come to see Julia Verecunda?'

'We have not seen her for some time, but with so much going on, that is to be expected.'

'She must be working hard at the moment, to support her husband?' I suggested, wide-eyed.

'Bound to be.'

The witness sounded so casual that I reckoned she believed it. Had no one in their party noticed how, when they encountered Vibius going about, they never saw his wife with him? I would expect a sharp-eyed mother to have spotted it, but perhaps Julia Verecunda kept her own counsel.

Would she have words with her daughter? Or would she approve, as Claudius Laeta and Claudia Arsinoë had both said? *She loves to see families disintegrate and to know she is responsible* . . . Had Julia Optata left Sextus because her mother encouraged it?

Here in the Forum, Verecunda continued as always, proudly bestowing maternal admiration on her son. Her head never turned. Yet her eyes moved. Her eyes were on me. She had spotted my conversation; her distrust looked acidic.

The freedwoman noticed and moved away from me. Very little showed that she was nervous, yet as she pulled her shawl tighter I saw her hand shaking. I, too, pretended to be unaware of Verecunda as I made off.

I marched to the other end of the Forum and, believe me, I went very fast.

29

A new flash of white drew me towards the Basilica Julia where I found Faustus with Sextus Vibius. They were advancing purposefully down the Sacred Way, striding to the Rostra, under the high shadow of the Capitol.

More people were with them than usual. I was loath to pull Faustus out of this large train of supporters, but he saw me and came over of his own accord. He looked troubled. I did not need to ask why. We walked along together.

'I tackled him.' He spoke quickly in a low voice. 'He admits Julia Optata is not at home. He says it is a normal visit away, with his complete agreement.'

Really? She had tripped off somewhere, at this crucial moment, taking all she owned? I remained convinced something was wrong. I would not push it. Intervention can go sour on you.

'There is comforting news, Tiberius. I found out she is *not* at her mother's, the obvious place if she ended her marriage.' I sensed coolness in his behaviour so wanted to reconcile with him. 'Forget I asked about her. I apologise. Apologise for me to Sextus. I shall meddle no more. But you do need to prepare a satisfactory public statement.'

'They will get hold of it, won't they?' Faustus was gloomy, I hoped he remembered people were already prodding at Sextus when I began exploring. I felt guilty all the same.

'You're not angry with me?'

'No, Albia.' He softened. 'Never.'

Faustus drew me in among the throng of people who wanted to hear Sextus. We were at the far northern end of the Forum, outside the Curia. The Rostra ran across almost the whole Forum's width. Behind it was the Umbilicus of Rome, a marble structure that represented the city's navel. In front stood the Golden Milestone, where all roads to Rome met. This was a sacred spot.

The tall base of the Rostra was adorned with ships' prows, memorials to sea-battles; some of the beaks were real prows taken from defeated vessels, though more had been created specially. The back and sides of the large platform had ornate balustrades but the front was open. Speakers stood up there, looking down the length of the Forum, crowded with monuments and statues, towards the Temple of the Divine Julius, whose eulogy had occurred right there.

Many famous and infamous speeches had been uttered from the Rostra, much brilliant oratory – and, inevitably, much tame tosh. Overcome by the occasion, as soon as their feet touched that legendary podium, all too many speakers succumbed to cliché and verbosity. They all thought they were Mark Antony. None came near him. That never stopped them. Very few let themselves be deterred by the rude Roman crowds heckling.

I saw Sextus eagerly clamber up to the great platform. When he took up a position, he looked dwarfed by the various columns that supported commemorative statues. Fellows in wreaths, with swagger sticks or scrolls, ill-advised Roman noses and very ugly sandalled feet, posed nobly all around him. There were too many, so from time to time the Senate had to insist on a cull.

It was the first time I had seen Vibius Marinus in action. He was not at all bad. We had given him a strong speech, which he must have read and absorbed, stewing over it all last night. He spoke without notes. That was correct procedure, in both law and politics. As far as I could tell, he had not made scribbles in the folds of his toga. If he had, they were only for reassurance and he never seemed to look down at the secret reminders.

He had the right style: he looked at his audience and spoke in an almost conversational manner. He came across as trustworthy and likeable. I felt glad to find that Sextus might be slapdash on occasions, but he had substance.

Faustus had made sure the crowd contained all their supporters, prominently at the front. The other candidates collected, most giving themselves a good view from the steep steps of the Temple of Saturn. Ennius had a much worse position at the Temple of Concord, as if the others had refused him space. Word had been spread about our man's intentions; none could afford to miss this, in case they needed to shout rebuttals. They brought their own supporters, who began catcalling early. Only a few people were unbiased members of the public. For all I knew, even some of those had been given incentives to come.

I spotted Gratus and his sister. For some reason, they were by themselves on the steps of the Temple of Vespasian, which had been squeezed in under the Capitol between the Temple of Concord and the Porticus of the Consenting Gods. It stood almost round a corner and gave hardly any view of the Rostra. Hiding there was a poor way to signal that they were in coalition with this speaker.

* * *

At first everything went well. The stories I had collected caused happily raucous shouts, while the jokes Faustus had written made all the crowd laugh, even those who were supposed to be supporting the insulted rivals. Sextus felt the buzz; he became positively thrilling. Everyone was with him, enjoying the speech, and he clearly enjoyed giving it.

Faustus and I listened, occasionally glancing at one another with smiles when our man reached one of our best lines.

'Why does he need a fierce hunting dog in Rome? He surely cannot intend to attack venerable priestesses. Is it for catching mice? I ask you seriously, my friends, what pathetic kind of man needs to rely on a *dog* to give him a public presence? If this creature means so much, why don't we elect the dog instead of his master, a new Incitatus?' Incitatus was that racehorse a mad emperor had once had elected as consul.

The crowd were laughing; some made barking sounds. Sniping at Trebonius Fulvo was easy: unseemly weight-training, the hard attitude, a dangerous dog that didn't respect religion, the fancy rings . . . Trebonius Fulvo listened with a faint smile, biding his time. As soon as Sextus paused for breath, he used his powerful barrel-chested voice: 'I cannot be all bad – at least I have a loyal wife! Day after day she proudly comes to support my efforts. In offering myself for public service, I for one am sustained by a strong domestic partnership.'

The loyal wife was with him; he took her hand and clasped it in the traditional pose of marital commitment, while she simpered at him adoringly the way politicians' loyal wives do when asked to perform in public. She looked older than Trebonius, a respectable woman of forty, forgetting her marital disappointments and horribly forgiving such a shameless fraud.

'Gruesome!' muttered Faustus. 'She must have seen through him years ago.'

'Sickening, yes – but it doesn't mean that when they are home she never complains that his feet smell, or tells him not to belch in front of her mother because he only does it to annoy the old crone . . .'

Trebonius went further onto the attack: 'So where, Vibius Marinus, is your own wife today? As usual, I look around and do not see her! I begin to wonder if the lovely Julia Optata has cruelly abandoned you! Is your marriage over?'

Sextus handled it. He gave Trebonius a pitying glance as if the man was recklessly misinformed: 'Trebonius, how good of you to enquire. Friends, let me tell you, I am much blessed in Julia Optata, but sometimes one must make a sacrifice. My dear wife has volunteered to visit her sister, who is due to give birth for the first time and is terrified. I miss my darling, but I must bear her absence. This is an act of kindness on her part, and may help produce a safe birth. Julia Optata and I have children, so she can offer useful experience.'

Trebonius came out of the exchange looking petty and inaccurate while Sextus boldly moved on to satirising Arulenus Crescens. The crowd knew that would be even more fun. They foretold ripe jokes about partying and eunuchs – always a favourite.

As their enjoyment swelled again, I was thinking that Sextus could have told us about the nervous pregnant sister – if it was true. His slipperiness continued to niggle at me. Even Faustus murmured, 'That was a surprise. When we spoke, Sextus only said Julia went on a visit.'

I decided to let Faustus come to terms with these conflicting stories in his own way. My way would be to dig deeper.

'Did Trebonius Fulvo *know* Julia is not at home?'

'How could he?' Faustus grumbled. 'Trebonius cannot have gained access, then gone up and inspected the apartment as you did!'

Then I remembered: I had told someone else yesterday. I looked across sideways to where Laia and her brother were standing. Laia noticed me turn in their direction. Was she feeling guilty? A mere shadow of communication passed between her and her brother. They were too far away for me to see if she said anything, though I thought not.

I took a deep breath. 'Have Laia Gratiana or her brother spoken to you today?'

'No.' Faustus gazed at me. 'No. Gratus politely left us alone to do the speech. He knew we were keyed up about it.'

'Do you think . . .?'

I saw Faustus take a conscious decision not to become annoyed, even though he shared my suspicions. 'I think nothing,' he declared. 'This is politics.'

Laia must have told her brother that Julia had left. For Gratus to pass this ammunition to Trebonius was spiteful, but he probably thought he had to start defending his own position. We already knew he was an opportunist. Gratus might want to extricate himself from the now-awkward partnership with Sextus. Before he openly chose to split, he might stir things up, see what came out of asking hard questions, make sure of his ground.

'I'm sorry I told Laia.'

'You can't be blamed. She was already dropping hints.'

'So much for loyalty!'

Faustus merely looked rueful. Knowing him, he blamed himself and his old enmity with Laia.

Sextus was drawing to a close. A roar of approval filled the north end of the Forum.

I asked quietly, 'How do you feel the speech has gone?'

Faustus smiled. I was relieved to see it. 'It went well!' he said. He tipped his head on one side, viewing me with a big, beaming grin, full of his usual warmth. 'Thank you for your help.'

Sextus jumped down from the Rostra, fired up with his success. He moved through the crowds, shaking many hands as he walked, until he reached us. People clapped him on the back so clouds of white dust arose from his toga. Even he started coughing.

At that point people almost barged into us. It was the Ennius Verecundus group. To my amazement his mother plonked herself right in front of us.

'That was a pretty piece of rubbish, Sextus Vibius!'

Close to, her skin was leathery, her black eyes glistening. Her high-rolled Livia topknot almost looked varnished. Standing straight as a battering ram and unmoved, she examined us, while Sextus very quietly leaned in and kissed her wrinkled cheek in greeting. I wondered how well he had known her before he was married, if at all, and how closely they had been connected since. Whatever their relationship, or his with Julia, he was maintaining correct respect for his mother-in-law in public. She looked annoyed but took it as her right.

The man was doubly gracious because Julia Verecunda visibly had no time for him. She jabbed an index finger so hard into his breastbone he would certainly be bruised. She seemed to be trying to bore a deep hole, but he only stepped back a little.

'Son-in-law! Tell that daughter of mine I expect to see her immediately.'

'I shall write and say that is what you wish,' agreed Sextus, mild and polite.

'Bring her back!' Julia Verecunda had a voice like charcoal rasping on the hot bars of a griddle. 'I want to hear her explanation of your falsehood. *Visiting a nervous sister?* You talk nonsense, Vibius Marinus. Somebody should tell those fools who applauded your rhetoric. Not one of my daughters is pregnant. Believe me, I would be the first to know!'

30

It seemed likely that my work for the Vibius campaign was done. If Faustus needed further help I would give it, but only if he asked. I was curious about the pickle his friend must be in domestically, but now I would retire gracefully.

Faustus and I made no arrangements to meet, though we parted on good terms. He followed Vibius down the Sacred Way. I veered towards the Basilica Aemilia. I made it look casual, as if I had business of my own there. In fact, this was one of those troughs in a case that generally make me want to terminate, and even if I ran into Nothokleptes with something to tell me, I felt I would no longer wish to hear it.

Well, maybe if it was disreputable.

Curses! I had forgotten to ask what Faustus had done with my donkey. Trust a magistrate to pinch your only means of transport, then the swine forgets he borrowed it and you never see it again.

Soon I had other things to think about. As I neared the elegant row of shops at the Porticus of Gaius and Lucius, I was hailed by Cyrus, the auction-house messenger. He said he was taking money to be banked after the Callistus auction; my Aunt Maia had released their earnings to clients, less our fees. We had done well. My father would be pleased.

As we always said in the family, it would buy him a new sail for his ridiculously elaborate fishing boat.

Nothokleptes took his time counting the bags of cash. He salted it away, pretending it was going into some high-income fund (in other words, his usual high-fee, low-interest, pension-for-him system). Comforted by the thought of his future profits, he leaned back and asked me, 'Have you found out what's going on with the Callisti?'

'Not entirely. Difficult cashflow, apparently. Why do you ask?'

'Oh, no reason.'

'Liar! Tell me your interest. Have they run out of money?'

'There is plenty, thank you, beloved Isis!'

'And more, with their gains from the auction.'

'Are you sending the funds to them at their house or direct to their banker?' Notho asked, looking eager to know.

'No idea. Maia Favonia will fix it all up. Why? Do they owe their own banker money?'

'Oh, he has the family savings in his care. He won't lose out.'

'Surprise! So what's going on?'

'Can't say. Client confidentiality.'

I scoffed. 'Stick that on a satyr's testicles with rosemary oil, and grill them lightly.'

'Flavia Albia, your poor mother would shudder to hear you.'

'She would cheer me on. Give, Notho!'

'Oh, it's nothing.'

'Do I have to drizzle rosemary oil on you and cook you too?'

Notho winced. 'It's only that old man Callistus operates in an old-fashioned way. He has never made his sons independent. He is not mean. They can have whatever cash they like, but his banker is only authorised to shell out on a signed requisition from the old man. Even if Callistus Valens goes to the country, which he generally does around now to avoid the heat, he packs off a messenger back to Rome every week to say how much can be released.'

'So?'

'No word from him. Primus went to ask for some readies, but had to be turned away.'

'A family fall-out?' I was intrigued.

'Not apparently. Primus wasn't expecting a rebuff. He stalked off looking like thunder, but he hasn't been emancipated so there was nothing he could do. The sons talk big, but their banker respects the old man.'

'And that is all you know?'

'Yes. There must have been some slip-up.'

'Promise there's nothing more?'

'Bankers never make promises. We know too much about life's uncertainties.'

Almost as wise as informers.

'This sounds dodgy,' I told Cyrus, as we left. 'I'm starting to wonder if the Callistus sons organised our auction to get round their old man and acquire some direct income. Have they quarrelled with him? Could they have emptied the old store without him knowing? They sound really desperate for the auction money. Must be glad it's over.'

'It's not.' Cyrus said. 'Gornia put a few things together to stretch it out for one more day. Most could have waited for the next big sale, but he wants to finish with that strongbox.'

'He's selling it again? What happened about the underbidder?'

'You know what people are like. When Gornia went and offered it, the fool lost confidence and convinced himself he no longer wanted it.'

I growled, 'Of course the idiot will turn up and bid again, as soon as he sees other people showing an interest. Serve him right if he ends up paying more for it.'

'Gornia has taken a real dislike to that chest. He can't wait to see it go.' Cyrus paused. 'You might drop in today – your pa would want someone on the scene. Gornia doesn't like the atmosphere. He went so far as to tell Lappius to bring extra men for security.'

'He's getting past it. The corpse in the box made him jumpy.'

'So we have to jolly him along,' said Cyrus.

Well, that was something to do. I bought hot flatbreads from a stall for Cyrus and me; then we turned back towards the Capitol, hiked around towards the Field of Mars and entered the Porticus of Pompey.

When we arrived there was only a modest crowd. Gornia was on the tribunal, selling a veneered cupboard; anyone who liked the finish would probably not see that a door was tied on with twine and a knob had gone missing.

The worn pelt and sagging frame of Ursa guarded the unsold goods. *Boy with a Thorn* was acting as another sentinel. The strongbox stood waiting. Nobody was taking notice of it. Everything seemed unexceptional.

Gornia liked to go to trouble. Using items for sale, he had created a small room-set, arranging a couch, tables, cupboards, stools. Lamps, some not even remotely erotic, hung from candelabrum stands. He had even set out a board and glass counters. Naturally people wandered in;

one member of the audience took his ease on the long chair. Every man who went that way tried making a move on the gaming board. They all tried ringing the tiny bells on a tintinnabulum assemblage. *That* was rude; they always are. Primitive people who think a nude phallus can ward off evil must know little about life.

Bidding opened on a bunch of weathered stone dinner couches that must have been stripped out when somebody remodelled their garden. The sloped three-person loungers were basic; they would be covered with cushions if anybody used them. But, excitingly, they came in a set with a large fountain niche, ornamented with shells and mosaic. It had a coy Birth of Venus (small breasts, big hips, half-heartedly veiling herself with a wisp of seaweed) flanked by a pair of extremely muscular sea-horses, who were having fun thrashing twinkly glass foam. A fine piece: I could see why it had been salvaged by the canny building team.

Five of them were here. Wide men in dusty one-armed tunics and heavy site boots, all looking and feeling out of place, but fixedly watching bids on their lot. They had a large squelchy wineskin of mulsum, that sustaining mix of honey and vinegar, with their own cups. Every time someone made a bid, the labourers winced, then gulped their drinks. It was pure amazement at the money they were about to make, a fortune to them.

These were men who worked long hours, very badly paid when compared with the wealthy house-owners and fashionable designers who commissioned them. Somehow, for once, they had managed a windfall. Gornia must have asked searching questions but we all knew there was prodigious waste when homes were renovated. Beautiful things were often thrown away and we liked to see good come out of a rubbish skip – especially since my father had once found a baby in one, now my sweet cousin Junillus. Salvage was in our blood.

When their lot sold, the workmen sloshed more mulsum into their cups, looking stunned.

I went up and explained what they needed to do now. They were happy to transport both couches and fountain to the new owner in their heavy-duty cart, and even offered him a cheap deal for installation. I said we would gladly receive more salvage from them, although they always had to demonstrate they had the right to it: our auction house would not become receivers of stolen goods.

At this point, the Callisti turned up: Secundus and the cousin, well attended by belligerent guards. Gornia glanced at me, though they parked themselves harmlessly at the back of the crowd.

Hardly had they started casting gloom with their heavy presence than the wife of Niger rushed into the auction circle, followed by a shabby man with sweat dripping off him, also going full pelt.

'Stop the sale!' She flung both arms wide as if shepherding some tricky goats. 'That chest belongs to my husband. You are not authorised to sell it!'

Gornia defused the situation by announcing he would auction off some wine vessels, while I ascertained the problem.

All the crowd perked up. The builders chose to stay and watch. Nobody paid any attention to Gornia's calls for bids on the wine kraters, which were, to tell the truth, disappointing. One had an enormous crack. People buy those things because they're smitten by their sheer size. Nobody uses the huge party mixing vessels afterwards: even empty, nobody can lift them. Most return in due course to be sold again. We welcome them back like long-lost sons and talk them up on 'rarity'.

Cornering Niger's hysterical wife, I kept my voice low. Auctioneers run into situations like this, but we knew how to defend our rights. 'It is true,' I said, 'your husband made a bid on this strongbox, but he never paid. The chest therefore reverts to the original owners, who have authorised us to put it up for sale a second time.'

'Titus Niger owns it!'

'Only if he bought it. Let me explain again.' I toughened up, while still playing reasonable. Grandpa, a ruthless charmer, would have cheered. 'If you are claiming you own this item, you must produce proof – our docket to say that Niger gave us the money.'

The wife was frantic. 'They won't pay his fee. He is going nuts about his lost time.'

'Then I suppose he might legitimately hold on to any item in his possession as collateral, but not this. Because we received no payment, we are selling the box again.'

'But—'

'No! Since this chest belonged to the Callisti, Niger must take up any dispute with them.' We were going round in circles. 'Anyway,' I demanded in mild annoyance, 'where is the famous Niger? What does the defaulter have to say for himself?'

His wife looked shifty. Her agent fixed his eyes upon the ground and made no comment. 'My husband is out of town right now.'

'Where?'

I realised his wife had no idea. That seemed slightly odd.

The sweaty man took a hand. 'I'm acting as arbiter. I subpoena the chest until its true ownership is decided.'

Hopeless. He was a cheapskate hireling who should have given the woman better advice right from the start and never have let her come near the auction. I reckoned he was someone Niger dealt with in his work: that was how the wife came to know him. But Niger himself was far out of his class.

'I do not accept your subpoena,' I stated firmly. 'Niger reneged. We asked the original owners for instructions and here we are, reselling. Any questions, go over there and take up your beef with the Callisti.' During this altercation Callistus Secundus and his cousin never moved, though they heard what was being said.

'This is a legal situation.' He was red-faced and pompous – but he had that nervous eye-twitch that revealed he felt deeply unsure of his position.

'Wrong.' I smiled coldly. 'This is an auction and we are proceeding with it.'

'I'm going to fetch the vigiles.'

'You do that.' I signalled to Gornia to shift the strongbox with all speed.

The so-called agent was so busy blustering he did not even notice my sign. 'I am going straight away and nobody is to touch that chest until I come back!'

'I hear you.' I would ignore him.

Niger's wife's agent hurried off in a new haze of sweat to annoy the law-and-order boyos. They would probably refuse to come, or more likely they would come tomorrow, when it was all safely over and no need for them to do anything. The woman cast a scared glance in the direction of the two Callisti, but could not pluck up courage to speak to them. Instead, she darted forwards and flung herself bodily on top of the strongbox. Lying there full-length, she glued herself to the lid, like a broad-beamed limpet, whimpering against the charred woodwork.

'Do not dribble on that valuable piece, madam!' Gornia nodded to Lappius, our largest minder, a big, peaceful, pock-marked man, who swung in and picked her up off it. He carried the flailing woman right to the edge of the crowd. Her large, flat, sandalled feet kicked out in all directions but Lappius set her down (because security operatives are courteous men – at least, ours are), then stood with his huge arms locked round her. He told her to shut up. She squealed. He played deaf. She called for help, so everybody near her edged away. She simmered down, though only slightly.

Gornia called time on the wine kraters, which would go back to store unsold again, then he announced the strongbox. The five builders who had sold the fountain niche had just stood their beakers of mulsum on it, which they lifted off shamefacedly.

It was far too heavy to carry about on display, so a junior porter who fancied himself as a circus performer pranced around it a couple of times, making 'Lo! This wondrous strongbox!' gestures. He was a daft imp.

'Thank you, Lucius,' said Gornia, solemnly.

That was when Callistus Primus hove into sight, coming down the porticus with a clutch of new security: matched toughs with short legs and no necks. I watched our own guards confer. They normally spent a lot of time bored, but a rumpus looked promising. Secundus and the cousin muttered to their own heavies.

Gornia kept going: 'This is a fine antique chest of exceptional size and armouring, and only ever in the possession of a single family . . .'

Primus closed on us. Scampering behind as best they could on high cork heels were the brothers' two prettied-up wives, plus Julia Laurentina, wife of their cousin. They had brought maids to tend their curls, carry their kerchiefs and pretend to be providing chaperonage.

Now it was Callistus Primus who held an outstretched arm above the strongbox and declaimed, 'Do not take offers on this box! I forbid the sale! This is an act of hideous impiety!'

That would have been fine. His family owned the box; we would not quibble.

Instead, Secundus ran forwards unexpectedly and barged Primus to one side so he fell into a pile of miscellaneous swags and moth-eaten curtains (some grey, some rainbow-striped, all horrible).

'You don't know!' Secundus yelled at Primus, falling on top of him.

'I bloody do!'

'We were told it wasn't him.' The cousin dragged Secundus upright again.

Still cradled in old curtaining, Primus sounded full of misery. 'You are a cloth-eared pair of innocents. You can't bear the truth.'

'Ignore this man!' bellowed Secundus, to the world at large. 'He's crazy. Just get on and sell the chest!'

'Sell it!' screamed the cousin, joining in with a wild squeak like an agitated Syrian hamster. 'Sell the damned thing now!'

'*Don't* sell it!' shrieked the wife of Niger, suddenly breaking free from Lappius and hurtling into their midst.

'What am I bid?' enquired Gornia, hopefully, from his plinth. 'Anybody start me?'

Only a lunatic would have placed a bid for an item in such an ownership dispute. The wiser dealers told him so laconically.

Even in ordinary circumstances this would have been an awkward moment to be joined by a substantial party of election candidates in their pristine whites. But, sure enough, into the Porticus of Pompey they all came strolling and smiling. These worthies were about to partake in circumstances that were in nobody's definition ordinary.

31

A bad situation ripened to glorious.

Deep-throated barks from a huge dog announced that Trebonius Fulvo, fired up by the taunts Vibius had thrown at him earlier, had sent for his hunting mastiff. The new Incitatus had never had such a tremendous day out. He broke away from his handler, simply by pulling his head out of his horrible spiked collar. Ecstatic, Inky bounded about; he urinated on the unsold lots, tore to shreds anything he could get into his slobbering mouth, then made a run at his master and lovingly jumped up at him.

The dog stood four feet tall with his four paws on the floor. This was an expensive, heavy beast that had apparently been bred for bringing down wild bulls, far too strong for Trebonius. Trying to avoid his pet's frantic licks, the candidate fell over in his chalk-white toga. Since he was turning away from the dog's tongue at the time, he landed face down or, as Inky saw with much delight, bottom up. The dog fell in lust with him. Insults would be easy now: never mind his respectable wife cooing gooily at him in public, Trebonius was a man whose dog had copulated with him, in full view of the baying public.

The thrilled crowd thought this was better than buying old platters and squashed couches. Dealers pushed in for a better view, forcing their way past the two massive metal wine kraters (*faux*-silver, *faux*-Celtic chasing, *faux pas* decidedly); both grandiose vessels toppled on their cranky stands and started rolling to and fro. Anyone caught behind the knees was felled, usually dragging someone else down with them.

The Callistus brothers were now engaged in violent fisticuffs. Invading Gornia's carefully created room set, they floundered about throwing punches. Primus broke a side-table. Secundus shattered lamps. Their cousin tried to intervene until they both turned on him. One of them yelled, 'Get this fool!' Heavies with cudgels rushed at the cousin, who soon had an ear torn half off and was reeling. Every time someone tumbled out of the mêlée, our laughing auction guards picked him up and threw him straight back in.

The three wives stood on the sidelines, squealing; it was impossible to tell if they wanted the fight to end or were calling for more blood.

Beside a colonnade, the struggle against the mastiff continued, Trebonius gasping helplessly while crude people cheered. Arulenus Crescens might look effeminate but he was a loyal co-candidate and carried a lot of weight, literally. He grabbed Dillius to help. Dillius looked squinty and sozzled, but they managed to rescue Trebonius.

Incitatus ran away. We saw him bounding towards the art gallery where, being a true dog, he was soon pulling down curtains. Yes, I do mean the fabled gold brocade hangings about which you may have read in reverent guidebooks. Soon the cries of horrified art-lovers were heart-rending.

Back at the auction, Vibius and Ennius showed their potential as men of law and order by taking on the fighting Callisti. Unexpectedly, the two candidates grappled the brothers until others came to help.

A wife plonked herself by each Callistus and loudly complained of being shown up. Their cousin was in deep trouble after his thrashing by the guards. Bent double, he started woozily vomiting into one of the wine kraters; I suspected he was concussed. His angry wife Julia Laurentina told him he was disgusting, though concerned dealers attended him. He was now floundering on top of the big wine vessel as if he had no idea where he was.

While Ennius still grappled Secundus, Julia Verecunda had to decide whether to approve of her son's initiative or reprimand him for joining a brawl. 'Keep out of it and let them kill one another!' He feigned not to hear her. Brave fellow.

Sextus loosened his hold on Primus because the older brother suddenly broke down. Sextus had to support his burly frame while Primus shuddered his heart out in what we all could see was unbearable grief.

For whom?

The three wives bunched together anxiously. I strode up to them. 'What on earth is going on?' None answered.

More people were arriving. One was Manlius Faustus, bringing Patchy back for me. Dromo and the boy were both riding the donkey, kicking at his flanks with their clumsy feet. Patchy crashed into Ursa, trying to shunt the lads off his back. The stuffed bear teetered and wobbled, then crashed to the floor. Her head fell off. Our porters cried out, grief-stricken. We had had Ursa a long time.

On his way here, Faustus had been accosted by a member of the public. This striking dignitary carried a jug in her left hand and a rattle in her right – not what most women would choose as accessories. Her veiled ringlets were crowned with a small mock-gold palmette, and over her long, heavily pleated tunic she had a many-folded shawl with a fringed edge, tied in a large knot of mystical design in the centre of her bust. (I agree: one fancy item too many. My sisters would have redesigned her outfit from scratch, with cries of horror.)

This woman was instantly recognisable as a priestess of Isis. All she needed was a snake wrapped round her wrist, but she had left it at home that day, probably because her arm was bandaged from thumb base to elbow. I remembered that Trebonius's dog had famously bitten her.

Isis was a respected foreign goddess in Rome, favoured by Vespasian and Titus, who had been in the east, and by Domitian, who had once taken refuge among the cult's followers when his life was threatened. Domitian had rebuilt the Temple of Isis and Serapis in fabulous style and this priestess carried herself as if she personified the goddess: Isis, the universal mother, mistress of all the elements, primordial child of time, sovereign of all matters spiritual, queen of the dead, queen of the sea, queen also of the immortals, the triple goddess of the underworld, the heavenly one . . . Not a neighbour to offend. To fend off the wrath of Isis you might need more than a phallic wind chime.

As soon as the wounded priestess spotted Trebonius Fulvo among the huddled candidates, she let out an eye-watering shriek of accusation. Incitatus heard her, turned round, saw somebody he recognised and hurtled up to greet her. The frightened priestess tried to deter him by battering him on the snout with her rattling sistrum.

The dog bit her again.

Manlius Faustus sounded a stentorian order: 'Someone catch that bloody hound for me!' As an aedile, he was responsible for escaped wild animals in public places. Unfortunately, as an aedile his person was sacrosanct, so he never had guards to help.

The five builders saw that nobody else was brave enough to tackle Inky, so they would have to. The men picked up their mulsum beakers (all they had to hand) and advanced on him. 'Here, boy!'

He nipped three of them, then shoved his great muzzle into a cup, lapping the honey and vinegar thirstily. I grew up with dogs. I grabbed a cord off the auctioned curtain swags, walked up quietly and, as he drank, fondled him between his ears. His fur looked smooth, but felt rough; he was not a dog anyone ever brushed. He growled as he considered whether being stroked offended his dignity, but he let me.

'Who's a good dog?' He wagged his tail. The tail caught a pile of ceramic platters, which shattered. 'Don't seem threatening,' I told the builders. We all smiled, staying very still and careful. I made a loop and tied it round Inky's mighty neck.

'Watch yourself, girl!'

'She's good with animals.' That was the quiet voice of Faustus, at my back. 'Albia, step away safely.'

'He just feels too hot and he needs a drink, don't you, precious?' Inky stopped drinking long enough to drag his hot rasping tongue across my hand. I had him under control, though I was scared stiff.

The builders had found lengths of rope from somewhere, as builders do; they configured a harness and delicately fitted it round the mastiff. Inky grew calmer. He sat when I told him to. So far, so good.

Manlius Faustus hauled Trebonius Fulvo out of the crowd.

Faustus formally asked the weeping priestess what compensation she wanted; with Egyptian alacrity, the handmaiden of Isis named a healthy price. Faustus called it fair (she was copiously bleeding) and doubled it because she had been bitten twice. The priestess serenely staunched the blood, using her shaggy shawl. Large numbers do not faze primordial daughters of time.

Faustus ordered Trebonius to pay up and avoid the need for a court case. 'No choice, man! You compensate the holy woman, or you pay the same as a fine.'

Trebonius agreed to settle, but would not consent to take Incitatus home. I informed Faustus how the dog had jumped Trebonius when he fell over. Faustus kept his face straight, just.

'Don't blame your dog,' I told Trebonius. 'It's not his fault. He needs a handler who likes and understands tough dogs. Just think about how your wife controls you.' Standing within earshot, she blinked and did not smile. 'You can manage him.'

'Not in Rome,' declared Faustus. 'This is not a city dog. Trebonius Fulvo, you are forbidden to let him rampage any more in our streets and public places. I order you to keep him on your country estate.'

Trebonius was still refusing to have him back at all. His wife agreed, which was probably because the dog caused havoc in her no doubt comfortable house. The original handler had vanished. To solve the dilemma, I volunteered that Incitatus could come home with me, but only for one night. If Inky behaved, Trebonius would have to take him back. If not, the dog would be put down. Manlius Faustus announced that was a proper solution, suggesting Trebonius should pay me for his dog's overnight boarding – and danger money.

'What's his proper name?'

'Consul.'

'No wonder he gets above himself!'

At that point everyone was settled and friendly. It was not to last.

32

The builders were leaving and offered to take Incitatus/Consul to Fountain Court for me. Gornia had slyly gathered a group of dealers around his little tribunal and once more asked for offers on the Callistus strongbox.

Manlius Faustus stood with his arms folded, now monitoring what went on. This was the first time I had realised that his allocated area, a quarter of the city, must include a slice of the Field of Mars.

Vibius had parked Callistus Primus on the couch in Gornia's room set. Secundus comforted his brother while Vibius went to investigate their concussed cousin. He was in serious trouble; he tried to stand up but slid to the ground, where he began having fits. Vibius called out for a stretcher-bearer. The Porticus of Pompey had attendants; Faustus struck off urgently to find them.

As the injured man lay racked by seizures, his wife knelt down and tried to help Sextus Vibius hold him steady. Her mother, Verecunda, marched up and told her not to bother. 'When are you intending to learn better?' She really was a vicious hag, putting on airs with her Livia lookalike tunic and hair, though in fact she was no better than any pinched, selfish, loveless old woman. If she had had a hard life, it might have excused her, but I could tell she had not.

'Oh, shut up, Mother!' Julia Laurentina hauled herself

upright and wildly struck out. She had no martial training and the swipe was off balance; it simply spun her on the spot, leaving Mama untouched.

Verecunda let out a disdainful snort. As she left the scene, she could not help taunting the Callistus brothers. 'How clever was that? You spent all your precious money trying to get this lightweight elected. You couldn't keep him in the running – and now you have both killed him!'

For a second I was baffled. Then it made sense. This previously unnamed Callistus cousin, Julia Laurentina's husband, must be Volusius Firmus. The name on the advertising plaque outside the Callistus house was Firmus, the porter had told me. Nobody had said he was a relative; I expect they thought I knew.

So, it was the Callisti who had lavished cash on bribing Abascantus. We were probably auctioning old Callistus stored items because the family had bankrupted themselves on their pointless attempt – and now Primus and Secundus had risked fatal damage to their cousin.

The auction stalled during the medical emergency. Out of the corner of my eye, I saw Dromo, Faustus's slave, poking through the wreckage of Ursa. He put the head on like a helmet. Dromo never had much tact or timing. Almost at once he pulled it off and hurled it as far as he could, shrieking '*Urrgh!* Maggots!'

This caused amusement to a bunch of red-tunic vigiles who had just arrived with Niger's wife's agent. Forgetting why they had been summoned, they started kicking the head around and laughing. People scrabbled out of reach in a hurry. Those close enough could see the maggots crawling.

The game stopped when Manlius Faustus returned with

a doctor and stretcher-bearers. After a swift examination, they picked up the limp form of Volusius Firmus and set off with him fast. Julia Laurentina sensibly removed her high-heeled sandals to run along behind them, like a devoted wife, barefoot.

The candidates' party also moved off, which unfortunately caught the attention of the Callistus brothers.

Callistus Primus finally stood up, wiping his eyes. The sight of Arulenus and Trebonius strangely enraged him. He ran at them, gesturing at the fatal strongbox. '*You bastards! You unfeeling, heartless bastards! How dare you show your faces here?*'

He was so angry I thought he would burst a blood vessel. Instead he shouted to his guards, 'Get the lid up! Get it up, I say! Then help me put this murderous pair of villains inside and see how they like it!'

It was no use telling him the strongbox was locked and its key at the Saepta Julia. He ordered his men to open it by any means; they started violently rocking it from side to side on its short charred legs. Our porters tried protesting, but to no avail.

A leg gave way. The men only pushed harder. The strongbox toppled over on to its back. Either the lock broke or it had been unfastened; the lid crashed open, flat on the ground. Something fell out.

Everyone jumped back. Shocked silence fell.

'Titan's tripes!' commented one of the vigiles. 'We've got a dead body.'

Correction, trusty man of law: we had *another* one.

33

First a man's bare arm flopped out. The rest of him jerkily followed, eerily affected by rigor. He lurched out, landing face down.

The vigiles shoved everyone back. He had to be dead. We could see that. One of the vigiles touched his neck to make sure, a routine gesture. 'He's cold.'

They rolled him face up. People craned to look. I pushed in myself, in case I recognised this one. I did. He was thin and lanky, wearing a beige tunic, with heavy acne scars. It was the missing agent, Niger.

His wife gasped, then fainted clean away.

34

Manlius Faustus took charge. You might think the candidates would want to stay and watch him, but when did men standing for office learn about their coming job? They were the quickest to leave. Other members of the public also vanished, not wanting to be involved in trouble. Faustus was stuck on his own.

The vigiles decided not to scarper while a magistrate was watching. Faustus instructed them to inspect the body for evidence of foul play. They peered at Niger, tweaked up sleeves and tunic hems, then announced that the dead man showed classic signs of having been beaten, shortly before death. This corpse was less than a day old. Faustus pronounced it murder.

The Callistus brothers forged a path through curious onlookers to inspect the remains of their former agent. Faustus asked them to identify him formally. Niger's wife came round from her faint; she indignantly claimed that task as hers, encouraged by the greaseball who was acting as her agent. So Faustus let them all do it, while he made notes.

He asked the Callistus brothers why they had ended up on bad terms with Niger; neither would answer. He told them to go home and await a visit, advising them to come up with a satisfactory story before they found themselves suspects.

Niger's wife's agent planted himself alongside her. He

must be thinking of that well-mopped first-storey apartment, not to mention the savings that Niger, like any careful freelance, would have stored up. Soon this man would be 'helping' his client deal with the funeral, after which he would probably console the dazed widow right into a new marriage . . .

I suggested we send for Fundanus. I assured the wife he would be reverent. With a deserving widow he might be. That way, too, he would pass on to me any useful information. I wanted to know what links there were between the two strongbox incarcerations. There was no way now I would abandon my enquiries into the first death.

Faustus tried to interrogate the weeping wife. He asked if Niger had had enemies, but she only wanted to protest that he was loved by everyone, especially all his wonderful, generous clients. She did say that the Callistus brothers had employed him quite recently, not simply to bid at the auction but, before that, for some errand to the countryside. Whatever rural task he had carried out had made his clients unhappy, she did not know why.

She sobbed that last night Niger had never come home. It was unusual behaviour, so the troubled wife was not entirely surprised to find he was dead.

I slipped off for a muttered consultation with Gornia. 'You know what I'm going to ask you. If we had that strongbox locked up and under guard all night, Gornia, how the hell did some villain open the lid and drop Niger into it?'

As I feared: last night our staff had sneaked off to have dinner. They had asked the Porticus nightwatchmen to keep an eye on things 'just for an hour'. I knew what that meant.

'So the porticus guards agreed, but mooched off and left our stuff unattended?'

They must have, Gornia conceded.

'For hours?'

Gornia looked despondent.

'Was anything taken?'

'No of course not, Albia. The porticus is locked up after sundown.'

'People can get in. It's a notorious place for assignations.'

'Lovers are too busy to steal things.'

'Though, oddly enough, not too busy to leave dead bodies behind!'

'Oh, go on, Flavia Albia. Don't beat me up about it – I'm an old man.'

We inspected the strongbox lock and found jemmy marks, shiny new skids across the old metalwork. Someone had forced the lock. They dumped Niger inside and dropped the lid again.

Faustus had noticed us talking and come over. I suggested, 'Whoever did this, Aedile, must have realised the chest was to be auctioned again. The body would be found. Are Niger's killers sending a message to the Callisti?'

Being Faustus, he thought about that in silence.

'What message?' asked Gornia. When nobody answered, he changed the subject tetchily. 'So what am I supposed to do about this bloody chest?'

Faustus stepped over Niger's body and peered inside it. This time he was definite. 'There are no clues. Nothing inside. Time to put an end to this fiasco. I order you to burn it. If the Callisti complain, tell them to see me. Destroy it as soon as possible, please.'

Gornia overcame conflicting emotions regarding the fee

we would have gained from selling the strongbox and his loathing of it; he agreed. From the sly wink he gave me while pulling at the broken lock, I knew he would first remove all the ironwork; there was money in that.

Fundanus arrived, sooner than expected. He had a nose for untimely death. Negotiations were swiftly concluded with the widow, via her agent, then the corpse was taken up and carried off. Niger's wife went home, escorted by her increasingly persistent agent.

Fundanus himself stuck around. Uncertain of Faustus, he took me aside. 'Would it be of interest if I told you I have seen that cove before?'

'It certainly would, Fundanus! When?'

'It was the day we torched that other stiff we scooped out. The second fellow turned up and asked for a viewing. He was just in time. An hour later, I had the pyre burning up nicely. According to him, it could be somebody he knew.'

'You showed him the corpse?' That was Faustus, not easily deluded. An aedile had to stop illegal gambling; Faustus had learned to spot surreptitious goings-on.

'I hope I did not do wrong, sir,' whined Fundanus, humbly.

'Get on with your story.'

'Of course, sir.' This was a new, creepy side of the bombastic undertaker. I preferred him when he was sounding off. 'Well, he took a peek, though not for long because, as Flavia Albia can corroborate, number one was in a, let us say, significantly poor condition.'

'Rotting?'

'Somewhat liquid, sir. We did our best on him but . . .' Fundanus shook his head mournfully. 'It really was as well we were ready to pyre him up.'

‘Did Niger put a name to number one?’ I coaxed, controlling my impatience.

‘Sadly, no. He stated that he must have been mistaken, this was nobody he knew. Then he hopped out of it, covering his nose. From evidence subsequently discovered, he threw up in the street outside.’

‘I can manage without that detail,’ muttered Faustus, at his most dour.

The undertaker turned to me. ‘I would have told you about this person’s visit, Flavia Albia, but since he did not know the corpse, I supposed there was no interest in it.’

‘I had told you I needed to know if anyone showed interest.’

‘And here I am telling you, Flavia Albia.’

‘Well, thanks for that!’

‘It is possible,’ warned Faustus, ominously, ‘if Albia had known your story earlier, number two might be alive now.’

‘I don’t see how!’ sneered Fundanus, more aggressive and showing his true colours.

‘And we might have named number one,’ continued Faustus. He regularly dealt with shirty householders and intransigent brothel-keepers. Nobody put him off.

Fundanus made a fast exit.

The atmosphere in the porticus changed as evening fell. News of the second dead body soon brought ghouls to our corner, keen to gawp at the strongbox with its sinister history. Deadbeats who hoped to find unattended goods after the auction turned up. Our staff hurried to tidy things away, knowing looters would descend. Felix had arrived outside to cart away any remaining goods. Some of the staff were off loading unsold lots and our own equipment, therefore we were thin on the ground.

Hooligans found the remains of Ursa, with predictable results. Shameless thieves tried to seize the two vast wine kraters, heavy though they were. Most of the armed guards belonging to other people had left, so we were now down to our own security and a handful of vigiles. Some of those had already sloped off, claiming they needed to be on fire-watch. Fortunately enough remained to whistle for reinforcements.

There was a brief air of menace, a swirl of unpleasant behaviour, then out of nowhere more troops arrived. They looked like Urban Cohorts, riot police, who were always taken seriously. The Urbans were barracked with the Praetorian Guard, and popped out periodically to thump people. Compensation was not paid even if their victims died.

The Urbans started doing what they liked to do. The troublemakers dispersed rapidly. Any moment now, the Urbans were going to turn on us.

Their centurion eyed up the aedile, obviously expecting him to act like a magistrate who meant business. Manlius Faustus surveyed Gornia, who was desperately tired and looked as if he had lived on air in a cave for a hundred years. Faustus turned to me instead. 'Flavia Albia, daughter of Falco, this auction has been a complete disgrace – and in the hallowed Porticus of Pompey. It is surely in breach of any licence you hold, which I shall need to inspect, incidentally. I will not tolerate such goings-on under my administration.'

Then he told two of the vigiles to put me on Patchy and take me to the Aventine, to the aediles' office. I croaked in surprise.

'Take her!' commanded Faustus. Gornia squeaked to me that he would tell someone, so not to worry.

I, too, was tired. It dawned on me only slowly: Tiberius Manlius Faustus, my so-called friend, this jumped-up pontificating aedile who had no common sense or discretion, was treating me like anyone on one of the watch lists that he supervised officially.

I was under arrest.

35

Soon I was cursing Gornia. He thought he was doing right, but I could have survived without the help he chose to summon. I had been in the aediles' building for about an hour. They were treating me politely. Everyone knew I knew Faustus. He had stayed behind to conclude business with the Urbans.

I had calmed down and was ready to laugh with him about him smartly removing me from a tricky situation. I was sitting in the courtyard. It had greenery. Patchy had been gorging himself on topiary, so when I reckoned he was about to burst, I sent him back with his boy, saying Gornia could ride him home if he wanted. I knew that first, once Faustus and the soldiers left the porticus, Gornia and the lads would make a bonfire of the strongbox and cook themselves a grilled supper over it. I was sorry to miss that.

Faustus took his time. While I was still waiting for him, I heard a horribly familiar voice in the entrance hallway: Petronius Longus, my father's best friend, his army buddy and long-time collaborator, husband to Aunt Maia, a retired vigiles investigator, frankly a man with not enough to do these days. To Gornia, he would seem the obvious person to extricate someone from custody. Not to me.

'Some bugger who doesn't know how to wipe his arse is holding my niece here!'

Good start, hoary uncle. The sensitive approach.

They let him in. No wonder. He was tall, solid and sure of himself. His once-brown hair had dulled to grey but his step remained sprightly and he paid attention to barbering. His boots were still the kind the vigiles wear for kicking people. Retirement hadn't mellowed him; it just gave him more time to make a nuisance of himself where he thought nuisance was required. That was most occasions, in Petro's opinion.

He was my father's age, just shy of fifty. Like Falco, he had always thought he knew it all, and nowadays he was even more certain the world was full of idiots and deviants.

He did not bother to hug me but sprawled on a bench, making himself at home. 'So you're in trouble! What's going on?'

Unfortunately, I saw Faustus enter the courtyard quietly at that moment. He must have popped into his office and was now casually dressed. I made 'be careful what you say' gestures, which could have applied to either, then prepared to introduce them.

They did not bother with me.

'Lucius Petronius Longus, ex Fourth Cohort of Vigiles. You can call me "sir".'

'Manlius Faustus, plebeian aedile. You should call me "sir", but I won't insist.'

'A smart talker! You're the latest lover-boy?' growled Petronius, incorrigibly.

'Better ask Albia.'

'Juno!' Seething, I shot Faustus an apologetic look. 'I apologise for my uncle.'

'Wait until you meet mine.' Faustus feigned amusement. From what I knew, his own uncle, Tullius, had a crude reputation.

Mine carried on, impervious: 'Your pa was checking up on some incomer, last time I saw him. Is this the dubious character?'

'I heard I was given the once-over,' Faustus intervened. 'Any idea what Didius Falco found out?'

Uncle Petro laughed, suggesting something terrible. He probably had no idea.

'Leave the aedile alone. He saved my life,' I protested.

Petro gave Faustus a sharp look. 'That true, son?'

Faustus kept it light. 'No need for a big proclamation. I found her dying on the floor so I picked her up, put her to bed and looked after her until her mother came.' He failed to spell out that he had not summoned my mother until a week later.

'That would be how Helena Justina came across you in her daughter's bedroom.'

'Oh, it didn't go down well?' Faustus twinkled like a lad about town.

'We all heard about it! Still, she's a big girl now.'

I complained, 'I am twenty-nine, an independent widow – and I am sitting here!'

'That's right,' agreed Uncle Petro, ever unflappable. 'Able to get into all sorts of trouble – and old enough to know where to look for it.' Warmed by his fine riposte, he settled his big frame more comfortably. 'So now you're in a pickle and I have to help you out.'

'While you're here, I expect you'd like a drink,' Faustus suggested to him.

'Now you're talking!' Holy Vestals, the boys were bonding.

Faustus waved up the only slave who was still around, the others having disappeared when the evening grew late. After a word in his ear, the boy went off. Petro filled in time by asking, 'Who do you normally deal with in the Fourth?' To him, his old cohort was the only one worth mentioning. He still mentioned it a lot.

'Titus Morellus, though he's currently on sick leave.'

'Took a blow at work, I heard?' Morellus had inherited Petro's job, allowing my uncle to look superior about his successor's supposed delicate health. 'How do you find him?'

'Fine, when he's available. He was struck down by a poisoner, nearly croaked. Albia and I were working that case.'

Petronius shook his head at me. 'Was that when you wrecked the old balcony? Plenty of memories were lost that day . . .'

'You and Father glugging wine on it and talking about women.'

'Sometimes even drinking the health of women we love and admire!' Petronius reproved me. He had not finished interrogating Faustus: 'So your remit covers both the Twelfth and Thirteenth regions here on the Aventine?'

'Plus the Transtiberina,' Faustus dutifully supplied.

'Good luck with that!'

'Yes, it's lively. I also look after half the Field of Mars, mainly theatres and porticos. A colleague handles the Pantheon and the Saepta, with all things north. With the Transtib and Circus Flaminius, obviously I liaise with the Seventh Cohort who are, between us two, a bit of a shower.'

'I'd not quarrel with that! Have much to do with Scaurus of the Fourth?' Petronius quizzed.

Faustus merely emitted a choking noise. When evaluating a cohort tribune, contempt was the correct response. Uncle Petro brightened further as the returning slave brought a flagon and two cups. He must have fetched them from indoors – he hadn't had time to go to a bar.

'I like a man who keeps a private stash in his office – and is prepared to share it. Fetch us one more beaker, son,' my uncle told the serving boy, nodding at me. He added to Faustus, with a heavy wink, 'I don't approve of women drinking, but after fifteen years in this family, I bend with the wind.'

'Best practice!' Faustus poured politely for my uncle and me, himself waiting for the extra cup.

Lucius Petronius quaffed, then admitted surprise at how good the aedile's private wine was. 'Setinum?'

'You can never go wrong,' Faustus acknowledged modestly.

Petronius stretched out his long legs, as if ready to pass a whole evening there. Faustus copied the action. With no rehearsal, my presumed lover was making himself an acceptable prospect. All he had to do now was actually want to woo me.

Petro was finally ready to start the real discussion. 'Let's get down to business. Neither of us likes what Albia does, but it keeps her happy. She earns a bit of pocket money, though she doesn't need the income. Her father's an auctioneer, for Jove's sake! She stays out of trouble – Falco and I have taught her that. She helps a few lamentable souls, where nobody else would bother. Between friends, I know she must be on your watch list of disreputable professions, but everything this one gets up to is harmless, I can vouch for that.'

I groaned. Lucius Petronius was acting the retired squaddie. He would drop the right word, as he saw it – and bury me much deeper. 'Oh, Petro, let me handle things myself, will you? Nothing is worse than some grey-haired, gnarly has-been who believes he knows the ropes, but whose day has passed.'

'She speaks her mind,' my unwanted referee growled at Faustus. 'Think you can handle it?'

Faustus gave him a resigned shrug – exactly what was called for. There was no point in fighting Lucius Petronius, and the aedile was wise to accept it.

'Let me fill you in. I was there in Londinium when Falco and Helena first hauled this nipper off the streets,' Petro confided, as if to a long-time drinking crony. 'The pair of them thought here was a poor urchin they could civilise. Good people, but ludicrous.'

'You believe civilising Albia is hopeless?' Faustus asked meekly. A deceptive man, his grey eyes were conveniently veiled by the shadow of a pergola. Aediles enjoyed the very best of civic gardening at their headquarters.

'No, I believe they did a good job!' snarled Petro. 'She's not a bloody Druid. She never hangs up mistletoe or croons at the moon. She can read, she dresses nicely, her heart's in the right place. People can take her anywhere. Well, almost. I wouldn't push it myself. She's a girl, she can be unpredictable. Once a month she's a termagant. Believe me, I'm father to several and I know what I'm talking about . . . What I'm saying is, wherever she came from, Albia is ours now, so you treat her decently.'

Faustus was deadly quiet. 'Albia is safe with me.'

'Ah, but are you safe with her?'

I saw Faustus smile faintly. 'Who knows? My fear is, your Albia could break my heart . . . But I believe she gives her loyalty to very few, and when she does, she is tenacious.'

My uncle considered that. I considered it myself.

I wondered if there was any point in me speaking on my own behalf. Deciding not, I served myself more wine. Faustus stretched out his arm for me to slosh him a top-up. Our familiarity was instantly observed.

'So what's your plan, Aedile?' quizzed Petro. 'Arresting Albia? Whatever's that for? You're a handsome package: I don't suppose this is the only way you can get women?'

Faustus let him tease. 'Petronius Longus, you know how things pan out in the Porticus of Pompey after dusk. The place pretends to be sophisticated, but that's crap.' Now he in turn spoke as a colleague. Two men of the law-and-order world. Compatriots in crime-fighting. 'The louts were hunting for a riot. Social dross adores a rumpus. Tensions run high in hot weather. Consequence: we had a roughhouse.' My uncle looked jealous to have missed it. 'Somebody had found a corpse, which always leads to silly behaviour. Judging the mood as dangerous, I took Albia into custody for her protection.'

'No charges, then?'

Faustus looked surprised. 'What would I charge her with?'

'Some magistrates I've bumped noses with would think of something.'

'Holy shit, I hope not. Don't force me to write out a damned docket!'

'Damned hassle . . .' Petronius approved. Since he had finished off the Setinum, he was ready to move. 'Everything seems quiet enough.'

'Certainly is up here. So,' Manlius Faustus suggested, 'I can take Flavia Albia home to her apartment and see Rodan locks the gate behind her safely.'

'Good try, hopeful Cupid!' Uncle Petro scoffed. 'No, thanks. This is a respectable young woman and I am her male relative, *in loco parentis* for the legendary Falco. I shall take that madman's daughter to ours for a bite of dinner, then escort her to her horrible dosshouse. No need for you to trouble, Aedile. No need at all.'

36

Cobnuts. Not only was I kidnapped from the aedile's grasp, but dragged off to eat with Petro and Maia. My uncle clearly hoped to wrench another flagon of Setinum from Faustus to bring away with us, but was disappointed.

Not as disappointed as me. I had felt sure this was an evening when Manlius Faustus, in the words of his friend Sextus, would have made his move. When we said goodbye, he kissed my cheek to annoy Uncle Petro; he was formal, yet his fingertips brushed my inner wrist, which was certainly not public etiquette. I could see he was stressed by a long day. Alone with me, Faustus would have shared his weariness; he would have taken comfort – and given solace in return. So, another chance lost, and every time it happened, the pattern became more established.

Cursing, I pretended to be annoyed because Faustus and I had had things to confer about. My uncle therefore nagged me over what those might be, giving me his professional thoughts, most of which I disagreed with.

Fortunately my aunt could cook.

They lived in a too-small apartment, given that Aunt Maia had two sons and a daughter still at home, another married daughter who visited on a daily basis, and now they shared the place with Petro's daughter and her baby. He was a grimly protective father, so no one had been surprised when his adored Petronilla rebelled and ended up pregnant by some unknown man. Well, she knew who he was. As we ate that night, every so often Petro let out a snide comment designed to goad her into naming the culprit so Petro could kill him, while she stubbornly kept silent. Petronilla had lived with her mother until her disgrace but, interestingly, the mother threw her out and it was her father who gave her refuge. None of us had expected that.

He ignored the baby when anyone was looking, but Maia had caught him dandling his grandson secretly. He called himself tough, but was an utter softie.

Petronius assumed Petronilla had got herself pregnant purely to annoy him. My wise aunt Maia thought it was an unfortunate accident and was glad Petronilla had had enough sense not to tie herself to whatever male disaster had landed her in trouble. She loved her father and had always been his darling. He was hideously traditional, yet when a crunch came, Lucius Petronius did not let her down.

It went for me, too, I knew that. Had I truly been in difficulty with the aedile, Lucius Petronius would have scooped me out of it. He had played the fool tonight, but only because nothing else was needed.

With Petronilla he refused to stop railing. In the end, Maia biffed his ear and sent him onto their sun terrace. Various children cleared dishes, which left her free to tackle me about Faustus.

I said nothing. What was there to say?

'Petronius says your fellow "seems all right".'

Juno and Minerva! I fought back with tactless enquiries

about the menopause, until my ear was biffed too. 'Ow! Girls' talk. You know you love it.'

'Don't push me, Albia.'

We settled down and discussed the auction. I brought her up to date on today's adventures.

Maia was round (too round, these days) and attractive, her hair still dark – aided by her daughter Cloelia, who was a hairdresser, and a good one, though even Cloelia had failed to tame Maia's curls. She coped well with being a step-grandmother but her youthful spirit remained. Maia had always been seen as headstrong. She had ideas. She spoke her mind. I didn't quibble with that – except when she spoke of my chances with Manlius Faustus, a man she had never met and couldn't judge, even if I wanted to have a chance with him, which, according to what I consistently told the family, I did not.

'Ideal,' commented Maia. 'No risk of Falco having to kill some twerp who can't keep his tozzle under his tunic.'

'He's pious.'

'He's unique, then!'

'Do you want me to tell you about the new strongbox incident or not?'

'I think I get it. This is a magic container. Every time the lid comes up, a bloated corpse pops out. Does my brother know? He'll shoot into this conundrum like a belaying pin up a sailor's arse.'

I had no idea where Maia had learned her nautical naughtiness. It was me who had been married to an ex-marine; her first husband was a horse vet. 'I am handling it. Don't say a word to Falco – or Helena.'

'You're right, she's as bad. What's your plan?'

I spelled out options. From choice, I wanted thoughts from Faustus, but I let my aunt be my sounding board. The first line of enquiry had to be: discover what had upset Callistus Primus so badly. I had suspicions.

'You think it's his father? The first body?' My aunt tossed that in without being asked.

'Oh, thank you, Maia! I do love solving a problem, then having my grand theories pre-empted.'

She smirked. Always the clever one in the family – and she knew it. 'Obvious. We took the auction instructions from the father, but since then only the sons have been involved. Primus and Secundus were insistent I send any money straight to them when I cashed up. If their father is dead, I suppose they can't touch anything else. They have no free cash – they admitted to me they had used up everything from under the mattress, getting their cousin elected.'

'Which he won't be. He lost the Emperor's favour, and now he's been seriously hurt. He could die.'

'So no bribes or fines will be coming in from that lucrative magistracy!' Maia had a cynical view of administration. 'I assume your lad is doing nicely out of his, by the way. All right: Manlius Faustus is too perfect to exploit the chance. I'm going off him rapidly . . . So why would Primus start blarting over an empty strongbox, unless he thinks it's linked to some terrible tragedy?'

'Bad memories? He might just have been remembering property they lost ten years ago to Mount Vesuvius,' I conjectured even-handedly.

'Rubbish! It must have deeper meaning.' Maia was always brisk.

'They could have lost family in the eruption, as we did.'

'Why sell the strongbox at all?' she demanded. 'If it has sentimental connections that still make him cry?'

'Maybe Secundus and Firmus put it in the sale without telling Primus.'

Maia refused to accept it. 'He came down to watch the bids first time, didn't he? With the others? Was he easy when Niger secured it?'

'He looked calm enough that day,' I confirmed, remembering how the two brothers and Firmus had stood and watched the strongbox being sold. 'So what about Niger? Have you come across him before?'

'Oh, yes. He acted as a negotiator for several people. Some folk don't like to come to auctions in person, perhaps out of shyness or fear that they'll get carried away and bid too much. Or simply the day and time are inconvenient for them.'

'Ever had anyone else go back on what their agent did?'

'No. Sometimes one receives an earful if he fails to buy a wanted piece, or pays too much. That's just the rough and tumble of patron and agent,' Maia told me. She added, 'And I've never seen anyone buy back their own goods before.'

I thought about it. 'If Primus really believes now that his father was the first dead man, I reckon at the original sale he wanted to see if anyone took an unhealthy interest, meaning they could be involved in his father's death. He wanted things to look normal, yet didn't want the strongbox to go to someone else.'

Maia followed my thinking. 'So back at the start he wanted the strongbox sold, for the money. He still thought that, once you told him someone had been dumped in it dead. But after he decided the corpse could be his own father's, he viewed the box in a horrible new light. No one else should treat his father's last resting place impiously. He tried to retrieve it discreetly, using Niger.'

I nodded. 'And then I know they all had a row. Secundus and Firmus didn't want to keep the chest because either they don't think the father was ever in it at all or they don't feel the empty container matters. From what they shouted at each other today, Secundus and Firmus cannot bear to believe the first dead man was Callistus Valens. They see Primus as wrongly fixated, while he blames them for wilful blindness to the truth.'

'Can't they just find out by looking at the dead man?'

'Tried it.' I told Maia what Fundanus had said about Niger going to view the corpse. 'Niger claimed he didn't recognise the man. So he's then gone back to the Caelian and told the three junior Callisti that it is not Senior.'

Maia frowned. 'So why is Primus so sure it was Valens? Why would Niger say no to that?'

'I don't know. It could be a genuine mistake. Niger had only recently started working for them. He may not have known the father well enough to recognise him. The body was in a repulsive state, Maia.'

'These three men,' mused my aunt, 'have some reason to fear the old one must be dead.'

'They all seem to care about him. What did you think?'

'Nice man,' said Maia, immediately. 'Something of a rarity!'

'So they are genuinely upset if something has happened to him . . . Niger's wife says he had been sent to the country on an errand earlier. In the week before the auction, the father had stopped sending messages, so let's say Niger was hired to investigate. He learned nothing. When I turn up to say a corpse has been found, Primus starts brooding. He tells Niger to get back the chest. Niger is also sent to check out the body – Primus knew its location from me. Niger pronounces that it is not Valens, which Secundus and Firmus accept, perhaps too readily. Primus doesn't believe it. He and the other two quarrel; they are all badly overwrought.'

'Why didn't Primus go and have a look himself?' asked Maia.

'Too late. Strongbox Man had been carried outside the city and cremated. He was taken immediately after Niger left.'

Maia wanted to be sure. 'We do believe the old man has gone missing?'

'Seems so. Callistus Valens always goes to the country in July to avoid the heat. This time he stopped authorising his banker to make payments to his boys – apparently unusual.'

'Oh, yes!' Maia showed off her knowledge. 'He's no miser. Happily splashes it.'

'That fits. I was told he never emancipated his sons, but was generous. They bet on chariots; their wives are kitted out with glamorous gear.'

'There's your answer. Valens has dropped off his twig. Primus is right.' Suddenly, as was her habit, Maia Favonia lost interest. 'Now, will you be safe to find your own way over to Fountain Court? I don't want that daft lump of mine taking you – he'll go in too many bars on his way back.'

I said I would be safe. I slipped out quietly while Lucius Petronius was snoozing on the sun terrace.

I was much closer to Maia, Petronius and their children than others in our family. Maia and Petro were always nostalgic about where and when they first got together as a couple. They were in Britain with Falco and Helena when my adoptive parents found me; we all travelled home to Italy in one large party so I got to know them. In some ways this was good. I arrived in Rome with firm family connections, which I admit helped me hold my own with more suspicious relations.

On the other hand, when you are given a new start in life, you do not necessarily want other people to know about your old existence.

It was a short hop to Fountain Court. As usual, I was discreet and achieved the walk without incident. On the streets it was dark, but too early yet for unbearably persistent drunks. Burglars were preoccupied. In the Street of the Armilustrium, I walked behind a group of vigiles. They failed to notice. None even looked down our alley; Fountain Court could have burned, for all they cared. At the corner, I stood listening for trouble, then trod carefully on the broken kerbs and slid through the familiar pungent darkness to the gate of my own building.

'If that's you,' shouted Rodan, our listless concierge, 'all I can say is, about time! Some man came demanding to see you.'

'Who was he?'

'No idea.'

'Manlius Faustus?' I pleaded, remembering his fingertips tickling my wrist.

'Some very important person from the Palace, according to him. A right rigid prick, if you ask me.'

'I didn't ask. What did the Palace Priapus want? Let me guess: you helpfully have no idea.'

Rodan finally poked his greasy head out from his insalubrious cubicle. A waft of fried onions billowed after him. His large untidy frame blocked the light from the lamps behind him. He never wasted much of Father's lamp oil on making the stairways safe, but used plenty on his own account. 'Don't be like that!' he whined plaintively. 'He says he has a message from his father.'

'Did he tell you this message, or write it down?'

'It's too long. He'll call back.'

'If I knew who he was, I could go and see him.'

'No, don't do that,' Rodan cheerfully told me. 'He said you're not to. He can't be seen with an informer at his official address.'

'The bastard!'

Rodan jeered, 'I told him you would say that.'

I intended to sit out on my bench for a while, thinking. A low growl warned me off. Incitatus. At least he was tied up, thanks to the builders, but I heard him racing to and fro on his length of rope, wanting to get his teeth into someone.

'Calm down, Consul!'

No chance of that. It was one of those intense Rome nights where the heat hardly drops from daytime. Everyone in the building would toss and turn in their beds in misery. Uncomfortable as everyone else, the mastiff barked and howled all night.

37

Most people who knew me would have expected me to give that dog a home. Wrong! I liked dogs, and generally I felt for the abandoned and unloved, but despite my personal history, or even because of it, I would not rescue strays. I've had enough fleas for one lifetime. I had no scope to devote myself to orphans, and I would never live with any creature that frightened me. Consul was more than a handful – he was so big he would always be dangerous. So, I was not stupid.

At first light I roused Rodan. 'Bloody hell, I need some sleep!' he moaned.

'Don't worry. He's going home today. I shall need you to help.'

We collected the dog; Rodan was strong enough to hold him – and, to a dog, he smelt very interesting. I had the address, so we went straight to the house of Trebonius Fulvo. We dumped Consul. He was theirs to dispose of as they chose. Maybe they would send him to a farm as Faustus had suggested. If not, I didn't want to know.

Rodan went home. I stayed and insisted on being granted an interview. Fortunately candidates rose early.

Trebonius breezed into the room where I had been helpfully picking dog-hairs off the couch cushions. I had built up a pile on the bronze arm of the furniture.

He had evidently taken breakfast and forgotten I might be peckish after babysitting his mastiff through a long night. Trebonius was thickset and muscular, with a large, almost shaved head and broad hook-nosed face, where your attention was gripped by that squinting eye with its opaque iris. Had he been leaner he could have passed for an old-time republican senator, but he lacked the experience-lines and gobble-neck. He was a pampered, modern go-getter. The gold rings said it.

'Trebonius Fulvo, your dog has been barking all night and I am too tired to be polite. I want to know one thing. Why does Callistus Primus think you killed his father?'

Trebonius did not waver. He was very sure of himself, ideal political material: my judgement, right or wrong. 'Is that what he meant yesterday? I was unaware his father died. However, I am not responsible.' He lowered his voice slightly. 'Are you telling me his old man was that corpse you found?'

'The first one? We don't know. Primus seems to think so. The only witness who could have confirmed it one way or the other is the second victim, the man who tumbled out of the same chest yesterday.'

'Neat coincidence! Is that why *he* was killed?'

'Seems possible.'

'I heard the first had rotted.'

'As you say.'

'You saw it?' People love the macabre.

'Unfortunately.'

'So why are you here asking questions, instead of the authorities?' Trebonius demanded bluntly.

I managed not to bridle. 'I dare say officials will trot along here in their own time. I won't wait. Two bodies have been found in the course of an auction run by our family business. That makes it my concern.'

'You're hooked up with Manlius Faustus, aren't you?' This man was as nosy about the living as the dead.

'I know him. Back to the point, please. Can you shed light on why Callistus Primus suspects you?'

Trebonius sniffed. 'Isn't it clear? My colleague and I – Arulenus and I – are campaign front-runners. This is on merit. Primus and his family bankrupted themselves on a failed effort to elect Volusius Firmus. Primus's accusation of me is based on raw jealousy. This may be understandable, but it's not a viable position. We had no need to attack his family, nor would we do it. There is no evidence, of course?' Trebonius barely allowed time for me to answer. 'Forget it. The poor man believes he has lost his father; in his grief, he is morbid and reckless.'

I sighed. We did not even know that the first corpse really was Callistus Valens. Even if so, nothing connected his dead body to Trebonius or Arulenus. In fact, nothing connected that body to anyone.

Blackening the Callistus name even more, Trebonius added, 'Primus and company threatened *us* with violence.'

'Care to elaborate?'

'Anonymous letters told us to withdraw or we would be harmed, killed even.'

This was new. 'Do you have those letters?'

'We burned them.'

Why are intimidation victims always so obtuse? 'What made you think the writer was one of the Callisti?'

'Firmus was still standing then. He always was a no-hoper. He needed any help his ridiculous backers could provide.'

'I see. You did not consider that Dillius, Ennius, Gratus or Vibius Marinus could be issuing such threats?'

Trebonius let out a full-chested, derisive laugh. 'A drunk, a wimp, a prig and a human grain bag?'

'Right! One more thing. Have you ever worked with the agent who has also died, Titus Niger?'

'Never.' By now Trebonius could see I had run out of questions and was giving up. With the pressure lifted, he became more reasonable, even helpful. 'I know of him. I can probably find out for you the names of people who have employed him. Get some of them to talk to you.'

I smiled wryly. 'I hope this isn't simply an election promise!' He passed it off, openly accepting that those were empty vows. 'That would be very helpful. Thank you, Trebonius.'

'I'm a reasonable man. Please assure Callistus I hope he finds his old father holed up safely at Crustumerium, just too busy screwing a pretty little goat-girl to write home.'

I would keep the goat-girl comment to myself, lest it inflame the situation further. I was jaded. Otherwise I might not have felt so grateful for his cooperation, nor so reassured by his bland offer to deliver names.

I learned to distrust Trebonius Fulvo as soon as I left. Two men who clearly worked for him were in the street outside with mops and buckets, washing down the carrying chair that must have been used by Trebonius's wife when she travelled around the city. Perhaps they were her bearers: they were sufficiently well built. Close to, the biggest looked as if he could pick up a bacon pig one-handed. The other was not small.

I recognised them. They were the two lark-about loafers who had parked themselves next to the strongbox when I was selling it on the first day of the auction.

38

When I arrived at the Stargazer, Junillus conducted a little mime of amazement at my early arrival. He was deaf, but capable of interpreting a tetchy reply, so when Faustus came along some time later, Junillus acted out another mime for him, warning him to expect a wild beast with fangs.

Faustus bent and kissed my cheek very gently before he sat down with me, miming extreme caution. Junillus grinned and gave him double olives. Faustus took one of the olives and placed it between my lips delicately, pretending to be feeding a particularly nasty parrot.

Chewing morosely, I greeted him. 'Tiberius.'

'Albiola.' He tipped his head to one side, also savouring a big purple Kalamata. 'What's the matter, darling heart?'

While I considered the endearment, I finished cleaning up the olive stone and flipped it onto a noggin saucer. 'Tired out. Incitatus kept us all awake. I took him home, which was an excuse to grill his master. Trebonius denies killing Valens, points out we have no proof, says the Callisti threatened him and virtually accuses Primus of mental instability. Next, he comes over all sweet and helpful, yet as I leave his house with his smooth promises of assistance, Jupiter, I only spy that he owns two lowlifes who behaved suspiciously by the strongbox at the auction. *If* the first corpse was Callistus, I don't suppose Trebonius put him in there, but he perhaps guessed who that body was.'

'Does he have a motive for murdering Callistus?'

'Not really. He looks a bully, but why bother? Yes, Callistus was heavily supporting a rival candidate, but the candidate withdrew because he lost his palace sponsor. It was nothing to do with Trebonius. All Trebonius and Arulenus have to do now is cruise to victory and try not to smirk too much.'

'Did you tackle the two men who work with him?'

'No, I needed to ponder what this means.' Chin up, I admitted to Faustus: 'Talk to you about it.'

He pushed the olive dish over towards me. 'I can prod them. What do they look like?' I described them. A big pig-lifter and a small one. 'Have you spoken to the Callisti?'

'I'm off to see Primus after this.'

'Want me to come?'

I shook my head. 'If you are not needed by Sextus, you could make an official visit to Trebonius, and double-check with Arulenus too. We have two corpses and those men have been publicly accused of killing one. I said you were bound to follow up.'

'Did Trebonius know Niger?'

'He said not. But he could be lying. He's a politician – not intending any insult to you.'

'Thanks!'

His food came and Faustus began eating, all the time surveying me. He did not actively soothe me. I would only have flared up angrily if he had tried. Nevertheless, I calmed down in his presence. As always, he seemed to be enjoying mine.

Neither of us spoke about Petronius and Maia yesterday.

'Someone from the Palace was looking for me last evening.

Tiberius, I wonder if it's a message from Claudius Laeta. The person left strict instructions I was not to bother him at work in case his reputation is fouled by contact with an informer.'

Faustus grinned. 'I could go there for you.'

'I have enough men taking over my life, Aedile, thank you.'

Faustus, who had been dipping his bread in olive oil, wiped his hands on a napkin. At the Stargazer this was not wise unless you brought your own. Most customers rubbed greasy hands up and down their work tunics. Even napkins in the clean-linen basket were habitually slept on by whatever flea-ridden cat the bar gave a home to at the time. I was going to mention it, when Tiberius dropped one of his wiped hands onto one of my own and held it.

Then he just sat there.

My cousin Junillus was about to come and clear the dishes, but decided not to. His disability had made him observant and given him tact. In this, he stood alone in our family.

Even if I had not been a sleepyhead that morning, I could have sat for a long time holding hands like that. In the end I could not help myself but blurted out, 'Are we in love?'

That question you should never ask. In my head I could hear Julia and Favonia screaming in pain to have a sister who so badly broke the rules.

'Of course!' Tiberius seemed surprised I needed to ask.

'Just like that? No uncertainty and misunderstandings? No misery? No endless analysing words and actions? No flouncing in a huff, no writing unreadable poetry?'

'Not our way.'

I took a breath into lungs that felt squeezed by iron bands.

Tiberius Manlius smiled at me. It was his special smile for me. He had smiled like that when he watched me at last waken peacefully, the day he was sure that, through his care, I had survived my illness.

He released my hand so he could pay Junillus. We both had business at the Caelian, so we walked there together, side by side but never speaking. We went different ways that morning. There were questions that needed to be asked and we were the people to do it. Eventually we would meet up and compare what we each had discovered. That was how we worked together.

It was another hot day, so the sun was shining. The glorious sun in Rome: shining, shining, shining.

Sometimes people asked me whether I felt glad I had been plucked from the wet, badly gravelled streets of my childhood and brought here to Rome. I was always glad. Even if I had had no other cause to say it (and there were plenty), Tiberius Manlius Faustus had given me reason today.

Then I reminded myself he was political. I ought to be careful, whatever he said. Even if this reticent man had spoken the truth about his feelings, eventually he would do what was best for his social position and his own career.

Who cared? Everybody thought we were having an affair. Sooner or later we would be.

39

When I saw Callistus Primus, he made reference to him breaking down in sobs yesterday. He acted as if he assumed I had come to ask after his cousin Firmus, given that our auction had provided the occasion of his wounding. For a mad moment, Primus seemed on the verge of wanting to sue us. I shot him an evil look, then reminded him whose guards had hit Firmus and who had told them to do it, in my hearing. We settled on him telling me Firmus was slowly recovering and me telling him Trebonius denied having killed Valens.

'Trebonius claims *he* received death threats and he assumes one of your family sent them.'

'No.'

'On oath?'

'All the gods are my witness.'

'Can you vouch for your brother and cousin?'

'Yes. And my father. Why would we?'

'I agree. It would have been stupid. While he was in the running, Volusius Firmus was favourite. You had no need to blackmail or beat up anybody else. And neither, as I see it, did anybody lean unfairly on you. Firmus dropped out due to—'

'Reasons beyond our control.'

'In dealing with the Emperor, Primus, reasons are beyond

anyone's control, as even the admired Abascantus has been shown . . . So, talk to me sensibly, please, about why you suspect your father has been murdered. Start at when he left Rome.'

Primus confirmed what I had mostly worked out. His father had set off on a normal summer visit to their estate in the country, at Crustumerium. When he failed to send back messages as usual, the brothers had despatched a slave, who returned to say Valens had never arrived at the farm.

'Something was very wrong,' I prompted, as Primus fell silent, musing. 'You were shocked and anxious, so you wanted someone other than a slave to go. You hired Niger to look into it? Someone more responsible who, you hoped, would check more carefully. But why didn't you or your brother go yourselves if you were so worried?'

'We had no idea it was so serious, and we were tied up here. My father had left us work, trying to make good our losses after the useless bid by our cousin. Firmus as well; too many tasks in Rome. Your auction was only one of our schemes – and bear in mind, this action was what my father wanted.'

'So you chose Niger. A man of affairs who acted as an agent for various people here on the Caelian. He had a good reputation, but had not worked for you before. How were you introduced to him?'

'My sister-in-law, Julia Laurentina, obtained his name from someone who recommended him. He seemed reliable. Efficient. Diplomatic. He went out to our estate for us but came back with bad news, worse than we thought: not only my father but his whole entourage seemed to have utterly vanished on the journey. Niger could not even find the litter he went in. Someone along the route claimed to have seen it standing empty by the roadside, but by the time Niger went there it had disappeared. Some farmhand has appropriated it. It's been cut up for firewood or turned into a hay wagon,' Primus concluded bitterly.

I thought it not impossible the farmhand could be tracked down. Now we knew the gravity of the situation, more stringent enquiries might flush someone out. Faustus might organise it. 'Who was with your father? Slaves? Would they have turned on him?'

'Oh, no.'

'If something bad happened, say an ambush or robbery, they may have simply run away.'

'Possibly.'

'Did he have valuables in his luggage?'

'Nothing significant. He doubles everything he needs at the estate and here. He goes so frequently, he travels light. It's a one-day journey if you really push it – he expected to reach his own bed that night. He had no need to carry cash.'

'Thieves might not know that.'

'No, but he has made the same journey many times for forty years.'

Primus looked so miserable I was gentle with him. 'I am sorry. Sorry about your father, and sorry to have to press you for answers. But you do want to know what has happened. So, tell me, what made you fear the body in the strongbox might be him?'

'By the time you told me a corpse had been found, I knew something terrible must have happened to my father. If he's alive, why have we not heard from him? If he was taken ill, he would have sent a slave back to tell us. If he was kidnapped, where is the ransom demand? He must be dead. And whoever did that knows something about us, knew we had a chest in storage. Our father, put in our strongbox: some twisted person thinks that is neat.'

'Apparently so. But who?' I asked. 'You were in such confusion over your father going missing, you genuinely reckoned Trebonius and Arulenus might be responsible?'

'Before Firmus had to drop out of the election, they did bluster and make menaces. Arulenus offered to break my cousin's legs. Plenty of people heard him.'

'You could have made a formal complaint.'

'We did! Father wanted to sue the swine. Arulenus knew we intended to do it. The only reason we refrained is that everyone knows he is already bankrupted by legal suits from that mistress he preyed on and lied to. But fear of a court case seemed another reason those two might go after our father.'

I thought not. A defendant doesn't usually kill his opponent, or they won't get any compensation in the case.

'Well, they still deny it. I myself have only spoken to Trebonius Fulvo but the pair seem to back each other up. Arulenus is to be formally questioned. Did your father have any other enemies?'

'Let me tell you, my father was the sweetest man on the Caelian.'

Primus spoke so fervently I believed him. 'Yes, everyone I speak to seems to have liked him. And, Primus, I can see how terribly his absence has affected you.'

Partly to distract him, I asked Primus if his mother was alive. She had died a couple of years ago. Before that, the couple had been married for over thirty years, a long and loving partnership that produced a close, happy family. Their sons were clearly decent. Their nephew also; Firmus had always lived with them because Callistus Valens and his father, whose name was Callistus Volusius, were brothers; after both his own parents died, Firmus was treated like a third son by Callistus Valens.

As I already knew, all three in the younger generation were married. Secundus had no children. Julia Laurentina, wife of Volusius Firmus, was expecting her first child, although so far it was only known to close members of the family. 'She has yet to tell her mother!' I commented, thinking of Julia Verecunda declaring to Sextus Vibius that she had no daughters pregnant.

'Laurentina doesn't get on with her mother!' answered Primus, rather forcefully.

'I gather few people do. When their paths crossed at the auction, I gained the impression the ferocious Verecunda thinks little of her son-in-law?' I meant Firmus, though in the Forum she had behaved the same to Vibius. Primus humphed and told me I was correct. I said that must have made life difficult while Firmus was standing for aedile, as a rival to her son. Primus agreed it had, though he implied no one regarded Ennius, then or now, as a meaningful candidate. I asked, 'Do you mind if I ask how Firmus and Julia Laurentina came to be married? Was it against her mother's wishes, or have relations deteriorated since?'

I thought an odd expression crossed his face. 'There was a brief period of thaw once,' Primus said, 'which quickly ended. But Julia Laurentina became a loyal wife, to her mother's intense irritation. She has been pregnant before, though sadly none survived. Should a child be born safely now, all connections with Verecunda will terminate. None of us would want her evil influence to affect an infant.' He was hard and definite about that.

Completing my survey, I said I knew Primus himself had a daughter.

'I do.' He did not elaborate.

Nevertheless, I asked whether his daughter had been close to her missing grandfather. At that point, Callistus Primus had to choke back tears again. He told me that his daughter, Julia Valentina, had nearly gone to the country also. She and her grandfather were extremely close (she had been named after him) and she would have been company for him.

He found it ghastly to contemplate. If his young daughter had gone for this holiday, she would probably have suffered the same fate as Valens. Had the girl been travelling in the litter with her grandparent, she too might have ended up trussed with rope, with her frail body also shoved into the old strongbox. I recalled the inoffensive, normal thirteen-year-old I glimpsed on my last visit here, and could understand her father's agitation.

I did wonder about the girl being yet another Julia, but I had already asked too many questions. Twiglets in the Callistus family tree hardly had bearing on my enquiries.

The two men I interviewed that morning, Primus and Trebonius, had similarities. They were of a type, typical plebeians. Both men ran businesses, with all the masculine bonhomie that brings, solid men, self-confident. They knew their work; they also knew it was necessary to act well, to impress colleagues and customers. I recognised that – I played the part myself, in a quieter, 'more suitably female' way. Trebonius Fulvo had carried himself well today, as ever; Callistus Primus was deflated, temporarily crushed by bereavement. I liked him more, more than I cared for Trebonius, and more than the first time I met him.

Before I left, I reminded Primus of that. 'I came to ask you about the body, immediately after we found it. You said, "Why don't you just shove the remains on a rubbish heap like anybody sensible?" I think now you understand why.'

Callistus Primus agreed sadly.

He said if I could help discover anything about his father's fate, the family would be grateful. I promised to do all I could and to tell them anything I found out.

40

What I should have done next was brace myself to invade the government office of the man who had come looking for me last night. If you call on somebody who is not there, always leave a message written on a tablet. Busy people like me need something physical to remind them to follow up. So I forgot all about him and instead I would nibble at details, retrace steps looking for missed clues, make mental checks on whether my deductions were logical – and, frankly, look for lunch.

People sneer, but I say that much of an informer's useful work is done at lunch. You spend the morning struggling to add to your store of knowledge; when you relax over your chunk of bread and salad ingredients, bright new ideas flood into your brain. At least, they do until you spot that the kitchen-hand has left a slug on your lettuce.

Since I was on the Caelian, where everybody seemed to live, it made sense to stroll round to the Vibius house to see if Faustus was there. I was pleased to find he was. Sextus had gone out canvassing, but my friend was talking to his mother, Marcella Vibia, and his father, though as always the father made no contribution. They happened to be having lunch. I exclaimed innocently, 'Oh, is it that time?' at which I was politely invited to join them.

To begin with I kept quiet. Muted slaves served me a

bowl of light food, then topped up everybody else. Today the two grandchildren were at home. Playing in a far corner of the courtyard, they were quite absorbed, though they ran over to us and were given filled flatbreads, which they carried back to their game.

Once the slaves had retreated, Faustus explained, 'We were talking about Sextus's wife just now.' It was the turn of Marcella Vibia to look unhappy, though she did not try to change the subject. Faustus said, 'Sextus is at the Forum, but heckling other people today. I was explaining that he is likely to garner more attacks about Julia Optata's absence. Without going behind his back, I was asking his mother if she can explain the situation.'

He *was* going behind his friend's back. Still, Sextus could hardly blame him.

'We understand it's difficult,' I told Vibia, trying to sound sympathetic even though I thought it was high time people came clean. 'I know there can be good explanations for everything. For instance, I was confused yesterday when Sextus told the crowd that Julia Optata is visiting a sister who is having a baby – only for their mother to declare categorically that none of her daughters is pregnant. Verecunda maintains she would be the first to know! However, only this morning – and please keep this between ourselves – I learned that Julia Laurentina, the wife of Volusius Firmus, is also expecting her first child. She hasn't enlightened her mother either. Indeed, I was told if that child is safely born, the Callistus family will cut themselves off, so its grandmother can't exert a baleful influence. So Julia Optata is looking after another sister in a similar position?'

'I believe they would prefer me not to say,' said Vibia,

unintentionally confirming my suggestion. 'Our Julia is cagy on the subject.'

'They come from a troubled family.' Faustus wanted to explore this.

'Yes.' Vibia would not exchange gossip.

'Where the mother seems aggressively unkind,' I put in.

'Yes.'

Marcella Vibia distracted herself, tempting her husband with sliced eggs. He was gaunt, only toying with food. You could tell he had lost interest in eating, and probably most kinds of personal care. Left to himself, he would fade away from self-neglect. His poor wife spent her days struggling with the problem.

I exchanged a veiled glance with Faustus. He eased the situation by helping me to something, then I spooned more for Vibia.

'You, too, must eat, Marcella Vibia.'

'Oh, don't worry about me.'

'We do,' insisted Tiberius.

'I have to look after my husband here, don't I, darling?' The old man responded, though in a vague, smiling way; he was not following the conversation. 'I can always find myself a little bite in quiet moments. So . . .' Finally, to avoid talking about herself, Vibia addressed our real issue. '. . . what did you want to ask me about our Julia, Tiberius?'

'I don't mean to pry. I am simply trying to understand.'

'Yes, yes.'

'Tell me about Julia and Sextus. They always seemed perfectly happy to me.'

I nearly chortled that how married couples *seem* is never a true guide, but we were trying to tease out information so I only asked gravely, 'Was it a marriage of love?' As a newcomer I could ask that, whereas Tiberius was supposed to know.

'I always thought so.' Vibia paused strategically before carrying on, 'When they first met, Julia absolutely doted on him. He was everything to her. There was never any question that he was the centre of her world – and, of course, Sextus returned her devotion, if in a more measured way.' Another of those pauses. 'She is a lovely, sweet girl. They have two wonderful little children.'

'Doesn't Julia have an older daughter?' Faustus asked.

'Yes.' Vibia gave another short response, not looking at him.

'So Julia Optata was married before?'

'She was very young. It must have been one of those disastrous liaisons that should never have been arranged in the first place. Luckily it was not allowed to drag on; there was a very swift divorce.'

'Who was she married to?' I asked, ever the informer.

'Oh, someone connected to her mother, as I understand it.'

'Ah.' Sometimes a family are so keen on burnishing a connection, they convince themselves a marriage will work even though the couple are incompatible. 'It sounds as if sense prevailed. And where is her daughter?'

'Lives with the father. Julia sees her occasionally. Now that things have settled down.'

'Settled down?' asked Faustus, lightly.

'How old is the child?' I queried, when there was no answer.

'At least twelve, she must be. The marriage was some time ago.'

'Have you met her?'

'No, she has never been here.' As I gazed at this most hospitable, reasonable of women, Vibia felt forced to add, 'I would welcome her, but it would upset Julia. We don't press it. Of course I would invite the girl – she ought to meet our two.' She glanced over to them, still happily lost in their private play. 'It seems hard, but we do what Julia wants.'

'You like Julia?'

'Julia?' Vibia blinked. 'Of course I do.'

It was Tiberius who laughed and teased, 'Come, come, isn't it traditional to have bad blood between a son's wife and his mother?'

'A great many things are considered traditional,' replied the mother of Sextus Vibius, coolly. 'Julia Verecunda certainly makes herself unpleasant – although I think she is like that with most people, relatives or not.' She hit back. 'How did you get along with your mother-in-law, Tiberius?'

'Badly.' It was his turn to be brief. 'She died years ago. I won't insult the woman.' I wondered if he blamed Laia Gratiana's mother for how Laia had turned out. 'How does Julia Optata get on with her own mother?'

'We have never seen much of the woman, luckily.'

'Julia Verecunda was very harsh on Sextus in the Forum yesterday.'

'Yes. I thought he was undeservedly polite to her. But that is how I brought him up,' said his own proud mother.

I moved the conversation forward as diplomatically as possible. 'Whatever happened in Julia's first marriage, she and Sextus now have a good partnership? This is what puzzles us, Marcella Vibia. Neither Faustus nor I can grasp why, in that case, Julia Optata should prefer the company of a sister when, if she cares about Sextus, her place is at his side. If her sister really needs her, why not have the sister here?'

'She wanted to be in the country,' Vibia explained, sounding feeble.

'Yet how can Julia have deserted Sextus at this time? How can he agree to it, apparently without minding?'

His mother trotted out the standard line: 'All I know is, the trip to the country was by agreement. "For the best" was how they described it.'

Impatient with being put off, I decided to speak the unspeakable. 'May I be honest? This is not easy to say . . . Somebody told me there are shocking rumours that your son beats his wife.'

'Never!' His mother seemed startled and shocked. She looked to her husband for help, but found none. 'That is a terrible accusation, Flavia Albia. Tiberius, help me out!'

Before he could speak, I took the burden on myself: 'I only want you to see why we are so concerned. Bad things are being said. Faustus and I accept it may be a mistake. But Julia Optata's odd absence has given rise to cruel stories, fabrications by worthless opponents. You have seen the rival candidates; some are dreadful men. But, Marcella Vibia, as friends to your son, we have to ask about it.'

Marcella Vibia was an old-fashioned type, who tried to resist having to talk behind her son's back. Frowning unhappily, she told us in a low voice, 'The marriage is volatile, I have to admit.'

'Oh?' asked Tiberius, speaking mildly but fixing her.

'They are both strong characters.'

'You mean they *fight?*' He sounded amazed. Presumably that was because of his long-term regard for Sextus.

'Oh, I don't know what goes on upstairs. I never interfere.'

At that, I smiled. 'Mothers who claim to keep out of things are generally covering up!'

Sextus's mother was still upset by the accusation against him. 'He has never had a temper. I taught him to respect even his slaves – certainly his wife! I cannot believe people are suggesting that he hits her.'

'Please tell me honestly,' said Tiberius, quietly, 'have you ever seen Julia looking bruised?'

Vibia's eyes widened. 'People have accidents. Sextus had a black eye once himself. They have moods. Sometimes awkward little stand-offs. One person leaves the house in a rage. Someone refuses to appear at breakfast. Excursions are cancelled unexpectedly, with no real reason given. It happens to everyone in married life. We never discuss it. Oh, I feel so disloyal, saying this!' Finally, Vibia admitted reluctantly, 'I know there have been a few tempests that I did not want to hear about. Now! Who wants to finish lunch with fruit?'

She made it clear she would say no more to us on the subject.

41

I watched the children for a while, struck by how little impact their parents' parting seemed to have. People will tell you very young children are resilient, though in my experience they feel things deeply. Frightened at what may happen if they say the wrong thing, they hide it. Of course, there are plenty of adults, too, who hope that not facing up to problems will make their pain go away.

There could be a very good reason why this boy and girl played so happily at the moment, why they had been exuberant the other day with their father, even though their mother was missing. When their parents were together, was there too much strain? Did they hate it? Children like their home to be peaceful and organised. Quarrels are frightening. Constant stress makes their lives dark and fearful.

'And what about your grandchildren?' I asked Vibia. I still wondered at Julia Optata for leaving them behind. She must have felt sure they were safe with her husband's parents. In fact, I had myself seen that, whatever the wife's position, the *children* seemed perfectly safe with Sextus.

'Oh, I am used to looking after them,' his mother replied breathlessly. 'Young people today – they expect to land everything on Grandmama and Grandpapa, while they go about their own concerns. We never mind. We love having them. It keeps us young.'

That hoary old myth!

But there was no getting anything more out of Vibia: she made the excuse that her husband must be settled in his afternoon nap and left us, taking him.

Tiberius and I were silent while the slaves came to clear lunch.

I remained silent afterwards, fanning myself gently with one hand. Eventually he instigated a discussion by murmuring, 'You don't believe a word of it.'

I sighed. 'He's your friend. What do you think?'

'I don't want to believe it.'

I could not be hard on Tiberius. I merely said, 'People never do.'

There was no strife between the two of us, even on this delicate subject. I knew what I thought about the situation and, even against his inclinations, Tiberius felt the same.

We sat on, quietly talking about other enquiries we had made that day. I reported on my two visits, to Trebonius and Primus. Faustus had been to see Arulenus, who stuck with the same story as his colleague: they had had no reason to attack Callistus Valens, and they had not done so. For their part, the Callisti had made aggressive legal moves to sue Arulenus for defamation and had also complained to the Senate that he offered threats of violence, in contravention of election rules. It had all gone quiet once Volusius Firmus stood down, so Arulenus was hoping to escape further trouble.

'Collusion.' I sniffed. 'Exactly what Trebonius told me. We have a rare instance of two politicians agreeing on something!'

'In order to further their own careers.' Faustus was equally cynical.

He had also visited the wife of Niger. Her pompous agent now had his feet under the table, literally, and had made it impossible to re-interview her. He was using the 'women must have guardians to speak for them' throw of the dice. It found no favour with Faustus, I was glad to see.

'How in Hades does that ridiculous fraud know what was said between the wife and her husband?' he raged. 'As far as I can gather, little was ever discussed at home – still, if I can ever manage a proper interview, there might be a useful detail to extract. Niger didn't keep her entirely isolated. She certainly met this buffoon she is now employing.'

'I want to ask her some time,' I said, 'if she knew another man who was seen at the auction talking to Niger. He bid on a statue. Intriguingly, he also fled without paying and has not been seen since.'

'A ruse? A double ruse, if Niger concocted some plan with him?'

'Not sure. They may have been mere acquaintances, who met that afternoon by chance. After all, Niger did not originally intend to default, and we know he was distraught when the Callisti changed their minds. Backing out damaged his reputation.'

Faustus winced. 'Oh, I heard all about that again from the widow. She is not sufficiently prostrate with grief to stop her insulting the Callisti!'

'I think she is wrong,' I disagreed. 'I am now seeing them as good sorts. The lost father seems to have been particularly well liked.'

At this juncture Sextus Vibius came home. He plumped himself down heavily on a seat, causing clouds of chalk dust to fly up. He seemed disgruntled.

To my surprise, Faustus at once tackled him, and head on. 'What's up? Let me guess – more hassle about your missing Julia?'

'People can be such pigs.' The words had force, yet Vibius spoke mildly.

'Well, you have revealed a weakness,' Faustus told him, none too sympathetically. 'In politics, that is an invitation to attack. Look, we have to talk about this. It's unacceptable that your rivals are harping on Julia Optata's absence from Rome. They are making a really bad accusation about you, and how you are supposed to have caused her to go.'

'Are they? What can that be?' Vibius looked bewildered. Apparently he was one of those men who are wilfully blind. The more gossip about him became public knowledge, the less aware he appeared to be.

No politician can afford to be so obtuse. I was completely unused to it. All the men close to me were as bright as campaign medals. Father, uncles, and now Tiberius. Holding a conversation with them was like scuffling in a constant race to be first to the point. They might not agree with you, but they knew not only what you were saying but why you said it.

Either Sextus was dumb or he was hiding something.

'Brace yourself,' Faustus instructed bleakly. 'People are saying Julia has left home in order to get away from you.' His friend continued to look disingenuous. 'All right, Sextus, I shall have to be blunt. People believe she has left you because you are violent.'

There was a silence. I stayed still, watching Vibius. He did not, like many violent men, instantly rage and deny it. He did not, like the clever ones, claim he could see why people might think that, then produce a slick, plausible explanation. He did not whine, thank the gods. Nor did he blame his wife for any behaviour of hers that had misled people.

Manlius Faustus held his gaze. His old friend looked straight back.

'Vibius Marinus, please tell me you are not a wife-beater.'

Vibius spoke solemnly: 'Manlius Faustus, I give you my word this is untrue.'

'In that case, I am sorry to have raised it.' Faustus was not letting up, however. I stayed out of the conversation. It sounded polite, yet must be painful. 'I have a proposition then, my Sextus. We have to bring Julia Optata back to Rome.'

'I can't do that.' Sextus was equally steady.

'Either you do it,' said Faustus, 'or I can't carry on as your mentor. I cannot and will not continue with a situation that is so pointlessly damaging to you.'

His friend leaned forwards on his couch indignantly. 'I need you! You know the condition of my father. My mother is utterly loyal, but this is men's work. I have no brothers or uncles. Where shall I turn, but to my oldest friend?'

'Don't blackmail me, please.'

'Don't *you* blackmail *me*!'

'It's not meant that way. This is what I must absolutely advise you.'

'She agreed to go.'

'Then she must agree to return.'

Vibius slumped back and looked glum.

'What are you afraid of?' I now asked him quietly. 'How long has she been gone? When did you last hear from her?' He looked grateful for my intervention, yet still said nothing. I risked more: 'If you and Julia Optata have quarrelled, will you allow Tiberius and me to talk to her? . . . You would do that for him, wouldn't you?' I asked Tiberius.

Tiberius remained steely, but backed me up. 'I am prepared to go out to see her, yes.' Sextus was weakening. 'You cannot leave Rome yourself, Sextus,' he continued. 'You're a candidate and remaining in town is axiomatic. You should write her a letter. Ask her to come home. I shall go, taking your letter, and I shall speak to her on your behalf. You're a good man and you ought to be elected. The Julia I have met will certainly see that.'

'She understands!' Sextus assured him.

'Then I shall plead with her to come back to help you. If Albia is willing, I should take her along with me. She can address Julia woman-to-woman.'

'I can do that,' I agreed, despite surprise at being asked.

'No time to waste, then. We'll go tomorrow.'

I assumed that was in case Sextus changed his mind.

42

We began our journey in darkness, fighting for passage with the last of the delivery carts. Faustus provided transport, a carpentum, the zippy two-wheel, two-mule carriage that his uncle used for going down to Ostia on warehouse business. There was room to have a driver. This permitted more conversation than if Faustus had taken the reins, not that he bothered to talk when we first set out.

He picked me up at Fountain Court. I was sleepy-eyed and wishing I could stay in bed. He put me in the back of the carriage, under a rug. He hunched in a cloak, up at the front with the taciturn driver. I felt the jolts as we went downhill, then was aware of curses and sick-making stops and starts as we dawdled through Rome, with all the other vehicles seeming to want to cross our path or travel against us.

We were travelling out past Fidenae, which is ten miles beyond Rome, an easy day's journey, except that from the Aventine it was necessary to go first either through or round the city in order to reach the Via Salaria, the ancient Salt Road that goes north. Rather than out and round, the driver went through. He headed down to the Embankment then up across the Field of Mars, along the Quirinal ridge and so found the Via Salaria somewhere near Domitian's new temple, built to glorify the Flavian family. Personally, I would not have chosen that way. But who listens to women?

Eventually I grew drowsy as the pace grew easier when we reached open country. The air seemed fresher. Light was beginning to filter in, but I fell asleep.

Later, I sensed food was being consumed. I scrambled forward and squeezed in on the driving seat, a narrow cross-bench. As he made room, Faustus handed me a bread roll from a basket, smelling warm from a baker's stall. Always organised, he also produced home-cooked clove-infused gammon to fold inside the opened roll.

The day brightened. Grassland and crops were now glowing gold beneath the summer sun. Cypress trees darkly dotted the landscape, singles or doubles or lines that often seemed planted together for no obvious reason. We passed olive groves and vineyards, heading towards the rolling Sabine Hills, though we would stop long before Reate, Vespasian's homeland. Occasional old Etruscan towns clustered on hilltops in the far distance, each dominated by a temple, each colourful with red pantiled roofs above their rocky grey escarpments.

We were chinking along at a racing pace. Faustus had told me the Vibius estate ought to be reachable today; a bonus of setting out so early was that if we forced the pace we almost had time to return tonight. It would partly depend on Julia: how willing she was to accept our request and how fast she packed for the journey.

Even though his uncle had invested in seriously good mules, this was not to be. We hit a long delay en route. It happened quite soon after Rome. We had reached the bridge over the Anio, which comes down from Tibur. That famously clear river wanders around, crossing both the Via Nomentina and the Via Salaria before it turns towards the sea and is consumed into the muddy Tiber.

Faustus had been sitting up and looking around. I presumed that was because annoying beggars often lurk under bridges. As vehicles slow down, they jump out at you, whining sad stories and wanting money. They can also snatch packages off the back of carts, unnoticed by less careful drivers and passengers.

There were a couple of them lurking under the span, but they were dopey. By the time they called out we had passed them and crossed over. Then, Faustus abruptly ordered our driver to stop. He was reluctant, while still so near the bridge, but he knew Tullius's nephew of old and grudgingly obeyed orders.

Faustus clambered over me, leaped out and set off across a nearby field. Caught short, presumably. The driver and I exchanged glances, then we, too, descended and made ourselves comfortable. For modesty, we chose bushes on different sides of the road, neither of us bothering to go as far as our companion, but staying near enough to protect the carriage.

Faustus was a long time gone. The driver stood up on the footboard, looking for him. He hollered out, at which I caught a faint reply. The driver shrugged and took his seat once more. Curious, I climbed down and made my way across the weedy field in the direction Faustus had taken. There seemed to be a kind of path, but it was one of those wobbly walk-along byways rural people have, which infuriatingly peter out. I had shoes on, not sandals, but was groaning to myself at the twigs that scratched me and the mud underfoot.

How come even parched ground in the country always

has puddles and cart-ruts full of foul squelchy substances into which you always step? So much safer in the city where you can see what's coming.

How do goats keep their hoofs clean? You never see a nanny wiping her slimed foot against a tussock, scowling with disgust.

Actually there were no goats in sight, though animals with unhygienic habits had passed this way regularly. Farm Boy, my husband, would have chuckled at my squeamishness – but he was also a strong lad who would have picked me up and carried me over the rough and smelly parts. He always thought it hilarious that, although I come from a province so remote it is mythical, I am utterly a city girl. Londinium is full of shacks, but it has streets with stalls and verandas to keep the rain off. I want fresh produce and regulations. And I don't want to encounter people my father describes as having hairy toes and three ears.

Bumpkins had been here. Faustus was in a clearing. It had been heavily trampled, and was full of sordid litter. While I tried to work out what the aedile was doing; I murmured, 'This is one of those places the lads of the village – assuming there is anything so cultured as a village nearby – bring shameless girls to fornicate in groups by moonlight.'

'Don't worry, that is not my plan for you.'

'Such a pity!'

'Wait your turn . . .'

The only reason he let me lead him into this banter was that his mind was not really on it. He was intent upon another task he had set himself.

The villagers must come often for entertainment. They had left ash from several fires. Outside the circle, though not very far out, I noticed human waste. On one side of the clearing stood a high pile of junk. This had attracted Manlius Faustus, who was single-mindedly picking the pile apart and inspecting every item he yanked out. In his careful way (the reason it took such a long time) the pieces of old wood, sections of wheel, twisted tree branches, amphorae, odd boots, oily rope ends, gourds, mouldy bread chunks and a half-carcass of a rotting sheep were meticulously sorted into neat lines, in categories of his own devising. The locals who came here were going to be extremely puzzled to discover this array some night soon.

I sat on what I took to be a log, cleaning my shoes with leaves, and cooed gently, 'Tell me your plan then, dear Aedile.'

'I think you'll see.'

'Not evident so far. But I have great faith in you, Tiberius.'

He looked up briefly, holding a dirty old garment between his fingertips. 'I knew you were the girl to bring!' He noticed what I was doing. 'What's that you're on?'

'Part of a fallen tree? Some result of accident or lightning?'

'I do not think so, city woman.'

I jumped up quickly, in case it was horrible.

Manlius Faustus positioned the tunic where he deemed it belonged in his collection, then came across to me. He stood with one arm round my waist, blissfully comfortable. I leaned my head on his shoulder. He leaned away – 'Hair tickling!' Still his arm remained, warm and heavy, fast round me.

We looked down at what had been my seat. It was a long, sturdy pole, weathered but properly shaped and finished by a good carpenter. Once painted, its colours were now peeling after soaking in dew. Faustus kicked aside the undergrowth and uncovered a metal socket into which it would be fixed, when this pole was used for lifting the equipage it belonged to. He picked them up, pole and socket, and carried them over to a carefully assembled group. I saw now that he had singled out pieces that belonged together: three uprights, one leg with a fancy foot, another pole, a half-round roof with decorated semi-circular ends, parts of a slatted mattress base, a shaped back support, various ripped curtains and the rods they had hung on. There was even the mattress, though that seemed to have been used by the villagers for some filthy purpose and he would not let me near it.

'This is all I can find, so the rest must have been used for firewood. If I carry the roof, will you be able to manage that leg for me, Albia? I want to take enough for a sure identification when we fetch it back to Rome.'

I picked up the leg gingerly. I knew, without Faustus spelling it out, I was now holding part of the litter in which Callistus Valens had set out on his ill-fated journey to his country estate.

43

It is an inescapable truth that when two strangers, who are courteous but slightly official in manner, ask, 'Excuse me, do you live around here?' all the locals will say no.

This held us up. We wasted the rest of the morning trying to get somebody to talk to us. Anybody. Only when we found a roadside snack stall did things improve. The stall-holder accepted we were only travellers, rather glum people, but prepared to eat savoury meatballs for lunch and drop sauce down our tunics quite normally. He could hardly deny that he lived nearby. The meatballs were warm; he had fetched them from his hovel, which we could see from the stall.

He knew who the night birds were, hooting rowdies who came and lit campfires. They collected on long summer nights to drink, sing, play crude musical instruments, knife one another in quarrels over women, and exchange stolen goods they had pilfered from passing wagons or from local farms. The snack-seller thought they must have found the Callistus litter and pulled it off the road for sport; he doubted they would have been involved in whatever ambush happened. Faustus agreed because he reckoned if robberies took place at the bridge on a regular basis the authorities would have set up preventive measures. If nothing else, they would have installed a bridge-keeper.

I said, yes, that would be a good way to ensure the authorities knew that when carriages were held up, the bridge-keeper did it.

Although to me the countryside is bare, plenty of people could be found. Once we squeezed evidence out of one lot, others spoke to us. We followed a trail through farmhands and road-menders to a small villa rustica close to the River Anio, where the field labourers admitted they had seen what happened. Their story was corroborated by the semi-professional beggars who sat by the bridge. Locals had leaned on hoes or lain under pine trees and watched it all. None, of course, had rescued the victim or bothered to report the incident afterwards. It was nothing to do with them. The people involved were city folk.

A group of 'foreigners' – that is, from Rome, which was at the most five miles away – had arrived early one morning, driving away the beggars and positioning themselves at the bridge. There were either five or six, or ten or fifteen, depending who was telling us. Before the beggars had had time to gather reinforcements to regain their squatters' rights, along came the Callistus litter with its bearers and attendants. Out jumped the men lying in wait. The attackers were shouting oaths and threats, wielding sticks and possibly daggers. The slaves made a stand initially, but their master put his head out of the litter and gave orders to save themselves; they all ran away across the fields and had not been seen since.

On his own then, the old man was dragged out into the road.

'Did they harm him?' asked Faustus. 'Did they knock him about?'

The witnesses said no; the attackers only surrounded him

and yelled at him. He bravely stood there, giving them shirty answers. He was certainly alive, when the witnesses last saw him, because he was tied up and marched away by his assailants, back towards Rome.

I asked, 'How exactly was he tied up?' Ropes round his arms.

Faustus asked if the witnesses could describe him. This elicited a picture of a mature or elderly man, sturdy-looking, fit enough to walk and to seem capable of making it to Rome.

'What was he wearing?' A blue tunic (they settled on this after a dispute about other colours) and good boots (no contention about that). Faustus looked at me; I nodded. This all matched Strongbox Man.

'What happened to his luggage?' Nobody knew. The country people swore devoutly that the men from Rome must have taken everything. Faustus and I wondered. But we were never going to identify who had plundered the litter. Primus had told me his father travelled light, taking nothing of real value. We did not pursue the subject.

The litter was originally left standing by the road, though it had vanished by the next day. We showed the pieces we had recovered, with mixed reactions. Nobody wanted to commit themselves to saying these parts came from the same vehicle, lest they be accused of knowing too much.

Taking away the victim seemed strange. We rounded up helpers and conducted a search of the immediate area, looking either for a body or for indications of a grave being dug recently. We found neither. It seemed definite that Callistus Valens had been forcibly returned to Rome. Either he was murdered there, or he died of stress during or after his ordeal: the shock of the ambush, the tiring, unexpected walk in extremely hot weather. Then his attackers had disposed of his body in his family's chest in store.

They had known about the chest, so they had known who he was. The attack and abduction had been planned.

Faustus bought rope from a man who had a table beside the road, where he sold nails and small hand tools for emergency repairs to carts. In weight and colour, the rope looked very like that I had seen binding Strongbox Man. The seller denied providing any for the assailants and maintained that he was asleep when the attack happened. Faustus only nodded grimly, then set about tying the litter parts we had salvaged to the roof of our own carpentum, aided by his driver.

We thanked everyone. Now old friends, they cheered us off.

'Were you prepared for this?' I asked Faustus, as we finally resumed our drive. 'Tiberius, were you looking out for signs of the attack?'

'I hardly dared hope to find clues. But I thought it was worth keeping an eye open. Callistus must have used this road if he was travelling to Crustumerium. That's beyond where we're going. It's a long drive in one day, but doable by a fit traveller. I know this road. The bridge over the Anio seemed a good place for an ambush.'

That was when the significance struck me. 'We are going to where you were brought up, aren't we?' He nodded. 'Shall I see your old home?'

'No.'

A monosyllable hardly answered me. I would have pressed a suspect who answered like that, but did not nag Tiberius.

After a while he opened up of his own accord, as I

expected. He told me the estate where he had spent his childhood had been sold by his uncle straight after his parents died. I already knew that his father and mother had passed away within a short time of one another, when Tiberius was sixteen. For a moment I thought Tullius had been insensitive, but Tiberius assured me selling the estate had been at his own request. 'I could never go back. Uncle Tullius wanted to wait in case I changed my mind. I insisted.'

To me, it seemed strange to give up your childhood. But I had never really had such roots and happy memories.

'You learn to live for today,' commented Tiberius, when I said so, 'if yesterday becomes too painful. At sixteen, it seemed the end of the world. I never expected a tomorrow.' Well, that was something with which I could identify. More willing to talk now, he added, 'This is partly why Marcella Vibia complains they saw so little of me. Apart from the fact we lived on the Aventine, when other people came to the country for the summer I would stay in Rome. Tullius has a villa by the sea at Neapolis. Occasionally I join him there.'

I took this opportunity to talk to him about personal things, as we rarely did. 'So that estate beyond Fidenae was your inheritance, or part of it?'

Tiberius chortled. 'Checking up whether I am solvent?'

I dug him in the ribs. 'I already know. My father gave you one of his searches.'

He turned to me. 'So give! What does he say?'

'Now I will tell you – but only because you mentioned Marcella Vibia. She wants you to make something of yourself. If you do try to spread your wings, wing-spreading needs collateral.'

'I'm not short of a bean.'

'You could be. Falco's verdict is that your uncle has fully

absorbed your inheritance into his business. He spent it on adding to his suite of warehouses and he keeps complete control.' Tiberius nodded thoughtfully. 'That may seem normal in a family, but will he release anything to you? You may find him tricky to deal with, should you ever want funds. Luckily, my father said if he can see the history after a cursory enquiry, the truth should be demonstrable in court. To be safe, you ought to get your hands on the old records and have copies made.'

'I don't envisage my uncle and me going to court!' exclaimed Tiberius.

'No. Avoid going to court. Father says you just need to convince Tullius you *could* do it.'

'Uncle Tullius has always been generous, especially when he supported me for aedile.'

'Still, make him acknowledge that some money is yours.'

'I see.'

'Well, you asked me.'

'I did.' At first I could not tell if Tiberius was annoyed. Then he said, 'I agree. It's easy to assume that one day my uncle will pass on and I shall inherit everything, so I don't need to bother now . . . But I am not a complete idiot, you know.'

'I never said you were.'

'No, but you think Tullius has grabbed everything and only grants me small change for sundries.'

'You never have to borrow for a bar bill . . . But I have no idea how you arrange your day-to-day finances. Why would I?'

'Do you care?'

'I care if he is cheating you. As your good friend, naturally I care.'

'It is not the same as the non-emancipated Callisti,' Tiberius assured me. 'I am not his son. Uncle Tullius never adopted me – which, to be honest, makes it easier. Strictly speaking, my head of household used to be a very remote male relative on my father's side, though even he died recently. So I am fully independent.'

'That's good!' I said, sounding cheerful.

'It is!' he agreed meaningfully.

'So, if you go to your uncle's banker, does the man hand over whatever you want?'

'Actually, yes, he does.'

'You never ask for much, though,' I guessed.

Suddenly Tiberius grinned. 'Don't be so sure! I bought a house last month.'

While I got over my surprise, he explained that during my time convalescing at the coast, he had felt at a loose end. Looking around for something to do, he saw and bought an investment property, which he intended to renovate. His uncle was as startled as I, but made no objection. It was somewhere I knew: on the Aventine, a house with a builder's yard alongside it, in Lesser Laurel Street. A client of mine, a woman who had died, once owned it. Faustus and I still knew her heir, a cheese-maker we both patronised.

'A hobby for you?' I suggested.

'Tullius saw it as that.'

'Stretching yourself?' I asked carefully. 'An addition to the family business?'

'Funnily enough, I seem to have the property deeds in my own name.' Tiberius kept his eyes on the road ahead. 'A little project to keep me out of trouble . . . Well, that is what my uncle thinks,' he murmured.

44

The long delay at the Anio bridge had upset our plans. As we approached the small town of Fidenae, we discussed what to do. If we continued to the Vibius estate, we would arrive so late we would have to ask to stay the night. Given that we might not receive a warm welcome from Julia Optata, we decided it was best-mannered to send our driver to warn her we were coming; we would stop at an inn and travel to the house first thing the next morning.

'Then she has time to think about it.'

'She has time to bunk off!' I warned.

Faustus risked sending Sextus's letter to Julia right away. Nervous of the effect it would have, I asked if he had seen it.

'Yes, he showed me. It's very bland. Not what I would write to you!'

'You did write to me.' We had exchanged brief notes a couple of times while I was at the coast.

'What did you think?' He was like a lad, flirting.

'I thought you composed your words too carefully – as if you feared my entire family would read it.'

'Did they? Sneak into your bedroom and look under your pillow?'

I answered him snootily: 'I have trained my sisters to be too scared of me; my brother would not be interested. My father leaves that sort of thing to my mother. My mother is beyond reproach, a condition not to be trusted, so I keep my letters in a locked box.'

He grinned. 'Ah, you kept them, then!'

By that time I was too tired from travelling to contrive a good riposte.

We had to stay at a Travellers' Rest, one that ever since has been known to us as the Cow with No Tail. That is the polite version. It had a real, more mundane name, the Mansio at Fidenae or similar. It was an ordinary mansio, indeed, a no-star mansio of such miserable ordinariness that it had no baths, no real kitchen, one dormitory, with six hard beds where we and several snoring travellers off the Via Salaria had to sleep in our clothes on top of rough covers with no pillows, trying to ignore each other. That was made easier by only having one very small window so it was quite dark, though very hot. Faustus put me in a corner, with himself on the outside in case any of the lumps in the other beds attempted molestation. After an evening at that mansio, they were too gloomy to try.

We had foolishly eaten there. A cauldron of vegetable water had had a lamb knuckle waved over it, with results that caused my still-weak insides to protest. Faustus said even he had indigestion. Once he realised I was feeling ill, which had made me anxious, he pushed his bed up against mine. I was curled up. Despite the suffocating heat, I was shivering. He wrapped himself round me, holding me still, sharing his warmth. 'Don't start anything!'

Only he could have said that. Only I could have found myself the last chaste man in Rome. Why, then, did I think he was close to giggling?

After a time, I demanded quietly, 'Why not?' Silence. 'Why don't you want me?'

On the back of my neck I felt hot breath as Tiberius muttered his reply. Somewhat intense, it seemed to be, 'I don't want a precious memory to be tied for ever to a sordid inn in a tiresome town that I meant never to come back to on, an errand that makes me uneasy, with three hairy nail-sellers from Noricum listening in.'

They were certainly nail-sellers: they had spent the whole evening discussing among themselves the best way to sell Norican nails. My companion had politely gone over for a few words, in the course of which he somehow obtained a bag clinking with samples. I queried this. He seemed very pleased with his free gift and said good nails always come in. I mused to myself on how, unknown to me before, the aedile Faustus was a typical man.

Now, despite the Norican presence, Tiberius whispered, 'Never, ever believe I do not want you, Albia.'

Accepting the situation, I relaxed in his grip. With nothing else worth doing, we both fell fast asleep.

The Norican nailers must have left and hit the road again before dawn. I think of them quite kindly now.

When a trickle of light finally forced its way through the tiny window, we awoke. During the night we must have adjusted position, maybe more than once. Faustus was now lying on his back, with me against his side. He still had an arm round me. It felt natural and familiar, as if we had been sleeping together in one bed for years.

'Stop thinking.'

'What?'

'Every time a busy little thought wafts through your

brain, your eyes move about and your lashes tickle.'

Everything seemed to tickle him. He was as ticklish as a baby. Hair, eyelashes . . . His responses to me seemed ridiculously acute.

The room was quiet. We were the only people left. I fidgeted, scratching a forearm. Creatures who lived in mattress straw had emerged during the darkness and eaten me. Tiberius stilled my wild scraping with a light hand on my wrist, stopping me drawing blood. He spat on a finger and applied it to my weals, so the drying spittle cooled the irritation.

I needed to stretch and must have edged closer against his hip. More of a squeeze than a movement. I never started anything. It was him, all his fault, all his choice.

He turned. Now he was lying over me, extremely close. In the dim light, his familiar face seemed soft and boyish after sleep. I had seen him absorbed yesterday, but nowhere near as single-minded as he was now. He sighed, but if it was resignation, he had given in and welcomed his decision.

'Tiberius—'

'Don't talk.'

I know people who would think this demanded half a scroll of comic dialogue as in a Greek drama. I, however, did not talk.

Tiberius dropped his head and began kissing me. We had kissed once before, pretending it was for disguise, once when on surveillance. The taste of him was just the same, but this was deliberate, him choosing me, me openly showing my response to him.

Whatever he had intended, or had not intended, neither of us could help ourselves any longer. We hardly changed position. We never undressed. The Cow with No Tail was not a place for nakedness. We made necessary adjustments, then held our breath for what would happen very fast and with profound intensity.

My waiting was over. Tiberius Manlius Faustus was making his move.

45

Our driver had chosen to remain at the Vibius estate last night. He had viewed the mansio stabling and guessed the rest. The stalls were not good enough for the wonderful mules of Tullius; the facilities for humans, where they existed, would disgust him. He came back for us early enough. If he thought us strangely silent, he made no comment.

He had delivered her husband's letter for Julia Optata last night, though had not personally seen her. That remained for us. She was a contained, dark-haired woman, still youthful, although she must be closer in age to Sextus than wives tended to be. She was the oldest of Julia Verecunda's children, the first daughter to have been subjected to the mother's hateful régime. She was plainly dressed, perhaps because she was in the country, though since we were coming she had put on earrings and a single-strand silver necklace.

People had called her quiet, and also sweet. I saw nothing of that. I found her guarded, and generally a blank.

There was a physical likeness to the sister I had met, Julia Laurentina. For reasons I could not explain, I liked the wife of Firmus better, even though she had been so aggressive: Julia Laurentina had seemed more honest. This secretive sister greeted Tiberius with a cool nod, then viewed the pair of us suspiciously.

It may not be tactful to visit a woman with marital difficulties when you are dreamy with new-found sexual fulfilment. We could not help that.

The way Julia played it was that she had come to the country because of her anxious sister, who never appeared. I did believe she existed: she had had her baby; we could hear it crying. I worked out what was going on: 'Your sister has problems with her husband? She has left her marital home and she does not want her man to find her?'

Julia Optata nervously confirmed this, begging us not to reveal to anyone that her sister was there.

Quarrels can happen during pregnancies. I don't mean, as male doctors have it, that women are full of turbulent emotions as their poor hysterical wombs expand. My work had taught me that impending children make *men* think hard about their lives. Not always for good reasons.

If the new mother's husband had reacted to fatherhood badly, it would explain all the mystery surrounding Julia Optata's exodus. They did not want him to know where his wife was. It would explain why the pregnant sister had fled to the Vibius estate. If the husband had behaved really badly, Julia and Sextus were giving her a safe and secret refuge.

Questioned by Faustus, Julia Optata said her sister's name was Julia Pomponia and the husband was Aspicius. Faustus did not know the man. Julia Optata lowered her voice and confided that, some years before, this sister had abandoned an approved first marriage, and shocked everyone by running away with somebody of a very much lower social status. What Laia Gratiana would snobbishly call 'a bit of rough', I supposed.

He turned out to be too rough. The couple never had

enough money and Aspicius was a villain. Julia Pomponia's relatives had tended to gloat, though one or two were helpful – but not her mother.

I asked, was this why Julia Verecunda had no idea she was to gain a grandchild? 'Presumably she was not best pleased when one of her daughters went, let us say, down-market?' Optata agreed. Pomponia was estranged from their mother. 'What is her rough husband – a soldier? Don't tell me she fell for that terrible cliché, a gladiator?'

Julia Optata looked shocked. 'No, he works in decorative crafts!' She came clean: 'Actually I'm afraid Aspicius is a hod-carrier on building sites.'

I managed not to snort at her snobbery. 'What's wrong with an honest job?' One thing that might be wrong was that the couple could not afford a child on a hod-carrier's wages. It's poorly paid, fitful work, depending on who gets hired for the day. 'I guess your brick-toting brother-in-law is good-looking?' Julia blushed and said yes, you could say that. But he toted not brick, but plaster, for frescos.

I wondered if Julia Optata had ogled her hunky, handsome brother-in-law too obviously and it had caused squabbling with Sextus. Not that Sextus seemed the jealous type.

That was just me. I had sex on my mind that morning.

Julia Optata addressed the subject of our visit. She had read the letter we had brought from her husband. Now her sister's baby had been safely born, Optata agreed to come back to Rome with us, accepting that the journey should be made that day. She would bring a maid. However, her sister would not be coming.

'She is preparing herself to go abroad, as soon as she is fit to travel.'

I raised my eyebrows. 'Isn't that rather extreme?' Then I backed down. 'Of course, it depends how anxious she is about her husband. I understand.'

'Someone we know has offered her a secure place at an estate where she can live,' Julia explained. 'The baby can romp among the Baetican olive groves, and if Pomponia should fall for another handsome piece of manhood out there, it won't matter.'

Inadvertently, perhaps, Julia Optata had revealed where her sister was going. Luckily, Faustus and I could keep a confidence. He glanced at me, but we made no comment.

The sister, Julia Pomponia, genuinely was no phantom. After Sextus's wife left us, saying she must supervise preparing her luggage, I made an excuse to use the facilities. Wandering about 'lost' afterwards, I saw the two women together. They were in a side room that opened onto a small courtyard. From my position, I could not see either sister properly or they would have noticed me. But this was another dark-haired woman of the same build, similar also to the third sister, Julia Laurentina, at the Callistus house. I suppose the three of them had some resemblance to their mother, though they were all much more modern in style. Pomponia sounded younger than the other two.

Heads together, Optata and Pomponia were discussing in low voices whether Julia Optata really should return to Sextus. It sounded like a conversation they had been having last night when she received his letter, and possibly on previous occasions.

'I cannot keep arguing about this. It will be easier if I go home now. I have already told that couple I will, so it's settled. Nothing will happen.'

'Promise?' asked her sister, sounding unconvinced.

'I promise.'

'And if I stay here, no one will find out where I am?' The sister sounded petrified.

'If you must. My going home should draw off attention anyway. I still don't see why you should be in hiding, when you have done nothing.'

'I will never go back to him! After what he did . . . And I shall never see or speak to her again.'

'She will work out why. You know I think that's dangerous.'

'I have the child to think about now.'

'Yes,' said Julia Optata, in a hollow-sounding voice. 'You will find that changes many things – although other things never change at all. Well, I want to see my children too; you understand that.'

'Go. Go to them,' urged the fugitive, Julia Pomponia. Then she added, still in a frightened voice, 'But please think about what I have said. Try not to see your eldest until everything calms down. Don't insist. Darling, if you go to their house, there is too much chance that family will see you know something.'

'Oh, not from me!' For once Julia Optata spoke up with real spirit. 'Have no fear, Pomponia. Nobody can keep things hidden quite as well as your big sister!'

They were parting from one another, standing up and embracing. I scampered back to sit on a long chair where Julia had left us, looking innocent, while I wondered when and how on the journey I would find an opportunity to report their cryptic interchange to Faustus.

46

Not much was said on our return journey. We took our time setting out and did not hurry: there was no point in arriving back in Rome before the wheeled-vehicle curfew ended. For me, this trip could have been a delightful country idyll. However, it was overcast by a constant sense of strain.

When we first went to the carpentum, Julia Optata asked about the woodwork lashed to its roof. We told her it came from the litter of Callistus Valens, who had been set upon, and she looked as frightened as her sister had just sounded.

She wanted little to do with Tiberius and me. Although she had come with us, she still behaved as if she was travelling on sufferance. Sometimes I caught her chewing her lip as she brooded. Was she worried how things would turn out once she was back with Sextus?

For part of the way I sat in the rear of the carriage with her and her maid, hoping I might glean something useful. But Julia Optata had not exaggerated when she boasted to her sister of being tight-lipped: she never conversed with staff and had placed me in the same excluded category. I knew better than to expect the maid to gossip in front of her mistress, and no opportunities materialised to get her on her own at rest-stops. Julia kept her close, probably on purpose. I gave up on both of them, to allow myself the luxury of travelling up front, next to Manlius Faustus.

He was not a man who smooched or even held hands in front of his uncle's driver. That hardly surprised me. Since I knew him, I was not disappointed either.

Other travellers were fascinated by the pieces of wrecked bodywork lashed to the roof of our own vehicle. People in carts coming the other way actually said hello. At one point a raffish young man overtook us, staring heavily, in a boy-racer chariot that must have cost his father much heartache; he turned round, came back for a second look, then asked Faustus if he would accept anything for the parts. He pressed but Faustus courteously declined.

It takes a real conniver to flog off evidence. My grandfather, for instance: he would have let it all go, for the right price. 'Looks like you have a knack. If you want a career,' I chortled to Faustus, 'you could well become a scrap-dealer.'

He thanked me for this careers advice but wondered if it might put off women. I said the kind of women he liked would love it. He then claimed that doing up the house in Lesser Laurel Street had made him think. Instead of closing down the builders' yard, he might keep it and go into business. I pointed out the previous owners renovated bars. He said, to a plebeian anything was acceptable, so long as it was lucrative. At least he had an insider view now of how much to bribe the district aedile.

That was the most exciting episode on our journey. We arrived back in Rome too early for our carriage to be allowed in. That gave us an excuse to persuade the driver to go round the city to a more convenient entrance than the Pincian Gate. We made him start a circle, but he lost his nerve at the Praetorians' Camp even though they were all inside 'resting' (on wineskins, by the sound of it). As soon as the gatekeepers opened up, he nipped in through the

Tiburtine Gate and flogged down all the way through the Fifth Region gardens. At the base of the Esquiline, where the Fifth joins the Second and Third Regions, we passed the enormous sanctuary of Isis and Serapis. I realised that this, rather than the other Temple of Isis beside the Saepta Julia, must have been where Trebonius Fulvo's dog first bit the priestess. We could have called in to see how her wounds were but by then we were keen to be home.

We did see Consul. He was racing about, barking at vehicles' wheels. 'Don't call him! He'll recognise us and jump in.'

A sturdy man whistled decisively, at which the huge dog slowed up and tentatively returned to his new trainer. A piece of stick was thrown for him to fetch. Consul seemed pitifully grateful to be praised when he retrieved it.

At the house on the Clivus Scauri, Faustus and I closely observed Julia Optata's return to her husband. He heard the carpentum and came to greet us in the atrium. Sextus embraced Julia; she clung to him. Their children then raced out, squealing with joy that their mother was back. His mother appeared, beaming. Even his father hovered, looking gently delighted to see everyone together.

It was all normal.

Absolutely normal.

So normal I would have felt ashamed I had ever doubted them – had I not overheard that telling exchange between the two sisters.

I finally managed to tell Faustus about it as we drove towards the Aventine. I could not remember full details of what had been a nebulous, allusive conversation. 'They knew what they meant, but did not spell it out in case of eavesdroppers.'

'I believe you,' he reassured me.

Not long afterwards, we arrived at Fountain Court. There we had one of those tricky moments when I had to decide whether to invite him in, as if something particular might be expected, while he would have to choose what to do about a perhaps unwanted invitation . . .

Stalling, I said I was exhausted. Faustus also looked weary; he hesitated but suggested meeting tomorrow for breakfast at the Stargazer. Afterwards we could collect the litter parts from the Vibius house where we had left them for convenience, then take these tragic relics to show to the Callisti. They would not have thanked us if we had brought the heartbreaking evidence of their father's fate so late in the evening.

Rodan for once was on the threshold, gawping. Tiberius passed me over into the cold porch of the Eagle Building, almost forgetting to say goodbye. I turned back, leaned in and kissed his cheek. 'Ugh, stubble!' he mumbled apologetically, rubbing a hand over his chin. In his tired state he seemed unsure of himself; with anyone else I would have thought he had regrets.

'That stiff down from the Palatine came back again,' grumbled Rodan.

'Next time tell him I shall come to see him.'

The mules wanted their stable. Their driver had had enough of us. While I stood talking to Rodan, Faustus was driven off.

I walked upstairs. Entering my apartment, I was glad to be alone. I needed to think. I wanted to dwell undisturbed on what had happened in the mansio, whether it was significant in our lives or would prove to be a one-night wonder. I felt I knew the answers – but that was dangerous. My heart had been broken once, many years ago, when I had believed I knew what a man intended.

My sisters would have cheered me on. 'Make him wait, Albia! Make him nervous . . .' Julia and Favonia had never been in love themselves, so they were full of theories. Ridiculous girls.

So I had finally lured Manlius Faustus into bed, and what a terrible bed we had chosen. The bedbugs' bites bothered me, just thinking about it. My bed, as I lay back on it, was a beautiful, expensive piece of furniture that had turned up at an auction long ago and been retrieved for private sale, especially for me. I had shared it with a husband. There were occasionally lovers, none who mattered. I could not pretend: a lover mattered now. My heart and body longed for him.

This is what you miss most as a widow. Not even the intercourse, really, because you can always arrange that somehow, but having someone solid and tolerant to loll against. Someone who drops an arm over you, during the night or early morning, wanting to make sure for himself that you are still there.

Everything about this bed was comfortable – except that I wished Tiberius was in it with me.

47

Double olives were waiting for me at the Stargazer. As Apollonius, today's waiter, jerked a thumb at the place already set for me, the man opposite kicked a stool further out so I could sit down more easily. His grey eyes were calmly welcoming. He had already watched me coming down the street. For once, I enjoyed being stared at.

I wore a blue gown I liked, intending to feel comfortable, and minimal ornament. When meeting a new lover you do not want to appear expensive. They get frightened off so easily.

Despite the very early hour, Tiberius looked newly shaved. He had chosen the neat approach. His tunic was centrally belted. His hair was unnaturally combed down. He was equipped today; I had passed his slave, sitting on the kerb outside, doggedly munching.

'Why didn't we take Dromo to Fidenae?'

'He was sound asleep when I set off. I hadn't the heart to wake him.'

'You sweetie!'

Apollonius dropped my bread roll. He picked it up and brushed it off before he served it decorously in a napkin. Tiberius reached and swapped rolls with me. He blew on the one that had been dropped, shifting dust and most of the cat-hairs it had picked up from the napkin.

I smiled. He smiled back at me. We both kept smiling as we ate.

After we paid Apollonius, Tiberius stopped in the street outside and kissed me, making it lingering.

We walked together to the Caelian, seeing Rome in the early morning, new-washed and full of marvels, like a foreign city when you are fresh off an ocean-going ship. In that first rapture, when you may notice the dead rat in the gutter but do not remark upon it to your bright-eyed companions.

We made our way to the Clivus Scauri where we reclaimed our evidence. The children were going off to school with their pedagogue. Julia Optata was questioning them about it, showing more animation than she had let us see at Fidenae or on the journey. Sextus appeared. 'You know I said I didn't want that school!' Even in front of Tiberius and me, the catch in her voice was embarrassing. She tripped off towards the stairs up to their apartment. Sextus gave us a silent shrug, then went after her.

We knew they were about to have a fight. Clearly they had argued about education before. I felt a chill, wondering how far this would go. I could see Tiberius also now felt doubtful about us bringing Julia home. If we were wrong, and Sextus was prone to violence, anything that happened to Julia Optata was our responsibility. Still, he had looked resigned, rather than angry.

We left with the Callistus evidence, perhaps faster than we originally meant to. We ourselves were too newly happy to want to witness other people squabbling.

* * *

We walked in silence, back down the street and round the corner to the Callistus house. Dromo dragged along behind us; he was laden with the litter parts and moaning.

I was amazed to see, sitting on the stone bench outside and waiting for admittance, Fundanus, the funeral director.

'Fundanus! I don't reckon to find you at a house where you have already conducted the funeral.'

As soon as we pulled up outside the door, Dromo let the litter pieces drop with a clatter. Indicating the pile, Faustus asked Fundanus, 'Does word fly so fast? You know Callistus Valens is the corpse? Even though we have not yet formally checked our evidence with his poor survivors?'

'I don't care what horrible clues you've dug up,' retorted Fundanus. 'I brought my own. Mind you step back and let me go in first, just in case they show any gratitude. I devoted a lot of time to this, and I don't want you stealing my thunder.'

'All yours.'

'What have you found, Fundanus?' I demanded. 'What's so special?'

Fundanus could not resist gloating. 'Only the boots! I bet you never noticed the boots, Flavia Albia? It takes someone clever to realise their significance.' We could see a pair of boot soles poking out of a cloth parcel he was clutching.

I disabused him coolly. 'I spotted the boots. I suppose you are going to tell us these boots were custom-made. The deceased had a walking impediment. His footwear was built up specially, to counteract a rollover?'

'Pronate!' cried Fundanus, a man who used technical terms like weapons.

'I expect you are very familiar with feet – you've bent enough of them, you cheapskate, squashing them onto short biers. Of course I noticed his boots, Fundanus. Your pyre slave had pinched them and I could see he found it almost impossible to walk in them. I imagine his hobbling eventually alerted even you.'

'I've dragged these boots around half the shoemakers in Rome, trying to find who made them and who for!'

'You could have just asked the people who believe the dead man is their relative. Take the easy route.' I smirked. 'As I shall.'

'You told me nobody knew who he was!'

'No one did – then. You have to keep up with the investigation, Fundanus. If I had known you cared, I would have sent over daily bulletins.' Faustus, aided by Dromo, who liked banging knockers, had successfully roused a door porter. 'Shall we go in?'

I had undoubtedly confirmed the undertaker's view that women were uncontrollable harpies. I flexed my fingers at him, like soul-snatching claws, but he failed to get it. He must have noticed I was with Faustus, at whom he shot a corrosive look to indicate the aedile was not punishing me hard enough. In which 'punish' was a verb where the meaning was both corrective and sexual.

'After you!' offered the aedile, smiling politely. Fundanus was impossible to crush with good manners, though Manlius Faustus had a good try.

We were early enough to find Primus, Secundus and Firmus all at home. Two of the wives were hastily made presentable (one in two shades of turquoise, one in amber and saffron); after delaying us while they chose outfits, they wafted in to listen amidst a delicate tinkling of bracelets, though not Julia Laurentina, who had morning sickness.

As we expected by then, the family all straight away recognised the damaged parts of the litter when we led them to the sorry pile on the floor of their atrium. Dromo moved pieces around and turned them, as if demonstrating goods at an auction; he must have noticed how it was done at the Porticus of Pompey.

There were cries of alarm, then tears. Once the family had comforted each other, wept some more, then dried their eyes, we moved elsewhere to talk. It was a squash in their reception salon. The room was full of wide-shouldered heavy men. Manlius Faustus was no stripling but the three Callisti and Fundanus made him look svelte.

The boots were gently unwrapped. As expected, Callistus Primus confirmed that his father had his footwear made with special insoles. He identified the boots and held them on his lap like precious treasures, but surprisingly he did not break down. Knowing the truth, meagre and tragic though it was, gave him more comfort than knowing nothing.

Faustus quietly related all we had been told about the ambush. The sons and nephew were full of questions: who carried off their father? Where did they take him? What happened to cause his death? Was that intended all along? Why put his body in the strongbox?

They had still had no contact from the slaves who had been with him. Since Primus assured us they were loyal, Faustus now said he would make enquiries of the vigiles, in case the slaves had been picked up and held as runaways. The Callisti could not bear to wait, so Faustus wrote notes then and there, using his powers as a magistrate to elicit fast answers; they sent messengers to several cohort tribunes, who were asked to reply to the aediles' office by midday.

While Faustus was briefing the messengers, I pointed out that the attack looked to be deliberately intended for Callistus Valens, so I asked again what enemies he could have had. Again, the family members swore he was a wonderful man, upon whom no one could have wished harm. If he had enemies they could not, or would not, name them.

I thought the brothers' two young wives glanced at one another, but they stuck with what their menfolk said. This was when I regretted that Julia Laurentina, whom I had got to know a little, had been unable to join us that morning. I could have judged her better than the two who were strangers to me. They were pleasant women, but what I called display models.

Fundanus announced that he had carried out a cremation because it could not wait. However, he had collected the ashes and saved them in a nice urn, in case anyone was ever able to claim them. The Callisti were naturally eager to have the remains, which they would solemnly deposit at their family mausoleum.

I reckoned Fundanus would certainly produce ashes for them, in a container that he would swiftly acquire now, at a value such a family would find palatable. If I knew him, he was bound to know a marble firm who would give him a good discount, so in due course he would make a tidy profit from the grateful Callisti. Whether he had really bothered to keep the ashes of Callistus Valens, I personally doubted.

Why should Fundanus have all the profit? As we left, I nabbed him on the doorstep and whispered that Gornia would give him a good price on the green glass urn in which we kept old bits of sealing wax at the Saepta Julia; it was a decent round-bellied shape and had its lid – well, a lid that looked all right on it.

Grandpa would have been proud of me.

'Valens's ring finger was chucked in your discards bucket!' I called after Fundanus, who raised a grimy hand in acknowledgement.

48

Manlius Faustus found the escort slaves.

He had asked five of the seven vigiles cohorts, no small undertaking, even though he had felt he could omit the Transtiberina and Aventine. I went with him to the office, to see whether his query had results.

Faustus was able to dismiss messengers from the Second, Third and Fourth Cohorts, none of whom had anything to report. The First's officer who dealt with runaways had grudgingly come in person because he had had contact with the group we were looking for: his men had picked them up on the Via Flaminia. They must have run away across country from the Anio bridge, following that smaller river until it met the Tiber where the Via Cassia and other roads met with the busy Via Flaminia, the triumphal route down from the north that then entered Rome across the Field of Mars.

'Their story made no sense,' the vigilis told us defensively. 'They came from the Mulvian Bridge, didn't they? Sir, that location causes us a lot of trouble.'

'The Mulvian Bridge is where members of the Catiline conspiracy were apprehended and arrested, allowing Cicero to have their incriminating letters read in the Senate.'

'Sorry, sir, you've lost me.'

'I apologise. I meant that for Flavia Albia. She has an

interest in political history.' The officer thought Faustus was ragging him to amuse me, so I copped a dirty look: an aedile's girlfriend, not merely female and flirtatious but having a dangerous passion for revolutionary events. He wanted to put me in a cell and I would not have liked what happened there. 'Do carry on, officer.'

'There's a big huddle of bars and brothels clustered at the bridgehead, frequented by disreputable elements. That Nero started it – he used to go out there for his private kicks. Folks still trip out from Rome every night to get lathered and fornicate, knowing they're beyond our jurisdiction. It's barely two miles out from the Flaminian Gate. They can get there and back on foot if they're minded, though most take transport of some kind. They have their orgies and come rolling back in all states. My cohort has to pick up the damage. With respect, it's not supposed to be our job to mop up vomit on the Via Flaminia every night – or even to pick up the rich drunks who are lying in the gutter, after their floozies totter off into the night disgusted with them. Sir!'

'I am sorry you have to put up with it. Were these slaves in a bad state?' enquired Faustus, mildly.

'I believe the rascals looked as if something had gone on with them, sir.'

'That's because something bad did befall them, and in particular their master.'

'Well, my lads wasn't to know that.'

'Did they ask?'

'Yes, but it was slaves. Naturally we don't believe any story slaves tell us. They claimed they was told to save themselves, then come home quick and tell someone – but they were bound to give us some excuse. And be fair,

Aedile, nobody had reported anyone of importance going missing, had they?'

'That is because they didn't know he was missing – because his slaves had not been able to tell anyone! Now that people do know, it's probably too late to be useful. So may I have the Callistus escorts given into my custody, please? Their master died; it looks like foul play. I need to question his people. Then they must go back to their kind owners.'

'No can do, with respect, sir.'

Faustus looked alarmed. 'Why not?'

'Once I know runaways actually belong somewhere, in this case the Caelimontium, my orders are always to march them off to the relevant cohort to deal with, which is the Fifth Cohort, sir.'

'So I suppose,' sighed Faustus with a wry smile, 'you got rid of them to the Fifth the minute you received my note indicating who these slaves were?'

'Well, it couldn't have been any quicker – we hadn't got around to processing them before.'

Faustus ignored the lack of logic; he was grim. 'I feel sorry for these slaves. They managed to reach the city and thought their troubles were over, but were picked up by a patrol, just for looking upset and lost. They were only acting as their master ordered. They were by no means runaways.'

'Yes, sir. Now you have explained it, I believe that was the case.'

'How long were they detained in your lock-up?'

The man looked shifty. He admitted the First Cohort had a backlog; he had had the slaves chained up as runaways for over a week. Purse-lipped, Faustus made notes on a waxed tablet in a way that made the officer even more anxious. 'You realise that, strictly speaking, you deprived these slaves' owners of their property, for which they are entitled to make a compensation claim?'

The man apologised for any inconvenience, which is what they always say. Faustus dismissed him.

The next man, from the Fifth Cohort, was in a flap.

'I don't know anything about these, sir, I'm afraid. They was just dumped on me this morning, right after we got your letter. I haven't had them taken home. I thought I ought to recce with you first. I didn't have time to interview them – I rushed right here.'

'Relax. I don't blame you. What's their condition?'

'None too good. But I've told the team to give them a wash and brush-up, so they don't look and smell so horrible. It's all nice people on the Caelian – they're not going to be too happy, I can tell you. I've got the slaves sat down at the station house with bowls of broth right now and the boys are speaking to them kindly. We'll try to perk them up a bit . . . I can have them delivered back home as soon as you give the say-so.'

'Have they said anything about what happened?'

'Only that there was an ambush and they fear the worst. The man in the litter shouted for them to run back to Rome and tell his family. Oh – and he gave them this, to show they hadn't run off and abandoned him, but he himself had sent them to get help.'

Onto the aedile's outstretched palm the officer placed a signet ring. It was heavy male jewellery, its gold now worn on the shank, with a stone of polished chalcedony bearing a carved ship to make a seal mark. The Callisti were river men and boat-builders.

I sighed. It seemed a long time since Fundanus had told me a ring was missing, presumably removed by a killer to prevent identification. This must be the very ring that had left a whitened mark on a finger of Strongbox Man, now known to be Callistus Valens. I could reunite it with his wedding ring, which I had at home, then give both to his sons. At least when they honoured the old bits of chicken bone and dogs' teeth that Fundanus hastily put together for them as a fake relic, they could place something of the man himself in the green glass urn that represented their lost father.

49

Faustus was happy to give me the signet ring, so I took a short walk to Fountain Court where I collected its partner. I tied them together with a snip of red thread, wrapped them in a handkerchief for safer keeping and put them in a pouch on my belt.

I had been neglecting my work. While I was home, I climbed the six flights of stairs to my office, to check for messages. There were none. Such is the life of a private informer. I had a quick tidy of the couch, rearranged pots on a shelf, threw out dead flowers and put the rubbish pail on the landing ready to take downstairs. Rodan was supposed to come up and empty it, but rarely did.

I was about to leave when I heard someone puffing on the stairs. A client at last – and one I knew. All dressed in her smartest stole, up struggled the wife of Titus Niger. Amazed, I brought her in, seated her on the clients' couch to recover her breath and waited for more surprises.

'Flavia Albia! I saw your notice.' I must have looked blank. 'In the Forum. Was that you? I thought it must be, and it said to come here.'

'Oh!' She meant my appeal for witnesses to help trace Strongbox Man. 'Well, we know who he is now, so I can take down the notice – or alter it because we know more about him . . . Now, what can I do for you? First, I don't think I know your name?'

'Claudia Galeria.'

A few swift questions ascertained why Galeria had come here alone. 'I don't like that fellow who has grappled on to me. I don't like him interfering in my business.'

'I imagine he's offering to deal with your late husband's estate?'

'Yes, he is.'

'You don't need a man for that.'

'Don't I? He's trying to take over everything. I was knocked sideways at first, but I am now ready to tackle things. He says I have to have a guardian or it is not legal. This is what I want to ask you about. I saw you at that auction; you looked as if you knew how things are done.'

Well, that summed up my work. I was pleased with her assessment.

'I can certainly help you get rid of that man, if that's what you would like.' He might retreat after a few well-chosen words from me or, if not, I could call in muscle to warn him off. 'Did Niger leave a will? If he bequeathed everything to you, all you have to do is this: find his assets, pay the right inheritance tax – I have an aunt who does figurework; she sometimes helps my clients – then you can enjoy your property in your own right, while you get over losing Niger. You don't want to be worried by anything financial while you are learning to cope with your loss. I can introduce you to a very sympathetic woman banker, if you have investments to look after. I have been widowed myself and I always advise my clients to stay in their house if possible, or at least the neighbourhood they know, and to remain single until they have passed at least two anniversaries.'

'That man said I had to marry again in six months.'

'Two or three years. Unenforceable anyway. Don't worry about it. He is probably scared you will see through him if you wait. He's right, because you already have done! Do you mind if I ask, did Niger leave things behind in a mess?'

'It's all neat,' his wife boasted, proud of him. 'He was organised. He did say if anything ever happened to him, I should marry again and he won't haunt me . . .'

'No, he didn't seem the haunting type.'

'He was all right. I cannot see the point,' complained Claudia Galeria, 'of passing from one man, who wasn't a bad one, straight to another, who could be anything.'

I told her cheerfully I could help her avoid that.

We settled for a proper client talk: what I could do, what I could not do, what she did not require or want, what I would charge her. 'The bonus is, unlike the fool you are dumping, you will never be asked to marry me.'

We laughed. She had been married to Niger for thirteen years. There had been many floors to mop, but basically she did not regret it; what more can you ask? 'I could buy a little slave now to do the floors and that, couldn't I?'

'You could. You'd have to train her to your high standards.'

'I might enjoy that!' She actually chuckled, and I could see she intended to do it. 'It's a relief talking to you, Flavia Albia.'

'This is my job. This is why people come to me.'

Then she said there was another thing she wanted to ask: could I put up a notice in the Forum, like the one I drew up about Valens, to ask people to come forward and tell us if they knew what had happened to Niger?

50

She had a point. No real effort had been made to look into Niger's demise. Once his body had fallen out of the chest at the auction, he had been carried off and cremated. Faustus and the vigiles had had too much to do at the time, calming the fighting factions in the Porticus of Pompey. Afterwards, even with Faustus taking charge, enquiries had dribbled to a halt.

In Rome, if nobody makes a complaint, people can die of obvious unnatural causes yet never be investigated. All you need is to ensure a nice quick funeral and no one contesting the will. That is how murderers get away with it.

I apologised to Galeria.

'It's not your fault, dear. Nobody is paying you for that, are they?'

I could have bragged about my constant struggle for truth and justice, but with such a down-to-earth woman it seemed better to give a queenly smile in agreement.

'Now look, Albia, I would hire you to find out who done him in, but as we just discussed, I'd rather spend the money on a girl to mop the floors. I'll give you what you say is the right money to put up a notice. Then I shall feel I have done my bit for Niger.'

'A wise approach.' I produced a new set of note tablets.

'But, Galeria, before I chalk up a notice, I need to ask some questions. There's no charge for this, incidentally. A man has been killed. Somebody did that, and I need to know what I'm going into.' Galeria looked frightened. I set the notebook to one side. 'Don't be scared. Look, I don't try to catch a murderer without having some idea about who he might be and where he might come jumping out from. This is for my safety, and your own.'

Galeria saw my point; she toughened up. 'I'll have a broom ready to whack him.'

'Excellent!'

'But what about you, dearie?'

'Don't worry about me. The last time a killer came looking for me, I shoved him off the balcony. That's why the window is blocked up.' Impressed, Galeria looked over at the folding doors, here in the main room of my office, once a good feature but now boarded with builders' safety panels. 'Now, we have to start with Niger. I'm going to ask you about his work in general, then what he had been doing specifically for the Callisti.'

When I interviewed her before, I had thought Claudia Galeria knew little about how Niger spent his time. Nevertheless, like many, she kept her eyes and ears open. She had quite a lot to tell me.

Until recently, Niger had worked for various people, one of whom was an extremely rich woman called Julia Terentia. Through some connection of hers he had been introduced to the Callistus family. 'That all started when they were looking for an election agent.'

'To help Volusius Firmus when he was standing for the aedilate?'

'Niger was finding things out for him to do with the rival

candidates.' Oh, that job! The sleaze pitch. I knew all about that. 'It fell through, though.'

'Yes, the man had to stand down . . .' A thought struck me. 'Firmus has a wife I've met, called Julia Laurentina. I don't suppose she is any relation to your Julia Terentia?'

'Yes, of course!' Galeria exclaimed in surprise. 'They are sisters. Laurentina asked Terentia if she could recommend an agent. That was how my Niger was offered the work.'

Another sister! Diana Aventina. How many Julias were there? (Four so far, plus a brother). And how intricately tangled were their links in the events I had to investigate? Claudius Laeta had given me a hint. I definitely ought to go back to him in the very near future, especially if he sent the man from the Palace who wanted to give me a 'message from his father'.

'Tell me about Julia Terentia.'

'She's the one who got away from her mother. She found her own husband well, she's done it twice.'

'Someone told me she was an unpleasant woman.' That had been Nothokleptes, not that I had taken his word.

'She just speaks her mind freely,' said Galeria; we nodded wisely.

Julia Terentia had inherited wealth from her first husband, for whom Niger had worked as a general negotiator. Terentia then remarried, to a sponger, Galeria called him, though he had not drained her resources entirely, as shown by the fact Terentia was still a regular benefactress to others. Her Saturnalia gifts to clients included the glass beakers I had already heard about. She also supported struggling relatives of her own.

'Terentia has one sister who is married to a difficult man

and has a terrible time. My Niger used to take money to them whenever Julia Terentia gave them a handout.'

'Handouts to Julia Pomponia?' I guessed. I was interested that the one who had run off with the hod-carrier was being helped by at least two of her sisters, Optata and Terentia. Were they all secretly banding together to defy their mother?

'Yes. Pomponia's husband works, but he gets in low company and drinks it all away. Every time Niger went there with a purse, he was supposed to warn them it was the last time.'

'Hopeless.' Every time someone says *this is the last time*, it impresses spongers less and less. Even I was seeing the wealthy Julia Terentia as a soft touch, though we had never met. 'Then Terentia procured further work for Niger, with the Callisti. Let's discuss that, Galeria.'

'He should never have done it. The election work was all right, but then it went wrong on him.'

'You mean, the strongbox? He thought not paying for it would damage his reputation?'

Galeria shook her head. 'He was upset, yes. But he could have told people the Callisti had had a disagreement among themselves, so it wasn't his fault. I said no one would care – well, he was only obeying their orders. But something much worse had happened. Something to do with the old man. Niger was going spare. He said he just didn't know what to do for the best.'

'Over what, Galeria?'

'There were two things, really. First, Albia, when he was asked to go and see that body – you know, the one that was found in that strongbox . . .' Her voice faltered. 'The box where some villain put my Niger afterwards.'

I helped her out, as she bit back tears: 'The Callistus family asked him to go to see whether the first corpse was their father. Niger said not, although I can tell you for certain that it was Valens. So what happened? Did Niger accidentally get it wrong? Was the body too degraded to recognise?'

Galeria was quick to defend him. 'Well, be fair, Niger didn't know the father well. He only met him once. And he told me that body was horrible. He could hardly bear to look at it.'

'But?'

'Niger was dead set in his mind that something else had happened. He had already been to their estate to see if he could find out why Valens had disappeared. He came up with nothing. Absolutely nothing. So he was convinced the old fellow had just bunked off for a few days, in his litter, taking his escort slaves, maybe a tryst with some secret girlfriend.'

I balked at that. Nothing had ever suggested Callistus Valens had had a mistress – or that, if he had, he needed to keep it hidden from his family. Some men like the thrill of leading a double life but everyone said Valens was a dear person. I doubted whether his relations would interfere.

Galeria saw my doubts. 'Or a gambling party? Men in a barn, playing with counters for a lot of money?'

'Two problems there, I think. The Callisti all like a flutter, but they generally bet on chariots. More importantly, at the time Valens was perturbed that they were short of cash, after their election efforts went bottom-side up. Valens doesn't sound like a man who would play games of chance, with meaningful stakes, at the same time as he left his lads desperately trying to recoup funds.'

'Well, then. My Niger was very soft-hearted. He didn't

want to have to tell those relatives that corpse was their father, not when it was in such a terrible state. If he had said it was, they would have rushed down there. He didn't want them to look at it. And he wasn't sure. Albia, he really was not sure.'

I managed not to show what I thought. Did Niger, the soft-hearted idiot, never think that the missing man's absence would eventually need an explanation? The Callisti would have to find out one day that Valens was dead.

'He should have just told them, shouldn't he?' Galeria quavered woefully.

'If he recognised the dead man, I think so.'

'The point is, he couldn't tell for certain. The funeral director hadn't bothered to do up the corpse nicely. He was all green and blue and bloated. Only afterwards – and this is the second thing, Albia – someone else said something to him, so poor Niger realised it must have been Valens.'

I sat up slightly. 'Who said what?'

Galeria saw how significant this was. 'A man he knew, Albia. Talking about the strongbox at the auction. After Niger bid for it, this fellow came up and got talking to him, then made a peculiar joke. He said that the Callistus brothers had just bought back their father's sarcophagus, hadn't they? Niger told him to be more sympathetic, and the man said he'd been told Callistus Valens had had it coming to him. He had had it coming for years and now he had paid.'

I tried to stay calm. 'Who was this man? Who was Niger talking to?'

'He wouldn't say,' sighed Galeria. 'Afterwards, talking to me, he felt the man knew more than he should do – he must have been there at the murder. Apparently he was that sort of man. Very strong. Handy with his fists. Up for any crooked scheme, if it would make money. Niger said there was nothing we could do about the situation so he didn't want me to know any more. It was safer if he didn't tell me who the man was.'

But I knew who it was. Our staff at the auction had witnessed that conversation. I remembered them telling me they had seen Niger talking to the man in the puce tunic.

That bastard had looked suspicious all along. All afternoon I had worried about what he was up to. I'd watched him bid for *The Boy with a Thorn in His Left Foot* as if that accounted for his presence. Then he never paid for it. All along, his real interest must have been the strongbox.

'The thing is,' said Claudia Galeria, 'my Niger had a conscience. He was always very straight. I worry that he might have gone to see the man again, and maybe the man didn't like to be asked about it.'

I believed it. Puce Tunic was stupid to have made his veiled comments to Niger but killers are often stupid. Perhaps, later, he regretted what he had said. He would certainly have seen his mistake once an anxious Niger turned up and tackled him. Cornered and threatened with exposure, a man who had finished off Valens might well kill Niger to silence him. After which he had lacked imagination to think up a new solution and just stuffed the second victim into the same strongbox as the first.

That left me with the urgent question: who was Puce Tunic?

51

There was nothing useful I could say until I discovered more evidence. I agreed to write a notice in the Forum requesting information.

As we drafted out wording, first briefly describing the victim, I mused on how different physically this couple had been. Galeria had now lost weight, presumably through grief, but she remained heavy in the body. I reckoned she ate to fend off troubles. Despite mundane appearances, her life had been a constant swivel between outward complaisance and inner anxiety.

Niger, on the other hand, had been so thin because he lived on his nerves, a man in a precarious profession, yet he had been good at it and was probably more secure than he let himself admit. When we first met, I had thought Galeria mouldered at home in ignorance of his work, but it was clear today that Niger had brought worries to share with her. He had only refused to name the man who knew about the murder of Callistus Valens because of the obvious danger to her.

Would that man see my notice?

I took Galeria with me. I let her watch me select a decent place and carefully chalk up our request: *Titus Niger, negotiator, fifty years old, slim build, found lately in the Porticus of*

Pompey, murdered. For information leading to his killer, his grieving friends will show their gratitude. Contact Flavia Albia, the Eagle Building, Fountain Court, the Aventine.

I remembered that his face was covered with acne scars, but I omitted that as a courtesy.

My original notice about Strongbox Man had been rubbed out by some apothecary to make space for his advert for virility pills. Rome contained quite enough virility.

After Galeria left me, I cleaned the wall and, as if scrawling arena graffiti, I wrote in different handwriting (I have several): *Defaulter in puce tunic, I know you and where you live!* The threat was meaningless, but it might shake him up.

I had not signed the notice, an omission that probably contravened civic regulations. It also seemed best not to leave a contact address. Apart from thwarting any advert-monitoring aedile, I did not want the killer turning up at my apartment. Rodan would probably let him in and serve him wine and almond biscuits.

I had not yet finished adorning public monuments. I do like to be thorough. I amused myself creating other anonymous works of art on behalf of Sextus Vibius. Faustus had not asked me for poster mischief, but he was an innocent. I played rough. The campaign was ending and we needed to turn screws. I discovered wall art came naturally to me.

Have a drink with Dillius, but be careful, he'll want several!

Arulenus Crescens is the aedile for us, says the guild of good-time boys.

But he doesn't pay up! sighs the eunuch Veronillus.

All the Forum purse-snatchers are supporting Trebonius Fulvo.

Some vicious rumour-monger had written *Marinus misses*

his wife – or does he just miss thumping her? I scrubbed that out and chalked instead the subtly suggestive, *Salvius Gratus is getting married: does his new wife know what I know about him?* Dodge the fallout from that, supremely pompous brother of most annoying Laia!

I nearly put up *Ennius is too fond of his mother* but even I declined that one. It was the really polite way of phrasing a really scurrilous insult, but I knew my own mama would be disappointed in me. A good mother's influence can be very far-reaching. Almost as far-reaching as that of a bad mother, as Ennius Verecundus and his sisters, the four stroppy Julias, undoubtedly had cause to know.

I strolled along to read the *Daily Gazette*. It told us the usual censored crud: news of far-fetched military victories by Our Master and God in Pannonia, celebrity births and scandalous elopements, relieved only by some wag denouncing on an unofficial pillar the absence of good poetry, worded as if advertising for a lost kitten: *Last seen mewing plaintively in the Minervan Games, when shall our hearts be lightened again by cunningly wrought epithets, when thrilled by sweetly scampering meter – all is now flea-ridden flattery and squeaking drivel framed for tyrants.* Someone must have listened to one of the Emperor's praise-your-Master-and-win-a-prize-from-him competitions. This crtitic was so angry about literary standards, he was risking the order to commit judicial suicide. Whoever he was, I could rule out any candidates for magistracies, and that went from plebeian aedile right up to consul.

Feeling surly about public life (hardly an unusual mood for me), I returned to the *Gazette*. In the individual notices at the end, I saw that the Callistus family had formally announced their head of household's death. No details of the attack on him were provided. In place of a funeral, they said a memorial would take place tonight, at a mausoleum on the Via Appia. I decided to go home, rest up for the afternoon, then join them for the ceremony. I could take Valens's rings to give to them there.

52

I spent that afternoon alone in my own apartment. I did a lot of thinking. It was the best kind: when your body lies at rest, good ideas flow into your brain unprompted.

Afterwards, I had the usual outfit dilemma, trying to decide whether the Callisti would favour white or black clothes for funerals. Whoever you ask will always argue about what is supposed to be traditional. I guessed the women would consider white more fashionable (and flattering), while the men would deem dark colours more appropriate on a sombre occasion.

I went in white. I owned no tunics that would qualify as brown or black. The nearest I had was the colour of damson juice and that had spangles on its hem. I had sewn them on myself so could easily unpick them, but why lose good decoration? Since my white gown had once been criticised as too gauzy, I wore a thick under-tunic, so I would be extremely hot. I sent down to the Saepta and borrowed Patchy again.

It was the most crowded funeral I had been to. Half the Tiber must have been empty of boats and boatmen that evening. Everyone who worked on the water must have known Callistus Valens at least slightly and many thought enough of him to trek out to his memorial. With no body to burn, the function was at least short. It took the form of a funeral feast, to celebrate a man for whom admiration and affection flowed freely.

In the sweet haze of meats being barbecued, I hunted for Primus, determined to give back his father's rings in time for them to be placed in the urn. In fact Primus and Secundus decided to keep one each. They thanked me, Secundus saying it would help to have these memorabilia. The brothers seemed to be friends again. They told me how the funeral director had been so thoughtful he had even included a finger in the ashes urn, symbolically saved for separate burial as is sometimes done.

'Yes, Fundanus is a kindly man!' I agreed gravely. 'No formality is too much trouble.'

A sacrifice had been made on a portable altar. It stood outside a small moss-covered private tomb, decorated with carved ships and oars. Valens's sons and nephew placed the green glass urn inside in a columbarium compartment, with prayers and brief speeches. Demountable seats and couches rapidly appeared and everyone sat down for a decent tuck-in.

They were a sensible family. Even their smart wives were moving around the company today, making the right noises, letting serious old cronies of Valens bore them silly with reminiscences, comforting anyone who wept. I thought it a shame Volusius Firmus had been prevented from standing as aedile: from the way he was talking to people here, he would have worked hard. Who knows? He might even have been honest.

The young daughter of Callistus Primus, Julia Valentina, was carefully handing round dishes of funeral meats. After she served me, I said to her father, 'You brought her up well, I can see.'

'We're proud of her.' As usual he cut off further discussion, making an excuse to go and greet someone. Undeterred, I sat down for the meal alongside Julia Laurentina, so I could ask her about the girl.

Laurentina kept a hand on her pregnant belly, fingers spread, to tell the world she was entering the sacred role of motherhood. The fact it was supposed to be a secret made no difference. I politely asked after her health and condition; she recounted the history of three children she had lost, before or soon after birth, then claimed she was being wise this time, while tearing into a charred leg of some funeral roast and washing it down with herb-infused wine.

I picked at a wheat cake. It was flavoured with cinnamon, very delicate. 'Young Julia Valentina served me this. She is so very shy and sweet, a credit to her upbringing. I can tell how fond of her you all are . . . Will you tell me about her? I know her parents are divorced.'

Mellowed by drinking toasts to her dead father-in-law, Laurentina shot me an astute glance, but started without much of a struggle. 'The marriage failed pretty well instantly. My niece was born after the divorce. Her father claimed her, as you see, though her mother engaged in a bitter battle to recover the child.'

I was startled. 'Good heavens. That sounds as if Primus snatched the baby.'

'No, I did!'

'What?'

Julia Laurentina looked amused by my shock. 'I had volunteered to be with my sister during her pregnancy and at the birth. Is that what you came digging for?'

It took a moment for her choice of words to strike me. 'Valentina's mother is your sister?' Which one was this?

'Julia Optata. Surely you knew?'

'Actually, no.' I was even more surprised. All I knew was that Sextus Vibius was polite in public to Primus; Faustus had said they had some connection, which he, culpably, never specified. Thanks for nothing, Aedile. That Sextus had a stepdaughter at the Callistus house might have been useful to know.

It was still unclear why his wife rarely saw her eldest child, though bad feeling between Primus and her might be the explanation. It did add colour to the elusive conversation I overheard at Fidenae between Optata and her sister Pomponia. In that, Julia Optata was hankering for maternal contact with her daughter yet, for some reason, Pomponia had warned her not to press for it just now.

'I gather there is coolness since the divorce, but do you see anything of Julia Optata?'

Laurentina, who lost no opportunity to be unpleasant, was enjoying my unease with the new information. 'Sometimes she is allowed to visit our house. Primus gives her a regulated meeting with her daughter. The two have lunch together in the garden, or something on those lines. She claims Primus makes it difficult, though I think he has been extremely gracious. We don't encourage such meetings but they are by no means forbidden. Valentina is always upset afterwards and takes days to settle.'

'And what of her mother's feelings?'

'Oh, Julia Optata doesn't speak to me! She still blames me for taking her baby.'

I chewed another wheat cake, catching crumbs in my cupped hand. 'And why did that happen?'

'After Valentina was born, Julia Optata was weak and in a sorry state, very low in spirits, lethargic and weepy. With the birth safely over, I was free to return to my husband. Most people thought I helped Primus to ensure a quiet life here. But no. I judged my sister incapable of looking after a child. While Julia Optata was sleeping, I simply picked up Valentina from her crib and carried her home with me. We organised a wet nurse and she has thrived ever since.'

'A hard decision for you, though?' I wondered whether the new mother's convenient sleep had been assisted by potions.

'No. I shall never apologise for it.'

I considered their wider family. 'What does your mother say about all this?'

Laurentina laughed softly. Under white veiling, complicated gold earrings tinkled at some movement. 'She gave me all Hades for interfering. Julia Optata was her eldest and in those days she could do no wrong. Well, not until our father married her again, into the Vibii, who were old friends of his. Mother was furious he did not consult her. Father died not long after. I suspect the sustained venom helped him into the underworld. Mama was equally wrathful that my sister went along with it, so they fell out too.'

'Vibius Marinus comes in for loathing, merely for being male?' I asked, remembering how nastily Julia Verecunda had treated him at that encounter in the Forum. 'I have the impression your mother does little to further her children's marriages – even where she arranged them.'

'Understatement!' Laurentina chortled frankly. 'Everyone knows how much she interferes. At the moment she's determined that both my sister Terentia and I will leave our husbands.' Terentia, the rich one, was now the only one of the four sisters I had not met. 'According to Mother we should marry them, make them dependent on us, then leave them in the lurch. We're all constantly nagged about it. At least Mother will leave Pomponia alone now she has escaped from Aspicius.'

'So tell me about that. I gather he's handsome but given to fights. Did she leave him because he frightens her?'

'Oh, he does! Mind you, he's always been the same so we can't see what's different this time.'

'The baby,' I deduced. 'Do people realise where she has gone into hiding?'

'It's pretty obvious – especially since that fool Vibius made his public pronouncement and told the whole world. His wife will beat him up over that, now she is home with him.' Laurentina saw my expression. 'Julia Optata will be furious he was so stupid.'

'All a sorry story of friction!' I commented. 'But you and Volusius Firmus have found genuine happiness?'

Laurentina groaned with relief. 'I can't tell you how it felt to come to a house full of peace and good feeling! I will never give that up. Vibius suits me fine.'

'And your sister Terentia feels the same about her husband?'

'She can do as she wants, of course. She has money. Mother never forgave her for going off and finding herself a millionaire first time round.'

'I did hear a snide rumour that her second husband sponges off her?'

'He's a joke. Still, what if he does cost money? She can afford it and he is what she wants. He drinks,' snapped Laurentina, swigging wine herself. 'Perhaps he guzzles to obliterate the fact that our terrible mother is endlessly trying to get his dear wife to leave him while, actually, he is attached to my sister and cannot bear to lose her. Everyone is so sure he cares only about Terentia's money that they don't see his loyalty. He truly loves my sister and she him. Is that so unbelievable? That was why she married him. In our family some of us treasure love. We have seen what happens without it. My mother,' Julia Laurentina announced, as formally as a trial judge, 'is an unforgiving, brooding, vindictive, manipulative bitch. She never forgets a slight and devotes herself to working against those who offend her, stand up to her, or boldly ignore her.'

I was thoughtful. So here we had a situation in which two of Verecunda's daughters (Laurentina and Terentia) had defied her and were sticking with their marriages while a third (Pomponia) had just given up on a man who seemed a threat. What about the fourth? 'Does your mother want Julia Optata to leave Vibius Marinus?'

Laurentina shrugged her shoulders. Her white stole descended and she replaced it gracefully, paying more attention to it than to me.

'That could explain some tension in their house,' I speculated. 'I've heard Julia Verecunda called the mother-in-law from Hades, excuse me saying so. Julia Optata has not been forgiven for making a happy second marriage?'

Laurentina then bestirred herself. She flashed me another of those wry glances. 'That assumes you think she and Vibius *are* happy!'

'Don't you?'

'I know what she's like.' Much as I wished it, she did not elaborate.

I sat quiet, nursing a wine cup, which I did not drink from, while my companion slumped, lulled by funeral wine. Eventually I reminded her of her secret suspicions the first time I saw her. 'Julia Laurentina, you feared from the start that the strongbox body might be your father-in-law, didn't you?'

'And wasn't I right?' she snarled, more her previous snappy self.

'Were you aware Valens had an enemy?'

'Everyone loved him.'

'Yet somebody went after him. Someone lay in wait and hauled him back to Rome. Whether they intended to kill him is uncertain, but they did, after which they stuffed him into that chest to rot. So somebody really did *not* love him.'

Julia Laurentina gave me a wide-eyed unpleasant stare. 'Oh, Flavia Albia, do you say somebody *hated* him?'

I almost felt she was taunting me for some error on my part, even if it was simply my ignorance. 'Do you know who? Are you protecting them?'

'No.'

'No idea even who it might be?'

Her answer was to stand up and leave the table, becoming impossibly high and mighty. 'This is my father-in-law's funeral. I suggest you stop your vile theorising right here.'

She was not sober. There could be several reasons for that: she was simply a lush; she was covering some personal unhappiness; or she did not want to face up to what had happened to Callistus Valens. I thought the latter. But she did not intend to tell me, and I would not break her resolve. She was correct: this was not an occasion for me to persist.

However, she suddenly turned back to me. 'One thing is certain,' she announced dramatically. 'If we ever know who caused the death of Valens, this family will deal with them!'

I acknowledged the bravado with a cool nod. In my business, you hear things like that at funerals all the time.

53

Not long afterwards, I left discreetly. I had shown my face. I had returned the rings. There seemed little chance of shedding more light on the death of Valens or the subsequent murder of Niger.

As I rode Patchy slowly back along the Via Appia, thoughts of Titus Niger gave me pause. Was it possible the surviving Callisti believed Niger had had some involvement in what happened to Valens? If they had such brooding suspicions, what happened to Niger himself could be the result. They would want to avenge their father. The three Callisti were hefty men who knew their minds and would not shirk a duty. I could entertain the idea that *they* might have killed the agent. It would be appropriate retaliation to incarcerate his body in the strongbox that had once contained their much-loved head of household.

Why would they distrust Niger? Perhaps because, like me, they noticed him talking to Puce Tunic at the auction. Racking my brains, I thought they had left the scene after that, not before. Niger was a relatively new employee for them, untried at best, and Primus had distrusted Niger's report after viewing Valens's body. If the Callisti suspected Puce Tunic of involvement in Valens's death, they might view Niger's speaking to him as proof of collusion. From what Galeria had told me, there had been no collusion, but the Callisti had not heard her story and, anyway, they were hot-headed.

Keen to solve this puzzle, I realised I was close to the villa of Claudius Laeta. It was evening, though not late. It seemed a perfect opportunity to call and see whether he had sent that persistent man to me at Fountain Court.

I was to be cruelly disappointed. The great double doors to the fine retirement villa were now swathed in dark garlands. Two sombre cypress trees stood at either side of the entrance. I knew before I knocked what the story would be. Claudius Laeta, the mighty imperial freedman, had gone to the gods of his own accord before Domitian could require it of him prematurely. He had lost his feud with the upstart Abascantus. He would be unable to assist Faustus and me. For Tiberius Claudius Laeta, there would be no more plotting.

54

My father's old crony had remained meticulous in his final illness and, though unable to write, he had summarised everything he had discovered, leaving a long message for Faustus and me in the charge of his son. He, too, was an imperial freedman, working in a secretariat. The slaves at the villa, who obviously respected their late master more than his son, sneakily gave me detailed instructions for finding Junior in his workplace lair, even though he had tried to put me off.

I had to go to Domitian's Palace. At least I knew the Emperor was not there, but still abroad. He rarely lived in Rome, preferring his fortress villa out at Alba Longa. That had not stopped him having another wondrous complex created for him here by the great architect Rabirius. I had to leave Patchy at a cryptoporticus gate and climb the steep Palatine on foot, through a long covered corridor. At least with the Emperor away, the Praetorian Guards were relaxed. My father had many a tale of having to bribe or bully his way past them, but today they were so relaxed I never saw any.

People came to the Imperial Palace to gawp at its inventive rooms with their exquisite décor. The crowds left behind dust and detritus to be swept up from the multicoloured marble. That meant I could borrow a broom and slide myself into the bureaucratic areas. The Palace slaves wore white, so my funeral outfit came in handy. All you have to do is keep your head lowered and look miserable while you continue very slowly sweeping. Everyone thinks you are a domestic slave. They don't even lower their voices while discussing their best friend's adultery. They pay over bribes right in front of you. If I had wanted to assassinate Domitian, I could have gone all the way into his bedroom and done him in with the borrowed broom.

I had good directions and soon found my way to the right office. It was a massive space with similar polished marble to that in the public rooms, but had comfortable loungers for bored bureaucrats to snooze on. I swept around these noble reading couches conscientiously before emitting a gentle cough, leaning my broom against a stupendously ornate scroll cupboard, and telling the lone occupant who I was.

His name was Tiberius Claudius Philippus. This was not his own suite; he was borrowing the élite workspace of Abascantus, who was still composting leaves elsewhere in disgrace. 'Practising?' I asked satirically. Philippus took it badly. I dragged up a seat with arms and feather cushions, which soon had me sneezing. 'Is Abascantus ever coming back?'

'My sources expect him to be replaced by Titinius Capito, an equestrian.' Domitian was aware that the imperial freedmen, an intelligent bunch, disliked him. He was starting to get round that by appointing new men from outside to high positions. It was a good opportunity for the middle rank – if they liked living dangerously.

'What do you think of Capito?'

'I cannot comment.'

'Oh, you despise him!'

Laeta's son omitted comment on that too.

He was bony, spare, between thirty and forty. Olive-skinned, he had a long face with a straight nose and fine eyes; I guessed his mother had been a beauty, no doubt an exotic slave who also served at court in some capacity. She could have been a topless wine waitress, but I did not rule out an intellectual role, librarian or correspondence secretary for one of the imperial women.

Philippus wore heavy white imperial livery, even though the Emperor was absent so he could have dressed down. Or dressed up, had he been a party person. Clearly not. He seemed joyless, though I gave him the benefit and called it grief for his father. Ambition, and probably rivalry with Laeta, oozed out of him. That must have been why he was working here alone, when everybody sensible was having dinner.

He began briskly: 'Now you have come here, despite my imprecations, let us despatch the task.' He told me his father had wanted me to know the history of the Callistus family.

'Yes, it looks sweetly intriguing,' I agreed, deliberately frivolous.

Philippus indicated with a scowl that intrigue was not his medium.

'Please listen carefully to save me having to repeat myself.'

'May I take notes?'

'Why not? Everything is in the public domain. My father had to dig for it, however. I hope you appreciate his extensive work on your behalf, despite his poor health.'

'He enjoyed research. I expect this little exercise cheered his misery in his last days.'

With a frown, Philippus placed bony elbows on the

smoothly polished citron wood of Abascantus's office table, putting his fingertips together. I broke in to say, 'My prime consideration is to discover the fate of Callistus Valens, who has died in murky circumstances.'

'I shall clarify that.'

'Go ahead, then.' I beamed graciously. I could pretty well hear his teeth grinding.

He recited what he had to tell me, with no recourse to notes. Being a bureaucrat, he had the good manners to pause if my shorthand lagged behind, though he sneered when it happened.

'Once there were two brothers, Callistus Valens and Callistus Volusius, also two sisters, Julia Firma and Julia Verecunda. Julia Verecunda passionately wanted to marry Callistus Primus. He never encouraged her, but she pursued him obsessively.'

'I bet that made him avoid her!' I interjected. 'She will not have liked him saying no. She always expects to get what she wants.'

'Valens rejected her. He married someone else, a thoroughly decent woman, by all accounts, and the couple were extremely happy.'

'I like that,' I said gravely, thinking of Manlius Faustus. 'I like people to find one another and live happy lives together.'

'You are very romantic, Flavia Albia.' A criticism, I gathered. 'Eventually Valens's wife died.'

'Well, at least she died happy.'

Even though I kept disturbing his flow, Philippus was forced to smile. He carried on gamely: 'Julia Verecunda was not merely spurned. She and her sister had never got on. They fought one another from childhood. After Julia

Verecunda was rejected by Valens, her sister upset her further. Julia Firma married his brother, Callistus Volusius.'

'Oh, sneaky! Was that deliberate?' I wondered.

'Whether it was or not, they, too, were happy. For Julia Verecunda that must have been even harder to bear. She took herself off and married Ennianus Optatus, generally regarded as mild-mannered.'

'More fool him for having her. Their son is Ennius Verecundus – the Mother's Boy candidate for aedile.'

'Precisely.'

'So far, so clear.' And doom-laden, I could already see that.

'It gets muddier,' gloated Philippus.

'I thought it might.'

'Listen, please, Flavia Albia. The two brothers were well established and well liked in the community. Callistus Valens ran a shipping fleet on the Tiber. Callistus Volusius had a boat-building business, which passed to his son after Volusius and his wife Julia Firma both died. At that point, Julia Verecunda suddenly initiated a thaw. She and Julia Firma had continued to feud until her sister's dying day, but for a short period Verecunda apparently mellowed. Perhaps losing her sister was the reason.'

'Or a convincing excuse,' I scoffed.

'Mother's Boy,' said Philippus, becoming more human as he picked up my nickname, 'has four sisters. They, and their marriages, are important. To trace their relationships, my father had to draw a chart.'

'Wonderful! May I see it?'

'When you leave.' Philippus had no faith in visual aids. Old school – an idiot. I cursed, but I could wait. 'When Verecunda had her theoretical change of heart, Valens accepted her overtures. As a result, the Callisti took three of Verecunda's daughters in marriage.'

'Three!' That was surely overdoing it.

'One daughter was given to the newly orphaned Volusius Firmus and, perhaps more surprisingly, two other daughters married the two sons that Callistus Valens had fathered.'

'Primus and Secundus,' I spelled out. 'This I know. The marriage of Volusius Firmus and Julia Laurentina survived; she is currently pregnant. The other two unions rapidly failed, with unhappy divorces. That may have been caused by Julia Verecunda's poisonous influence on her daughters.'

Philippus nodded. 'Cynics think she always intended to cause grief to the Callisti, as a punishment for Valens having refused her.'

I nodded. 'If so, the most scandalous breakdown will have particularly pleased her: when Julia Pomponia, who was the wife of Callistus Secundus, left him. Ran away and married a hod-carrier, hunky, but trouble. Aren't they all? A building-site Adonis. One of the other sisters now has to give them cash handouts. They have just produced a child, but are estranged.'

'Julia Pomponia and one Aspicius,' agreed Philippus. 'Callistus Secundus has regarded Pomponia very bitterly ever since she deserted him. His brother, Primus, similarly loathes his ex-wife, Julia Optata.'

'By whom he had a daughter, Julia Valentina. Acrimonious custody battle,' I said. 'I have seen the girlie – she looks normal, considering the permanent bad feeling between her parents. Valentina's mother, Julia Optata, took as second husband Vibius Marinus, the candidate my friend the aedile is supporting. Marinus and Primus seem to have no quarrel.'

'Unusual in this family!'

'I don't know why Primus ended up on such awful terms with Julia Optata. People say they were simply young and ill suited. But I learned yesterday that, understandably, she has never forgiven the Callisti for taking away her newborn baby.'

'My father tried to look up law-court records,' said Philippus. 'He found none. Bitter or not, the custody battle must have been settled privately. Nor is there anything in our records to explain the divorce.'

I smiled. 'And Domitian takes such a keen interest in people's divorces! Still, they wouldn't be the first plebeians who don't believe in lawyers . . . I am starting to see why your admired father, Laeta, said the election list was too closely interwoven.'

'My father believed Firmus standing for aedile led directly to the death of Callistus Valens,' Philippus told me. 'If you are as quick as you seem, Flavia Albia, you may wonder whether there is still feuding within this complicated family.'

'Oh, no doubt of it!' I exclaimed. 'Clearly, things came to a head during the election campaign.'

Once again I had jumped in, annoying Philippus. 'The situation became vitriolic. My good father wanted to impress upon you Julia Verecunda's lasting hatred for Callistus Valens.'

'I hear you,' I assured the po-face. 'Candidate rivalry must have been a nightmare. On one side, the Callisti must have strongly opposed Ennius Verecundus, whose horrible hostile mother is his most visible supporter. She in turn would have opposed Firmus, and also Vibius. Then when Firmus was forced to drop out of the contest it placed Ennius more securely in the running.'

'My father saw that as critical,' Philippus managed to put in.

'How did it happen?' I demanded. 'Firmus was the favourite, Caesar's candidate. His family paid over squillions to gain that. It put them deep in financial trouble, all for nothing. I'd like to know your colleague's involvement. We all assume that Abascantus being sent off for a rest-cure was why Firmus gave up. But here's a worse scenario. Can Julia Verecunda have worked some trick specifically to shove Firmus out? Is she capable? Does she have contacts at court, influence over Abascantus? If the Callisti even suspected she was responsible for Firmus losing out, they would be incandescent.'

Philippus glanced around the finely decorated suite he had 'borrowed' from Abascantus. We could hear the evening silence. Nobody was listening in. It was so quiet that if the marble cladding moved on a contracting wall, as the day's heat died, we would notice the subtle creak. 'I have no reason to think my senior colleague went back on whatever he had promised the Callisti.'

'Oh, so he covered his tracks?' I mocked. Philippus did not deny that. 'Olympus! Can it be that Abascantus took money from both sides?'

'The relevant issue,' Philippus hedged, in a tight voice, 'is that Julia Verecunda openly hates all the candidates opposing Ennius, but what she hated most intensely was having one of the Callisti in her son's way.'

He stared at me significantly.

I blinked back, not quite with him.

'These are my father's words to you, Flavia Albia. Think of how much Julia Verecunda hated Callistus Valens.'

I could follow that.

Bribing Abascantus to remove the Emperor's backing from Volusius Firmus was vicious and probably illegal, but no different from tactics any candidate deployed. Julia Verecunda ought to have been satisfied. To anyone normal, ejecting Firmus from the campaign should have been enough.

'So Verecunda never forgave Valens,' I mused. 'Even when she pretended to thaw, it was a ploy to get closer so she could cause him misery through marital strife. His rejection years ago still dominates her existence.'

In my youth I had been in the same position. I knew how it hurt. How you threatened the direst punishment for the rat who betrayed you, by day and by night brooded upon him and threatened his destruction . . . I grew up, changed by the experience yet moving on from my loss, which is what most people do. I learned to be content, on occasions even happy. Other men had become more important to me.

Julia Verecunda never mellowed. She married, a man who sounded harmless, and she had a large family, but nothing gave her consolation. She never forgot. She never forgave. At one point she pretended to be reconciled, married three of her girls into Valens's family as a peacemaking gesture, but she had sent them to the Callisti full of hate.

Assuming the Callisti had responded to their let-down over Firmus with quietness and dignity, a woman who liked to cause sorrow would be left disappointed. I had seen her gloat in public over Firmus stepping down. That was not enough. A woman of such ingrained, obsessive bitterness would want Valens to know this was his fault for refusing her.

That was the answer. *She* went after Valens. It was Julia Verecunda who had had him hijacked on the way to Crustumerium. She had had him brought back to Rome ignominiously, roped up and on foot, like a criminal. When he arrived, she intended to confront him with his old crime.

The long walk in the July heat had proved too much for him. He had died. It seemed to me that she would not have wanted him to die, not before she had a chance to make him understand the retribution she was exacting. If he died before they came face to face, she had probably not forgiven him for that either. She had been denied her chance of vengeance. No wonder she had had his corpse thrust into his own strongbox, hidden in a neglected storeroom, where she meant his remains to rot for ever.

55

Before he dismissed me, Philippus surprised me with a request. Apparently his father had told him to maintain contact with Falco. I said firmly, as my mother would want, that my father had retired from all that.

'You mean, the current régime is not to his taste!' Philippus responded astutely.

'Everything comes to an end.' Philippus could take that as referring to Falco giving up imperial work – or to my hope for Domitian's régime.

'Should the opportunity arise, maybe you would accept commissions, Flavia Albia. We do have women who carry out special tasks.'

Here was Philippus trying to set up his own network, just like his father. I chortled. 'So Perella is still cutting throats? Hades, that dangerous woman ought to hang up her tambourine and castanets. Good as she was, she can't still be going about in disguise as a dancer!' Perella was a legendary agent, but worked undercover. Philippus blinked at my inside knowledge. 'Not for me,' I disabused him. 'I'm not a spy. I hate spies.' I had reasons for saying that. My intense feelings must have been obvious.

'I know nothing of a tambourine!' he claimed. 'Well, please bear it in mind.'

Philippus was a smug bastard. He had no concept of

ever being turned down. (He had not dealt with me before.) Distrusting him deeply, I wondered if he would respond to rejection as malevolently as Julia Verecunda. I could imagine it. You collaborated with these ambitious officials at your peril.

Riding Patchy back to the Aventine, I blanked out his invitation.

Philippus had given me a scroll, prepared by his father, showing the intertwined Callistus and Verecundus family tree. Patchy knew his way, so as the donkey reluctantly trotted homeward, continually stopping to nose at people's flower tubs, I unrolled the scroll on my lap for an initial scrutiny.

Most was familiar. I understood why Laeta had been so annoyed at the interconnection of those on the aedilate list. I already knew that two candidates, Volusius Firmus (originally) and Vibius Marinus, were brothers-in-law of a third, Ennius Verecundus. There was one extra surprise: only now did I see that Julia Terentia, the sister who had found her own rich husband, was in fact married to Dillius Surus, he who enjoyed his drink. (Niger's wife Galeria regarded him as a sponger, but Laurentina had said the couple were genuinely affectionate.) I now recalled that, before I knew who Terentia was, Nothokleptes had said he envied her investment in Baetican olive oil – and Baetica was where the fleeing Julia Pomponia had been offered a refuge.

So that made a fourth knot in the candidates' tangled relationships.

Once I rerolled the document, I used the slow journey from the Palatine, round the Circus Maximus and up my own hill, to add to the significant case against Julia Verecunda.

THE CALLISTUS FAMILY **A FAMILY WITH TOO MANY JULIAS**

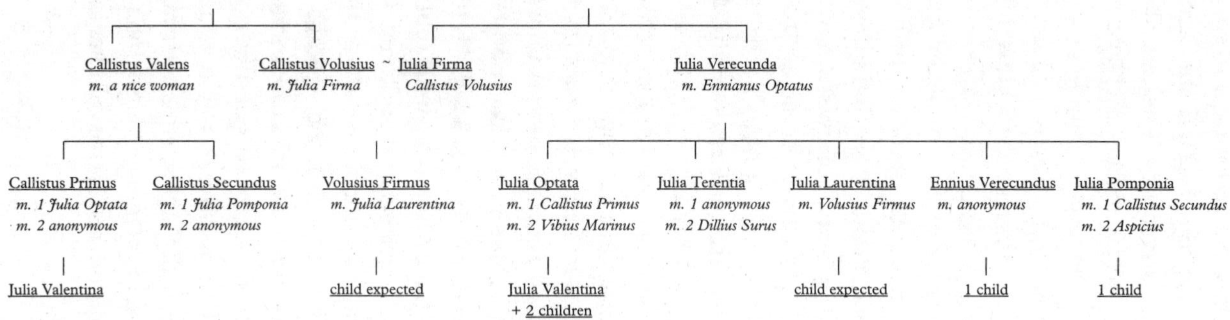

I suspected she had looked for – and found – someone she could employ to attack Valens; she had chosen someone from within her own family. The man I called Puce Tunic would be a possibility, if I could place him on that family tree – and I now believed I could.

What if he was Aspicius? Everything I had heard about Julia Pomponia's low-grade, feckless husband made him obvious for dirty work. Always up for a fight or a dodgy deal and, more important, he never had enough money. The rich daughter, Julia Terentia, provided financial help but she had threatened to stop. So I guessed Aspicius would readily accept any black commission, if his mother-in-law paid enough. A hod-carrier could probably call on associates to help arrange an ambush. He would certainly be strong enough to carry a corpse on his shoulder and shove it into a chest.

If Aspicius had organised the snatch on the Via Salaria and his wife had found out, that explained why Julia Pomponia fled. *I will never go back to him! After what he did . . . And I shall never see or speak to her again . . .* That must have been a reference to her mother. Pomponia would not want her newborn to have a killer for a father, especially one acting for her own obnoxious mother. Besides, even though in youth she had abandoned her first husband, Callistus Secundus, prior to her elopement she must have known Valens as a decent father-in-law.

All the sisters must be in a dilemma. How could they reconcile loyalty to Valens, a good man, with his death at the hands of their relatives? I had heard Julia Pomponia tell her sister fearfully, *If you go to their house . . . that family will see you know something . . .* So Julia Optata also knew the truth. Pomponia must have told her what had happened to Valens, and how Aspicius was involved. She would have had to explain why she needed to hide. But even after she had left him, out of fear or misplaced loyalty Pomponia might not have wanted anyone else to turn Aspicius in.

That explained, too, why their sister Julia Laurentina was so anxious. She intended to stay married to Volusius Firmus and to remain on good terms with his family. If her mother had caused Valens's death, while employing a disreputable brother-in-law, Laurentina's position was difficult. I myself thought the Callisti would be understanding, but all this must be hard for her – and just when she, too, was expecting a child.

What to do now?

Some informers would have gone straight to Julia Verecunda and confronted her. It would be a pointless exercise, and dangerous. She was unlikely to confess and might turn vicious. I certainly would not see her without taking a witness, and any interview would be safer with armed back-up.

Nor was I ready to enlighten the Callistus family. Julia Laurentina was right to keep her own counsel. She knew them. I, too, was sure they would explode at the news. Both brothers and the nephew used bodyguards. They got physical themselves. They might well respond violently.

All this needed to be relayed urgently to Manlius Faustus. Criminal investigations were not his responsibility, especially on the Caelian, out of his area, but he and I together could safely conduct further interviews, including one with the hod-carrier, if we could find him. Then, when it came to arrests, Faustus had vigiles contacts.

I went first to his office, but he was not there. It was now late. I could travel about because there were always lights on bar counters and glimmers from lamps lit to signal the all-clear to adulterous lovers. Still, I would go home now and try to find Tiberius in the morning, having breakfast at the Stargazer, for instance.

Leaving the Temple of Ceres, which was next to the aediles' office, I had to steer Patchy down Lesser Laurel Street, so I paused at the house Tiberius had bought. I knew this hilltop street extremely well, and had been inside the property, both the working yard and its adjacent home. That was of modest size, but in a desirable location on the main historic summit of the Aventine, among some of its most prestigious temples.

Renovation work was continuing by torchlight. The place badly needed to be cleared. Any neighbours must be complaining, though when the local aedile is himself being a menace, people are stuck.

I wondered if Faustus turned up to chivvy his men after his other business finished at the end of the day, but again he was absent. I knew the foreman slightly, so we fell into conversation. He reckoned Manlius Faustus was having doubts about whether to do up the place and sell it for profit. 'He says he wouldn't mind living here himself, if he gets married.'

I grinned. 'Cunning. He's been single for ten years. Supposedly living here himself could be a ploy to make you work to a higher standard!'

'No, he's bringing some woman along to look.'

What woman? He had not asked me. With slight foreboding, I bade him farewell and rode on.

This made up my mind. I knew where Faustus lived. I had been there too. What I had to say was so important I would go to his house and leave a message.

It was not too far from Fountain Court – indeed, since it was past the donkey boy's bedtime, I dropped him off there. I went on alone. I knew the streets and felt safe even at night. Faustus' home lay beyond my horrible alley, further across the hill. But we were really as close neighbours as all those people who lived on the Caelian.

Faustus and his uncle resided in a smart area to the west of the Street of the Plane Trees. Their house was a part-block, double-storeyed atrium residence: prime real estate, as befitted people who owned half of the warehouses nearby, above the Lavernal Gate.

I found it from memory. I nervously approached the double front doors, up three marble steps, each with a rose urn, the expensively trained standard trees in full flower this month and dripping after a recent watering. The aged porter did not remember me. Even so, he allowed in a declared friend of the young master. I already knew this was not a pompous household. It was well run but had a comfortable atmosphere.

The porter said Faustus was out. I was growing tired of that refrain. Wherever was he?

'Is Dromo here?'

Yes, but fast asleep.

A slave went for writing materials so I could leave a note. I stood by the porter's cubicle and tried to admire the frescos. There was no reason to feel guilty, yet I did. Last time, when I barely knew Tiberius, I had been sneaked in here by somebody else for a secret tour of the reception rooms. This time, being here without his knowledge made me even more uncomfortable. This wasn't a suspect's house where I would seize any chance to explore. I barely entered the atrium, with its roofed shrine to their household gods and images of ancestors. A worn plaque showing a young couple side by side was probably a memorial of his parents. I had taken no notice before, but now it mattered.

A secretary, yawning, turned up to take dictation. I composed a brief letter telling Tiberius in three or four sentences what I thought had happened to Valens and the need for us to act. Being under mildly curious scrutiny from the staff quashed any temptation to add endearments. I was handed the stylus and signed the tablet myself.

I nearly got away with this. Luck was not with me, however. Just as I breathed freely and was about to leave, a man stalked in from the street. He had his own house key but was not Tiberius. He came in, demanding loudly, 'Whose is that disgusting donkey left tied to our ring outside? One of you go out and give it a kick up the street!'

My heart sank. Alone, at the end of a long hot day when I was drained of energy, I had to make friends with my friend's uncle, Tullius.

56

Someone I once knew had accused Tullius of lewd and predatory behaviour. Even Faustus acknowledged they were very different characters. Still, this man had taken in an orphaned nephew, brought him up, then stayed on good terms while they had lived together for most of the past twenty years. I had never heard Tiberius make a complaint.

Face to face, I saw little physical resemblance between the two men, nor any between the uncle and that young woman in the ancestral plaque who must have been his sister. The uncle was bulky though not gross. He must be sixty, sixty plus. He had a bald crown, inquisitive light brown eyes, and a contemptuous manner. I knew why that was. Even though he asked, 'And who are you?' he knew. 'Don't tell me – the cheeky piece who has been luring my nephew away from home!'

Quietly, I answered: 'My name is Flavia Albia, daughter of the equestrian Didius Falco and the noble Helena Justina. I do have the friendship of Tiberius Manlius –' I deliberately chose to use his first two names rather than the more formal last two. The Roman naming system is so subtle, and I knew how to deploy it. 'I apologise for coming so late. I have been assisting your nephew with his election work. We uncovered foul play and I badly need to give him information.'

'"Election assistance" – that's a new word for an old game!' Tullius screwed up his eyes, which gave him a piggy expression. 'Well, this is a useful meeting, young woman!' He folded his arms aggressively.

I decided there was no point in holding back. 'I see. You think I am a graspy little gold-digger and this is your chance to see me off.'

Good move. My calm words surprised him. He expected me to be defensive, not to come straight out with my own challenge.

With anyone else, I would have suggested we relocate to somewhere private. Here, we had the porter, the secretary and several slaves, who had popped out to greet their returning master, a rash of attentive people who had heard him come home. In view of what I had been told about his crude habits, I chose not to be alone with him. So we held our conversation there in the atrium, with an eager audience.

I had to be very careful. Faustus wanted to avoid a quarrel. It was wise for me to cultivate good relations with his uncle.

'You had your fun,' sneered Tullius. 'Him too, I gather!'

He looked me up and down, his meaning unmistakable. I wondered what he made of my white funeral-going drapery: thoroughly discreet, with minimal jewellery and the formal veil I had automatically lifted over my hair. I watched him assess me, as people so often did when I was working. He would be puzzled by the grave appearance that belied my smart talk. He had expected three-inch cork heels and thick lead face paint, with layers of gold necklace – probably loaded onto me by Faustus. He could not know that Faustus's idea of a love-gift was a stone bench, but even so Tullius was bemused by his nephew's taste in girlfriends.

'Tullius Icilius . . .' Nobody seemed to use it, but I knew

his cognomen from my father's investigation. Indeed, I knew much more about this man than he would expect. *Good at what he does*, had been Falco's verdict. *Apparently without undue use of sharp practice. A sly mover and a hard-working money hound.* Thank you, Father! 'Tullius Icilius, it is late. If you want to say something important, do. But please remember that your nephew has chosen to be friends with me.'

'And now he'll see sense.' That old line!

'You haven't been watching closely enough. He has changed.' I sounded sure.

'Oh, no!' So did Tullius.

'I have seen the alteration.' I remembered Tiberius when we first met: hard, belligerent, short-tempered – simply unsure how to wield his magisterial authority, I now realised. For a time it had made him unpleasant to deal with. That was how I had ended up stabbing his hand with a meat skewer. He learned; he calmed down. I calmed down too. I spoke very levelly now. 'Other people have commented on the alteration. He spent thirty years doing nothing, then he acquired the aedilate. You must have thought this was simply good for your business contacts, good for prestige. You underestimated the results. Never mind how other men approach such a post, your nephew took it on and mastered it. And when the work and his ability to carry it out thrilled him, he discovered himself. A cliché, perhaps, yet true.'

His uncle shrugged and admitted without drama, 'Yes, he surprised us.'

'Take my advice. Unless you accept the new Tiberius, you will lose him.'

This time Tullius laughed out loud. 'You imagine I shall lose him to *you*?'

'Well, I do like the new version, as he knows. But he makes his own choices,' I said. 'One thing I respect is that, since you had him at sixteen, some of Tiberius Manlius as he is today must be your creation.'

'Oh, you are a clever one!' Tullius scorned this as flattery, though I had meant what I said.

I had argued with much more dangerous men than him; undermined a few of them. 'May I go home now, please?'

Not yet. My argument with Tullius Icilius had hardly started.

We stayed in the atrium, the staff gathered on the sidelines. They all stood still with their eyes cast down, trying to look unobtrusive in case Tullius dismissed them. I thought he enjoyed having an audience. He lolled his well-padded posterior against a heavy side-table, a man who loved holding forth when he assumed he had control. I stood erect. I must have been healthier and stronger than when I had returned to Rome.

Now Tullius dumped his clincher on me. He began by saying there were ambitious plans for Tiberius who, I was assured, would go along with them. His uncle bragged that financial control of their business affairs was kept in his hands, limiting his nephew's freedom of action. He had accustomed Tiberius to a soft life, a luxury he would want not to lose. Unfortunately, I saw the force of that argument.

His uncle said Tiberius did not even realise how privileged his life had been. He had never concerned himself with the family business; to illustrate that, some years ago Tiberius had been allocated a warehouse in his own name yet he had not done anything with it.

'What's in it?' I asked automatically.

'Nothing.'

'Is it secure? Is it waterproof?' My questions clearly surprised Tullius. 'He should hire guards and acquire tenants.' Not the solution Tullius had intended! He didn't want me beefing up his nephew to use his resources. 'I expect Tiberius Manlius shied away from competition with you, who are the expert. But he evidently has thoughts of striking out on his own now, proven by that property he has bought in Lesser Laurel Street.'

Tullius scoffed. Tiberius had acquired it but had no funds for its refurbishment.

'Of course you may refuse him finance,' I conceded. I paused, letting the threat make its own point. 'You would suffer if he decided to force you. He could do that. He manifestly has his own money, even though you have always taken charge. But a split would be stupid. Everybody loses when a good family business is broken up.' Again, Tullius had not expected me to speak so shrewdly. Again, sadly, it made no impression on him.

That was when the uncle utterly floored me. He crowed that he was delighted when Faustus went into home-buying. Nothing could have been better. The reason would be announced at a musical evening tomorrow, an elegant gathering of influential plebeians to celebrate the end of the political campaign. This election party would be at the house of Marcia Balbilla, a social climber I knew was close friends with Laia Gratiana.

Manlius Faustus, his uncle told me, had so impressed everyone as an aedile that among his social circle – a circle in which, Tullius pointed out pleasantly, I had no standing – he was happily forgiven any youthful indiscretion. At the soirée tomorrow he would be welcomed back by those he had once offended. Tomorrow when Laia's brother, Salvius Gratus, made the formal announcement of his planned wedding, Tullius Icilius would give their friends yet more good news. The election coalition between Gratus and Vibius had borne unexpected fruit. Old friendships had been rekindled. To the joy of both their families, his nephew Faustus was to be married again to Laia Gratiana.

57

I never saw that coming.

It had to be true. It is how such things are done. Despite everything, despite how Tiberius spoke to me and looked at me, even though he was in love, I accepted he would see the benefit of a good social alliance. He had obeyed his uncle for twenty years. He valued what his uncle had done for him. Everything he himself owned was tied up with the warehouses and he was inured to agreeing with whatever was asked, for the sake of the family business in which he shared. But it would be a disaster.

I was startled and angry. Indeed, I was so angry on my friend's behalf, I risked appearing quite naïve. 'That's a wicked proposal. I believed you must have affection for your nephew – how wrong I was! He and Laia Gratiana were always incompatible. If he failed her in their marriage, that is why. Nothing has changed; they cannot begin to communicate, neither of them even wants to. I am astonished she has agreed to this, though of course if her brother asks it of her, she is a dutiful woman. Nobody who cares for Tiberius could doom him to that again. You cannot care, or you would know this plan is selfish, cruel and dangerous.'

I could not go on.

Head high, I turned away. Behind me I heard Tullius order me out of their house, but I left of my own accord. He might now regret letting his slaves hear what I said to him. They all liked Tiberius, who was a generous, kindly master.

Somehow, unaware of how I made the journey, I went home to Fountain Court. In my heart, I was hoping I might find Tiberius there but the apartment was empty.

58

I spent another sleepless night, though it was not the heat that distressed me.

By morning I was strangely reconciled. I accepted I was losing him.

Was it a measure of my love that I never at any point raged against Tiberius? I wished no harm on him. I felt no fury. I was only clear that, if he did marry Laia, I could have no more to do with him. For one thing, if he allowed himself to be pitched into that arid marriage again, I would be bitterly disappointed in him. I had thought he had more self-regard.

I was desolate myself yet, to my surprise, my first thoughts were to protect Tiberius. Despite that, I did not want to see him. I rejected breakfast at the Stargazer, though it seemed probable he would be there, looking for me. I made myself scarce, carrying out domestic errands that took me away from the apartment, then hid at my parents' house. I was trying to avoid a falling-out. That was interesting, because once I would have torn right in to confront and censure him.

Bored, I emerged and bought a snack lunch, which I ate alone in the deserted enclosure called the Armilustrium. Tiberius knew it as a place I went to, though he did not come there to find me. That was good. I had not bought enough food to share.

I found myself making a comparison between myself, in this eerie mood of tolerance, and the brooding wrath of Julia Verecunda when she lost the man she had set her heart on. I wondered if the difference was that I loved mine, whereas she had only coveted Valens possessively. I wanted an equal companion. She wanted power.

People with that fault in their nature are prone to jealousy and suspicion, even if their elective choice accepts them. Many lose lovers through their extreme behaviour. Verecunda probably never stood a chance with Valens. Over-possessiveness can be very well hidden, but a strong character will resist its controlling nature. Valens was too wise to be trapped.

I was genuinely not jealous of Laia Gratiana. I feared what Faustus would do, yet I knew he did not want her. His heart belonged to me. Yet would he act upon it?

At one low point, the idea flitted into my mind that maybe he planned to show the house in Lesser Laurel Street to Laia Gratiana. It was extremely convenient for the Temple of Ceres, where she held her implacable sway in the cult.

No. Laia would not like that house. She definitely would not want to live next to a building yard. On the other hand *I* would never object to a man who had his work premises next door to where he lived. The first suggestion I would make, in fact, was to knock a door through for direct access into the yard from the house . . . This was too dangerous a dream.

Sad but calm, I left the Armilustrium and made my way home.

Stepping into the cold gloom of the entrance to the Eagle Building, I heard male voices. Faustus was there. I saw him sitting on the bench he had bought for me, holding court with his slave, Dromo, and my porter, Rodan. They were discussing the elections, seriously, man to man. I stood out of sight, listening.

Faustus was reporting on the likely outcome of their campaign. 'The lobbying is over and names will go forward to the Senate. Of course, the level of support they have managed to gather – or not! – will influence the vote. The hard candidates, Trebonius Fulvo and Arulenus Crescens, have streaked ahead.'

Rodan naturally thought that good. He had been a feeble gladiator, retired by his trainer because his only habit was losing. Still, he liked men who went to the gym. 'Brilliant!'

'Well, they have worked for it and deserve it.' Faustus was a fair man. 'After them is the woozy one, Dillius Surus.'

Dromo chuckled. 'He'll have good experience for regulating bars.'

'I think he drinks at home,' Faustus demurred, smiling.

'What about the others, Master? What about that fellow you like?'

'Trickier, Dromo. The last three are neck and neck. Ennius is about to be connected to a tragic scandal, bad enough to damn him. Otherwise, my man and his co-runner seem to be heading for a tie. If so, a helpful senator says he'll get up and propose placing them in the traditional order – that is, precedence to married men with children. Vibius is married and a father of two. Gratus is getting married, but has no children.'

'Can he adopt some?'

'I don't think it counts, Rodan. Otherwise people standing for election would all foster orphans just for the voting period!'

I stepped out into view. Watching Tiberius closely, I saw his face light when he saw me. 'Albia, there you are!'

Expressionless, I walked over to them. Dromo slipped off the bench to make space for me, but I remained standing.

'Who is your useful senator?'

'Camillus Aelianus made the offer.'

'Aulus!' The surly one.

'Yes, I was surprised. But your uncle seems to mean it.'

Faustus signalled to his slave and the porter to leave us, saying we had things to discuss. That was truer than he knew.

I did sit, at the other end of the bench. He held out a hand for me to move closer, but I pretended not to notice.

It was more than a day since we were last together, when we interviewed the vigiles about Valens's slaves. I said I had no more news, so Faustus should give his catch-up first.

He stared at me curiously, but then began. He made no reference to his uncle. Tullius could not have said anything. 'Yesterday first: I saw the Callisti. They owned up that their slaves say Valens recognised the leader of the group who attacked him.'

'Aspicius?'

'Yes. Valens told them to run home and warn the family, as we know. But with Valens dead, only the slaves are witnesses to who took part in the ambush. In law they have to be tortured to give usable evidence. The family do not want that.'

I sighed. 'Can we squeeze a confession out of Aspicius? He could be offered a deal, if he implicates Julia Verecunda.'

Faustus pulled a face. 'Unfortunately we can't find him.'

Groaning at that, I asked, 'What have you tried?'

They had started with a vigiles search of the hod-carrier's workplace and home. Aspicius had not been seen in his usual haunts for days. He had left the site where he worked, and neighbours said he had not been home. They told the vigiles he had been brooding about his missing wife, claiming he knew where Pomponia had gone. Faustus feared Aspicius might follow her to Fidenae, so he had spent most of yesterday and half the night racing back there with mounted men to rescue her.

'We brought the woman and baby back to a safe house in Rome. She made a fuss but I insisted.'

'Does she admit to knowing what her husband did?'

'There was no time to interrogate her. We came back in the dark. It's a damned long way, even for cavalry.'

'You can ride?'

'Country upbringing.'

'You looked whacked.' He was tired out, and no wonder.

'Yes, I am.' My man was pleading to be comforted; it was hard not to respond.

Instead, I reported my own fears that the Callisti would go after Aspicius. Faustus had already thought of that: he had told the vigiles to send him word if any suspicious bodies turned up.

We discussed Julia Verecunda. I explained her history with Valens, her tireless jealousy and manipulative nature, her attempts to subvert her daughters' marriages, and how Philippus and I thought she must have paid money to abort the election hopes of Volusius Firmus. Faustus said that yesterday the Callistus brothers and Firmus had evidently worked out who must have employed Aspicius.

I asked if anyone had interviewed her. Faustus had attempted it this morning. At her most old-fashioned, Julia

Verecunda had claimed the full privilege of a Roman matron to have a male relative speak on her behalf.

'Oh, no. Not Ennius?'

'Yes, Mother's Boy! But don't despair,' Faustus told me. 'Ennius came good. He surprised me. He must have amazed his mother.'

'What with?'

'Well, whether or not Julia Verecunda intended that Valens should die, ultimately she organised the ambush and caused his death, which cannot be ignored. Ennius asked me not to put her to a public trial. Instead – and I agreed this, so I hope it meets with your approval – he has called a full family council in the ancient tradition. You know what that means, Albia?'

'The charges against his mother will be judged by her assembled family. The family will give their verdict; the family will decide any punishment.'

'Exactly. Ennius will preside. He gave the impression he is going to be tough on her. It takes place later today. I shall be present as an observer,' said Faustus. 'You can accompany me, if you would like.'

I nodded.

It was the hottest part of the day. We were burning up in the courtyard. I stood and said I would see Faustus later. I was going indoors, and made it obvious that he was not invited. He stood up too. He looked hurt, but made no attempt to follow me.

A while later I looked out. I saw Faustus sprawled dead asleep on the stone bench, in full sun.

I called up Dromo. 'Your master will catch sunstroke.

Wake him and tell him to come indoors to rest in the cool on my reading couch. Then go to his house and fetch him a clean, dry tunic for when he goes out later. Better bring two, formal and informal, because I don't know whether he intends going as an aedile or a private citizen.'

I put out a pillow and a jug of water. I heard Faustus come in. I stayed in my bedroom with the door firmly shut.

All the same, I was glad I had taken care of him. Glad, too, simply knowing he was here close by.

59

The Verecundus council was held at the Temple of Claudius. Temples are used for special meetings, of the Senate, for example. The family wanted a place with solemn religious significance, somewhere large enough to hold them all, and on the Caelian Hill where they lived. I presume they did not consider the fact that this temple had been begun by Agrippina, widow of the Divine Claudius, after she had killed off her imperial spouse with the fabled dish of poisoned mushrooms. How divinely appropriate that she, too, had been a domestic murderess.

Agrippina, the tigerish mother of Nero, eventually met retribution at the hands of her son. Also apt!

Lack of interest in Claudius meant it had taken several emperors to complete this temple, which stood high on an enormous man-made platform. The cost of its earthworks and engineers had not helped. Massive arched colonnades surrounded the huge sanctuary, with rows of trees shading its interior enclosure. Partly encircled by the crook-backed line of the Aqua Claudia, which brought the waters of the River Anio to Rome, in Nero's time this area had been subsumed into his lavish Golden House. Elaborate nymphaea had once fed fountains and cascades that clothed half of the Caelian in sheets of sparkling water. It would have been a beautiful tribute to his adoptive father had Nero ever completed it, but he called himself an artist and artists notoriously abandon projects.

Vespasian owed his career to Claudius. He finished the job. He reduced the beautiful waterworks system to a more economic level but otherwise he turned a neglected eyesore into a striking structure. Despite that, no one had ever really loved the place.

The fabulous monument's footprint was larger than that of the new amphitheatre, which lay across the road from it at a slight angle. The back of the temple's platform had been cut into the long main ridge of the Caelian, while the front occupied one of the most elevated positions in Rome. Steep stairs led up from lower levels, deterring all but very fit visitors. The temple stared across to the Palatine Hill, as if to remind new generations of emperors that even the so-called divine could be despatched by wicked wives and quickly forgotten.

We met in one of the awe-inspiring colonnades. The main temple would have dwarfed our group. Tall-backed thrones had been set out. It was early evening. Everywhere here seemed deserted. Faustus and I sat a little behind the rest. It had been agreed with Ennius that the meeting was private so we would remain silent and not keep a record.

All five children of Verecunda came. Four brought a spouse each, the husbands all looking subdued. One grandchild, Julia Valentina, was deemed old enough. She arrived from the Callistus house with Julia Laurentina and Volusius Firmus; she sat with them, though her mother rushed over to kiss her when she arrived.

I had forgotten that Julia Optata would bring Sextus

Vibius. He nodded to Faustus, then took no part in the formalities.

A whisper of gold silk and a waft of expensive perfume announced Julia Terentia, with her husband, the tipsy candidate, Dillius Surus. She was the only sister I had not yet met, physically like the others though looking even more pugnacious. She and the wavering Dillius held hands tightly, no doubt to emphasise to her hostile mother how fond of each other they were. The fourth sister, Julia Pomponia, was brought by a protective escort. She alone had no husband with her; Aspicius would not show his face lest he be arrested.

Last of the five siblings was Ennius Verecundus, no longer smiling as he had done so inanely during the campaign. His pale wife arrived on his arm, then sat leaning towards him; I found her manner indicative. I deduced that when they were alone in private they held long conversations. The pale thing was a traditional confidante and her presence was giving Ennius courage. I bet she had advised him what to say.

Last, the mother stomped in. Her freedwoman followed her and two male guards; she waved them away truculently. After they stood back on the edge of the circle, Julia Verecunda was left looking old, frail and alone. That was deliberate theatre. Nobody would have called her vulnerable. Without actually refusing to appear at the council, she showed she was here on sufferance. She was swathed in black, with a long Livia veil.

At first I thought she intended to remain covered, but she put the veil back from her face because it hid the glares that she directed at everyone. Even silent, she emitted loathing for everyone present. Now that I knew her history,

I saw near-mania in the way her eyes darted to anyone who spoke. I could imagine the decades of long-distance envy she had sent towards her happier sister, the vengeful thoughts she had aimed at Callistus Valens.

She did not care that he was dead. She would have obliterated all of us, and never shown remorse.

I had attended a family council once before. They have the force of law. Ours had been a last resort in combating some truly terrible crimes; in retrospect, attending that meeting twelve years ago had marked my true growing up. I wondered, would the same be true for young Julia Valentina, brought to witness proceedings as a bereaved granddaughter? I had been a little older than her. At thirteen, she sat twisting her girl's skinny bracelet and dangling her feet, visibly awed by the occasion.

Ennius took charge. He was thorough, yet did not allow delaying tactics or emotional outbursts. He said the purpose of the council was to ensure his mother's rights as a citizen: not to have anyone lay hands on her nor have her liberty constrained. As a woman she would be accorded the decency of a private judgement. She had the right to a trial. Her family would judge her actions and, if they found her guilty, would decide what happened to her. It might also be necessary to compensate the Callisti for their loss. Ennius had promised Callistus Primus that a council was being held and that he would be told the outcome.

Ennius stated the charges: that his mother had arranged the attack on Callistus Valens, employing her son-in-law Aspicius; during his ordeal Valens had somehow perished; his body had been impiously concealed. There were witnesses to the initial attack and the corpse had now been identified. Aspicius had gone on the run, which argued his guilt.

Ennius asked if Julia Verecunda wanted to say anything. She refused to speak.

I had seen killers take the stubborn, silent route. Sometimes they, or their slaves or associates, were persuaded through the use of torture. Ennius pointed out that he would prevent that.

Others then made statements. They spoke solemnly. The rest listened without interruption.

Julia Pomponia, Aspicius's wife, was the most important witness. She stated that early in July her mother had come to their house to see her husband about some special task, for which Aspicius was paid money. At first Pomponia was unaware what had been discussed. After the event, Aspicius told her all about the attack. According to him, Callistus Valens collapsed of heat exhaustion when they reached Rome. He was not beaten up, but died of natural causes. An accident, Aspicius claimed; there had been no intention to kill him. Verecunda had said that the point of capturing Valens was so she could humiliate him, avenge his rejection of her all those years ago, and gloat about how she had punished his family since. She had arrived on the scene soon after Valens died. She ordered the incarceration of the body in the strongbox in the storeroom. She decided they would keep Valens's death a secret from his family, to cause them more distress as they agonised over what could have happened.

Next, Julia Optata gave witness. It was the first time I had seen Sextus's wife speaking at any length. She managed to come across as the sweet woman Marcella Vibia had once called her. Julia confirmed that Pomponia had told her the same story, terrified of what Aspicius would do to her and the new baby when it came. Pomponia had been so frightened that Julia Optata helped her escape the marital home, after which another sister was intending to give her refuge overseas. Julia Optata added that yesterday Aspicius had turned up at the Vibius house. He believed his wife was there, and demanded access to 'deal with' Pomponia. He issued wild threats, terrified everybody, then stormed off.

Next was Julia Laurentina, Firmus's wife. She reported news from her brother-in-law, Callistus Primus, not present because he was no longer a relative. He had now ascertained from Palace sources that a senior official called Titinius Capito had been paid by Julia Verecunda to remove the Emperor's grant allowing Volusius Firmus to call himself 'Caesar's candidate'.

At that, Firmus himself growled from where he was seated that he would never be able to stand for election again, due to lack of funds. Julia Laurentina resumed her seat, putting an arm round him.

Julia Terentia was the last sister to give testimony. Among that self-assured bunch, she came across as the most confident. Making much of her power derived from her money, she confirmed that for many years she had supported the hard-up Pomponia and Aspicius, as a favour to her impoverished sister. In light of Aspicius's irresponsible behaviour, she had recently warned them she would stop paying. All he did with the money was go to bars where he started fights. Julia Terentia knew that cutting off handouts left the couple in great hardship, but she saw no other option. She had advised Pomponia to leave him. Terentia said Aspicius had come to her house yesterday, too. When he threatened the occupants, Dillius hurled a big amphora at him, then chased him away.

Ennius then read out a statement from Claudia Galeria, wife of Titus Niger, that a chilling conversation had left her husband in no doubt that Aspicius, who was gloating about it, had been party to the death of Valens. Niger had gone to see Aspicius about this and was himself murdered.

A brief discussion followed. The women, trained by their mother never to hold back, denounced her fiercely. Her son managed to be more moderate. Pretty soon he declared they had heard enough. He gave his mother one more chance to defend herself. She snorted, then pointedly replaced her veil over her face.

Ennius offered them a secret ballot; they all chose to put up hands openly. They voted. Their verdict was unanimous: Julia Verecunda had not planned to kill Callistus Valens, so was not guilty of murder. But she had caused his death by planning the attack and paying the man who had carried it out. Aspicius was found guilty in his absence; Julia Pomponia would be divorced from him and sent abroad for safety, while the family would cooperate with the vigiles manhunt.

Ennius pronounced his mother's punishment. She would be taken to a distant temple on the family's land, where she must permanently remain. She would live in the charge of the priestess, with the family providing maintenance. Anyone who wanted could visit her, but she must not return to Rome.

In addition, they would make a payment to Claudia Galeria in compensation for her husband's murder. A suitable sum would also be paid for the death of Callistus Valens. In further settlement, they would pay the surviving Callisti a sum equal to what they had spent on their thwarted campaign for Volusius Firmus.

60

As Ennius supervised the departure of his still-silent mother, the group began breaking up. The sisters swooped for farewell kisses; it would have been impossible for a stranger to tell which women were on good terms, which not speaking to one another. The girl, Valentina, was passed among them to be kissed. Sisters kissed brothers-in-law and vice versa. Brothers-in-law shook hands. Only Ennius made any gesture of farewell to Julia Verecunda who, oddly enough, accepted her son's embrace.

A temple attendant must have been waiting until the council finished. A messenger was led up, wanting to see Faustus. While they stepped aside, I had a quick word with Sextus Vibius, wishing him well for the election. He puffed out his cheeks, a relief of tension after the meeting. Then he grinned and asked teasingly, 'Made his move yet?'

It was really too painful to answer, but somehow I managed to laugh back at him.

His wife whisked up, looking peeved. 'Leave my husband alone!' She spoke lightly enough, but with an undertone I did not like. Sextus and I had barely spoken. Any familiarity was on his side. I would much rather he had not teased me.

The others were leaving. Julia Optata took her husband away, giving him a little biff on the arm as they went. It looked playful, though not playful enough. Something about her action, and how he moved out of the way, perturbed me.

I stood waiting for Faustus, thinking.

After he finished with the messenger, he came to collect me; he raised his brows in enquiry because he could tell I was puzzling. 'Tiberius, why would you call somebody a grain bag?'

'A what?'

'A "human grain bag"? In a context where it was definitely an insult.'

Everyone else had gone. Just the two of us now, we started to walk through the high colonnade, our shoes striking clops on the expensive marble slabs. I explained how Trebonius Fulvo had once dismissively listed out his rivals to me: *a drunk, a wimp, a prig and a human grain bag.* Dillius, Ennius, Gratus – and that grain bag was Vibius Marinus.

Troubled, Tiberius suggested an explanation: 'Trebonius is a gym-frequenter. Apart from its agricultural meaning, sacks of grain are used for training boxers. They are hung up to be whacked, sufficiently firm to take meaningful practice punches, but with enough give in them not to cause physical harm.'

I sighed. 'Oh dear. I have a horrible feeling. Julia Optata just showed extraordinary suspicion when all I was doing was chatting to Sextus.'

Faustus whistled through his teeth, very softly. He knew what I was suggesting. 'Now I am worried too. Did we have it wrong? Is the violent one not Sextus but *Julia*? Does she keep losing her temper and battering him?'

'Sextus vowed to you he never hits his wife, and I don't think he lied. We ourselves have seen what happens with them.' I said. 'It felt extremely unpleasant. In front of us, Julia Optata snapped at Sextus over the children's schooling; when he went off to talk to her, he looked very anxious. Now I think he may have been expecting violence.'

Tiberius explored the idea. 'If this is true, did she behave in the same way when she was married to Callistus Primus?'

'Primus wouldn't stand for it. That might be why he divorced her, and so rapidly,' I said. 'And why the circumstances were hushed up.'

Faustus agreed. 'It's why her sister, who must have known the situation, took away the newborn baby, saying Julia Optata should not bring up a child – and why Primus insisted on custody.'

'He only lets Julia Optata see Valentina with careful arrangements,' I said. 'Mind you, he never acknowledges any of this. He blanks all questions.'

'Because he has to protect the child from scandal,' explained Faustus. 'That's why reasons for the divorce have never surfaced and the battle for his daughter ended with a private settlement.'

'Julia Optata's mother knows,' I decided. 'Optata and Verecunda share the same traits. Not only a violent temper but unjust suspicion, especially where men are involved.'

We began to descend the long flight of steps out of the complex, which was steep. Tiberius offered me an arm; for safety I took it. He was still working out answers. 'This is why Sextus and Julia rarely socialise. This is really why she left Rome when Sextus kept saying obliquely, "We agreed it is best." Julia may genuinely not like crowds and she clearly wanted to look after her sister Pomponia. But the main reason was to ensure that Sextus never had to appear in the Forum showing the marks of domestic injury.'

We reached street level and walked on, round the back of the Palatine, towards the Circus Maximus.

'This is extraordinary.' Tiberius seemed baffled.

'It happens.' I lifted his hand, ruefully showing him the scars where I had once stabbed him.

'Ah, you would not do that now.' True. I could never hurt him; indeed, I would fight to protect him. 'Besides, the difference is, Albiola, I was seriously in the wrong on that occasion. *I* would never offend you in that way nowadays.'

I nearly took him to task on what his uncle had said, but this was the wrong time. 'Tiberius, even when a husband hits his wife, the situation tends to be well concealed. How much more so, when the wife is dangerous? A man, letting a woman batter him? It makes him no more than a slave. Think of the shame for Sextus. For her too, if she admits her temperament.'

Tiberius sighed gloomily. 'We brought her back to him. What have we done, Albia?'

I had no answer.

As we carried on past the great curve of the Circus, we fell silent. When we spoke again, Tiberius changed the subject. He told me the messenger at the temple had come to say the vigiles had found a body. It sounded like Aspicius. The corpse had been dragged out of the Tiber that morning, an apparent drowning. If no one came forward to claim ownership, the man would be cremated at public expense and all record of him discreetly lost.

We agreed not to pursue the matter officially. Tiberius would tip the nod to Ennius, and let him decide whether to warn his sister Pomponia that she had probably lost her husband. We could never prove how Aspicius had ended up in the river, but we knew three substantial, capable men with detailed knowledge of the Tiber. They might, if they thought someone deserved it, get together on the riverbank with him. One might hold his feet, one take his arms, the third push his head underwater until he stopped kicking . . .

If that was what the Callisti had done to Aspicius, there was nothing to gain by accusing them and we agreed we could not blame them.

In a muted mood, we continued to walk down the long, far length of the Circus, up the hill on the crooked Vicus Publicius, then onwards to my building in Fountain Court. There, when I went up to my apartment, Tiberius followed. I let him come in with me. All the way home, I suppose I never looked at him. Indoors, he turned me so I was facing him. Hands on my shoulders he stared at me. He knew I was upset with him.

Tipping his head, he simply asked me, 'What have I done?'

61

I loved the man. I adored his straightforward openness with me.

'You have not done it yet.'

'There's hope, then!'

I choked a little, throwing my arms round him, burying my face against his chest. When I let go, I told him in plain words how I had met his uncle and what Tullius had said.

His mouth dropped open slightly. I knew then: Tiberius had not been keeping this from me; he had not known himself. 'It will never happen!'

I covered my face.

'Albia!' Tiberius was stricken. 'What must you have been thinking? Oh, my Albia!'

There was no time to discuss it. He would have to take action immediately: the announcement was to be made that very evening. If a marriage was announced, and if Tiberius later refused to go through with it, he stood no chance of salvaging his relationship with Tullius, let alone calming the wrath of Laia and her brother. He cared about all that. He was a pragmatist.

For the Verecundus council he had worn his aedile's white tunic, with its magisterial purple bands. While he buffed up to look like a man who could be admitted to a musical evening (a quick hair comb), I did question why his uncle was plunging him into this without prior discussion.

'All my fault,' he admitted sheepishly. 'The idea was run past me, I have to say. I never took it seriously. Uncle Tullius is so desperate, I suppose he took silence for agreement.'

'For heaven's sake! You need to learn to talk to people.'

'I'm sure you will teach me! Look, I must go to this bloody lyre party. Do you want to come?'

I badly wanted to hear what he was going to say, but ending the proposal (which her friends probably knew about) would be a public slap in the face for Laia Gratiana; my presence could only inflame the situation more. 'No. You have to go alone.'

On the threshold, he grasped both my hands. 'Have faith.'

If I had known in advance how long he would be gone, having faith while I waited would have been much easier.

It grew dark. I gave up on him. I cursed him, I wept, I dried my eyes and ate something. I would have got drunk but had no wine at home. I decided to send Rodan to buy a huge cheap amphora with which I could end my sorrows while writing a suitably dreadful suicide note, but as I opened the apartment door, a kerfuffle met me.

Struggling upstairs with a handcart was the aedile's slave, Dromo. It was laden with scrolls, some in scroll boxes, some bundled and tied together, more clasped awkwardly under the arm of the overheated, agitated boy. He was too tired even to complain.

'Stop, Dromo. Where are you going and what are all those?'

'Stuff!' He clumped the wheels up to the next landing and came to a halt, his handcart dangerously teetering. 'I'm always having to haul stuff about for him.'

'Scrolls? Tell me, Dromo.'

'Old scrolls he's gone and got from that warehouse, that one right over the Caelian with the boozy clerk. We've been scratching around and loading things for hours. It's all his uncle's accounts and no one is to tell Tullius we've got them. I'm supposed to lug my cart all on my own right up to the sixth floor of this awful building where you live, and tonight I've got to sleep up there to protect the stuff.'

'And where is your master now?'

'Getting even more stuff from our house.'

'Go on, then,' I said heartlessly. 'Only four more flights and you'll come to my office.' I softened. 'There's a good couch you can lie on, and you can sleep in as long as you like tomorrow morning.'

'Oh, I see!' Dromo gave me a disgusted look. He knew why I was saying that. 'Are we coming to live here? It's horrible. Oh, don't do that to me!'

'Ask him tomorrow.'

Tiberius arrived soon afterwards. *He* had a large bundle, which he dropped on the floor with a thud. In answer to my quizzical look, he listed, 'Tunics, comb, strigil, spare belts, spare boots, knife and napkin, absolutely *lots* of writing tools for copying old documents.'

'Isn't thirty-six rather old to run away from home?' I asked.

'Thirty-seven. I believe in waiting until you are old enough to enjoy things.' Suddenly, he became sweetly uncertain. 'Should I have asked you?'

'Not necessary. Tell me what happened with your uncle.'

'I tried not to quarrel, but the conversation was painful and at the moment he wants no more to do with me. He will not make life easy, though he may come round one day . . . As a courtesy I spoke to Laia and her brother, gaining more enemies for life. Afterwards, I went to the old grain warehouse and extracted all my uncle's records, as your father suggested. Now I have to say something.'

I went up to him. 'Tell me tomorrow.'

'No. This is it. I wake every morning with my heart lightening because I may see you. I want to wake to find you there in my arms. I have to be with you.'

'You are,' I said, winding myself round him experimentally.

He glanced at the couch, but I said if he was staying for good, we should migrate to the bed. I led him there, meeting little resistance, though he did try muttering self-consciously, 'I may not be up to much. I went all the way to Fidenae and back on horseback yesterday . . .'

Kind-hearted, I gave him some help with undressing. 'You'll manage. You had a good long sleep this afternoon.'

He began to assist me in taking off my own clothes, acquiring a new interest in exploring what was under them. 'A good sleep! That was cunning, Flavia Albia. Were you, in a previous life, a strategist for Hannibal?'

'Don't talk.' He smiled. He knew what came next even before he let me kiss him. Now it was my turn. Flavia Albia was making her move.

Epilogue

For us, this was our beginning. For others involved, it ought to have been the end of their unhappiness, though for some that was never to be.

Tiberius and I became absorbed in our own lives, yet we had news occasionally. The Verecundus family council's decisions were all put in hand. The Callisti accepted their settlement. As far as we ever knew, the two families then managed to exist on friendly terms.

The results of the political campaign were as Tiberius had predicted to Dromo and Rodan, except that Ennius Verecundus formally withdrew. He would stand again, once time had passed. In January, the candidates went to the Senate and made formal speeches recommending themselves, supported by friends who backed them. First Trebonius, then Arulenus were easily elected, comfortably trailed by Dillius. That left one more place, for which Vibius and Gratus gained equal votes. My uncle, Camillus Aelianus, stood up and suggested his colleagues give precedence to Vibius on the grounds that he had been married and was father to two children. The motion was passed: Vibius would be the fourth aedile designate.

I say 'had been married' for a reason. By the time of the vote, his status had altered. For him, there had been a tragic coda.

One day at mid-morning, Julia Optata was found at the bottom of a flight of stairs at home, dead. We were not called to the scene, never saw the evidence. Next thing, her body had been gathered up and we were attending her funeral.

Friends were invited to the house afterwards, so we had a chance to look discreetly at where she was found. I remembered taking that staircase, which led up from the ground floor to the apartment Sextus and Julia shared. I had thought it unusually safe. *The treads were clean natural stone, spaced evenly and well designed. Small windows lit them. A handrail, so rare in Rome's ramshackle tenements, made the climb easier . . .*

After the other mourners had left, Sextus told us two that he wanted to explain. His mother, tight-lipped, went away to another room, leading his father. Sextus sat on a couch with one arm round each of his small children. He said he intended them to know about their mother, to love her, but to know her life had been difficult.

'I killed her. That is, I was responsible. But of course it was an accident.'

If anyone asked, he said he would be open in public. There had been too much secrecy. Sextus did not want his children or himself to be the subject of any more unfortunate rumours. All the best politicians take that line, I thought.

He confessed that throughout their marriage Julia had attacked him. On the day she died, they had been fighting again. She was furious that Sextus had announced in public that she was with a pregnant sister, revealing to Aspicius where his frightened wife might be. Her angry tirade worsened until, as so often before, Julia started shouting and beating Sextus. He tried to escape by leaving the apartment, intending to go down to his parents. Julia rushed after him and they struggled together on the stairs. She lost her balance and fell. It was a terrible accident. Sextus said he had loved her and was heartbroken.

We had to accept what he told us.

In private afterwards, at home, Tiberius and I thought his story was all too convenient. While he had spoken to us so earnestly, his eyes flickered like those of a guilty man lying. Most of his story might have been true, but we were afraid he had taken his chance and deliberately pushed her.

If Sextus had killed Julia, he would get away with it. Even if questions were asked, he was a plausible man. If necessary, depositions would be made by family and friends that, sad as it was, Julia had regularly attacked him. The tragic results were not his fault; it had been self-defence.

Sextus carried it off beautifully, ironically as trained by us. He told Tiberius that even if cruel people had suspicions, he would be able to rehabilitate himself. Once in office, when he started repaying favours, the public would soon forget. His reputation remained pure – or at least as pure as any other politician's.

Tiberius, no fool and a good man, was subsequently cool with him. I found my feelings affected unexpectedly. I could never say I had liked Julia Optata; I certainly pitied her husband for what he had endured with her. But I felt belated sympathy; I saw the sadness of her life.

On the surface, Tiberius continued his friendship with Vibius and was always kind to his two children. A wise partner does not come between her man and his best friend.

Luckily, at heart, mine shared my reserve. So Sextus Vibius Marinus would not be invited to our home, when we had one, as often as he once might have been.

We would have our own home. But that is another story.

THE

LINDSEY DAVIS

NEWSLETTER